Grave Beginnings

A Case File From: The Grave Report

R.R. Virdi

Grave Beginnings
A Case File From: The Grave Report
R.R. Virdi

Copyright R.R. Virdi 2013

Acknowledgements

To Jennifer Romstedt. Thank you for all your help in going through this book picking out the things to improve.

Cayleigh Stickler for going through it with laser-like focus and being a great copy editor. I hope to work with you for a long time to come.

And, of course, to Michelle Dunbar, for the most amazing editing experience I have ever had. You not only saved this work, but made it shine. You made editing fun, and proved that editors are magical creatures capable of wonderment and more! Thank you so much.

To Lacey Sutton for all her kindness, support and help in formatting this novel. Thank you.

Chapter One

I woke in complete darkness. It was narrow, cramped, and I was surrounded by wood. A disconcertingly musty, rotting smell filled the small area; not to mention the lack of air. I was dead and buried in a coffin...again.

Worse still, I was running out of air fast and I couldn't see a thing. Not exactly the best combination of circumstances. Fortunately, I've been in similar situations before, so I know how to get out of them.

See, coffins aren't really designed for keeping bodies locked in. If you're lying in one, you're either dead, unless you're me, or buried alive. Coffins are simple constructions. Nothing but planks of wood nailed together with some hinges to keep the lid shut. There's always a way out of a situation like that; you just have to find it.

Before you suffocate.

I tried to remain calm in an effort to conserve what little air there was, but something was bothering me. It was the space, or rather, lack of it. Although there generally isn't much room in a coffin, I've been in enough of them to know I was seriously cramped. Running my hands around the coffin, I brushed against something that was certainly not wood. It was stone-like, rough here, rigid there, smooth in some places with gaps in between.

"Sunuvabitch!"

It was bone.

I was stuffed in somebody else's coffin. My first clue that I was buried in a hurry and without ceremony. That meant there might be a way out, hopefully. Unfortunately, I was blanking on the how bit. It happens when there's a brain-damaging lack of air.

Suffocating doesn't even crack the top twenty worst ways to die. It's somewhat peaceful, *if* you can get over the psychological part of being buried alive or, in my case, dead. Your lungs get heavy, your eyelids follow, and you sort of go to sleep.

I rubbed my hands together to release some tension, pausing as my fingertips brushed against a cool metal band strapped around my wrist.

I was wearing a watch!

Now, if you're stuck in a coffin with a watch, keys or anything sharp or blunt, there's still a way out. Albeit a painful way, but it's still a way. I slipped the watch off, clenching my hand and setting it over my closed fist. The watch made a poor set of makeshift brass knuckles, but it would have to do.

The smell and feel of the coffin told me it was old, meaning the wood wouldn't be as strong. I punched the roof with all the strength I could muster. The watch face shattered with the first blow. Tiny flecks of broken glass bit into my aching fingers. With a determined snarl, I worked through the pain, pumping my fist harder, willing the wood to splinter above me.

I can feel pain like everyone else, and I haven't gotten as used to it as I would have liked by now.

I kept punching, trying not to waste any effort. It took a lot to ensure every blow was calculated, hard and delivered to the same spot. My arms and lungs felt like they were made of lead. I was getting tired, my movements sluggish, not to mention the watch tearing into my skin. My knuckles and fingers were bleeding and I'd definitely broken some of the smaller bones in my hand, but I was soon rewarded with the lovely sound of wood splintering.

Now, some survival experts will tell you that survival is about perseverance and they're right. I've been inside a lot of people and picked up their skills and memories, but at the cost of many of my own.

So I continued hammering away at the small crack,

listening to *thud* after *thud* as my fist impacted the roof. The wood was giving way, but my hand was suffering for it. You know it's bad when you're losing sensation in a body part. The pain became a distant numbness, but still, I kept going. The watch had dug halfway into my fingers and knuckles, and after what seemed like the thousandth punch, something sprinkled onto my eyes, nose, and mouth.

Dirt!

I jammed my fingers into the crack, prying the jagged wood apart. It bit into my flesh as I pulled hard. Eventually, it split, and a mountain of dirt came crashing in to bury me—again.

I spat soil from my mouth, rolling onto my stomach, sweeping dirt beneath me as I turned. Packing it into a tight layer, I got onto my hands and knees, pushing against the lid with my back. It rose briefly, showering me with even more dirt. I repeated the process as the pile of soil beneath me grew, applying more of my strength to the roof. It rose higher. More dirt followed along with something else, air! Musty, dirty air, but it was the sweetest smelling air to me. I lay directly against the half-broken coffin lid. A massive crack ran from top to bottom. Arching my back, I placed my knees against it, giving one final push.

It didn't rise so much as crack in two. Dirt rained down on me, but I was free. I clawed my way out with my left hand, my right hand completely useless from the feverish punching. Dirt found its way into my eyes, nose, mouth, and ears. After an eternity of digging, I made my way out of the grave and onto fresh open ground. The air felt as thick as soup, and it tasted delicious. It was lung nectar to me.

My eyes itched and I rubbed them vigorously. When my vision cleared, I was greeted with a dark, starless sky. The landscape was caked with the glow of bright lights radiating from the mass of buildings towering in the distance.

"Ah, New York," I said, warmed by the sudden flash of memories the concrete jungle evoked from me. I've spent many of my cases racing through the city's gritty underbelly, and then there were the few times I was rewarded with a chance to see some of its glory. I remembered the mouth-watering smell of hot dogs from my favorite food cart on Broadway and the scent of spring leaves in Central Park. Too bad it was winter.

My right hand twitched. I was getting some feeling back in it, and it hurt like hell. I should probably mention that when I'm inside a body, I break many of life's rules. I can regenerate from certain injuries, such as having my right hand bludgeoned into oblivion or even a bullet wound. If it didn't kill me, that is.

It should be obvious by now that I'm not exactly normal. Completely broken and non-functional hand? No problem, heals damn near instantly. Hell, I've been shot before and ended up fine after a little rest. I don't really need hospitals… The sort-of dead generally don't.

I turned around to get a better look at the grave I'd exited. The name on the headstone read Emmanuel Suarez.

"Sorry about that, Emmanuel. Nice to meet you. I'm Vincent Graves."

Well, Vincent Graves isn't my real name. I've been doing this job for so long, and been inside so many people, I can't actually remember my real name. Vincent Graves seems to fit with my line of work. I have so many memories in my head that it's hard to tell which are mine and which belong to the hundreds of people whose bodies I've occupied. Every time I'm in someone, I get fragments of their memories. They all stay with me, to my misfortune, but the skills and memories I've picked up have saved my life many times over, so they're worth it.

I looked myself up and down to see if there was anything to clue me into who this body belonged to and what killed him.

I? He? We?

Ah hell, I didn't know how to refer to myself since I wasn't using my own body. I would…if I still had mine, but I lost it a long time ago. "Strange and mysterious circumstances" took it from me. Never having solved my own death leaves me free to solve other people's murders.

Ones caused by "strange and mysterious circumstances," which is another way of saying the supernatural did it.

I should probably point out that I'm not a ghost or a poltergeist. There are dozens of types of undead, and I don't have the time to explain their differences. To keep it short: a ghost is an imprint of a person, a recording of a person's memories and behaviors. I'm not a shadow of the person I once was. I'm still me—sort of, minus the body. In essence, I'm something more complete.

I'm a soul.

We're all souls. You, me, that annoying kid next door banging on his drums at two in the morning 'cause he didn't take his ADHD medicine. The difference between everyone else and me is that I'm only a soul. Simply put: I'm you without the body. See, you're not really a person with a soul inside you. You're a soul with a physical form to play with; get drunk with, have sex, and all the other things you can think of. When someone dies, his or her soul leaves their body and goes… Well, I never really figured that part out, but in a nutshell, your soul is what makes you, you. It's what defines you, what makes you the either great or asinine person you are. Without a soul, you're a meat suit. One I can jump in and out of.

I was wearing what would have been an impressive navy blue pinstriped suit, had it not been covered with dirt, and a black dress shirt. The black leather Italian dress shoes looked expensive and somehow managed to retain a glossy shine. Other than that, all I had on me was a broken and expensive-looking watch. As far as clues go, it wasn't much to go on. I groaned at how much work I had ahead of me to figure out who this guy was.

"So, I'm a really well-dressed, well-off man in New York. That narrows it down to…goddammit!" I'm not too keen on the almighty and those up high, mostly because I have the feeling they're responsible for me being stuck in this gig. It doesn't pay well. Actually, it doesn't pay at all. Not to mention, it's probably a great source of amusement to whoever's in charge.

Disembodied cosmic assholes.

A clatter of noise tore me away from my metaphysical musings. I whirled around to face the source. Standing about ten feet from me, this whole time probably, was an elderly man. He had short, graying hair with a very pronounced widow's peak, severe crow's feet and a tired, worn face. He stood slack-jawed, staring at me, no doubt flabbergasted by the fact I'd burst out of a grave. His dark and simple overalls were speckled with dirt. Lying at his feet was the shovel that most likely caused the noise when he had dropped it.

He and I stared at each other for a good while before I said, "Well whaddya know? You really can dig your way here from China!"

He collapsed to the ground, which at his age could have been fatal, but I was hoping it wasn't. Not because I was worried... Ok, maybe a bit worried. I was hoping that he was unconscious so I wouldn't run the chance of having to come back as him.

He died via heart attack caused by "strange and mysterious" circumstances: a dead guy rising out of a grave. Yes. That fit the criteria for my line of work.

I mean, how would that even work? Would I have to hunt myself down? Case solved! I killed him by freaking him the hell out.

I checked his pulse, releasing a sigh of relief that he was still breathing and decided it best to get the hell out of there.

I hit the sidewalk, setting a fast pace and keeping both hands in my pocket to hide my bleeding, watch-encrusted hand until it healed. Too bad the watch wouldn't. It was a Rolex—emphasis on *was*.

I kept my eyes open for the first church I could I find. It didn't matter if it was Catholic, Protestant, Episcopal or even one of those Scientology ones. It would be empty, save for one person.

Ten minutes later, I found a nice, quiet, little Catholic church and entered it. A lone figure was sitting with his back turned to me...in the first and furthest pew. Apparently it was too much for him to sit in one closer to the entrance. As I drew closer, I noticed that he was scrawling in a small, black Moleskine notebook. He snapped it shut when he rose from his seat, turning to face me.

He was a handsome guy; I'll give him that. A few locks of chin-length, wavy blonde hair fell over his glacier blue eyes. They were framed by a pair of dark, thin, rectangular glasses, the color contrasting his fair skin. He tucked the notebook into his khaki pants and his pen into...I swear to god, the pocket protector on his full-length white-collared shirt. He clasped his hands together, resting them in front of his waist as he slightly rocked back and forth in his brown oxford-style shoes. All in all, he looked like an I.T. guy who could've done a fair bit of modeling on the side. And I looked like, well, I really didn't know what I looked like yet.

Graveyards aren't known for their overabundance of mirrors, but I had a feeling that I didn't look all too well. Dead guys who come back to life generally don't.

He smiled politely. "Vincent, nice to see you," he said, holding out his hand.

I shook it and grunted a greeting. As much as I liked the guy, I didn't completely trust him. I had worked with him for...well, I don't remember, but it seemed like forever. In all that time, I'd never really got to know him. I didn't know where he was from, how he got into this, or even his real name. All I knew was that when I started a case, I would head to the nearest church and he would be there—alone. He'd give me my time limit, maybe a clue and send me on my way. I asked him his name once. He looked around a bit, smiled, and said, "Call me Church."

Friggin' wiseass.

"Ow!" I yelped as Church clasped my left forearm, pushing my sleeve out of the way. A burning sensation overwhelmed me, and when he let go, there was a big red mark on my skin. It looked like I had been sunburned. A big, black number twenty-four emblazoned into my arm, which made it feel like a cow's ass.

Branding me with a magical countdown tattoo was how

Church gave me my time limit. The number would decrease with every hour that went by until I either solved the case or failed. Although come to think of it, I've never failed, and I don't plan to. I have cut some pretty close though. Really close, minutes close.

"You know, Vincent, you scream every time I do that," Church said, not quite smiling. His eyes shone with amusement.

Ass.

"First of all," I said, trying to clear up the misunderstanding, "I don't scream. I exclaim though onomatopoeia."

"That's called a scream, Vincent."

"And secondly," I said as if he hadn't spoken at all, "it hurts every time you do that!"

"I thought you would have been accustomed to pain by now," he said, still not smiling. The corners of his mouth twitching didn't escape my notice though.

"Being accustomed to and not feeling it are two completely different things. And what's with the twenty-four hours? I'm not Kiefer Sutherland. Last case I got seventy-two!"

"Forty-eight," Church corrected.

"Whatever! Still more than I have now and plus, I was in a little boy last time so my memory isn't that great…"

His eyebrows rose slightly at that.

"Yeah…that came out slightly more pedophile-ish than it sounded in my head."

"Yes," Church replied.

"The point still stands. I had more before. Why is that?" I argued, my voice taking on a bit of heat.

"You get as much as you need," he said sternly.

"Well, I want it changed!"

He grabbed my arm, and the searing heat enveloped my forearm again. When he removed it, the tattoo had changed.

To thir-frickin-teen!

"Thirteen hours!" I exclaimed.

"You said you wanted it changed," Church said flatly.

"What happened to as long as I need?"

"Thirteen is enough," he said matter of factly. "I was being generous giving you twenty-four."

Now I'm not one to beg. I've still got a bit of pride left, as long as you don't count some of the embarrassing ways I've died over the years. But, I'm also proud of the fact I've never once failed to solve a case. So, here I was, stuck in a situation where I'd have to beg and lose my pride in order to get more time to well, save my pride...

"The hell you were!" I snarled. "Come on, Church. I need more time. I've never failed a case before, and I'm not about to start now." I pleaded which isn't begging. It's asking with a desperate passion. It's not begging. It just isn't.

Pride intact.

"You won't fail," he said in the same matter-of-fact tone.

Did Church just pay me a compliment?

"So, you're going to give me twenty-four hours then, right?"

"No."

So much for the begging—er, pleading!

"I could really use that extra time, Church."

"Here," he said as if I hadn't spoken at all. He thrust a saddle brown leather journal into my hands. My journal filled with knowledge, lore and tidbits of wisdom I'd gathered over the years.

Yes, I've managed to accumulate some wisdom.

The journal was a veritable encyclopedia of every supernatural nasty I had come across or heard of, and how to stop it. Description, motives, preferences, mythology, and, of course, the most efficient ways to gank 'em. I take it with me on every case and then hand it back to Church for safekeeping. Think of it as *"The Graves' How-To Manual of Badassery"*...ness...ism...s?

How do you even pluralize badass?

I took it from him without saying a word, not like there was much I could say at this point. I'd just gone from twenty-four hours to thirteen and without a single lead to go on. I decided to keep my mouth wisely shut, lest he shave off more time. Some of that wisdom I mentioned beforehand: wisdom in silence!

Church plopped something atop my journal. "I've been thinking, Vincent. You could use another one of these."

I looked down to see a different version of the journal. The leather was a rich burgundy and it was a bit smaller than my other one. The question was: why did Church think I needed another journal? My original one wasn't even close to full and this one was, well, tiny. I arched an eyebrow, shooting him a quizzical look. "What gives?"

"For your memory."

"Huh?" was my all-too-clever reply.

"It might do you some good to keep a personal record of your cases, your thoughts and such, as opposed to just knowledge on monsters and mythos. I'll hold onto it, same as I do the other one. You can peruse it in your free time, keep your memories together," Church said casually.

Translation: This will help you keep your shit together.

"A diary?" I said.

"Or a journal," he said, shrugging nonchalantly.

"Not much of a difference."

"The difference depends on you, Vincent."

Whatever the hell that means… What's the difference between a journal and a diary anyway?

"I'm not a writer, Church, I'm a paranormal investigator...hunter... Ah hell, I don't know what I am!"

Church just stared at me, silent. He was creepy when he did that, creepy…er.

"Fine, but keep in mind that I kill things, not punctuate sentences, so don't expect high-quality work the first time 'round."

There was a flash of a smirk, just a flash when Church spoke. "Don't worry, I won't."

Smartass.

"Well, since you come bearing gifts and seeing how as you've cut my time nearly in half, I don't suppose you could, oh I don't know, give me a fucking lead?"

"Watch," he replied.

"Watch what? The hell does that mean?" I clenched my fists. "Oh!" Undoing the strap that was still around my knuckles, I looked the Rolex over. There were no discernable markings on the smashed face, or the band, nothing to point me in the right direction anyway. It wasn't until I looked at the rear of the watch that I found something.

Engraved in tiny letters were the words: *Congratulations on thirty years of service, Norman Smith, from your friends at the AMNH.*

It was one of those celebratory watches companies gave to employees, equivocal to a high school ring. Except to earn this one, you actually had to do some work.

At least now I had a name. Norman Smith, Smith— probably the most common last name in the world, the Caucasian version of Nguyen. I was in New York, looking for a guy named Smith... What's that popular saying these days?

Fuck my life?

Still, it was more than I had a few minutes ago. Whatever AMNH was, it was tied to Norman's life, to his work.

"Thanks, Church," I said, finally looking up from the watch, but he was gone; no sound, no movement, no nothing. He was just gone. I hated when he did that. It reminded me that Church was higher up and more involved in the supernatural world than I had originally thought.

I had always thought of him as my paranormal parole officer, guiding me, making sure I stayed out of trouble and so on. I was starting to realize that he was something more.

I searched around the pew where Church had been sitting. Lying at the end was a thick white paperback book. I drew closer, realizing it was a copy of the local white pages. I picked it up and began flipping through it. As it turns out, New York doesn't have a bazillion Norman Smiths.

It has *only* ninety-five.

I looked up in no particular direction. "Was it too much

to just write his address down on a piece of paper?" I shouted. My hand spasmed and I dropped the book. It landed splayed open. When I picked it up, I saw a neatly drawn, bright red oval around an address in the Upper West Side of Manhattan.

"Oh, sorry," I muttered somewhat apologetically.

I was currently somewhere in Lower Manhattan. By car, it would take about twenty minutes to get where I needed to be. By public transport, half an hour. Either was fine by me, *if* I had the cash, which I didn't.

"Uh, Church, I don't suppose you could've left me some money? You know, case funds for investigational expenses?"

No answer and no money lying around the pew. So, I had to walk through New York, in the winter. Oh, and I had one helluva short deadline.

Fantastic.

Chapter Two

One of the perks of being just a soul is that cold weather doesn't bother you much. I mean, sure, I feel it but it's more of an annoyance than a hindrance. Another benefit is that it takes more than a one-hour trek to leave me winded. Pissed off that I had to walk in the first place, sure, but not tiring. The time spent at church with Church (say *that* ten times fast) and the time it took huffing my soulful ass from Lower Manhattan had cost me.

I was an hour down already.

I let out a low whistle when I finally found Norman's home. It was an old townhouse, built around the early 1900s, easily five, maybe six, stories high. It was painted in some kind of peach color. Maybe it was peach, I don't know.

I'm not much of a writer or even a painter for that matter, so sue me.

The steps leading up to the door were the same peach-like hue as the building; the door itself was a highly polished oak. I was inside a carpenter once, who was killed by a type of Nymph for cutting down some sacred tree. The Nymph ate his heart in retaliation. Seemed like a bit of an overreaction to me: he cuts down a tree and she eats his heart. No one ever said that supernatural entities were known for their sense of fair karma. Anyway, I know my wood when I see it.

On the left of the door were two very plain-looking windows. They didn't seem to belong with the rest of the house. Not that I would know. It's not as if I've ever inhabited a décor specialist.

A glimpse of pale yellow caught my attention. I turned to see a pastel yellow Lamborghini Miura parked on the street... Ok, Mr. Norman Smith was very well off indeed. Home in Upper Manhattan and a classic Lamborghini. Sometimes there's a little jealous vindictive part of me that feels people like this shouldn't be getting my services. Especially considering the fact I can't even charge them.

Hell, I'm dead and so are they. The universe is seriously screwed up.

Deciding that I had done enough sightseeing and appraising for one day, I strolled up to Mr. Smith's door and tried the doorknob. It was locked.

Of course, it's never that easy. Just once I wish it were though.

I pushed against the door, trying to see if maybe I could find a way to force it open, but it wouldn't budge. That was some seriously solid wood. I checked under the rather plain-looking doormat. No key. There was nothing else to look at nearby bar the stupid miniature cactus, the bulbous looking type.

There was a somewhat painful *pang* in my head as a vision blurred through my mind. A familiar, yet meatier looking, hand reached towards the prickly little cactus, its wrist adorned with the same Rolex I had smashed to bits earlier. It was a memory from Norman Smith.

Following his lead, I reached for the cactus, praying this hunch was right. I grabbed it tentatively, surprised the needles didn't pierce my skin. They plunged inward instead, and as soon as I let go, they sprang back out. I squeezed the cactus harder and the bulb caved in like one of those squeaky dog toys. I yanked it, and it popped loose with a sound much like a plunger being pulled from a toilet. I looked inside the pot and smiled.

Clever. Hiding the spare key under any old potted plant might not have been too smart, but a cactus? Who would be stupid enough to take that risk?

Aside from me, of course. But, I do have the advantage of the deceased's memories...which I unfortunately have no control over. They just pop in and out at their leisure.

I acted as natural as I could as I inserted the key into the keyhole and unlocked Mr. Smith's door.

"Wow!"

The door opened into a beautiful and massive living room, adorned with all manner of exquisite things: a chandelier with rows of expensive crystals and minute clay sculptures surrounded by protective glass. Two luxurious, white leather armchairs in the corner and beside them, a wine-colored suede couch. The floors were the same oaken wood as the door, but highly polished. While on the walls, paintings hung with price tags still attached. The mantelpiece was furnished with two solid gold candleholders and two fire pokers: one was a typical, solid charred black, but the other was solid silver and engraved. Both were held in two equally beautiful silver brackets, embossed in elegant designs.

The guy had a solid silver engraved fire poker... Who the hell buys stuff like that?

I wondered if I would ever be able to afford a place like this. You know, if I wasn't dead and could charge people the exorbitant fees I ought to be charging for this kind of work. I liked to think I could... Delusions of grandeur are a perk of having severe mental issues due to having many different memories inside me.

As I continued on, I noticed that every floor was as ostentatious and opulent as the first. Mr. Smith's kitchen was amazing! It had cherry cabinets, mahogany floors, and a Subzero fridge. Too bad it wasn't stocked.

Hey, a dead guy's gotta eat too!

Oh, and everything in the kitchen was that new touch technology crap, no buttons or knobs in there. Well, except maybe Mr. Smith when he was alive, because who pays for this high-tech crap anyway?

Just setting foot in the man's gym made me feel like I had to check my wallet (which I didn't have) for a membership card. It was a professional and posh-looking setup. He had a bar in the far corner with juicers and other fitness-oriented culinary equipment dotting the counter. Machines lined the walls. Padded flooring, dumbbell racks, medicine balls...you name it, he had it.

His home even had five outdoor terraces, one of which boasted a brand new hot tub. It's not wrong to hate someone I've never met before, whose body and home I'm currently inhabiting, is it? I just about managed to make it to the upstairs bedroom without my jaw dragging across the floor.

It was very tidy. Someone was either a clean freak, or they had something to hide. Considering that I had woken up buried in someone else's grave, I was gonna go with option number two. Pulling out drawers, I threw his clothes unceremoniously across the room, looking for more clues as to who Norman Smith was...is. Chances were that not everyone knew he was dead. It's not like there was a proper funeral for him.

I finally managed to find his wallet, one of those metal-locking types you see on infomercials, the kind guaranteed to prevent your credit card info from being stolen.

And what a surprise—it was engraved. This guy seriously had a thing about that, like he had to show off to the world or something. Some people just *have* to let everyone know what a douche they are.

It was filled with premium credit cards. The kind you get when you can blow six figures a year on purchases. Black cards, Platinum, and a whole bunch of other nonsensically named cards. What I wanted was tucked away in the back. Prying his driver's license free, I studied the face staring back at me. Something felt off.

I hurried to the bathroom, although calling it that was an understatement. It was more like an entertainment center with bathing facilities. Flat panel televisions were everywhere: on the walls, on the mirrors—even the shower! Don't get me started on that shower. It was one of those walk in ones, made of some beautiful stone and surrounded by glass. Only it was large enough to fit the entire women's volleyball team in it. Not that I fantasize about that kind of stuff. I'm a consummate professional.

That wasn't why I came to the bathroom though. I shot a look at the driver's license. The man was light skinned, had a fair bit of flesh on his face, and a bit of double chin going on. There were no whiskers, and his eyes were a clear icy sort of blue, but tired looking. Wrinkles lined the corners of his eyes and forehead. An extra mass of darkened skin drooped beneath his eyes and his champagne hair looked thin on top. He looked like a workaholic whose stress was finally catching up to him.

So why did the guy in the mirror look like an Abercrombie and Fitch model? The double chin was tucked away somewhere because I had a jaw of finely chiseled granite. My blonde hair was thick and luxuriant, combed back in a posh look. The skin was supple and tight, no wrinkles or dark bags under the eyes. This guy looked like he was in his late twenties. Which was a little strange considering that his license put him in his fifties. The man in the license could have easily weighed in at a hefty two-fifty, but the one in the mirror was a trim, modelesque one-eighty. Yeah, something was very wrong.

I stuck my mug closer to the mirror. Not for vanity's sake, mind you. I wanted a better look. I ran my healed right hand through the blonde locks and sighed. "Man, still not a ginger."

I've done this hundreds of times and never once came back as a ginger. I've always wanted to see what being a redhead is like. I'll settle for sleeping with one instead. Find out first hand if what they say about them never getting any sleep is true.

I shook my head vigorously, clearing that line of thought from my mind. All these memories and influences inside my noggin, there's bound to be hormoned up male teenagers in there somewhere.

What I was having trouble processing was how a guy goes from being the model of stress and obesity to, well, looking like a model, and then winds up dead, and buried in far better shape than when he was alive?

That fit under the "strange and mysterious" label.

I still had no idea what Norman did. With only half a day left to solve this case, I went into demolition mode, tearing apart the bedroom with reckless abandon.

The search turned up nothing but an unusually high number of um…adult material. Well, maybe not unusually high. The guy was an out of shape workaholic.

Looking around, I noticed the door to a closet. It was lined with suits, but none of them were anywhere near the quality as the one Norman was wearing when he took his dirt nap. They were cheap, average-looking suits. The kind you'd expect a high school principal to wear. Some were tattered and frayed, others had patches you knew weren't for the style.

I didn't need a vast amount of detective knowledge to know that none of this felt right. I was wearing the only designer suit this guy owned, and then there was the Rolex. He had a multimillion-dollar place in Upper Manhattan but could only afford one nice suit? I didn't know what it all meant yet, but I was sure it was connected…somehow. Although the how part was eluding me.

I rummaged through the suits, looking for anything that would help me pinpoint the cause of death. Every suit turned up empty until I reached a shiny brown suit with yellow pinstripes. I couldn't believe he actually had one of those. I dug around a bit, turning out a few loose threads, some change, used tissues (gross), and…an I.D. badge!

It read Norman Smith, Curator of the American Museum of Natural History.

AMNH. Well, now I knew where he had gotten the watch.

That set off more bells in my head. A curator of a museum, even one as prestigious as the one he worked at, didn't make the kind of salary needed to live in a place like this. A curator makes maybe seventy grand, tops; there were some out there closer to a hundred grand. I've never heard of one making enough to support a million-dollar lifestyle however. Unless there were dirty dealings going on. It's not unheard of for people to be involved in black market antiquity dealings.

The only problem with that theory was that if he was dealing with the black market, he would certainly make the money to live this kind of lifestyle, but it would be somewhat hard to keep the opulence quiet. Secondly, if he had died as a result of a black market deal gone bad, I wouldn't be on this case. I only dealt with the whole supernatural thing.

So here's what I had: a museum curator going from portly and balding to model status, an average middle-class salary supporting a million-dollar lifestyle, and no clues to how he wound up dead in another guy's coffin.

Basically, I had nothing, except the fact that people might not know that he was dead. So maybe it was due time Mr. Smith returned to work.

Chapter Three

It was late so the museum was shut down for the night, but that wouldn't be a problem for the curator of the place. Norman probably had a set of keys lying around somewhere. If it came down to it, I was certain I could persuade a guard to let me in, assuming they recognized me in the newfound SlimFast glory. It made sense to go in late though. The museum would be relatively empty so I could search for clues without disturbance. Plus, I didn't really have the luxury of sleeping till morning, not with the tight clock I was on.

I only had ten hours left.

I did, however, have the time for a shower. Well, I made time. I was covered in graveyard dirt, smelled like a rotting corpse, and had blood encrusting one of my hands. It would have been weird trying to explain all that to anyone I ran into.

So I stripped down and stepped onto the cool, rough, stone floor of the shower, taking a few moments to discern what the various knobs and such did. After about five minutes, I was able to get the shower started, and it was heaven. It had fifty million different massage and water pressure settings. You know, the fancy ones with names like gentle rain and thunderstorm. I may have dallied just a bit, letting out a series of pleasurable moans as the warm water batted my borrowed skin. I could've stayed in there forever, groaning under the sensation of my body loosening up. It struck me that my pleasurable moaning could be seriously misconstrued for something else. Thankfully, no one was around to hear me.

I stepped out and instantly regretted it. Just once, I wish I could live a normal day. I want to shower, go work some normal job, and then come home and sleep.

But I couldn't, so here I am.

I pulled the designer suit back on. The dirt was easy enough to brush off, and besides, I wanted the murderer to recognize him. Normal or supernatural, it's a shock when the person you've killed comes back from the grave. I needed a reaction, something more to go on. I pocketed the damaged watch, clipped the I.D badge on, and searched for a set of keys.

I dug around for a bit and found a key and a piece of paper on a small nightstand. The paper turned out to be a will, nestled beside a photograph of a younger looking Norman next to an older version of himself. They had their arms around each other, and in the background was a small wooded creek. After a quick read, I found that the will belonged to Norman's father. He had recently passed away and left him the classic Lamborghini sitting outside. Apparently, one of Norman's greatest wishes was inheriting that car. At least that's what his father said in the will. Well, at least I could rule the car out for being acquired through foul play.

I snatched the key up and that's when another flash of memory hit me. Norman tossed a small ringlet with several keys into the bottom drawer of the nightstand. I opened the bottom drawer gently. There was really no point to tearing the place up now that I knew where the keys were. The drawer turned out to be a disheveled mess. There was crap everywhere! Pens, all manner of papers like credit card applications, bills, cruise trip info, a little can of shoe polish, an electric razor, and…measuring tape? What the hell?

After digging through the random assortment of things, I managed to find the ring of keys I had seen in Norman's vision. I didn't know what they were for yet, but at least I had them. I added the car and house key to the ring and headed downstairs, locking the door as I stepped outside. Opening the door to the pastel Lambo, I clambered into the car. It was a bit of an effort since the seats were so low, more a case of falling in abruptly than getting in. Still, I was inside.

I let out a low whistle as I looked around. Polished, rich black leather, and equally polished wood and metal adorned the car. Even the gated plating around the shifter was polished. Wow, they didn't make cars like this anymore. Well, they did, but I couldn't afford them. It's not like I have a bank account.

I put the key in and started her up. The car thrummed to life with a guttural growl—a deep, bubbling basso beehive. It vibrated like it was shivering in the New York winter, so I decided to let it warm up even though I was low on time. I didn't want to be responsible for killing a classic. These old cars could be difficult at times.

I haven't actually been in a mechanic yet, so I think some of the car knowledge must be my own. Maybe I was a mechanic before all of this started. I honestly have no clue.

After waiting ten to fifteen minutes, I depressed the clutch, which was much harder than I thought it would be, slipped the car into first gear, and drove off. Fortunately, it wasn't snowing. It's a strange thing about New York. Every winter it snows and rains as it always has, but every time it does, people forget how to drive despite having lived there all their lives.

It didn't take much time to get to the museum, about ten minutes give or take. I pulled into the garage near the west pavilion and entered through the Columbus Avenue entrance. I had a pretty good idea of the layout because of the memories flooding through my brain. From experience, whenever the deceased's memories increased, it was a sure sign that whatever killed them was nearby. It's like getting the heebie-jeebies, but receiving flash after flash of random memories instead.

So far, so good. The keys Norman had on him granted me access, and I was now strolling through a corridor alone—in the dark. If ever there was a time and place to be jumped by a supernatural baddy, it was now, but nothing of the sort happened. Most people—sane people—would have been relieved not to run into a monster. Not me. At this point, I would have preferred it.

I was running out of time and didn't have much to go on. I would have liked being attacked. I could kill whatever it was that had killed Norman and be done.

But none of that happened.

I strolled along the corridor, passing a sign for an IMAX theater. A film about the moon and desolation and some such was playing. Would've been nice to be able to stop and watch it, but I was pressed for time and the museum was closed. Then there's the fact I'm not entirely interested in the moon, unless I'm on a werewolf case...and I've had a few of those.

I walked past the theater and reached the small mammals section—a wooden hall with minute, glass-walled exhibits featuring mostly rodents. There were different types of squirrels, wolverines, minks, badgers and something called a marten… I had been in a Marten once. Didn't look similar. The one I was in was quite the hefty guy. Although, he was furry too.

I shuddered at the recollection. It wasn't one of my fondest memories.

Something odd bothered me as I carried on walking. I had made it a fair bit into the museum and hadn't run into a single security guard. It was somewhat eerie. I'd thought there would've been some people around. Night was when some museum staff would be setting up exhibits.

I kept on walking and passed a café, the North American Mammal section, a rose gallery, and some cosmic path thingy. That's when I finally saw a sign for the security office.

I followed the signs, hoping to find someone who would recognize me. At least then I could start asking questions, maybe get my bearings on this case. I passed the Theodore Roosevelt Memorial Hall on my way there but didn't stop to look. With all of my paranormal experiences over the years, I wouldn't be surprised if the statue came to life and started yelling at me. I was very short on time and didn't need to be yelled at by Robin Williams. That conversation would never end.

As I drew nearer to the office, a gruff voice rang out.

"Hey!"

I spun around. The man was shorter than Norman. I'd put him around five foot ten. He was portly and porcine-faced, cheeks flushed and pink, beady little weasel brown eyes, and a nose that looked like it was constantly being thumbed up.

Porcine, yup.

He had slicked-back dark hair, and his face looked like it was stuck in a perpetual state of scowling. He was dressed like a rent-a-cop and had a swagger to match, the kind that belonged to those high school kids who needed a constant power trip to feel in charge. He walked towards me with his chest puffed out, stretching the fabric of his uniform.

"There's Stiller," I muttered in an attempt to keep myself amused. If I didn't do that, I'd go insane...er.

He pointed his massive flashlight at me as he got closer. When I mean massive, I mean this thing was as long as a nightstick. Clearly someone was compensating. He shone the light into my face, causing me to squint.

"Who are you?" he barked.

"I'm Norman. Norman Smith...the curator," I said, letting the word 'curator' hang in the air.

"Oh!" he exclaimed. "I'm sorry sir. Sorry. I didn't, um..."

Damn right, asshole. Shouting at me and shining a light in my face.

Before I could speak he ran the light up and down my body again, blinding me a second time. "What happened to you? You don't look the same at all. You look younger and you lost a lot of weight!"

I showed him my I.D badge and smiled. "Native American sweat lodge. The pounds melted right off!"

"Really?" He asked, sounding genuinely shocked. Ah, bless him; stupid people are the universe's gift to the intelligent. Make fun of them while you can, and enjoy it.

I looked down at his little security tag. "Hey listen, Rick, I need some help, and you're just the guy I'm looking for." He nodded, but otherwise remained silent. "Do you happen to remember what I've been doing for the past few days?"

He looked a bit confused but answered nonetheless. "Yeah, you were doing something with that new Middle Eastern exhibit. It's not open yet. You were doing some stuff with the archaeologists, cataloging or something."

Now I had something. Middle Eastern exhibit, which meant…nada.

"Say, um, could you point me in the right direction, Rick?"

He rolled his weasely eyes and pointed the way.

I strolled in the direction he had pointed for maybe a minute before coming to a set of double doors, the kind you see in some grocery stores, leading to some back room filled with stock and whatnot. I pushed through them and saw what looked like an endless corridor branching off into many other halls.

"Fantastic," I muttered.

"What's fantastic?" asked a girlish voice.

I suddenly remembered those cartoons where someone gets so scared their soul jumps out of their body for a second. That nearly happened to me. *Nearly*, not did. I am a fearless paranormal investigator. I've killed all manner of monsters before, but occasionally the voice of a random stranger in the same hallway might surprise me. I made this quite clear in my response.

"Fuck me!" I yelped.

I whipped to my side to see a young girl in her early twenties. She was about five-four, long, wavy, raven-black hair. She had smoky, brown eyes that just smoldered and oozed sexuality. She was leaning against the wall in a tight leather jacket worn over a gray t-shirt. The shirt was peppered with strategically placed tears that showed a bit too much skin. Her dark blue, form-fitting jeans were cut short at the top and were worn low, revealing a taut midsection. The jeans were ripped in certain places and went all the way down to her buckled, black combat boots. She stared at me with an arched eyebrow.

"Put that out, now!" I growled at her.

She was smoking…in the American Museum of Natural History! Kids these days… They're just, well, assholes.

She looked at me the way any young kid would when their parents told them to do something that irked them. It was a haughty, defiant look. "Who died and made you my dad?" she asked.

Kids. Assholes. Getting uppity with her elders was bad enough, but smoking in a frickin' museum?

"I'm the curator," I said in a flat tone, pointing to the I.D card clipped to my suit.

Her eyes widened, and the only sound that came out of her mouth was a meep! She hastily removed, put out, and stowed her cigarette, staring at me like a deer caught in a pair of headlights.

"How did you get back here?" I asked her.

"My… Um…my dad works here. He lets me come with him sometimes…" she said trailing off.

Considering that I wasn't going to be here too long, I didn't really care all too much about her smoking. I decided against fetching security; after all, she could be helpful. If her father worked here, then maybe I could go to him, try and get some answers or leads that would put me closer to solving Norman's death. Of course, that would depend on her cooperating, like telling me who her father was and where exactly he was working at the moment. If I called security on her, well, chances were she wouldn't be all that helpful then.

"Where's your father now?"

She turned her head, avoiding eye contact with me, which was weird. I wasn't that intimidating, was I? She raised her arm and pointed to a corridor on the far left. "Down that way. He's cataloging for the Middle Eastern collection."

The girl had gone from rude and defiant to shy and

quiet. Weird. I heard something about kids having personality disorders from too many video games these days. Whatever it was, at least she was being helpful. As I looked her over again, I noticed that she went to a lot of work to avoid meeting my eyes.

"Do I, uh, know you?" I asked.

She shook her head vigorously but said nothing.

"You sure? I mean, if your father works here, are you sure we've never met?"

"Nope," she said briskly.

I decided not to push it. She was clearly on edge, probably worrying about getting in trouble for smoking. Kids can look as aggressive and badass as they want with their leather jackets, combat boots and cigarettes, but they're still kids and kids scare easy.

"Hey, the cigarette thing? I'll forget I saw it if you promise not to do it again, alright?" I said in a calm and reassuring tone.

She nodded and mumbled, "Thanks."

I thought it best to leave her alone, and I headed down the hall, hoping to find her father and some answers. I was only walking for a minute or two before I came to another set of doors. I pushed them open and stopped, my jaw hanging open.

"Oh… Damn," I breathed. I have a way with words.

I'd say I was standing in a warehouse, except I've never been in one this big before, on top of which, it was filled with priceless artifacts and pieces. There was row after row of heavy-duty metal shelves towering up to the ceiling. Each rack was crammed with sealed wooden crates, and some were holding glass containers resembling oversized aquariums.

A rapid *clacking* sound snapped me out of my reverie. I turned to the source of the noise to see a young woman walking towards me, transfixed on a clipboard in her hands. She was dressed in a pair of khakis with a pair of comfortable work-safety shoes in black. I put her at five foot eight, so a fair bit taller than the girl I'd met in the hall.

She wore a loose-fitting shirt—long-sleeved, white, and rolled up to her elbows. The glint around her neck revealed an expensive gold necklace, with a heavily jeweled pendant fastened at the end. It was a golden flat oval, encrusted with several small emeralds. The stones complemented her beautiful emerald eyes, which were framed by a pair of dark brown half-moon glasses.

Her cute heart-shaped face gave her a sexy librarian look. Her brunette hair, fastened into a simple, out-of-the-way ponytail, the glasses, and work clothes…somehow; she managed to pull it off effortlessly.

I never knew women who worked in museums could look so…well…man… I've heard stories of really attractive women working in offices and as librarians and all that, but couldn't remember seeing one with my own eyes. Hearing and seeing are two different things.

I snapped back to reality and remembered why I was here. I cleared my throat to help get her attention.

Her head snapped up, and she gave a startled shake and a yelp as she stared at me in complete shock. She looked me over in a state of utter disbelief. "Norman?" At least she recognized me, which was quite the surprise. "Wow, you look great! How'd you change so quick?"

"Green tea diet," I quipped. "It's the latest trend. The pounds just fade away, and my complexion has never been better."

She snorted. "Yeah, okay. More like liposuction."

I raised an eyebrow.

"Um, sorry. It's just that I saw you the day before yesterday, and you were, well…not in the best of shape. Now you look twenty years younger. What else could you have done to change so fast?"

"P90X?" I replied.

She rolled her eyes and suppressed a laugh.

I was starting to like this gal.

"So what are you doing down here?" She seemed surprised to see me meandering around the warehouse.

I let my gaze wander around the warehouse before

quipping, "Searching for the Ark of the Covenant." Leaning forward, I added in a whisper, "I think it's on one of the shelves. Shhh!"

She threw her head back and actually let out a snorty laugh. It was, dare I say, adorable?

Her body arched back during the laugh, throwing her chest forwards. It prompted me to steal a quick glance at her identification card. It hung just a little lower than her pendant from a simple red lanyard. Her name read: Marsha Morressy.

She caught me looking but didn't realize what I was looking at, "Uh, nice view there, Norman?"

My head jolted back up. "No..."

It was her turn to arch an eyebrow.

"I mean." Come on, quick thinkin' time. "I was admiring the pendant. Who gave it to you?"

"Oh, that..."

Whew, disaster averted.

"James gave it to me." She smiled. "We haven't been together that long. I didn't think he could afford to splurge on something like this, but—"

"James?" I tilted my head.

"You know...James. You've been hovering over him for nearly a week, even called him to your office a couple of times."

There was a painful stabbing sensation in my head. Norman's memories flooded my mind again, too fast for me to make any sense of them, but fast enough to cause a frickin' aneurysm.

Figures.

"You...okay there, Norman?" Marsha asked, concern filling her voice.

"Yeah, great," I replied, my voice hoarse.

"You get a bad night's sleep or something?"

"You could say that. Felt like I woke up from a dirt nap," I said in a flat tone.

"At least you weren't actually taking a real dirt nap. Could you imagine that? Being dead?"

"Oh, I think I could," I answered.

Her eyes widened a fraction, and she shook her head. "Don't take this the wrong way, Norman, but you're acting weird."

"Yeah, there's a lot of weird going on in my life right now, but all that aside, can you refresh my memory? James?"

"He's cataloging the items we brought in for the new Middle Eastern exhibit. He's back there right now. Poor guy's been pulling all-nighters this week."

So this was the guy everything was pointing to. I really hoped he had some answers because I sure as hell didn't. All I had were leads to a person, not some supernatural baddy, and I don't deal in normal.

"Uh, Norman?" Marsha asked, waving a hand in front of my face. "You there? You sort of glazed over for a sec."

"Yeah, right, sorry. Lost in thought. Yeah, I remember James now. I met his daughter down the hall earlier. She seemed uh—"

"His daughter?" she interjected.

"Uh, yeah. That's what she said."

"He never told me he had a daughter!" She sounded scandalized. I don't know why.

"Does it matter?" I asked stupidly.

"It does to me," she scoffed. "We've been seeing each other since I started working here."

"How long have you been working here Marsha? Exactly, I mean."

"The museum called me in at the start of the cataloging—about a month, I suppose," she clipped.

Okay, now I had something. Not much, but something. She was a new employee, which meant she probably didn't know much about the museum or the other employees. Well, aside from James and—

"Where did you say his daughter was?" she asked, cutting off my train of thought.

"Down the hall, near the doors leading back to the museum. Why?"

She didn't answer, but huffed an angry breath, storming

off in the direction I had mentioned.

"Uh, Marsha… James?"

"That way," she snapped, accentuating the way with a stab of her finger.

What was it with people and pointing? Is it really that hard to say, "Hey, I'll take you there, come on," and then just show me the way?

But I knew better than to ask again. Angry girlfriend charging off to meet the haughty stuck-up young adult daughter of her boyfriend. I was smart enough not to get involved in that storm. Norman had already died once. He didn't need to die again.

Cause of death: Laceration by fingernails. Not a good way to go.

I didn't have much time, so I hoofed it over to a tiny hall with only a few grayish-blue doors in it. One had a small, scrawled sign that indicated it was the Middle East section. I pushed the door open and entered a sparsely filled room, which was odd considering how much stuff they had in the warehouse.

There were a few cultural items arranged on a table: fragile looking plates adorned with artwork, brass cups, clay pots, an oil lamp. A bronze mask with some demonic face was noticeable. An aged, worn-looking Shamshir—a Middle Eastern sword—sat beside some metal pitchers. While in an alcove, rugs that had managed to retain their beauty and quality despite their age, leaned against the wall. On a smaller table, a collection of bracelets had been set out with a small, hexagonal trinket. None of the jewelry was heavily lined with gems, like Marsha's necklace was.

In the middle of the cacophony of antiques was a wiry little man. His medium-length, black hair hung down his back in a disheveled mess. A few days' growth of beard spread over his mug, and his dark brown eyes were lined with stress. He reminded me of Norman's license, haggard and plain worn out.

Marsha said the guy had been working all-nighters. Some people are committed, but I didn't get a sense of that with James.

His dark blue work shirt, the kind mechanics and probably archeologists in the field wore, was heavily wrinkled. There were what looked to be sweat stains on it, and his simple blue jeans were just as rumpled. Overall, it looked like the guy hadn't slept, showered, or shaved in days. Even under normal circumstances, this guy was definitely not a looker.

Yet somehow, he and Marsha were dating. Talk about lucky.

He looked up at me and in a weary voice said, "Norman, I'm surprised," which was odd, because he certainly didn't seem like it. He recognized me straight away, despite all the obvious changes that Norman had gone through. "I was beginning to worry. I haven't seen you for a couple of days," he continued almost robotically.

"Yeah, well, I'm back now. Just came to uh...check up and take a look around."

He shot me an oblique look but otherwise remained silent. James returned to his work, writing fervently on the sheets of paper scattered around him.

I hovered over him for a while, looking around the room several times, but finding nothing suspicious, I decided to take a more direct route.

"Say, James, have you noticed anything weird going on around here? Anything strange?"

He gave me another weary look. "You mean how you look twenty years younger all of the sudden? Not to mention the weight loss?"

"Uh, yeah, like that."

"You're telling me you don't remember changes to your own body, Norman?"

"Well, no one seems to believe it was the magic of Pilates," I quipped.

He gave me a strange look. "You seriously don't remember?"

This guy knew something. The hard part was getting him to reveal something without making him suspicious. I had to be subtle.

"Just messin' with ya, James. I had some lipo done and then hit a Korean day spa."

He just sat there—motionless.

"So?" I said, breaking the awkward silence. "What do you think about the new me, huh?"

"You look great," he replied in a weary monotone.

"Don't get all excited now at my miraculous transformation."

No response. His brown eyes met mine as he let out an exasperated sigh.

"So, uh, aside from me and my whole day spa rejuvenation thing, anything else weird going on, James? Anything strange and mysterious? Maybe a walking reanimated dinosaur? Shrieking presidents portrayed by actors? An asinine monkey or two?"

See, subtle.

"Nothing," he replied a little too quickly. There was a hint of trepidation in his voice, the first bit of emotion James had shown during our conversation, not to mention the worrying glance he shot at one of the tables.

He knew something.

I had to get him out of the way so I could take a closer look at things. "Oh, James, by the way, I may have forgotten to mention something."

"And what's that, Norman?"

"I met your daughter earlier. She was smoking—inside."

He let out another exasperated sigh and mumbled an apology.

Well, that worked...

"And I bumped into Marsha earlier. We had a little chat about your daughter. Apparently, she wasn't aware you had one."

James shot up, ramming me out of the way, and tore out of the room, presumably after Marsha.

Ingenious.

Sometimes my brilliance amazes even myself. Want a guy to leave a room in a hurry? Tell him you revealed he had a daughter to the girlfriend he's been keeping it a secret from. Then watch him take off in an attempt to save his own ass.

Still, I could search the room now.

I scrounged around the room, turning over objects, scouring through James' notes. I found absolutely nothing, not so much as a single frickin' clue. Half an hour wasted from my already short clock, and what was even more annoying was that James hadn't come back yet. I mean, I figured he would have after thirty minutes.

How long does a conversation about a secret daughter take anyway?

This case was definitely one of the more difficult ones. By now I should have had some sort of lead, but all I had was a lot of nothing.

That's when I remembered what Marsha and Rick mentioned earlier; Norman had been hovering around James for nearly a week, keeping his own records. It was fair to assume they would be lying around the curator's office someplace. All I had to do was find them, once I found the office, and I was sure Rick would help me out if I asked.

Not that I was keen on having another conversation with Mr. Not So Bright, but he was competent at pointing in a general direction.

My hand was on the doorknob, about to turn it, when I heard a pair of voices. Some part of me, or Norman I guess, thought it better to wait. I pressed my ear against the door and tried to take in what was being said.

That's when my head started panging again. Chances were that whatever had done in poor…well, not so poor Norman, was right outside the door. I tried to work through the pain and listen, but it was difficult. It escalated to the point where it felt like an entire hornet's nest was buzzing around inside my head.

"Norman's acting weird. It's like he doesn't know, or is pretending not to know," one of the voices said. I couldn't properly make it out, partly because of the enormous, supernaturally inspired headache was distorting their voices.

Their voices should have been clear, maybe a little muffled due to the walls, but I couldn't get a clear reading on the first speaker's voice.

"More like he *doesn't* know, and more importantly, he shouldn't," the second voice said. It was more distorted than the first, carrying an unnatural baritone to it. I swear I could feel some slight reverberations in the air.

Whoakay, that was definitely in my "strange and mysterious" category.

"What makes you say that?" the first speaker asked.

"Because," the second voice began rather calmly, "he's dead, or at least should be."

"What!" the first voice exclaimed.

"Yes," the second voice continued, disturbingly nonchalant. "I should know. I killed him."

Hell, it sounded like this thing didn't even bat an eyelash when it did in Norman.

"You...you...ka...killed him!" the first voice sputtered in disbelief.

"Technically, he killed himself. Although, I think it would be more accurate to say he killed himself via my services," the second voice replied. "What is it you mortals call it? Semantics?"

And that was Yahtzee on the location and identity of the monster that did in Norman. Well, minus the identity part. Part of me wanted to fling open the door, surprise the pair of them, and waste 'em, but reason won out. I still didn't know what supernatural creature I was dealing with, and if I came out prematurely I could be in a whole world of hurt. I had no idea how to kill it quickly and efficiently. All a confrontation would lead to was my dying for the umpteenth time.

It had nothing to do with me being afraid of a paranormal baddie that sent shockwaves through the air when it frickin' spoke!

Nope, I wasn't scared at all. I am a consummate badass at ganking monsters. I just thought it best to listen to a bit more and get my bearings. Be prepared and all that.

Discretion is a part of valor; being sneaky and planning, searching for your opponent's weakness, *then* taking them out.

Yup, not afraid.

"Well...well, he's um back," the first voice said in a nervous stammer. "So what do we do?"

"I don't think that is Norman at all, but whatever it is, it's a threat," the second voice said.

Crap...cover blown.

"How do you know it isn't him?"

"Because..." the second speaker began in a tone like that of a teacher explaining something to a child, "the dead don't come back to life on their own."

"But—" the first voice began.

"No, I did not intervene. That was not the deal," the second voice explained.

Deal? So whatever killed Norman liked to deal, huh? Well, that actually narrowed it down quite a bit. I was starting to get a handle on what *it* might actually be.

"So what do we do?" the first speaker asked again.

"We kill him—it—again," the second voice said in an eerily neutral tone. Seriously, that calm about killing someone? Monster all the way through.

Wait a second. Kill him? Kill me? I thought in a jolt of sudden and panicked realization.

The. Fuck. You. Will! I thought as I ground my teeth furiously.

"You're right. It has to be done, doesn't it?" the first voice said with resignation.

"Yes, he's digging too deep, whoever or whatever he is," agreed the second speaker.

"Part of me still doesn't like it. Killing a person. I don't like it."

"But—" The second voice began.

"No, I agree with you," the first voice interrupted, sullenly, "I just don't know what to do. I just wish he was out of our way."

"I'll take care of it," the second voice said in a tone a

mother would take when reassuring her child.

I had just about had enough of hearing them plotting to kill me. It was time to go crashing through the door all heroic-like, kicking their asses up between their ears... Except, it didn't really go down like that. As soon as I made a move to fling the door open, my body erupted in agonizing pain.

Millions of microscopic claws were tearing at me, at my insides. It felt like I had dozens of fishhooks inside of me, all being pulled at exactly the same moment. I had no other way to describe it. It's like someone was trying to pull my insides out. I didn't scream. I wasn't going to give whatever it was the satisfaction of hearing me shriek in agony.

So I blacked out.

Chapter Four

Blacking out isn't so bad. What's bad is not knowing whether you're going to wake up again. It could very well be that your last blackout was in fact, well, your last blackout.

Fortunately, that wasn't the case. I had no desire to die so early into a case. Dying comes later, after I solve it.

There is a proper order to things, you know.

I awoke on an uncomfortable wooden surface, staring up at a simple, yet beautiful ceiling. Intersecting wooden beams, stained in a dark cherry finish, zigzagged their way across. A pair of ornate chandeliers hung parallel to one another, illuminating the complex architecture above. There was an archway directly above me. Painted into it were a series of rectangular portraits of angelic figures. Small archway-shaped windows were built into the sides. Divided into four parts, each were stained an individual color. No doubt they helped bathe the church in a beautiful glow in the mornings.

But it wasn't morning now; it was night, so the only light I could see was the piercing glare from the chandeliers.

"Wuzza hell?" was my oh-so-coherent response.

"You blacked out," replied a familiar, kind, and clear voice.

Waking up sucks. Why? Because you can't feel the pain that caused you to black out when you're unconscious, but you can as soon as you wake.

I groaned and reached for the back of the pew, gingerly hauling myself up. My entire body ached and panged, not to mention the parts that spasmed as if I had been electrocuted. It was hard holding onto the back of the pew.

The muscles in my arms were contracting and twitching at a frantic pace. I didn't really have a choice, though. I gritted through and faced my rescuer, eager to find out what caused the blackout.

I rolled my neck a few times to loosen the stiffened muscles, and regretted it. My entire body convulsed as the muscles around my neck twinged.

"Don't stress yourself." His voice was gentle, but then he often spoke in a soft tone.

I finally managed to turn my head to face him, although the muscles in my neck didn't so much turn as grind. It was like trying to turn rusted gears. Whatever had knocked me out did a helluva job in kicking both my physical and incorporeal ass.

I mean, I was hurting on a metaphysical level, which is…a lot!

"So?" he said simply.

"So?" I asked indignantly. "What the hell happened, Church?"

He sat there staring at me for a moment, thinking, I guess, of how best to describe my ass kicking. He pursed his lips and rested his chin in both hands, brushing a few locks of wavy, blonde hair aside when they fell over his glasses. His arctic blue eyes didn't blink the entire time he sat staring at me, and we sat in silence for a while.

Personal note: Do not get in staring contest with Church—ever.

Creepy.

When he did speak, he didn't give me the answer I was looking for. "Something unexpected," was all he managed to say.

"No kiddin' something unexpected happened! I feel like I swallowed a taser set on full!" I growled.

"I thought it felt more like fishhooks tearing at your insides?"

"That too… Wait, uh, how did you know about that?" I asked, dumbfounded.

He didn't answer. I mean, why bother when you can

remain silent and appear all omniscient-like.

Another few moments passed in silence before he spoke again. "*It* tried to kill you, you know?" There was a shade of sadness in his voice, just a shade, but it was there.

"Aw shucks, Church. I didn't know you cared that much. Uh, wait, dumb question again, but why didn't it kill me?"

"Because I rescued you," he said, as if it were obvious.

"Oh, uh, how?"

Silence.

Why explain anything to me? I mean it's not as if I'm constantly putting myself in danger working for him. I don't even *want* to work for him in the first place, but it's not like he gives me much of a choice...

I know, I know. I've got some pent-up hostility caused by being...pent up in dead people over and over again. It's like supernatural PTSD or something. I get angry. It's normal in my line of work

"Ok, Church. Let's try another one. Why did you save me?"

"Because I couldn't let it do *that* to you. It was"—he pursed his lips again—"wrong."

"Ok..." I exhaled in frustration, rubbing my temples, giving Church a chance to catch on to the fact I was getting a little pissed. "Let's try this again but how's about you give me an answer that, oh, I don't know, makes some fucking sense!"

"It was tearing your soul out of Norman's body, trying to rip you out."

I had never seen Church freak out before, but he had actually shuddered when he said that. Whatever that creature was, and whatever it had tried to do to me must've been all sorts of wrong to creep Church out.

"And why is that so bad, Church?"

"You just..." He paused to inhale deeply. "You just can't do that to a soul. It's wrong." He said with utter finality.

Anything that rattled Church, I had to be seriously wary

of. I've faced some pretty nasty things in my time, but none of them had ever caused him to blink. Hell, forget blinking, I can't remember a time when Church got involved before, aside from giving me a few tips here and there. This time though, Church, the man of little or no words, actually saved my soulful rear end.

My left forearm itched, feeling hot, like I had a rash or something. I pulled the suit's sleeve back to see my tattoo had changed. I had thirteen hours again.

Church had reset my time. Church had given me more time? Church had thrown me a frickin' bone?

Wow.

I nodded at the tattoo and then turned my gaze back to Church. "What gives?"

"You need more time now, after what happened. So I gave it to you."

"Uh, thanks."

He nodded.

"Uh, Church?"

"Yes, Vincent?"

"Look, if you, ah, saved me and all... You know something, right?"

He stared at me; emotionless. No tells, no signs, no nothing.

"You know something that I don't, right?"

His face remained neutral, but his eyes shone with amusement. "Of course, lots of things," he said nonchalantly.

Asshat.

"Look, Church, I'm a bit lost on this case—"

"Yes," he interjected.

Deep breaths. Try not to punch Church, try not to punch Church. I settled for rubbing my forehead again, right between my eyebrows with my thumb and forefinger, just so he'd get the message.

Church, you can be a major dick.

I exhaled in exasperation before speaking again. "I could use a bit of help, a finger in the right direction, a clue, something."

"Can't," he said through gritted teeth. It was like he actually had trouble getting the word out.

Weird.

"Uh, dumb question numero dos for the evening, Church."

He rolled his eyes at that.

I get no respect.

"Why not?" I asked.

"Pushed it," he replied.

"Pushed what?"

"I've already interfered too much by saving you, by allotting you more time, I can't do much more…sorry," he said. Strange… He actually, genuinely seemed sorry.

That, and he had answered a question in a complete and somewhat helpful sentence.

"What? You've got rules, too, Church?"

"Many. Harsher, far stricter than yours."

"You got a boss too?" I asked.

Silence.

"Yeah, well, I hope he or she is infinitely more vague and mysterious to you than you are with me!"

I could've sworn to god that Church was actually fighting not to smile when I said that. Church's boss was a dick too. Justice!

"Well," I said, clapping my hands together, which wasn't smart because it sent painful jolts up my arms. "I think it's time for me to get back to work." I tentatively got up from the pew and walked past Church. As I did, he gently placed a hand on my shoulder.

"Vincent," he said softly.

"Yeah?"

"You've still got friends, you know?"

I arched a quizzical eyebrow at him and snorted. "Yeah? What friends?"

He handed me a phone card. Seriously, not good ole cash or a cell phone, but a phone card.

I looked at him perplexed, waving the card to

accentuate the fact that I had no idea who I was supposed to call with it.

"You've met beings with access to vast pools of information and knowledge. Beings that owe you," he said.

"Oh…right." I sighed. I wasn't all that keen on talking or meeting with some of those beings. I say *beings* 'cause they aren't people. Literally.

"You have someone in mind, Graves?" Church asked, although I suspected he knew the answer to that one. Hell, I had a feeling Church knew exactly who I was going to call.

"Yeah, I do, I'm gonna need a bit of cash though."

He didn't say anything, but produced a clean crisp twenty-dollar bill out of his pocket. It, well it wasn't even folded or creased.

The hell?

I took the bill from him, folding it as I slipped it into my own pocket, "Thanks for spoiling me, Church."

He didn't feel the need to reply to that of course.

"So, I guess I'll be going then?"

He nodded.

I took several steps towards the door before realizing I had no idea where the nearest payphone was.

"Uh, Church—"

"Two blocks to your left, outside an organic food store. He likes raspberry, by the way," he said matter-of-factly.

Right, so not only can Church pull money out of nowhere, but apparently he's psychic as well. My boss is frickin' Criss Angel.

I pushed through the heavy wooden door and left the church. My eyes struggled to adjust to the night sky, and the cold wind nipped a little. It was uncomfortable, but then, my job always is.

"I swear, one of these days I had better end up inside a dead guy on a Caribbean getaway with a smoking hot missus or something," I muttered to no one in particular.

I walked along the streets for a while, grumbling to myself, drawing strange looks from passersby. Guess that was a normal reaction. I mean, it was obvious I was talking to myself; there was no Bluetooth on my ears. I finally made it to the organic food store, and the payphone was outside, just like Church said it would be.

It was a tiny place with a real homey look to it. A giant whiteboard hung outside with the day's deals and specials, written in marker. The windows had thin, olive-green wooden paneling around the edges, matching the décor at the top of the building, where the store's name was printed in giant white letters. Through the windows you could see a display of pumpkins and other massive fruits.

Is a pumpkin a fruit or vegetable?

Whatever.

The windows were full of organic and healthy foodstuffs that looked as if they were good for you—some of which might have actually tasted good, like the pie. I opened the door, and a soft chime tinkled above my head as I stepped inside. The floors were made of massive burgundy tiles upon which sat rows of handmade shelves filled with neatly packed glass containers. More whiteboards peppered the walls, displaying a variety of multicolored messages.

"Need help?" a sweet feminine voice called.

I turned to look at the counter. It was waist high and ran a pretty good length down the store. Wooden baskets lined the top, the kind you see at farmers' markets, and filled with an assortment of fruits and vegetables. The few shelves the counter had were stocked with an assortment of granola and energy bars, trail mix packets, and organic gum.

When the hell did they make organic gum? Wasn't gum always organic? Gum's just rubber, right? I puttered around with those thoughts before turning my attention back to the source of the voice.

The girl behind the counter was a pretty eyeful, five-five, one-ten maybe. Her blonde hair was pulled into a neat, short ponytail that bobbed whenever she moved her head. Cute smile, white teeth, and come-to-bed brown eyes. She couldn't have been out of her early twenties, probably a college student working part-time. She wore a dark brown t-shirt that seemed a little too tight. Across her chest in bright white letters was the word: HOMEGROWN in all capitals. On the bottom, closer to her midriff it read in equally bright white letters, organic shirt.

How the hell do you make an organic shirt?

"Yeah," I began, "I'm looking for raspberry preserves, honey, chocolate syrup and, uh, some spiced gin if you have it?"

Both of her pale blonde eyebrows shot up. "You can find them in the first three aisles. The gin and condoms will be in the last two."

"Uh, condoms? I didn't say I wanted those."

"Didn't have to with that list." She threw me a wicked smile. Seriously, it needed to be grounded or something. "I like the cherry flavored ones," she added in a seductive tone.

"Listen, I'm nearly three times your age and—"

She laughed. "You don't have to lie. Just say not interested. You're not going to hurt my feelings, you know?"

What was she talking about?

Right, Norman had made some sort of deal that had gotten him a supernatural facelift; he looked like a male model rather than an elderly pudgy guy.

"Sorry," I mumbled and shambled off to the aisles she had pointed to, gathering up supplies. I know they seemed odd, and I know the conclusion most people would draw, like the girl did, but there is a reason I needed them. I put them into a small plastic basket with crappy weak handles and headed back to the cashier.

I placed the cart on the counter and she began pulling them out, ringing them up one by one, occasionally glancing up to look at me.

"You know," she began, shooting me another devious smile, "a little whipped cream wouldn't hurt your night."

"I, uh, don't have that kind of night planned," I replied, trying to keep my voice as neutral as possible, but damn did she make it hard.

She rolled her eyes.

Seriously? Why does everyone have such a low opinion of me? Church thinks he's smarter than me. This girl thought I was a pervert with some culinary-based kinks. I die multiple times, fight and suffer at the hands of supernatural creatures, and I do so for the good of humanity. A little appreciation and kindness would be nice.

She rang up the final item and I paid her the total, telling her to keep the change. I wanted to get out of there and back to work, Church may have given me an extension, but I still had nothing to go on and that needed to change fast.

I strolled out of the store and up to the payphone. Dialing the number on the phone card earned me a select amount of prepaid minutes. I reached into one of Norman's pockets and pulled out my journal, flipping through a number of pages before I found the one I was looking for.

Since I had done a bazillion cases around the world, I've managed to make a few contacts here and there of both the human and supernatural variety. Contacts with knowledge and power. Contacts I could rely upon and some, well, that I couldn't. The one I was about to call...well, I had never managed to find out just how far I could trust him.

I took a deep breath and dialed the number I had written inside my journal.

"Hello?" squeaked a high-pitched girlish voice.

"I need to meet with him—now!" I said rather forcefully. It might've sounded like I was being rude, but I wasn't. Some creatures in the supernatural world need to be spoken to like that. You can't appear timid to them or their secretaries, not even on the phone. It's a sign of weakness.

"He's...he's busy at the moment and—"

"I said now!" I said, putting a bit of an edge into my voice.

"But, he's...he won't be able to. He's involved," she stammered.

I cleared my throat. "Oh, sure, I understand—"

She let out a sigh of relief.

"He's got a fucking hour! Tell him to get his short ass to Central Park, chop chop!" I growled.

She inhaled sharply, and I bet she was sweating bullets

on the other side. I'm pretty sure she did not want to relay that message to her employer.

"Tell him it's Graves. He owes me, and I'm calling it in."

The only acknowledgement I got from her was a little *meep*!

"Central Park," I repeated. "One hour."

She didn't reply. She just hung up.

Some people just don't have the manners to say goodbye. What's this world coming to?

Now I had to haul my kinky assortment of sweets and alcohol down to Central Park for a supernatural swap of sorts.

I rolled up my sleeve, checking my time beneath the streetlight.

Thirteen hours.

Good. My little shopping trip and phone call hadn't quite eaten up an hour, but the walk to Central Park might knock me down to twelve.

"Well, at least the pain's stopped," I muttered as I walked to the park.

I passed several small shops, but one in particular caught my eye. A Cantonese restaurant with high rectangular glass windows stained with a series of translucent orange tigers. Fifteen to twenty feet from the ground were rows of metal rods protruding from the building. Several pieces of black fabric with golden embroidery were stretched over them. I never learned what those things were called, but they were like mini tents, hanging over the edges of the building for aesthetics, I guess. The golden lettering atop read: The Golden Tiger.

My stomach let out an embarrassing grumble as I continued past. A faint aroma of spices and meat wafted out of the place, stirring me right up. I may technically be dead, but when I'm in someone's body I still get hungry. My pace slowed. I turned back to the narrow entrance framed by two minute bronze tigers. I hadn't eaten all day and was debating on whether to go in or not.

Dying and solving cases over and over again is hard on a guy. You work up quite an appetite and develop a real appreciation for food.

My stomach panged again. I was torn between food and the possibility of information.

"Dammit!" I growled.

Ignoring my stomach's pleas, I stormed past the restaurant. I didn't want to give into temptation and do a double take back to the place. Better to leave the restaurant behind me as quick as I could. My stomach did not agree with that idea, and it continued to make the point clear as I walked on.

I sighed aloud. "God," I said to no one in particular. "This info better be damn good."

I stuffed my hands deep into Norman's fancy suit pockets, hunched against the wind, grumbling as I strode as quickly as I could towards Central Park.

Chapter Five

Central Park at night is just breathtaking. No other word can do it justice. I strolled down an unbroken dirt pathway. Waist-high metal fences ran alongside it, behind which were rows of little black poles adorned with an orb-like light fixture on top. The minute balls of light illuminated the nearby trees. There wasn't a single leaf on them, and yet it was all so eerily beautiful. There's something about seeing nature at night, even in the dead of winter when the trees are bare. There's an honesty of sorts; no overwhelming cacophony of colors. It's just...simple.

Simplicity isn't something I come across too often so I've developed a fondness for it.

I carried on down the pathway for a bit, glancing at the benches as I searched for my informant. I knew he would be seated amongst them. This part of the park was his favorite area. I had first met him here in the spring, and it was a different scene altogether, though that might have had something to do with the fact that it was also morning then. The tree limbs were blanketed in pinkish red leaves, the pathway was littered with hundreds of them. It was a pink carpet of sorts. It was really something and still is. I haven't come across too many places that you could find beautiful all times of day, all the year-round, but then Central Park wasn't just any normal place.

Central Park was a place of magic.

There are places of magic all around the world, places attuned to the different elements of life, and they clearly show it. Central Park was as in tune with Mother Earth as they come. This was a place of nature and beauty, a place that represented life, even if it did have a few man-made pieces dotted around. Just like certain places in the world, some creatures in the supernatural world were in tune with particular elements. It's important to keep that mind.

Whether you're summoning them or calling them for a meeting, make sure the place you choose to meet is appropriate. If it's a creature of the earth, of nature, then Central Park is your best bet for making them feel comfortable, and that's very important to many a supernatural being.

That was why I brought the strange assortment of sweet items and gin with me. Supernatural creatures have many rules, traditions, and the like that need to be observed. Many of these creatures are big on offerings. They just can't resist. The one I was seeking had quite the sweet tooth. However, like I said before, they're big on tradition, so it's not like I could've bought him a bunch of Snickers bars and Pixie sticks—*especially*—the Pixie sticks. They would've gone over bad. Oh, they're sweet all right, but it's all about *traditional* offerings, and they aren't. That and the fact Pixies aren't held in too high regard by many creatures. Pixies are paranormal pranksters, and, well, they're assholes.

This was about being old-school—*proper* offerings and tributes. It was about constancy in a way, creatures of the earth are all about that. See, like the earth, earthy supernatural beings are stubborn, grounded, fixed and resolute. These aren't the kind of creatures that take to change very well, which is why my offering of sweets had to be very, very old-school and organic. Hence why I chose the raspberry preserves and honey. Yes, the chocolate syrup was less traditional, but the bottle said organic so that counts for something. It couldn't hurt to sweeten the deal as it were.

Then there was the gin, which might seem like the odd one out in my assortment of goods.

What can I say? Alcohol is the stupidity-inducing glue that binds the paranormal and normal together. Even the supernatural like getting a buzz every now and again.

"Graves," called out a deep grating voice, shaking me

from my reverie.

He was small for a man, but then, technically, he wasn't really a man. He was four-foot-two with a lump on his head. I think the politically correct term for a person of that stature is dwarf? Except the supernatural don't care much for politically correct, so much as correct. He wasn't a dwarf at all. My diminutive friend here was a gnome, and calling a gnome a dwarf...well, them's fightin' words to their kind.

I don't know what happened between them, but dwarves and gnomes loathe each other. I wouldn't go so far as to call it hate, more like they can't stand each other. Apparently they can't tolerate the sight or smell of one another. Yeah, I don't get the smell thing, but then again, I don't have heightened senses like they do. I guess that's nature's way of compensating for making them so short. I don't know if the two races have ever gone to war over anything, but I do know it's not a good idea to get a group of dwarves and gnomes together in the same room. It'd be like a supernatural Hiroshima. Yeah, it's that bad!

It was general advice to those in the supernatural world to not confuse the two races.

It's considered a grave insult to them.

So then, how do you tell the difference?

Well, take the foreshortened being in front of me. While dwarves and gnomes are about the same height, they differ in builds. The gnome before me was averagely built, while a dwarf would resemble a waddling barrel. A gnome can easily be confused for a dwarf...like politically correct dwarf not supernatural dwarf. I mean, a gnome is just like a really short person.

A dwarf is a really short person on anabolic steroids or like that human growth hormone crap. They're like little gorillas: some parts just aren't properly proportioned. They have massive chests and stomachs, the kind you'd see on professional strongmen who pull frickin' trucks. They have short arms that are really filled in. Their forearms are as thick as the average person's biceps, but they have strangely slender wrists that lead out to freakishly big hands. Oh, and one more thing, probably the most important: dwarves are beardless.

Yeah, shocker!

Tolkien got that bit wrong.

I think it's somewhat safe to say that if you happen to see a vertically challenged person with a nice beard, they're a gnome. If they're built like minute bodybuilders, they're dwarves. There is the off chance you might actually run into a normal, everyday small person, in which case you'll probably get your ass kicked. If you do happen to run into a gnome or dwarf and mix them up, then you will also get your ass kicked. More thoroughly since members of both races are several times stronger than humans.

This gnome could easily whoop me, even at four-foot-two. He wouldn't break a sweat, nor dirty his immaculate black & gray pinstripe suit. Then there were the golden, jewel-encrusted rings on his teeny, tiny hands; those would hurt—a lot.

Gnomes have a bit of a thing for gems, makes sense seeing as they're the best gem cutters in existence. Actually, many of them are in the precious stone business. He definitely looked like an elite businessman; slick suit, fancy rings and a neatly trimmed beard; it was all salt-and-pepper. Gnome beards tend to grow gray much quicker than the rest of their hair. I don't know why. Chalk it up to another supernatural quirk. As I said though, this gnome wasn't in the business of gems; he dealt in something far more important in my line of work.

Knowledge.

Most people have heard the saying "knowledge is power." Well, in my trade it couldn't ring more true. You have knowledge of a supernatural creature, what it is, what it feeds off, how it hunts or operates, and eventually you will find a way to kill it. This little guy here had access to boundless knowledge.

The word gnome hails all the way from the ancient Greek word *gnosis*, which means knowledge. That's what gnomes are: they are diminutive beings of knowledge. Hence why I called this little meeting. But there is a catch—there always is, isn't there? Knowledge is power, right? Well, who in their right mind forks over power for free? There's always a price. Thankfully, with this guy it was a small offering, maybe a favor, but hopefully not the last one.

He sat there quietly, regarding me with his hands clasped. The light from the lamps glinted from the gold rings adorning his hands. His eyes were tiny, deep brown rings, and with his unnaturally large pupils. They were more black than brown. It was just odd. He had a crooked beak of a nose that wasn't very characteristic of a gnome. I think someone, or something, had decided to break it for him at some point. His short black hair was neatly combed and parted. Gnomes don't look anything like those stupid garden ornaments; this guy was the model of a New York hot-shot executive.

Believe it or not, he was the king of info. He ran a multibillion-dollar consulting firm and, of course, some enterprises that catered to the supernatural clientele. Which I'm sure netted him all manner of other goods in exchange for his services.

Even after knowing all that, and as large a big shot as he was, his feet dangled off the park bench like a little child. It was hilarious. If he were actually a short person, then yes, it would be wrong to laugh. Since he was a supernatural creature, normal rules of courtesy don't apply. Like I mentioned before though, several times stronger than a normal person, so I kept my laugh on the inside.

I didn't want to be pancaked by a supernatural midget. My pride had already been wounded begging Church earlier. I didn't need an ass-whooping from a gnome as well.

"Well?" he said, sighing in exasperation.

"Nice night, huh, Gnosis?" I replied.

As our little exchange had revealed, his name was Gnosis. This guy was the first gnome. He was their origin, their forefather, and what not. A heavy hitter in the supernatural world. Not necessarily in terms of strength, but what he knew. He had access to knowledge that could procure him the services of nearly anyone.

This tiny four-foot guy could buy anyone or anything, and that made him extremely dangerous.

"Why do you insist on bantering?" he said, interrupting my thoughts rather rudely. "I know you're on a tight deadline, but I have a problem of my own so get to it," he said in an agitated tone.

First things first though. "Here," I said, handing him the grocery bag of goods.

He rummaged through them, and his eyes lit up when he saw the raspberry preserves and honey. He was like a kid at Christmas.

They're big on that old-school, sweet stuff.

Holding up the chocolate syrup, he snorted, "Really?"

I shrugged. "Don't knock it till you try it. Take it for a whirl with the missus. Maybe you'll like it."

He sighed again. "You don't know my wife."

Ouch, supernatural marital problem. Not getting involved in that. There was a part of my brain that wanted to ask if his wife had a beard, verify my theory. I told that part of my brain to shut up.

"Spiced gin?" he said, surprised. "Someone's been doing their homework." The grin on his face was more than enough to know that I had scored some brownie points.

"I accept your offer, Vincent Graves, and, in return, offer you my services in accordance to the value of your gifts and—"

"Whoa, whoa, whoa! You owe me one, too. I saved your munchkin butt with that whole troll thing. If I remember correctly, you were going to be eaten. Screw all that equal to the value of my gift crap! You're helping me until I figure this case out, got it?" I growled.

"Fine, fine," he grumbled dejectedly. "What do you want to know?"

I started by showing Norman's driver's license photo and then put both my hands on either side of my face, framing it to accentuate my point.

"Interesting," he mused.

"Not the word I would've gone for considering he ended up in a grave," I retorted.

"What else?" he asked.

I told him about Norman's job and how he had somehow managed to get a pad in Upper Manhattan. Told him about the Rolex, the premium credit cards, and how he'd come by a classic car.

He let out a low whistle.

"Yeah, not too shabby for a museum curator, huh, Gnosis?"

He shook his head in agreement.

"So?" I said, letting the question hang in the air.

"That's not much to go on, Graves. You'll have to give me something more—not to mention this will take time," he replied.

"How much time? I need answers now."

"Then you had better give me some more information. Your case isn't the only thing in my world at the moment. I'm preoccupied." He said in a rough voice.

"What's up?"

"Somebody stole from me," he said simply, except with him it wasn't so simple. When he found that somebody, they were going to pay, big time.

It was my turn to let out a low whistle. "Who's dumb enough to steal from you?"

"You'd be surprised, Graves. In fact, I'm constantly surprised by the stupidity of your species. Yet you surprise me by not being nearly as dumb as the rest of your kind."

"Gee, thanks! What can I say? I'm an overachiever."

He snorted.

What the hell?

"What did they steal?" I asked, trying to change the subject from the degradation of, well, me.

I could hear his teeth grinding. "They stole several gemstones that I had passed down through my family. They were stolen from a great descendant of mine. They mean a great deal to me."

"Ah, gotcha. Somebody stole your family jewels, huh?

Well, I'm certain you'll have your hands on them soon
enough."

He tilted his head and just stared at me.

"Yeah that wasn't, uh...yeah..." I said.

He didn't say anything but I was sure he was changing
his opinion of me. The whole not-as-stupid-as-everyone-else
thing. I'm pretty sure I was now ranked alongside everyone
else in the stupid category.

"Uh, how about we get back to helping me out with my
case, huh?" I said, attempting to bring the subject back to
my investigation.

"Yes, let's," he said.

"When I went digging around the museum for leads,
several people told me that Norman was involved in one of
the new exhibits they plan on displaying," I informed
Gnosis.

"What is the nature of the exhibit?"

"Ah, it's Middle Eastern Antiquities, things of that
sort," I answered.

"Hmm, that doesn't help much either. Did you find
anything curious in your search?"

"Zilch."

"You're not making this easy, Graves." He grumbled.

"If it were easy I wouldn't require the services of one of
the world's best information brokers." A little flattery never
hurts. Supernatural creatures have egos too, and they need
to be stroked every so often.

"I *am* the best information broker in the world. Don't
forget that," he replied firmly.

"Well, this shouldn't be that hard for you then, should
it?" I retorted.

He grunted.

"I do remember something else," I began.

"Which is?" he asked.

I had to be very careful explaining the next bit to him. I
couldn't let him know about my near departure from
Norman's body or Church's rescue of me. Not because of
my pride or anything, but because I couldn't let him know

something like that could be done to me. Most beings, Gnosis included, knew I could be killed physically but then I'd just come back again. I couldn't risk him knowing there was a way to harm my soul, and I couldn't let him know about Church. Church knew about Gnosis, but I wasn't sure if Gnosis knew about Church. Amazing information broker or not, I was not going to risk that.

I took a deep breath before beginning, and then told him about overhearing the distorted conversation and about Norman making some sort of deal.

"Now that is interesting," he mumbled, more to himself than me.

"Painful, too," I added.

"And the creature made no mention of how it killed Norman?" he asked.

"No. Just that it was responsible, and that technically it was Norman's fault," I replied.

"Hmm, it must have been referring to the deal."

"That's what I was thinking, but what I don't know is if it killed Norman after the deal was made, as payment? Or, if whatever deal Norman made actually got him killed?"

"Interesting questions. I'm not sure at the moment, but deals…hmm," he mused.

"That must narrow it down to a handful, right? I mean I haven't run across anything that makes deals, but there can't be that many things out there that do, right?"

"No, not many. Not many at all, but still enough that we cannot be sure what you're dealing with," Gnosis replied.

"Well, give me something. You *are* the best information broker after all," I said dryly.

"I'm not omniscient, Graves!" growled Gnosis. It was odd seeing something so small growl at me. It would have been somewhat adorable if, you know, he couldn't bludgeon me to a pulp.

"Well whatever it is, it was able to knock me out without coming in physical contact with me. Does that help?" I asked, being careful not to mention that it had almost succeeded in ripping my soul from Norman's body.

"No, it only raises more questions," he said frowning.

"Great," I said sarcastically. "More of those and no answers."

"How then, do you suppose you get an answer? Or any answer for that matter, Graves?"

"You give 'em to me?" I quipped.

"You ask a question," Gnosis answered.

"Right, well, now I'm asking what the hell killed Norman frickin' Smith!" I snarled.

He shrugged rather nonchalantly.

"Wait a minute," I said aloud. "This thing likes to make deals, right?"

"It would appear so."

"It was rhetorical. I was talking to myself," I grumbled.

"Then perhaps you should refrain from speaking aloud when talking to yourself, especially when you happen to be talking to someone with whom you were asking a multitude of questions," he said rather smugly. A tiny grin appeared on his bearded face.

"I think I'll let the troll eat the short, smart ass gnome next time. Trust me when I say that you won't be the snack that smiles back!"

His smile vanished.

Damn straight. Respect!

"What I was getting at, Gnosis, was that maybe this thing didn't only make a deal with poor Norman here. I'm thinking that maybe it's tried to do in other people. I mean, why not? Most monsters will keep going if the pickings are there, and this is the American Museum of Natural History. There are thousands of people coming in every day and all the full-time employees. It would be easy to get one of them. Maybe there are some other employees who know what this thing is—maybe they've already had dealings with the creature," I rattled off.

"You said it was also speaking to someone else? Someone who didn't handle the notion of murder too well," Gnosis added.

"Right," I said nodding. "So it's got a buddy at the

museum."

"Or a hostage," Gnosis replied. "If it's as dangerous as you make it out to be, then it's quite possible that the employee isn't helping it by choice."

"Great," I muttered. "Now I have to save somebody in addition to ganking the monster and solving the case?"

"Isn't that what you do?"

"Not really. It's not in the job description to begin with," I answered.

Gnosis snorted rather derisively. "As if you had a job description. If you did, what then would it say? Face it, Graves. You pretty much do what you are forced to do," he chortled.

"You don't know anything about me, Gnosis! Anything!" I snarled.

"You're right," he conceded. "But I know a bit about who you were."

What?

"You know something about my past? My *actual* past?" I asked, my voice shaking.

He smiled. It was like looking at a shark—all teeth and just a little bit terrifying. "Of course."

This diminutive little creature knew something about who I was—who I *really* was before I died. I had to know. I had no clue how I had been thrust into this life, about who I was before, about what killed me; this could end it all.

But Gnosis had no intention of telling me.

"Graves, I know what you're thinking, and the answer is no," he said with utter finality.

"Why?" I growled.

"Because all knowledge has a price and you have nothing to pay for the value of this information."

"But…" I started.

"Nothing, Graves."

I'm sure he could hear my teeth grating; he's lucky that I have immense levels of restraint because I wanted to throttle the ugly little gnome and force it out of him.

"I suggest you stick to your current case," he said, trying

to get me to drop the subject.

It worked. He was right; this case was first priority…for now. I made sure to let him know.

"Fine, we drop this for now, but, Gnosis, you *are* going to give me that info," I said in a dangerously quiet tone.

He didn't respond, blink, or make any acknowledgement that he had heard me. It didn't matter though. He knew I was dangerous and could carry out my threat if I wanted. He may be stronger than me, but I knew how to hurt and kill all manner of supernatural creatures, including gnomes.

"So back to my case. I want any and all information you have about any employees in the past month or so who have had incredible bouts of luck. Anything out of the ordinary: winning the lottery, changes in appearance, strange or sudden deaths—the works. I want to know anything and everything about anyone to come through that museum."

Gnosis nodded in agreement.

"And, Gnosis?" I said, letting the words linger in the air for a moment. "I want that info tonight."

He inhaled so sharply it sounded more like a hiss. "Tonight?"

"Yes."

I could hear his teeth grinding away in his jaw. Good. Now he knew what it felt like. He had to comply. As I said before, there are many rules when dealing with the supernatural. When you do a deal, both sides *have* to follow them. The rules aren't suggestions or guidelines, they're ironclad. We dealt, we agreed and now he had to deliver.

"Fine!" he snapped. "But this is a tall order."

"Step up, little man."

"You're pushing it Graves!" His nostrils flared.

I gave him an indifferent shrug. I was angry—angry at the fact he knew something about me and refused to share it. Maybe there were rules about trading information, but still, it was *my* past. I had a right to know.

"Don't burn bridges with those that can help you, Graves," he warned.

"Well, we'll see just how helpful you are, Gnosis. Info. Tonight," I said with such finality he knew our conversation was over. I started walking away from him when he called out.

"Graves, don't bother calling me again."

I replied without turning or breaking my stride. "You still owe me one, Gnosis. Till we're even, I'm calling you whenever the hell I feel like it."

I told you, you have to be rough with the supernatural; it's like being the new kid at school. You either put on your best scowl and make people respect you, or they walk right over you. I may have been amazingly rude to Gnosis, but it reminded him not to screw with me, or screw me over with the info. Maybe he didn't like me anymore after that conversation, but so what? He respected me, and maybe became a little bit wary of me. Those two are infinitely more important in my line of work than being liked.

I walked through the park for a while, thinking to myself, trying to sort through the maddening mess in my head. The conversation with Gnosis, and the fact the little imp knew something about my past was too much. I decided to stick with focusing on Norman's murder, but all I knew was that whatever killed him could hurt you from a distance. Oh, and it liked to make deals.

Two very ambiguous bits of information. I knew a lot of things that could attack someone from a distance, but nothing that had a penchant for making bargains.

I figured the best thing to do would be to head back to Norman's place and wait for Gnosis to deliver on the info I needed. I didn't want to sit around waiting, wasting my already diminishing timeline, but I didn't have much of a choice. So that's what I did. I headed back to what was home for now, whistling as I walked through Central Park.

Chapter Six

As I walked through the park, I noticed a small figure watching me in the distance. They were too far away to make out any of their features, but I could tell they were dressed in a hoodie and sweats. They watched me intently—too intently.

They were spying on me! I guess they must've tailed me to see who I was meeting with, which meant they had seen Gnosis. Instinct told me this was the person working with the monster. Catching this punk meant I could interrogate them and find out what the hell I was dealing with.

Apparently, that same train of thought had crossed Shorty's mind because they bolted.

"Dammit!" I took off after them. Now I can run fast, much faster than the average person and for considerably longer, but even with my enhanced speed, Short Round was able to outrun me. I don't know how, but they were constantly putting more and more distance between us, which was definitely not normal.

They were either on some form of paranormal speed or were paranormal themselves.

I kept running though. Tearing out of the park, I hit the streets hard. They sprinted down the sidewalk, barreling into people and pushing others aside. Even with the darkness, I had a fairly clear line of sight. I could see them a good two hundred feet ahead of me, give or take a little.

I guess they had finally gotten tired of running, or had gotten smart, because they stopped and darted through the doors of the nearest building.

I pumped my legs harder, skidding to a halt when I

reached the building they had run into.

A familiar and intoxicating aroma filled my nose and caused my stomach to grumble. I was back at the Golden Tiger. Shorty had gotten clever and decided to blend in with a larger crowd.

This was great for me though. Now they were trapped inside the restaurant. If I could find them, I would not only get myself some real info, but maybe even grab a meal because I was starving.

I rubbed my hands together and walked towards the entrance. The tiger statue on the right side was missing...

A deep guttural sound echoed behind me. The patrons seated nearest the windows looked in my direction and began shrieking.

"Oh, sonuvabitch!"

I whirled about to see, no doubt, the monster right behind me.

"Holy shit!" I yelped when I saw the source of the noise. Somehow, the garden sized bronze statue had found a way to become a full-sized beast made of solid gold—and it was fucking alive! Even in the supernatural world that's weird.

Now I've dealt with many a supernatural creature before, and been inside a number of skilled and talented people, but none of that prepared me for this.

So I ran.

I pushed Norman's body beyond its natural endurance in my desperation to get away. Although I have the enhanced abilities of running fast and hitting harder, even they have their limits. It's kind of like being a zombie, minus the rotting, the stench, and just, well, the general stupidity. Think of it like those moments where you see soccer moms lifting up a minivan on an adrenaline rush; I can do that—most of the time.

So when I run, I run damn fast, which in most cases would leave whatever's tailing me far behind. But, of course, today was the day I just couldn't catch a break. The eight hundred pound plus golden tiger was managing to hang onto my borrowed ass.

It's frightening enough having a tiger chasing you. Add to that the fact that this one was made of solid metal and had claws capable of gouging out bits of sidewalk. Well, you can guess how frickin' terrified I was.

What really bothered me was the fact that as I tore past people—scared and screaming—none of them were on their phones calling the cops or animal control. Nope.

They were taking fucking pictures!

What the hell is wrong with people these days?

It was a miracle I managed to see where I was going amidst the flashing lights from people's phones.

They were distracting, and the tiger certainly thought so too. It paused for a moment, snarling at some of the people snapping away. That elicited more screams. People turned and ran, which is absolutely the worst thing to do when a massive cat is staring at you.

All predators have a chase instinct, so if a big tiger's roaring and you decide to run, it's going to chase you down. Chances were, if they'd backed away slowly, it would have left them alone and continued pursuing me. They didn't do that.

So why did I run? Well, I knew that that tiger was going to try and kill me regardless of what I did. New York doesn't have solid gold tigers that appear out of nowhere. That's supernatural, and if it's supernatural, it's likely going to be after me.

Now, was it a good thing the tiger lost focus on me?

Yes.

Was it a good thing that it was about to chase down and devour a New York couple?

Probably not.

My bosses would be beyond pissed if tomorrow's New York Times read: "Solid Gold Tiger Eats Stupid Couple Who Were Taking Photos of It With Their Camera Phone."

So I did the only thing I could, I reached down and grabbed a crumpled up soda can—there's always litter in New York—and hurled it at the tiger. It made a noticeable *clank* as it made impact with the tiger's skull. Man, did that piss it off.

It snapped its head in my direction and let out the loudest roar I had heard yet, then came bounding after me. Each leap tore up bits of road and sidewalk.

It was times like this that reminded me just how much I hated my job, but then, who doesn't?

Fortunately, I was nowhere near tired yet, so I could keep running at an intense pace for a fair while. I was hoping the tiger might just get bored and give up.

It could happen…

I sprinted as fast as I could, occasionally dashing through the busy New York streets and traffic in the hopes a car would pancake the tiger. No such luck. Every car either swerved to avoid it or slammed the brakes.

Apparently solid gold tigers that are chasing me down are on the endangered list, so no one wanted to help me kill it.

I had only been running for a few minutes, but it seemed like an hour and I was getting nowhere. The tiger didn't show any signs of slowing down either.

There was a fairly narrow-looking alleyway up ahead. I was hoping that I'd be able to lose the tiger there, considering how much larger it was than me. I bolted towards it, putting every bit of pep in my step as I dove into the alley. I looked down it and realized it was a dead end, but it was at least lined with several dumpsters.

As disgusting as dumpsters are, New York dumpsters even more so, it's much better to dive into one of them than be eviscerated by a supernatural metal tiger. I drew closer to the nearest dumpster, and noticed something at the very end of the alleyway—a ladder! It was partially retracted, meaning that I would have to jump to reach it, *if* I could reach it, but if I did, I could avoid being kitty chow.

So I abandoned my plan of diving into a dumpster and dashed towards the end of the alley. I was nearly there when Whiskers came barreling down the alley behind me. I turned my head as I ran, wanting to see how much Fur Ball was gaining on me. The answer—a lot! It was too thick to avoid hitting the dumpster as it ran past. I thought it would slow down and try to squeeze through, buying me time.

Nope.

The friggin' feline just bounded over it. The eight hundred pound plus golden tiger hopped over the dumpster and never broke its stride.

Not fair at all.

I finally managed to make it to the retracted ladder; it hung there in its rusted and disused glory, leading up to the small, typical New York alley fire escape. It was a bit higher than I had originally thought. I missed it on my first jump, but got lucky on the second. I clasped the cold steel ladder, my weight sending it crashing down to the alley floor. Mittens' deep guttural snarls and snuffles grew louder as it drew closer. My hands impacted the cold steel hard as I rapidly scrambled up the ladder. That was when the large cat decided to pounce; it landed in the exact spot I was at seconds before. The weight of the tiger's impact caused the pavement to crack.

Okay…

I managed to make it up the ladder and onto the first of the metal balconies that comprised the fire escape. I collapsed against the railings and exhaled more in relief than exhaustion. The tiger plodded around below, obviously furious that it had failed to kill me.

"Ha, ha ha, ha ha!" I laughed loudly. There is something about surviving near evisceration that makes you appreciative of things like laughter. "Screw you, Tony!" I shouted. Something about surviving also makes you appreciate the ability to be vindictive.

The tiger let out another menacing growl.

Tigers can't understand human speech…right?

I got my answer the next second when the tiger stopped pacing and tensed its body. Its muscles were coiling visibly.

"Well…shit."

The next instant, the tiger was sailing through the air, about to land on the first balcony of the fire escape. My legs hammered against metal as I scampered up the first flight of stairs rather awkwardly. I barely managed to get out of the way when the enraged supernatural cat landed with a very audible *thunk*. I fought to keep my balance as the entire structure shook. The rusted metal groaned, and I could swear bolts were beginning to loosen.

Someone needed to lay off their Frosted Flakes.

The tiger didn't hesitate; it pounced again, launching itself up the first flight of stairs towards me. I didn't sidestep so much as collapse and roll out of the way as it leapt towards me once again. Its front paws were outstretched like it was going to give me a hug, an eight hundred pound razor-sharp hug. I bounced back onto my feet and ran up the second flight of stairs as the ballistic kitty missile crashed into the railings. I staggered as the entire fire escape jolted violently. I'm sure the sound of metal tearing from brick would have filled my eardrums if they weren't already being deafened by the tiger's angry roars.

By now, lights were flicking on in the windows of the apartments overlooking the fire escape. I could hear a noisy, terrified commotion from inside. Well, little did they know it, but it was a helluva lot more terrifying outside.

I clambered up the last few stairs of the second flight, my hands and knees panging as they hit the metal stairs over and over. I just made it to the next balcony when the tiger swept a paw at my legs. It missed—narrowly. The tips of its claws grazed my left calf, slicing the flesh open with ease. Fiery hot pain lanced up my leg; my calf muscle was twitching in shock, but worst of all, I was bleeding.

The tiger had spilt blood; no way was it going to give up the chase now.

Great...

I grabbed onto the cold steel of the support railing and hauled myself up, limping towards the next flight of stairs. The tiger followed at a leisurely pace. It was stalking me now. Why not? It had hurt me, and it knew it. Why waste more energy chasing me? I had dictated the pace of the chase so far. Now it was the tiger's turn. There was no rush;

it wanted to kill me nice and slow.

Supernatural douche kitty.

My calf was making it hard to ascend the third flight of stairs; my teeth were eroding each other at this point. They ground hard in my attempt to grit through the pain. There was hope yet though. The tiger covered the last flight of stairs in a simple, graceful leap. Its considerable weight once again caused the rusted metalwork to shudder and sway. The fire escape was beginning to lean towards the other side of the alley. Soon it would give in completely and crash to the ground—anything that went with it would be crushed.

And, suddenly, I had a way to kill this overgrown ornament!

"Hey, schizo cat! Come get some!" I snarled defiantly, goading the already enraged tiger.

The giant feline let out the most disturbing noise I had ever heard in response to my insult; it wasn't another deafening roar though. The tiger made the deepest guttural sound ever, an intense and heavy reverberation coming from its throat. A very low and menacing sound, kind of like when someone's voice drops to a dangerously quiet whisper: the "I'm going to kill you slowly and painfully" whisper.

So, I had successfully pissed off a supernatural solid gold tiger. Not my smartest moment.

The tiger charged with the most unnatural burst of speed I had seen yet. It was a golden four-legged cannonball...coming straight at me.

I used every bit of strength I had to hurl myself out of the way, crashing into the sides of the fire escape in the process and bouncing my sternum off the unforgiving metal structure.

Mittens, though, plowed straight into the railings, broke through them and went sailing towards the concrete in a snarling fury. It landed with an earth-shattering *crunch*; the pavement cracked beneath its weight.

And then what I was waiting for happened. The tiger's last impact against the fire escape caused the entire structure to become unstable. It wobbled uncontrollably. Seconds later, the inevitable happened. Five floors of rusted metalwork came loose and went crashing to the ground—with me inside.

"This is gonna hurt," I muttered to myself as the world around me sank. The impact was a hellish symphony of metal groaning, wrenching, screeching, me quite possibly screaming, and the painful, high-pitched wail of a very large cat.

The pain wasn't all too great either. My everything hurt, but at least I remained conscious.

"Ohhhhh," I groaned unintelligibly. My neck panged excruciatingly as I turned to look at the scene of carnage around me. Rusted metalwork lay around me in a mangled heap.

"Snowball?" I coughed, "You there?"

No answer.

I grabbed a piece of the wrecked metal framework and hauled myself up—slowly, *very* slowly. A combination of white-hot and dull, throbbing pain seared through me. I could make out voices coming through the apartment windows, but my head was a bit too battered to make out what they were saying.

After the spinning stopped, I looked around for the tiger, but there wasn't a trace of it beneath the metalwork. I scrambled free of the twisted heap of junk and began rummaging through the debris.

Nothing.

There was no body, no crunched up golden tiger limbs, not even a not-so-fuzzy gold-plated tail. Nothing.

My head started to get back in order and my hearing followed. I was able to make out the distinct sound of sirens that undoubtedly belonged to New York's finest. My little tiger escapade through the busy streets had attracted some attention. Last thing I needed was to be detained by the cops.

"Dammit." I cursed under my breath. Grabbing hold of a bit of once railing, I hauled myself up from one knee. The entire area from my thigh down to my shin erupted in pain.

"Errgh!" I groaned. My hands shook the railing as I fought against the pain. That's when I felt it. I removed my hands from the rails, teetering a bit from the lack of support. My hands were covered in a fine, powdery substance. It was difficult to make out the color at night, but it looked black. I rubbed my index and middle finger against my thumb. The powder was fine and soft, like black baby powder. I cautiously sniffed it; it smelt like the aftermath of a fire.

The hell was soot doing here?

I took another careful look around the scene. It was everywhere, like a giant balloon filled with the stuff had burst. When the tiger had been crushed, it had left an enormous amount of soot residue, but why? This was getting frustrating. What did a golden tiger have to do with soot? Every time I thought I had a lead, I was dealt another series of questions.

A barrage of red and blue lights began cascading over the walls of the alleyway. The cops were close or already here, waiting right outside the alley for little old me. I looked the other way, forgetting it was a dead end.

I didn't have much choice. I placed my right hand against the wall and staggered towards the flashing lights. As I drew closer to the street, I saw half a dozen police officers standing outside their cars. Some had drawn their firearms, pointing them down the alley—at me. Others had their hands on their weapons, ready to draw if necessary. There was one other person, and *man*, did she stand out amongst the boys in blue.

It was her face that made her stand out. It wasn't some indiscernible mug that blended in with the cops in the background. She had a striking beauty. Her oval face bore a bit of a smirk, the kind of smirk you wore when catching someone in the act of doing something bad…like me. The car's headlights illuminated her face, showing off her flawless beige skin, tinged with the slightest hint of gold. Deep brown eyes glowed with amusement. Her eyebrows were slightly darker than her chestnut brown hair; one of them rose a fraction of an inch, further accentuating the fact that she found all of this to be rather amusing. She wore her hair straight, loose, and let it fall down to the bottom of her shoulders.

She wasn't in the uniform of a cop. Nope. This woman wore oh-so-fashionable black. She wore what looked like comfortable flat-bottomed work shoes; the kind that went with a suit but ones you could actually run in. Her outfit was an all-black pantsuit combo. Her suit was double-breasted with notched lapels, unbuttoned to reveal a pristine white dress shirt with turquoise pinstripes. Definitely *not* the attire of NYPD.

Fan-friggin-tastic. It wasn't just the cops I had managed to attract.

She confirmed my fears when she walked up to me and produced a small rectangular leather wallet, in which were two sheets of paper. The top one contained a small intricate seal belonging to the Department of Justice. Atop the piece of rectangular paper, in very clear blue letters, were the words Federal Bureau of Investigation. In the center, in massive letters, were the initials FBI, and to the right, it had a small picture of the woman before me. I couldn't make out the rest, but I didn't need to. It would read Special Agent, her name, and a serial number. In the bottom right-hand corner of the wallet was a glistening gold shield shaped badge, the top of which had an eagle sprouting out of it.

"Fuckin' feds," I muttered under my breath.

"What was that?" she asked sharply.

I exercised my Fifth Amendment right and promptly shut the hell up. Unfortunately, it didn't stop *her* from talking though.

"I'm Special Agent Camilla Ortiz. I'd very much appreciate it if you could accompany me downtown to answer a few questions," she said in a rather sweet voice. Guess she was the good cop.

"What if I say no?"

A wolfish smile replaced her smirk as she brushed aside her suit, revealing a holstered Glock Model 22.

"Oh," was all I had to say.

"So?" She said, letting the question hang in the air.

"Well, I'd love to, but I'm sweaty, I'm tired, I'm bleeding, I've missed my shows, and I could really use a spa treatment now. So girlfriend to girlfriend, I think I'm gonna go home now and eat some Baskin Robbins and have some me time," I replied. So much for staying silent.

Her look of amusement returned. "Cute," she said.

"I can be," I smiled.

"Cuff him," were the last words she said before two officers deemed it necessary to force me to my knees and place me in handcuffs.

As they were escorting me into the back of the car, I shot her a quick look, grinned and said, "You know, this is a really rough way to get a date. You could've just asked me out, you know?"

I could've sworn a smile flashed across her face, just for a second. She shook her head and scoffed. That's when the cops shoved me rather unceremoniously into the back seat of the car and slammed the door on me.

If I paid taxes, I would have made a sarcastic comment about taxpayer dollars at work and hindering supernatural detectives trying to save the world...or at least a museum. This was seriously going to eat into my time limit. Church was not going to be happy.

Chapter Seven

It was about a thirty-minute drive from Manhattan down to Federal Plaza, where the New York division of the FBI was located. In that time, my shredded calf had managed to heal, which was nice. I did a bit of bantering with the officers, who were kind enough to chauffeur me literally downtown. Well, down state I guess.

They didn't like my banter.

Flashes of lights bombarded the windows of the car. There were reporters outside, snapping away at "the person of interest" everybody assumed was me. Well, technically I guess it was me, but if we get down to it, it was really the animated golden tiger. Somehow, I didn't think they would buy that story.

I was ushered out of the car rather forcefully, which was when I noticed the group of reporters was considerably larger than I had first thought. Much larger. There must have been dozens, literally dozens. My late night tiger excursion must have really garnered some attention, but then I guess if a massive tiger chases people down the streets of New York, it's bound to make the news.

The reporters all tried to shove their way towards me—microphones, cameras, and all—trying to ask me questions, but they were restrained by a group of stone-faced men.

"My, aren't I the popular one?" I said.

I guess one of the men escorting me must've heard that because I received a good shove, an indication to keep moving and stop talking.

"Asshat," I muttered dejectedly.

I was led into the building and escorted to an elevator. I

wasn't paying all too much attention to what was happening. My calf had healed and I wasn't leaving a trail of blood everywhere, but my head was still somewhat groggy. I probably had a concussion. Definitely not the first time it's happened either. I was going in and out of a coherent state of mind. All I remember is my body—well, Norman's body—being pushed and pulled along.

Manhandling at its best. Seriously, no concern for the disembodied spirit inhabiting the body of their recently deceased fellow man—who was now suffering from a concussion.

Bright, and somewhat painful, light bombarded my eyes like a sledgehammer as I was forced into a small cold room and shoved into a chair. I propped my head atop my closed fists and rested my elbows on the table before me. They didn't bother to take the handcuffs off, which just went to show how much they trusted me. I waited there for less than five minutes before some scrawny little man came in and gave me a quick look-over, a physical really. They apparently wanted to make sure I was fit enough to answer their questions.

"So now you care?" I mumbled, struggling to stay awake.

He ignored me and shined an annoyingly bright light into my right eye, waved it out sideways and then back again. He repeated the process on my left eye before turning to speak to someone behind him. "It's possible he might be suffering from a concussion—"

"You think, House?" I grumbled.

"But," he said, continuing as if I hadn't spoken at all, "he's lucid enough to answer some simple questions."

"Make sure," replied a familiar feminine voice.

He ran another series of small physical checks, even asking me to identify how many fingers he was holding up. I told him where he could put all four of his fingers. He didn't like that response.

Apparently, being able to give a snarky answer like that indicates that one is indeed coherent enough to answer questions.

Yippee…

"I'm sure you remember me?" the feminine voice said as the top doc was getting ready to leave. She leaned casually against the side of the doorway.

A smile crossed my face as I held up my still shackled hands. "I never forget a woman who puts me in a pair of these."

She calmly walked to my side of the table and produced a small key from her pocket, shooting me a molten-hot smile as she undid my handcuffs. Boy, she was good. She knew how to play off her looks and the whole situation. Let the bruised and battered suspect be manhandled by a bunch of angry guys, then let the beautiful woman remove your handcuffs and bat her lashes at you. What guy wouldn't warm up and confess to that?

Me.

"Better?" she asked.

I rubbed my hands together and then massaged my wrists. "Not really. I thought things were about to get interesting, the kinky kind of interesting."

Her smile broadened. "They still might."

Damn, she was good.

"So," she began, "would you like to tell me what you were doing in the alleyway?"

"Not really, no."

"So you're going to be uncooperative in a federal investigation, hm? Should I put the handcuffs back on?" Her attitude changed fast. I guess the good cop bit was over.

Great.

"Ah, well, you know, sticks and stones and whips and chains and all that," I replied. A smirk made its way across my face.

She let out a sigh of exasperation. "Would you like to explain why I'm hearing nonstop about sightings of"—she paused for a good moment before speaking—"a giant, golden tiger terrorizing the streets?"

I didn't answer.

"Eyewitnesses are saying you were running away from it." She shook her head in disbelief. "I still can't believe any of this."

I merely shrugged.

"So what *really* happened?" she asked, a bit of heat entering her voice. She wasn't playing games anymore.

"You wouldn't believe me," I replied.

"Was is some sort of ridiculous prank gone wrong?"

I kept my mouth shut.

She exhaled again, clearly getting wound up by my lack of cooperation. "Why am I being told that people have videos of you running away from this...tiger? Why were people running away from you?"

"Nobody wants to play with me—"

She slapped her hands on the table, glaring at me. Guess that made her bad cop now.

My reaction must've been obvious because she backed away, hands up in a gesture of placation. Guess she was a woman used to getting her answers.

I'm not the cooperative type.

"You know, you'd have an easier time getting my phone number," I quipped.

I could hear her teeth starting to grind.

Before she could speak, a tall, solid-built man entered the room. He was African American and dressed in a similar fashion to her. Well, his suit was a bit more masculine-looking, if there is such a thing when it comes to generic suits. He was holding a thin manila envelope, which he handed to her. She muttered a quick thanks, and the man bobbed his head before leaving.

The next few minutes went by in what would have been disturbing silence if I weren't so accustomed to situations like this. Unfortunately, I was. The envelope, no doubt, contained something pertaining to this whole fiasco. She stood with her back to me, engaged in its contents, using the silence to unnerve me. Unbeknownst to her, I knew how to play along.

I started humming fairly loudly, tapping my feet

rhythmically on the floor and drumming my fingers across the tabletop, hoping to press her buttons a bit more. The idea was to wind her up to the point where she would get so frustrated, she wouldn't want to deal with me any longer. If I was lucky—and I deserved a lucky break by now—she would cave and let me go.

Apparently, she was better than I thought.

"So, Norman Smith, fifty-eight years of age." She paused for a moment to look me over. She must have been taken aback by Norman's unnaturally youthful appearance. "Curator of the American Museum of Natural History and currently residing in one seriously overpriced townhouse in Upper Manhattan." She finished with an appreciative whistle.

I forgot the feds had access to all that information.

"Now, Norman. May I call you Norman?"

I nodded.

"Now, Norman," she repeated, "would you like to tell me how a curator is able to afford a place like this?"

I knew what she was doing. She was trying to scare me by implying that I, or rather Norman, was doing something shady to make some extra cash. By blackmailing me, or making it look like she was planning to, she hoped to scare me into cooperating.

"I'm a really hard worker. Take a look," I said, holding up Norman's battered Rolex. "Been working for 'em for thirty years. They gave me a watch and everything."

She seemed unfazed by my semi-witty response. "So if we get a warrant to search your place, we won't find anything out of the ordinary?"

"No," I answered flatly.

"Why do you seem so certain?"

Because I haven't found anything, I thought to myself. Aloud however, I responded rather nonchalantly, "'Cause there's nothing to find."

"Maybe we'll take a look anyway," she replied. "Sate my curiosity, Norman. You're an interesting person."

"Not really."

"I beg to differ. You're doing exceptionally well for someone in your position, and now you're making news headlines and destroying property," she said with a dangerous smile.

Right, I had forgotten about the whole wrecking the fire escape thing. She could charge me with that.

"So?"

"So, what?" I replied.

"You going to tell me what in God's name happened out there tonight, or am I going to have to make things difficult?" she asked sternly. It was more of a command than a question.

I shrugged. "I told you, you're not going to believe me."

"Try me," she repeated, only this time through gritted teeth.

"I thought I heard a gunshot, did what any sane person would do, I ran. So did many others. That's what caused the panic," I lied.

"Bullshit!" She sounded as resolute as anyone would when stating an obvious and irrefutable fact. She didn't even consider an alternative possibility. She was either really good at picking up on when someone was lying, or it was something else.

"What do you want me to tell you?"

"How about the truth?" she replied. "Something that has a tiger in it?"

"You really think that's possible?" I asked incredulously.

"Whether or not it is possible is largely irrelevant at this moment."

"Isn't it? I figured it would be the most relevant thing," I said.

"Right now, what I want from you, Norman, is the truth. I want to hear what *you* believe." she said, stone-faced. She had the look of a woman who was done playing games.

"I don't know, maybe a tiger got loose from the zoo or something, went on a rampage, if that's what you want to hear, and yes, I ran from it. Happy?"

She shook her head in disappointment. "And here I

thought you weren't going to lie to me this time. As soon as we got the reports of a loose tiger on the streets, we got in touch with anything and everything wildlife related in the area to see if any of them had lost a tiger. They didn't."

I shrugged once again. "I don't know what to tell you."

"How about the truth? Try again, and make sure the tiger stays in the story."

I remained silent.

"So what was it? An exotic pet you had that got loose?" she asked. "That almost makes sense," she muttered, more to herself than me.

"Trust me, there's no sense involved in this whatsoever."

"Then tell me, maybe I can make sense of it." Her voice was almost a plea when she said it, almost. There was still a fair bit of anger in it as well.

What the hell. I had already wasted enough time arguing and avoiding her. Maybe the truth would get me out of here. Not likely, but it was all I had left. So I told her. "Look, yes, there was a tiger, but I honestly have no idea where it came from. As for it chasing me, I ran. It's a big cat. That's what they do when you run. That, and I managed to piss it off. Some stupid couple was busy snapping pictures of it, and it didn't take too kindly to that. I threw something at the damn thing to get its attention, it chased me into an alleyway, and I scrambled up the fire escape."

"Truth," she said so firmly, it was as if she really did know that was the actual truth, even if she had a hard time believing it.

"And how do you know that?" I asked, rather interested in how she could be so sure.

It was her turn to shrug casually. "I just do. I've always just been able to tell. Call it a hunch or woman's intuition."

"Impressive," I muttered.

She shrugged again, trying to make it seem nonchalant, but there was a bit of pride in her face, showing that she appreciated the compliment.

"So?" I asked.

"So?" she repeated right back.

"Are we done here?"

"I don't know, Norman, are we? Is there anything else you have left to tell me? Anything that's going to make things easier for me? It will only make things easier for you. Keep that in mind."

I shook my head. I couldn't think of anything else left to share, but I did still have a question lingering on my mind. "So, are you charging me with anything, Agent Ortiz?"

"Well, I could. The destruction of property—"

"Hey, that wasn't my fault!" I blurted out. "If you're running away from a tiger and jump up a rusted, poorly maintained fire escape to *escape*, which is what it's for, whose fault is that? It's the building manager's fault!"

"But...I'm not going to," she finished.

"Oh," was all I was able say. It's hard to come up with a decent reply after you've gone on the defensive like that. "So, I can leave now, right?"

She nodded and gestured towards the door.

I got up gingerly and shuffled towards it. As I was about to leave, she spoke again.

"Norman..."

I turned to look at her.

"If I find out that you're responsible for this, for endangering the public, I. Will. Lock. You. Up. And throw away the key." Her frosty tone left no doubt on whether or not she would carry out that threat. She most assuredly would.

I nodded and left, getting all manner of looks as I walked in the direction of the elevator. Some were confused looks while others were downright nasty glares. Guess my little adventure made quite a bit of people upset. Screw 'em. They weren't the ones being chased.

The worst part of all this wasn't being brought in for questioning nor the attention I attracted, it was the fact that I was getting close and yet, at the same time remained clueless. I had had a lead, almost caught that person, and somehow ended up being chased by an animated tiger statue. I had never seen magic like that at work. Was the person magical, or were they the very monster I was hunting? No magic in my experience could warp reality like that, animate something, not to mention enlarge it to that scale and give it a pissed off predisposition towards me.

That realization impressed upon me just how careful I had to be. I was starting to feel a little out of my depth, a sensation I hadn't experienced in a long time.

And I didn't like it.

I waited on the curb for any cab to pass by. It's New York; there's *always* a cab somewhere. Hailing one is the problem. I finally got one about ten minutes later. I gave the cabbie Norman's address, leaned back against the seat, and enjoyed my chance to rest.

Chapter Eight

I had gotten back home, well, Norman's home, relatively quicker than it had taken to get to the FBI headquarters. Weird, guess cabbies knew something the feds didn't on driving. I paid the man with one of Norman's unnecessary premium credit cards. If the cab driver thought it a bit showy, he didn't mention it. He took it, swiped it, and I was done.

I stepped out of the cab and was confronted by the familiar sight of Norman's Manhattan townhouse. It looked exactly the same as when I had left it, with the exception of the little man sitting atop the lowest step.

He was about four-foot-two, dressed in a grayish-blue plaid shirt, dark blue-gray jeans, and a gray-green bowler cap. He had a wiry, coarse-looking beard. It was the color of sandalwood, an orangey reddish-brown. It matched the strands of equally wiry reddish hair falling from beneath his cap and his wispy eyebrows. His oceanic eyes were narrowed, and from the clenched setting of his jaw, I'd say it was clear the man was ticked.

Except, he wasn't really a man. He was a gnome. Someone working for Gnosis, I figured. He held a rather full-looking binder; the hard plastic kind children use in elementary school. After one look at me, he stood up and took a few steps forward.

I extended my right hand for a handshake and said, "Hey," as pleasantly as I could.

My hand stung as the next instant I had the binder jammed into it. The hard plastic dug into the soft flesh of my hand, not enough to break the skin but still… Ouch!

"The hell's got your Pampers in a bunch, Rumpelstiltskin?" I asked.

When he spoke, he answered with a Cockney English accent. "You're a right arsehole, you know that?"

"Me? What'd I do?"

"I've been waiting 'ere bloody ages! I've got things to do, you know? You're not the only person I've got to visit tonight," he said tersely.

"Santa's got you on toy delivery or somethin'?" I quipped.

"Oh, real funny! Yeah, you're a right comedian, aren't ya?" He scowled. "Tosser," he muttered below his breath.

Tosser? I thought, confused.

"Well, seeing how as you're so upset, why don't you Oompa Loompa your way out of here, Cabbage Patch?" I snapped in response to his insult. At least, I think it was an insult.

Tosser isn't in my vocabulary.

His teensy hands closed into fists, his knuckles cracked, and I was reminded that a gnome could kick a person's ass with ease. I may know how to kill 'em, but I wasn't prepared to at that moment. I had other concerns. Plus, I didn't think Gnosis would appreciate me killing his hired help, though at the moment, that's not how it would likely go down. The doctors would be pretty baffled at how to remove my head from up my ass because this tiny guy could surely do that to me.

I put my hands up, open palms, gesturing for him to calm down.

He did.

Whew. Not that I was actually sweating going toe-to-toe with the little guy, except that I was, but he didn't need to know that. Like I said, they have to respect you, maybe even fear you a bit. Most things in the supernatural world that know of me are, well, terrified of me. I know I don't come off as terrifying, but think about it: I can't really be killed, and if I am, I don't stay dead. I've had years of nonstop cases that have led me to figure out how to hunt and kill a variety of supernatural creatures. The biggest thing, of course, is that I *have* hunted down and killed a vast amount of these creatures effectively, so yeah.

Enough bragging and bolstering my ego. It just needed explaining that Vincent Graves ain't a pushover!

I muttered a gruff thanks to the gnome and told him to go on his way.

He did.

See? That's how you deal with the supernatural.

I thumbed open the binder as I ascended the steps to Norman's house, unlocking the heavy oak door and slipping quietly inside. I shut the door behind me with one hand and flipped through the pages of the file with my other. It was everything I had asked for, and more. Gnosis had provided me with an abundance of info: the name of every employee who had ever worked at the museum, the ones still working there, and anyone hired more recently.

It was amazing.

The little guy really went the distance, but then, he would. Gnosis was the best information broker in the supernatural world for a reason. No one had ever been let down by the quality of his work and as such, he could demand outrageous prices. Prices that were *always* paid, in some form or another. Gnosis never failed to collect on a debt.

There was too much info to go through in one sitting; although, I was hoping I wouldn't need to go through everything to find what I was looking for.

"Errgh!" I moaned, rolling my shoulders and neck. They were stiff and aching, not to mention the fatigue threatening to overwhelm me. I thought about my previous heavenly experience in Norman's shower and convinced myself I needed another.

I headed upstairs, passing the kitchen and gym on the way up to Norman's disheveled bedroom.

When I got there, I stepped into the bathroom and glanced at the gigantic mirror fixed above the sink. I wanted a better look at the sorry state I was in. It wasn't too bad though. Norman's hair was a bit messy. He looked like someone who'd taken a high-speed drive in a convertible; nothing a shower and comb couldn't fix. The eyes, however, they showed signs of real fatigue. As for the suit, well, that was done for—tattered and torn from all of the running and jumping with the tiger. I didn't have to look at it to know any of that.

But I did.

The tear from the tiger's claws had shredded a large section of fabric. That, and along with the frays and rips falling to the ground in a crumbling fire escape, yeah, you could say the suit was done. There were stains on it too— sweat, dirt, grease, and signs of soot.

The soot that was my only clue, and I was most definitely going to wash it the hell off. I didn't need it on me for it to have value.

I planned on flipping through my journal for any reference connected to soot in the supernatural world. Anything that left it as a residue, was constructed of it, or used in any type of magic. There *had* to be a connection. There always was. No reason that would change now. Delving into my journal was going to be the best bet I had. That and scouring through the information Gnosis had provided.

But first, that shower I sorely needed.

I went into Norman's walk-in closet and rummaged through his less-than-stellar collection of clothing. Don't get me wrong, I'm not a diva or anything, but still... If I'm going to be running around in someone else's body, I'm gonna look damn good doing it.

I settled for a clean dress shirt, a pair of navy blue jeans, and slightly worn but nice-looking, black, polished boots. Not the most amazing of styling choices, I know. Compared to his other clothes though, well, it's like the saying goes: keep it simple stupid.

I've been in some very fashion-conscious people before. To my displeasure, some of the fashion sense has stuck.

After picking out my new attire, I sauntered back to the

bathroom, hung the clothes over the metallic towel warmer, and stripped. I turned on the shower but didn't hop in immediately. I stood there mulling things over while the shower got up to a nice temperature. After a considerable amount of steam filled the massive bathroom and fogged up the mirrors, I stepped inside.

The heat, more than anything, was an immense relief. Every ache, pang, and dull throb seemed to vanish. "Ohhhh my god!" I groaned.

After twenty minutes of steaming hot nirvana, I stepped out of the shower and wrapped a towel around my waist. It was a thick, plushy material, black and embroidered in gold lettering with Norman's initials.

What man does things like this?

I shook my head to clear that train of thought. Walking up to the mirror, I checked my reflection again, hoping to see a better-looking visage. Norman's previously haggard face looked considerably better. The eyes and skin didn't seem as sunken and sallow as before; the stress had been washed away.

I had to keep wiping the mirror while inspecting myself. The built-up steam kept fogging over it. After the fifth time, I noticed something strange—strange in the supernatural sense.

Steam doesn't tend to emanate from one's mouth, but I could see my breath when I exhaled. I felt it as well—the sudden drop in temperature. My muscles were shaking. No, shivering as the temperature continued to plummet. The mirror was the biggest indicator that something was going horribly wrong. Heavy condensation caused by the steam was transforming into crystalline shapes over the glass.

An icy cool fog permeated the place. It was really disconcerting because I knew what was coming.

I had experienced this before.

I looked around frantically, trying to work out the creature's most likely point of entry.

A crackling noise filled the room, breaking my concentration. The glass paneling around the walk-in shower developed an intricate pattern of cracks, spiraling in every direction like a web. They spread rapidly, seeping deeper into the glass.

Upon reaching its breaking point, the brittle material shattered! The room erupted into a frenzy of glass daggers hurtling towards me. I hit the floor hard, avoiding the worst of the carnage.

At least the important bits are covered, I thought.

The towel offered a little protection, but the rest of my body found no respite. Glass bit into my back, scalp, arms, and more. In conjunction with the already freezing temperatures, the glass felt like shards of ice that sank into my flesh with a frigid bite.

I shook from the unforgiving temperature as well as the shock, but the worst was yet to come. This was just a warning. The caulking between the tiles was no longer white. A thick, black, gelatinous substance oozed in its place, forcing itself through the tiles. They lifted from their foundations, some breaking off completely as the liquid tar kept pouring in, bit by inky bit. The entire wall leaked the substance now, dripping towards the floor where it would soon pool together.

The scene unfolding before me was like those ones in the movies where a crack springs in a dam; water begins to leak until the whole dam bursts open. The only difference, well in my situation, was that the dam was going to leave me stuck with one of the horrors of the supernatural world.

It all happened in an eerie kind of silence, save for the occasional cracking of tiles. My mind told me to run, but my body didn't get the memo. I was transfixed by the sight until, finally, the entire wall exploded, much like the glass.

This time, I hurled myself out of the bathroom, flying across Norman's bedroom, landing with an abrupt *thud*. Fragments of tile shot out in every direction, but I scrambled for the door, managing to kick the door shut at the last second. Porcelain struck the bathroom side of the door, shattering against it, sounding like heavy rain.

The door opened, but I wasn't the one who opened it.

All the heat in the room vanished in a raspy sort of *hiss*. I rose awkwardly, staring at the monstrosity forming in Norman's bathroom. The pool of thick, murky liquid coalesced, rising and falling at the same time. A figure rose from the ground as rivulets of the black tar-like substance rolled down its mass. It was like watching one of those decorative waterfalls that recirculated water, except this one kept rising. When it was the height of a fully-grown man, its shape became more defined. A small mass of the liquid protruded from the body, extending forward to take on an oval shape.

I was unprepared for this, literally caught with my pants down—well off! In my line of work, jumping from body to body, it's difficult to carry materials to fight off any creatures I'm ambushed by.

And I get ambushed a lot!

I stood there gawking as the creature's sides filled out. Narrow shoulders sprouted from the sides of its scrawny, inky neck. The rest of its body, if you could call it that, wasn't really shaped like a man's. It was long and sinuous—serpent like. Its lengthy, decrepit-looking arms hung limply at its sides. Long spider-like fingers wriggled the way a newborn infant would move its digits for the first time.

"Great," I growled.

Most people think of Wraiths as something related to ghosts, but they aren't. They aren't related in the slightest. Like I said before, a ghost is an imprint of the person left behind; a supernatural memoir. Most are harmless, and formed when someone dies in a horrible manner that more often than not, remains unresolved. They need closure to move on. Part of what I do prevents ghosts from being born.

Wraiths are abominations, shadow and horror given form. They were animals—bound to serve more powerful beings as supernatural attack dogs. It would be wrong to say they were mindless killing machines however. They were *intelligent* killing machines. Think of a baboon: feral, intelligent—as many primates are—but forget about the brightly colored ass part. Wraiths might not be as smart as humans, but they're smart enough. They can hunt, rationalize, and some can even speak.

Wraiths are a perversion, even in the supernatural world. They're aimless, with no purpose but to be controlled. They feed off human emotions and, eventually, their life force. They feed off heat too, which is why the room had grown so frosty as quick as it did. They make the world around them become cold, physically and emotionally. You grow more and more depressed the longer you remain in their presence.

It hung there for a moment, motionless, save for the constant trickle of dark fluid running down its body. The Wraith balanced itself on its snakelike, inky tail, staring at me, head moving from side to side in a serpent-like manner.

Shivers shot through my body as the Wraith emitted a slow, eerie hiss. Recognizing its prey, it slithered forwards, well, glided. Suspended in midair, it moved effortlessly with a slow, sinuous grace.

I knew how to hurt Wraiths, how to trap and fend them off, but all of that required me doing one very important thing.

To fucking run like hell!

So I did.

I charged out of Norman's room, just managing to reach the staircase as the Wraith lunged with its thin, elongated hands.

"Gyah!" I yelped as its strike narrowly missed.

It let out a nasty hiss similar to the sound made by icy water hitting hot metal.

Guess it was mad it had missed.

Too fucking bad!

It snapped sideways—literally. The top half of its body swung in a different direction, separate from the rest of it, and then it lurched forwards with the speed of a frickin' cobra.

"Dammit!" I struggled to keep hold of my towel as I ran, trying to keep it from falling…as if that mattered. It's weird. Even while being chased by a supernatural horror, society's conditioning about modesty is pretty damn strong. In a life-threatening situation, I was more worried about my towel falling and revealing all of my—well, not even mine, but Norman's—junk.

I ran awkwardly, but as fast as I could, swerving in hopes of avoiding Inky's clutches. So far, so good.

I didn't know what else to do. Wraiths are notoriously hard to kill. One of the only ways to hurt them is with a few select pure metals and minerals; salt and iron for example.

I ran through Norman's gym, hoping to find something to stave off my attacker. Everything was either high-quality plastic or stainless steel. One of the weight racks looked like it was made of heavy cast iron, but I couldn't exactly throw one of those at it. I decided to keep running until I hit the kitchen.

I came flying in, diving over the central counter, and landing stark naked on the floor behind it. Scrambling to my feet, I tore through the cupboards and shelves in front of me, searching for salt.

"Yes!" I shouted in triumphant joy, holding an unopened bag of salt in my hand. Now, I know salt isn't the most threatening of things, unless you get some in your eye, but it's not about looking menacing. What it *is* about is the principles and rules of the supernatural world. Wraiths are abominations, perversions and essentially impure.

Salt is the opposite. It is part of the earth, of nature, a life giver in many ways. It's pure and has purpose, a boon of the world; whereas, Wraiths are a stain upon it. Simply put, look at it like fire and water. Water puts out fire; both of those things are part of our world and have their uses.

The whole myth about spilling salt and throwing some over your shoulder to "blind the devil?" Well, this is where it comes from. Salt interferes with the essence of Wraiths, and many other dark creatures from the supernatural world. It makes them lose the ability to hold their being together. In a way, it's like pulling a piece out of a Jenga tower. It wobbles a bit until it stabilizes, or you decide to put the piece back in.

That's what salt does to Wraiths.

And now I had me some!

I whirled around in my naked glory and ripped the top of the bag wide open, sending one of my hands crashing inside. I held a good fist-sized amount just as the Wraith came slithering in.

It released another angry hiss, sending another wave of shivers up my spine. As it entered, the temperature plummeted to degrees that could have adverse effects on certain parts of Norman's anatomy.

"Come get me, you Jiffy Lube reject!" I snarled defiantly.

It let out a venomous sound, a massive inhalation of air different from the sounds it made earlier. It sounded like a high-powered vacuum cleaner.

I flung my salt-filled hand in a wide arc, sending a shower of the coarse, white substance flying across the room, hitting the Wraith.

The effect was instantaneous.

The Wraith reared up like a bucking bronco, its hands flailing wildly before itself, as if trying to ward off a swarm of insects. It wasn't hissing, rasping or making vacuum cleaner noises anymore—it was shrieking in agony.

It was like fingernails on a chalkboard: excruciatingly loud, disturbing and chilling.

You should've seen the effect the salt had on its body as it writhed and flailed. The inky substance comprising the Wraith's body was bubbling. It looked like a boiling tar pit as a series of bubbles formed and burst across its body in rapid succession. There was hissing as well, only this time it wasn't emanating from the creature's mouth, but from the hideous black steam spouting from different parts of the creature's body.

"Someone needs to cut back on their sodium intake. Too much of this stuff will kill ya," I quipped.

Its pain-induced writhing began to slow. It was beginning to recover, and here I was wasting time with jokes.

I bolted towards the monstrosity—not the smartest move, I know—but now I had something to tip the scale in my favor. I tossed another handful of salt at the beast, and the Wraith twitched violently in agony. I rushed to pour more salt around the creature, forming a solid white circle.

Making an unbreakable circle of salt is an excellent way to trap many a monster. It creates an impassable barrier, trapping the creature inside. If it tried to cross, well, it'd be like going through an electric fence. Bottom line, the Wraith wasn't going to get through until I let it.

Score one for Graves!

Of course, now I had the problem of having a pissed off Wraith trapped in the kitchen with no clue what to do about it. I couldn't exactly leave it here until my case was finished. Somebody might come across it, and then what? I'd be leaving a booby trap for some poor innocent person, and the Wraith, being the killing machine it is, would feed on them.

I stood there for a moment, pondering my next move, when something really unexpected happened.

"Release us," rasped the Wraith.

It fucking spoke! I had heard that some Wraiths could talk, but I had never come across one that could.

"Well," I began, rubbing my hands together excitedly. "Now things are getting interesting."

"Release us, mortal..."

"Uh, I'm gonna have to go with *no* on that one, sludge ball."

The Wraith bristled at that remark. Apparently, it took offense at being called that. Well, too bad.

"Release us, and you die quick."

"Yeah, but if you stay in the circle you can't kill me. Clever, huh?"

The Wraith didn't respond.

"Wait a minute," I said aloud. "Why am I sitting here arguing with you when I could get the information I need out of you...and why am I doing this naked?"

"Stupid creature," it hissed angrily.

I narrowed my eyes. Okay, I was *really* going to enjoy this.

"Don't go anywhere," I chided as I grabbed my towel from the other side of the room, wrapping it around my waist to retain some dignity in the situation. As if the Wraith cared.

I had an idea, and it was a damn good one too, but it depended on one thing—a rope. I doubted Norman would have something like that lying around.

I searched his kitchen, first floor and bedroom, but found nothing. It was only when I passed through the gym on my way back to the Wraith that I noticed a lengthy metal chain lying atop one of the weight racks. I went over to inspect it. It was the kind used by hardcore weightlifters to look badass or whatever. I honestly didn't know what they used it for, but that was irrelevant. It wasn't made out of stainless steel, but pure good ole iron!

I didn't bother to get dressed between all of this. Due to the situation, I figured that was a waste of time, something I certainly did not have a great deal of. I headed to the kitchen and grabbed the torn bag of salt, strolling past the Wraith as I did.

It lunged at me—fast—hitting thin air and bouncing with a shriek, writhing in agony. Clearly it had forgotten about the salt circle and reacted on its predatory need to feed when I had walked by.

Lesson learned, bitch! Don't mess with Vincent Graves.

"Tsk tsk tsk!" I said, waving an admonishing finger at it. "Now now, Inky! Behave."

I could swear that the thing shot me a murderous look, even while writhing in agony. It looked me straight in the face for a brief second and held that look.

It had no eyes! How in the hell did it do that? There were no facial features, save for a sludgy opening that was a mouth, but it could give me a death look?

Creepy.

Of course, I didn't let it see that it had freaked me out. I had to appear in control and unfazed, which I somewhat was.

I walked past the creature. It had settled down and was calmly following me with its head, sitting there trapped and balancing on its coiled tail. I waved goodbye to it as I headed up to Norman's destroyed bathroom.

"Thank god the tub's intact," I muttered as I walked over to it and turned on the cold water. I leaned over the side of the tub and reached for the rubber stopper, grabbed it, and placed it into the drain hole. The tub filled with cold water. Once it reached a few inches I dropped the iron chain into it.

"Here goes nothing," I said. What I was about to do was more theory than anything else, but I was hoping it would be crazy enough to work. I poured the remaining salt into the water and ran my hand through the tub. After a few seconds, and being satisfied that most of the salt had dissolved, I removed the iron chain from the briny solution.

Salt and iron could hurt a Wraith, but what I was really wondering was what an iron chain submerged in salt water could do. I needed answers. What I was about to do could be considered vile, and I was pretty sure the Geneva Convention had something, or many things, banning it. Then again, those rules didn't apply to supernatural horrors, so fuck it!

I held the chain in both hands and gave it a forceful tug to check its integrity. It went taut and held strong, good news for me, bad for the Wraith.

Time to get me some answers.

I walked back down to the kitchen where the pent-up Wraith was still trapped. It continued to balance on its tail, swaying much like a cobra and looking ready to strike at any moment. Except it couldn't, not as long as it remained inside the circle. Well, I guess it could try, but I was sure the outcome of its last attempt was still fresh in its mind.

I adjusted my towel again, not wanting it to drop off as I was about to "forcefully interrogate" the Wraith. God, that would have been embarrassing.

"Okay, you toxic snot-ball," I growled. "Time to fess

up!"

The Wraith hung there, still and silent. Its swaying stopped; its posture remained tense.

Okay then.

"Last chance, you overgrown Rorschach! I know something has a hold of you. I wanna know who, what, when, where, why…all of it!" I said menacingly, jerking the chain in a threatening manner to accentuate my point.

It tilted its inkblot head to the side rather quizzically. Maybe it was thinking of a response; I don't know what goes on in their heads. Then it responded in a quiet, whisper-like hiss. "We will feast on your soul… Slowly, slowly, we will suck your soul, slowly."

"So that's a no, huh?" I shrugged. "'Kay then. Now we do it the hard way!" I had no idea if this was going to work, but I couldn't let my uncertainty show. I released the chain from the grip of my right hand, leaving it hanging from my left. I swung it as hard as I could at the creature's throat. It lashed the Wraith's neck, coiling around it, but that wasn't what I was focusing on because my question had been answered.

The Wraith erupted into the loudest fit of shrieking I had seen or heard yet. It spasmed violently as it flailed inside the circle. The saltwater-dipped iron chain was working, and it was the only safe way to interrogate the creature. I couldn't very well step into the circle myself. That would be suicide. This way I could reach into the circle without the risk of breaking it, while keeping myself out of harm's way.

What I was doing could have easily been considered torture. *Alright,* it was torture, but it was a Wraith, a remorseless killing machine, so I didn't feel one bit of guilt.

Wraiths don't feel compassion or love. All they have is an insatiable hunger. That's why they're horrors. Imagine something that only cares about consuming, killing anything to satisfy a hunger that can never be sated. Nothing is enough; no amount of humans killed will ever be enough. They are blights upon nature. You can't change them or convince them to stop killing. They're not some convict who you can try to "correct." They are, and always will be, a weapon made to be enthralled by other more powerful beings.

Wraiths are supernatural hitmen.

So, yes, I was going to torture the sonuvabitch until I got any information I could out of it. I knew it knew something useful. Like I said, Wraiths are contract killers, minus the contract part. Something out there, and I had an inkling it was the monster I was really after, had put this Wraith in its thrall and sent it after me. I wanted to know what, and where it was now.

The Wraith hadn't stopped shrieking yet. It wouldn't so long as I had the chain around its sludgy throat. I gave the chain a few shakes until it fell off. The Wraith collapsed into a coiled state, heaving with effort to recover from what I had put it through.

"Ready to talk now? If not, we could always go for another round. How 'bout it?" I said, holding up the chain for it so see.

The Wraith surged forwards so fast I would've missed it had I blinked. It collided with the magical barrier created by the salt and recoiled instantly, erupting into another fit of agony.

I tapped a finger to my forehead. "Ah ah ah. Bad supernatural nasty, bad!" I scolded.

I waited patiently, okay, not so patiently, as the Wraith endured its third or fourth bout of excruciating pain.

Welcome to my world, I thought.

After several moments passed, the creature began to rise. Once at full height, it stared at me, hard.

"Had enough yet?"

It rasped heavily, but made no attempt to answer me.

"Round two it is," I said, holding the chain up high, giving the Wraith a good view of it.

"Wait!" it hissed loudly.

I didn't. I swung my arm back, readying up for another lash.

"Wait!" it pleaded. Yes, it actually pleaded, like with its

hands up and everything.

"What?" I snarled.

"We will answer. It will ask, and we will answer," it heaved.

"S'pose I can't ask you to cut out the Gollum act, can I?"

"We don't...comprehend."

Guess not.

"What in hell?" gasped a feminine voice.

I whirled around. Not more than fifteen feet from me stood Agent Ortiz. She was frozen in place, her Glock drawn and held at chest level, pointed not at the Wraith, but me. There was a hideous, black, ink-like monstrosity in the same room and her gun was leveled at *me*.

Seriously?

"Wha...wha... What is that thing?" she stammered.

I should've known something like this could have happened. After all, she had Norman's address, but still, I didn't expect her to come barging inside. I know the tiger fiasco had her riled up, but you can't just storm into a suspect's home.

The Wraith didn't give a damn about what was going through either of our minds. It turned to face Agent Ortiz and let out a menacing hiss.

She fainted.

"Uh, don't go anywhere," I said to the Wraith, dropping the chain as I darted over to catch the falling FBI agent. She was fairly light, but then I also had a fair bit of enhanced strength, so carrying her wasn't too bad. I carried her all the way downstairs to Norman's lavishly decorated living room, placing her as gently as I could on his couch. Hopefully, she would remain unconscious, at least until I finished dealing with the Wraith.

After leaving her safely ensconced atop Norman's couch, I walked back upstairs and returned to the trapped Wraith.

"Sorry about that. The feds have never been good with manners. Always busting down a door or two. It's just so rude. So, where were we?" I asked. "Oh, that's right, Slime Ball," I said, remembering what I wanted to ask it before Agent Ortiz had interrupted. "I wanna know who or what made you their bitch! Who sent you?"

"We do not know," it answered.

"Too bad," I said, picking up the fallen chain. I raised it over my head and was about to send it into another cast when the Wraith spoke up.

"We do not know!" it rasped loudly. "She forced us. She bound us, but we did not see."

She? I wondered. Well, now I had something, sort of. I still didn't know if the monster was really female or masquerading as a human female. Although, it wouldn't matter in the end.

"What else do you know? And how do you even know it's a female?" I asked.

"We felt it, felt her. We felt her essence when she bound us." It exhaled in a serpent-like hiss.

"Wait, you can tell a monster's gender by feeling it's...essence?" I said in a befuddled tone.

"Yes," was its all too simplistic reply.

"How?"

It didn't answer.

"How?" I snarled. If there are things like that, then I needed to know. Any technique or ability I could use to glean info was always useful.

"Not for mortals, only Wraiths," it supplied matter-of-factly. "It is, nothing more, it is."

I took that to mean that only Wraiths could do it, like they possessed some kind of supernatural monster gender sensor. Maybe it was a way for them to tell who their new boss was, since Wraiths were used frequently by all manner of powerful creatures. Maybe it was a way to garner a bit of payback. I'm not sure if Wraiths cared about that, but if I were one of them and I was made into something's bitch, I would.

That logic made sense. I mean, why not? Wraiths fed on humans for their souls, the essence of power that lay inside them. Monsters had power too; power that could be fed upon if a Wraith was strong enough or had the jump on them. Maybe it could feed on a creature that had previously enthralled it. That notion intrigued me.

"Can you feed on whatever is binding you now?" I asked. That bit of knowledge could prove useful. Maybe I could turn this thing on whatever was pulling its inky strings.

"Yes..."

Sweet, I thought.

"And no," it finished.

"Uh, why not?"

"She is stronger, far stronger, older, and ancient," it replied.

Huh? Well then, I had gotten a pretty damn good answer from the Wraith. Why was it that the one thing in the universe that could supply me with a good answer was a Wraith and not my intelligent, and apparently omniscient, boss, Church?

"So this creature, it's old—very old?" I asked.

"Yes," hissed the Wraith.

"But you don't know what it is, right?"

"Yes," it repeated.

"Wait, yes as in you do know, or yes as in you don't?"

"Yes."

"Sonuvabitch," I muttered. "What *is* the creature that had you bound?"

"We do not know," it replied.

I sighed; it took all of that to elicit that response.

"If I release you," I began hesitantly, "what are the odds you'll get some payback on the thing binding you, and not try to peel my face off?"

"We will not peel your face off—"

"Oh good, because it isn't mine. It's kind of on loan, but the guy wasn't really using it 'cause he's dead and—"

"We will feast on your soul," it hissed, cutting me off.

"Well...that sucks. You sure?"

"We will feast on your soul. We will devour your essence and leave your corpse to rot," it hissed, literally spitting out its hatred as small drops of black ooze spurted from its mouth.

Guess that settled it. I wasn't left with any choice other than to kill it. I whipped the chain into an arc-like swing as fast I could, wrapping it around the Wraith's face. Small bubbles formed then burst. Black steam shot out of it as its shrieks pierced my ears. I didn't stop there, though. I yanked hard on the chain, forcing the monster to collide with the salt barrier. Its screams doubled; in fact everything intensified—the bubbles forming and bursting across its body, the steam billowing out of it, and, of course, its agony.

It didn't last long, a minute at the most. The worst part was the damage done to my hearing from its incessant shrieking. It seemed cold, cruel even, but it wasn't. The truth of the matter was, if I let that thing go, it would either report back to its master or come after me again. Or, since it was weakened from the torture, if I had let it go, it would have sought out some poor innocent human being to regain its strength.

I. Could. Not. Allow. That.

That's who I am. As cold and cruel as it might seem, it would have been crueler to let that thing go. Anyone it killed after being set free would have been on me. I'm not really in the business of saving people, but I'll be damned if I'm gonna stand by and let them die.

The Wraith's death wasn't anything spectacular. It didn't burst into an explosion of tar-like goo that went splattering everywhere; it just sort of collapsed. The mass of inky, black liquid fell in on itself like a structure that had lost its foundation. Inside the circle of pristine white salt lay a dirty, disgusting mass of black goo.

"That's gonna be a bitch to clean," I muttered. Not that it was my problem. That task would go to whoever was selling this place once they found out Norman was dead.

Back to business. I had wasted enough time on the Wraith, but at least I had gotten a clue out of it. All that, and all I was rewarded was with a gender, but still, it was more than I had before.

She and soot…best clues ever.

I headed back to Norman's bathroom. "Damn," I sighed. The clothes I had lain out to wear were ruined. Holes from the glass had peppered both the shirt and jeans, and, if that wasn't enough, the ice that had coated the glass had melted so the clothes were soaking wet.

I shook my head and muttered a curse as I walked back into Norman's bedroom. I tore through the previously ransacked dresser, looking for a new set of threads. I settled on a plain, black, full-sleeve shirt because black is oh-so-slimming and in style in New York, and then I picked out a pair of olive-green khakis. This guy had a weird assortment of clothes.

It was too late to go back to the museum to dig for more clues. Only the security guards would be there now, and the last thing I wanted to do was get into another IQ-deadening conversation with Rick. I decided it best to go over the information Gnosis had provided and cross-reference it with my journal.

Chapter Nine

I found where I had left the binder Gnosis' fiery featured and tempered friend had given me and then began searching for my journal. I searched everywhere, atop and below every fixture, in the clothes I had been wearing previously, but I couldn't find it.

"Goddammit!" That journal had everything I had ever recorded in it. It *was* everything to me; it was the only damn possession I really had.

"Trouble?" murmured a voice.

Agent Ortiz stood in the doorway of Norman's bedroom, both hands at the sides of her head, massaging her temples. She looked a bit groggy.

"Yeah," I said softly. I didn't want to give her anymore headache. "I can't find my journal."

"You mean this thing?" she said, holding up my missing journal.

"How'd you get that?!"

"I confiscated it while we were taking you up for questioning," she replied. "You were slipping in and out of consciousness. I didn't think you'd notice, or mind."

"You...you?" I stammered in the face of this sacrilege. *Take my journal? Like hell!*

I stormed over to her and snatched it out of her hands in a none-too-polite manner. The lady may have just fainted, but no one takes my damn journal!

"You're welcome," she muttered bitterly.

I snorted dismissively in response.

"I had a chance to go through it after we let you go. It was"—she inhaled heavily—"quite a read."

"So…what? You came all the way back here to return my property or something?" I asked, bemused.

"Something like that," she whispered.

"Awful late to be making deliveries," I said.

"Well, I decided to keep an eye on you after the tiger incident, especially after flipping through that journal of yours."

"You think I'm crazy, don't you?" I asked, already knowing her answer. I mean, who wouldn't think I was insane after a flip through my notes?

"I think…" she started. "I don't know what to think. At first, yes. I thought you were crazy. I was outside when I heard the screams. I forced my way in and then"—she stopped for a moment, biting her lip—"then I saw…that thing." She shuddered at that last bit.

"And now?" I asked quietly.

"Now"—she exhaled—"now, I just want to know what the hell's going on. No bullshit, just the truth."

"I'm hunting a murderer," I said. "So far, it's been responsible for the deaths of employees at the American Museum of Natural History."

"How many?" she asked.

"At the moment, only one I'm sure of."

"And…that thing…the thing in the kitchen was a…?"

"A Wraith," I said simply.

She sighed. "And I'm supposed to know what it is because…?"

I rolled my eyes and beckoned her to follow me, making sure to grab the info Gnosis had given me as I led her down to the kitchen. I also made damn sure to keep a death grip on my journal, lest Agent Ortiz decided to take another looksy without my consent.

I pointed at the large pile of noxious black goo smeared across the floor. "That," I said, "was a Wraith."

"Thanks for the in-depth description there, Britannica," she replied.

I huffed out a heavy breath. "A Wraith is a supernatural horror—"

She snorted. "Yeah, I worked that part out for myself."

I narrowed my eyes. "Quiet, smartass," I retorted.

Her eyes widened for a split second and then narrowed. Her hands balled into fists and found their way to being planted on her hips. She stood there in that pose women adopt when they're quivering in anger.

A pose that meant you were in trouble if you were either their boyfriend or husband. Seeing how I was neither, I didn't care.

I rolled on as if nothing had happened. "So, what was I saying? Oh yeah, a Wraith is sort of a supernatural contract killer, only minus the contract. They're bound into the service of a powerful being who lets 'em loose on their target."

"Wait, so...there are *more* of those things? And you can just trap one and make it do what you want?" she asked horrified.

I shrugged. "Well, yeah, pretty much."

She looked scandalized. "Isn't there some, I don't know, some sort of rules or regulations around that kind of stuff? You can't just hire assassins, it's...it's illegal!"

I snorted loudly. "Yeah, because the creepy crawlies of the supernatural world really care about everyday vanilla human laws."

She gave me a withering look; apparently law and order meant a great deal to her. Right, she was a fed.

"Sorry, really aren't many rules governing that kind of stuff in the world I'm involved in, and the rules there are— are just plain crazy. I don't make 'em. I'm just stuck trying to play by 'em," I said.

She blinked several times, shaking her head before signaling me to continue.

"'Kay, well that Wraith you saw was sent to kill me. I'm guessing because I'm drawing closer to whatever's responsible for the murder I'm investigating."

"So, what is it?"

"What is what?" I asked, confused.

She looked at me as if I were a simple child. "The thing

responsible for the murder?"

"Oh," I said, sounding foolish. "I, uh, well, you see, I haven't gotten that far yet."

"You what?" she exclaimed indignantly.

"I haven't gotten that far yet," I repeated in a softer tone.

"Let me get this straight. You rampage through the streets of New York with an angry tiger, terrify dozens of people—"

"The tiger thing wasn't my fault!"

"I'm not finished!" she said, raising her voice above mine. "You make my workload shoot through the roof, my stress levels are following, you push my levels of reasoning into unexplainable bounds—"

"But I—" I tried muttering sheepishly.

She shot me a death look for trying to interrupt her again, so I stayed quiet.

"You cause me to confront a horrifying monster and knock me out—"

"Technically, you fainted," I corrected.

She gave me another dagger and nails look. This time, I resolved to try harder to stay quiet.

"And after putting me through all of this, in *one* night, we arrive at the point where after all of this has transpired, and you've got nothing! Am I right?" she finished, her chest heaving heavily. Her face flushed with anger. If looks could kill...

"Yup," I answered.

"Yup? Is that all you have to say?" she asked menacingly.

"Yup," I repeated.

She put her right hand up to her forehead and winced. "I think I'm going to have an aneurysm."

"You sure you're not just going to faint again?"

She looked at me with cold, hard fury.

I shut up.

After a moment of silence, she walked closer to the puddle of black goo, kneeling and extending a finger to touch it.

"NO!" I shouted.

Her hand jerked back, and she looked at me, confused.

"I really wouldn't touch that if I were you, or if I were me, so yeah, no touchy."

"Why? It's dead, isn't it?"

"Yeah, but would you touch any other puddle of toxic-looking black stuff?"

"My," she said with a little huff of breath, "you really have a way with words, don't you?"

"Yeah, I'm a regular wordsmith," I replied with a cheery smile.

"A...wordsmith?"

"Yeah you know, like blacksmiths make stuff, a wordsmith smiths words..."

She didn't respond to that.

"Look"—I sighed—"you wouldn't touch radioactive material, right?"

She nodded in agreement.

"Well, that's what Wraith remains are like. They're toxic in a different way. Their remains can poison people, corrupt them," I explained.

"I don't follow."

"If you touch that, think of it as ingesting a psychoactive drug. It would mess with your mind, only in a truly spooky way. It would corrupt you—make you turn aggressive, cruel, angry, cold, and just plain evil. You're essentially ingesting the essence of that Wraith; you're letting it make you into what it was, only you'd still be human, sort of."

I could see her visibly make an effort to repress the urge to shiver.

"Okay," she began slowly, "so, this Wraith thing was sent to stop you from getting close to the murderer, right?"

"Right."

"And the tiger thing, same reason?"

"Looks that way," I answered.

"So, and I can't believe I'm about to ask this, have you

ever run across anything like this before?"

"Sorta, kinda, not really, maybe," I quipped.

She let out an exasperated sigh.

"I'm not sure. I've dealt with hundreds of monsters and had hundreds, if not thousands, of cases. My memory's not so great with all of them," I said defensively.

"Hence the journal," she said.

"Hence the *journals*. I've got one for case notes on all the baddies out there, and another for me noggin'," I said, giving my head a playful knock.

"So, what now?" she asked.

"Now I make some coffee and do some heavy reading," I said, holding up my journal and the binder from Gnosis. "Care to join me?"

"For coffee?" she asked incredulously, "Not the choice of drink I'd go with if I had just witnessed an unexplainable paranormal event and lost consciousness."

"You fainted," I reminded her.

"Black," she said firmly.

"Uh, I'm sure there's cream and sugar here somewhere."

"Black," she repeated. "The way my head feels, I'm going to need it to really kick."

She sat down on one of the stools near the kitchen island, legs crossed and her hands clasped, fingers intertwined. She looked haggard, vulnerable.

But then again, who wouldn't after witnessing what she had? One minute, monsters are imaginary. The next, you run into one being interrogated by a guy dressed only in a bath towel. That right there is a recipe for years of psychotherapy.

While the coffee was being made, I plopped down next to her, laying both my journal and the binder across the marble-top island. I slid the binder over to her. I figured as someone with a background in investigation, she might spot something amiss in the info Gnosis had given me. I stuck with the paranormal and monsters bit in my journal. Made sense.

I flipped through my journal with no success for about ten minutes. When the coffee was ready, I got up and fetched some ceramic mugs from Norman's cupboards. I gave Agent Ortiz her coffee straight-up black like she asked. As for me, I loaded it up with sugar, honey, and milk.

It's not like I can get diabetes, so I might as well enjoy the sweeter things in life. Norman's body was technically dead, so it's not like it'd do any harm.

After another ten minutes of perusing, Ortiz spoke up. "Where exactly did you say you got all of this information from?"

"I didn't."

She stared at me levelly for a good long while. I guess trying to make me tell her. Yeah, that wasn't going to work.

"So, how's your coffee?" I asked, trying to change the subject.

"Black, burnt, bitter," she replied in rapid succession.

"A bit of sugar and milk could take care of that," I offered.

"It's impressive, this collection of information. It's more than I could have gotten using Bureau resources legally," she said, raising an inquiring eyebrow.

"Good thing I didn't ask the Bureau then."

"Fine, play it that way," she resigned with a sigh.

I will, thank you very much. I liked the notion of getting a little, and insignificant as it may have been, vindictive pleasure at stumping a fed.

I had gotten halfway through my journal by now and still had nothing. I hadn't the foggiest idea of what could be responsible for Norman's murder. I was getting close to throwing something in a fit of frustration.

"Huh, this is strange," Ortiz murmured to herself.

"What is?" I leaned over to get a better look.

"Herman Burke, sixty-seven years of age, died about three weeks ago from a heart attack," she answered.

"So...? At his age that isn't really uncommon," I said, a bit confused at why she had brought this up.

"Well, it says here that he *was* a museum employee

before quitting a week before his death."

"Still not seeing a connection between the old geezer and a golden magical tiger and the Wraith," I responded.

"Well," she began, "it says he quit his position as a custodian soon after he…won the lottery and—"

"Good for him," I supplied lazily, "still don't see it."

"*And,*" she continued, "his heart attack occurred during…uh, a heavy romp session with his twenty-seven-year-old girlfriend—a girlfriend who happens to be a professional model."

"Wow, way to go buddy. Talk about going out with a bang."

"Not funny," Ortiz said.

"It kind of is, but wait, what? This guy wins the lottery, ends up dating a model, and then just, poof, heart failure all in a week?" I said perplexed.

"Strange isn't it?"

"More like an act of god," I snorted. "That guy had some serious luck."

"Yeah, I'll say. Winning the lottery and getting a model—every man's dream, I bet. Guess wishes do come true," she said.

It had been a while since I had felt a pang from Norman's memory, but the one going through my skull now was a whopper; one helluva painful light bulb moment.

"What did you just say?" I asked her.

"What? I said wishes do come true?"

"Son. Of. A. Bitch," I cursed below my breath.

"What?" she asked eagerly.

"I know what's behind all of this," I said triumphantly.

"What?"

"Is there an address listed in there for where the janitor lives…lived?" I asked quickly.

"Yeah," she said, skimming down the page for the information I had asked for. "He's got a place down on Fifth Avenue. A penthouse in The Premiere Hotel."

"I bet he does," I mumbled, more to myself.

"Why do you say that?"

"Wishes. That's what it's all been about. This house, the way Norman looks, everything!" I blurted.

"Um…" she said slowly, "now you've completely lost me. I was with you up until the monsters and murder. Now you sound crazy."

And then it clicked. The clues were right before me; I just hadn't noticed them.

"Dammit!" I swore.

"What now?" she asked, exasperated.

I bolted upstairs to Norman's bedroom and tore through the place looking for the will left to Norman by his father. I grabbed it and read it over again. It was right before my eyes. And if that wasn't enough, I rubbed the top right corner of the will where it was covered in heavy dust. Only it wasn't dust as I had first thought—it was soot.

I folded up the will, stuffing it into a pocket, and ran down to where Agent Ortiz sat waiting for an explanation.

"Find something?" she asked.

"Yeah. Now come on!" I said hurriedly, grabbing my journals and the binder of info.

"Where?"

"Herman's penthouse. You've got your car outside?"

She nodded.

I ran past her and grabbed the fallen chain I had used to interrogate the Wraith. It would probably come in handy. Chances were, I wasn't going to face another Wraith, but it was still a bit of salt and iron. That combo could put a hurting on a good number of supernatural monsters if need be. I led her downstairs to Norman's living room, the one full of outrageously expensive upholstery and silverware, like that stupid silver…

"Grab that!" I shouted, pointing to the ornate silver fire poker fastened between the silver brackets along the mantelpiece.

"But, why? What's going on?" she huffed, partly in anger, partly in confusion, with just a little bit of eagerness. She went and removed the fire poker like I had asked though.

"Something out there is granting belated birthday wishes, and I'm gonna go blow out their candles!" I snarled.

"That is the cheesiest, dumbest thing I have ever heard," she said in a flat tone.

"Just shut up and drive!" I growled, flinging the heavy door open and racing outside.

Chapter Ten

"How much longer?" I grumbled.

She turned her head and gave me a look that made me feel like I was an impetuous child. "Are we really going to do this? Really?"

"What?"

She shook her head in disbelief and muttered "Men," as if it were a curse.

"I'm on a deadline. I can't afford to waste time because you can't drive," I snarled.

"Excuse me?" she said, her voice taking on an edge.

"You heard me," I replied haughtily.

We bantered like that for a few minutes.

When my forearm started to throb, I glanced down and realized just how much time had passed.

I had six hours left to find, confront, and kill Norman's murderer. That might sound like a lot of time, but it's really not.

"What's that?" said Agent Ortiz, leaning over for a better look.

A car horn blew loudly, and she turned the wheel sharply, causing the car to swerve.

"Eyes on the road! Eyes on the fucking road!" I yelped.

"Oh my god. Calm down, you pansy!" she berated. "And you fight monsters?" she said the last part disbelievingly.

"Most monsters don't come barreling at me with the speed and weight of an automobile!" I retorted.

"Whatever you say, tough guy," she scoffed.

Seriously?

"So, what is it, Norman?"

"It's my countdown timer," I answered.

"Pardon?"

"Countdown timer," I repeated. "You know, the numbers keep going down until—"

"Yes, thank you, Einstein," she said tartly. "What is it counting down to?"

"Oh, how much time I have left to solve this case," I replied. "When it runs out, my case is sort of over, regardless of whether I solve it or not."

"You…you have a…magical countdown tattoo?" she said, her voice filled with disbelief.

"Yeah, I know."

"No. No, you really don't. That's just, it's not right. It's downright weird and unnatural."

I shrugged.

"So, what? At the end of your time limit, even if there's a monster left out there, you have to, what…move on?" she said, not quite believing that I could do such a thing.

"Yes," I said through gritted teeth.

"And have you?"

"No," I said rather stonily. "Never failed yet. It's a good incentive, if you think about it."

"Well, then, let's hurry up and make sure you keep your spotless track record, Magnum P.I."

I snorted, "Magnum's got it a bit easier than me. He doesn't deal with things that have magical powers, can twist reality, ooze through walls, and suck out your soul, and whatnot."

"Not to mention that he's fictional," she added.

"About an hour or two ago, you most likely thought monsters were fictional."

"Yeah," she said quietly. "Good point." She looked straight ahead at the road in an eerie, frozen sort of way, like she was glazing out. Something deep must have been running through her head. So I gave her a bit of quiet time to process her thoughts.

She exhaled heavily and muttered, "Monsters," as a

curse.

"Yeah," I said softly. "How are you taking it?"

She shook her head and shut her eyes. Only for a second, thankfully. She was driving, and I had already had one scare in the car with her. "I don't know how I'm taking it," she responded. "Truth be told, I think I'm still numb to it in a way, almost in denial." She finished with a shrug.

"Sorry," I whispered as apologetically as I could.

"For what?"

"For dragging you into all of this, for making you aware, I guess. For—" I started.

"For letting me know the truth?" she said a bit forcefully. "For letting me know there really are things that go bump in the night?"

"Yes," I said, bitterly.

"Why? What's wrong with knowing the truth?"

"Stop the car," I ordered.

"What?" she exclaimed.

"Stop. The. Car," I repeated, only slower.

"I thought we were in a hurry? Your countdown?" she exhaled and shook her head before continuing. "Your countdown tattoo." She forced those words out, and who could honestly blame her? I would find saying that aloud difficult too, if I were in her shoes.

She stopped the car, though; that's what mattered. I could make my point very clear.

"Look there," I said pointing to a smiling couple walking hand in hand down the sidewalk.

"What exactly am I supposed to notice?" she said, confused, and not quite grasping my point yet.

"They don't have a care in the world at the moment. That's all they have, all they're in—the moment," I said. "You think they would be like that if they knew the things I knew? What you now know? That there are monsters lurking out there? Well?"

"I...I...don't—" Ortiz stammered.

"No. No, they wouldn't. You know how I know? Because I can't go ten minutes without wondering what's lurking out there. If there's some supernatural nasty waiting for payback or to strike at some innocent bystander. They don't know, thus they don't care. Their thoughts aren't occupied with that. They can be…normal," I finished sullenly.

A soft hand reached out and grabbed my—Norman's—hand in a comfortable and reassuring grip. I looked over and saw Agent Ortiz staring at me rather intently, a hint of sadness shadowed her face.

"I'm sorry," she said quietly. "Sorry that you're stuck in this life."

I didn't say anything. I looked down at my knees, no, not even my knees. Norman's goddamn knees because I didn't have my own! I couldn't even remember my own knees. Hell, I couldn't remember my own face, my own frickin' name!

"How long?" she whispered.

"How long what?"

"How long have you been doing this?" she asked.

I shook my head. "I don't know. I can't remember. Years, a decade maybe, it's all too blurry," I said hoarsely.

"You don't even have an idea?" Ortiz said, sounding extremely surprised.

"Nope, not a clue. I remember the cases, most of them anyway. I can't remember the years, though it feels like forever."

"Some sort of amnesia?" she asked.

I shrugged.

"Anything else?"

"I can't remember my real name," I told her in a hushed voice. It scared me to admit that out loud. I never had before.

"So…Norman Smith isn't your real name then? You, what, had it changed?" she asked.

I shrugged again. I didn't know what to say. I couldn't tell her the truth, and I couldn't lie to her either.

"So, the whole museum job is what, a cover or something like that?" she said.

"Something like that," I agreed with a small nod of my head.

"Hm," she said, biting her lower lip. I could see her going through the mental gymnastics of sorting all of this out. It must've been quite the show in her head. After a few moments of us just sitting there quiet, she turned to me. "After this is over, I'm going to see if I can help you, Norman."

I couldn't quite look her in the eyes when I said, "Thank you." It wouldn't have been sincere. She didn't know that there wasn't going to be an *after this* for her and I once the case was done. I would be whisked out of Norman's body and shoved inside another meat suit.

Rinse and repeat. That's my life. I just tie up the loose ends, wrap things up as it were. There really wasn't much afterwards in the end.

"We should get going," I said, my voice a bit gruff. I found it hard to speak after what she had just said. It was hard on me. I've never been done a kindness or been offered one by a stranger before. I didn't know how to take it. Monsters sure, those I can deal with: run, fight, and gank 'em.

Kindness though? That was something I wasn't used to.

She must've noticed me struggling with those thoughts. Probably didn't know what I was thinking, but she must've known it was a lot. Women always seem to notice that somehow. Maybe they have their own supernatural powers; who knows? She didn't press me for any more answers though. I appreciated how she left me alone to sift through my thoughts as we drove off once again.

We got to The Premiere Hotel promptly, but the trip had carved out another hour of my time. My guess was that we were already on the edge of the last hour when we had left. Eight down, five left to solve the case.

No pressure.

We hurried into the hotel and up to the front desk. At this hour, it was a miracle anyone was still there, but, then again, this was *The* Premiere, so I guess it wasn't all that surprising.

"Hi, welcome to The Premiere," said a sweet and sugary voice. "My name's Stephanie. How may I help you?" I looked over to see a pretty-looking brunette woman in her mid-thirties. Her hair was cut in a very sleek bob cut. A few rogue strands had managed to find their way in front of her caramel brown eyes. As haggard as I was, without sleep and whatnot, I could still notice the subtle application of makeup, the cream foundation that layered and managed her skin flawlessly.

I'm a detective first. I pick up on stuff like that.

She stood there with a picture-perfect, white smile, the kind they could use in toothpaste commercials. How did they find someone this good looking to work a graveyard shift at a hotel? Well, considering what hotel it was, she was probably making a good deal of money for a front desk associate.

"Yeah, hi—" I started a bit too roughly.

"Hello," Agent Ortiz cut me off in a gentle and friendly tone. "We'd like to take a look at the penthouse belonging to a Mr. Herman Burke?"

"I uh…um," stammered Stephanie. "I'm sorry, but I can't do—"

Agent Ortiz apparently didn't care what Ms. Stephanie had to say. She held up a hand. Women code for shut up.

Stephanie stopped talking.

I made a mental note. I really needed to learn that move.

Agent Ortiz whipped out the magical badge of a Federal Bureau of Investigation agent.

"We know that Mr. Burke's penthouse hasn't been sold yet, nor have the contents of his home been removed either. We're looking into the cause of his death. It could possibly be a murder investigation."

The word murder was enough to make Stephanie's eyes widen like a doe caught in headlights. She muttered something unintelligible and vanished beneath the front desk for a moment.

Poor girl was probably frightened out of her mind. Between the possibility of a murder and a federal agent waving a badge in your face, who wouldn't be?

She popped back up an instant later with a keycard. No normal metal keys here. No, siree. This was *The* Premiere. A state-of-the-art, high-class place I would probably never be able to afford, not even for a night's stay.

Agent Ortiz beckoned for me to follow her as she walked towards the elevators. I raced up beside her and fell in step. "You know," I said, "you didn't have to scare the poor girl."

She didn't respond, just shot me a challenging look. I guess that meant she knew what she was doing.

"She didn't have to let us through," I told her.

"No, she didn't, but she didn't know that," replied Agent Ortiz, rather smugly.

"Well, maybe someone should let her know that she could ask to see a warrant, so the next time some fed doesn't scare the daylights out of her," I said a bit gratingly. I knew what Agent Ortiz had done was the quickest way to get us access, but still, I don't like seeing people get taken advantage of, especially by the government.

"Did you forget the part about us trying to solve a murder and stopping a monster?" she breathed heavily.

"Ixnay on the onstermay in public please," I said calmly.

"You ixnay!" she growled.

Okay, when a woman repeats what you say and very harshly—you ixnay.

We made it to the elevator and she jammed a finger into the call down button a tad too forcefully. She tapped her foot impatiently as we waited, arms tightly folded in front of her.

Yup, she was pissed.

She turned to look at me. "I had to scare the girl," she began in a defensive tone. "It kept her from thinking straight and expedited the process."

I let out a low whistle. "Expedited, huh?"

She let out a low, challenging growl.

I shut up again.

"Besides," she said, huffing, "how would you have handled it?"

"I wouldn't have," I said nonchalantly.

"What?"

"I would've just walked past her, up to his home, and forced my way in," I answered.

"You can't do that here," she said, waving the card in front of my face to accentuate her point. "Electronic keycards."

"I can do a lot of things that you can't," I said matter-of-factly.

I guess she took that as a challenge. It wasn't, but she didn't know that. "Oh really?" she said, her voice filled with an edge.

I responded in a singsong voice. "Anything you can do, I can do better."

Her teeth ground together.

"I can do anything better than you," I finished singing.

The elevator *donged,* and she stepped inside, fast. I was under the impression that at this point she was willing to leave me behind without a second thought. Actually, I think she wanted to leave me behind.

I leapt in and whispered. "Yes I can..." in a musical voice.

I didn't have to turn my head to know what she was doing. I could practically feel her glower.

I don't get much amusement in my line of work.

"You're insane," she muttered.

"Certifiably," I agreed, rapping a fist against my head.

After a few minutes of silence, and the elevator stopping on the first few floors to let people in and out, she decided she had had enough of the peaceful quiet.

"So...how would you do it?" she asked.

"Do what?"

"Force your way in," she said, as if it were obvious.

"Oh...that, I don't know," I said, shrugging indifferently.

"So you can't do it?"

I snorted. "I know this game, and, by the way, yes, I can. I'd have to see the door first."

"You've done this before?" she asked, trying to make it sound casual, but I could detect a little something more. She was a federal agent after all, and I could very well be confessing to breaking and entering.

I kept my trap shut.

"Let's assume it's a normal door, no electronic entry necessary. How would you do it?" she asked. I could hear the eagerness for an answer in her voice.

"Trade secret," I replied, bringing my index finger up to my lips a bit dramatically and making a *shushing* sound.

"You know," she warned, "doing those kind of things could bring you to the attention of law enforcement—more."

I gave her a nonchalant shrug, showing her I didn't care. I didn't, and I don't. I really don't.

"Right, tough guy doesn't care about getting caught by the authorities, but has a panic attack in my car, is that it?" she said wryly.

"Remind me how we met?" I asked her.

She was quiet, but I could see her jaw working furiously.

We were on the sixth floor by now, the elevator taking its sweet time to take us to the top.

"How many floors are there?" I growled edgily.

"Twelve."

I groaned.

The remaining floors passed by so agonizingly slow. It was mind numbingly slow. I think you get by now—it was really slow and it got on my nerves.

Dong went the elevator as we reached the twelfth and final floor. We walked down a red-carpeted hall, which, unlike most hotels, had few doors in it. Normally, you'd see rows of them, each door leading to rooms of varying sizes, depending on what you paid for. Here, however, there were only three, one presumably for each of the penthouses located on the floor.

"Which one's the one we're looking for?" I asked Agent Ortiz.

She nodded ahead, indicating the door at the end of the hall, the last door, in fact.

I made an exaggerated bow and flourish of my hands. "After you."

"Nutcase," she muttered below her breath in a tone that sounded half-curse and half-amusement.

I followed her to the door at the end of the hall, which sounded way more ominous than it actually was.

It was a heavy, solid-looking metal door. There was nothing ornate about it, clearly an example of function over form, built to keep things out.

We both let out a low and impressed whistle. It was damn impressive, and we both knew the home inside would only be more mind-boggling.

"So," she smiled, turning her head to look at me. "How'd you get past this?"

I smiled back. I honestly had no idea how I would've gotten past this door, but she didn't need to know that. When in doubt, ambiguity is the way to go. "I have my ways," I said in a vague manner.

She snorted. "Yeah, okay, what might those be?"

I waggled my fingers around in a mysterious manner and said, "Secrets."

She rolled her eyes and slipped the keycard into the electronic lock slot located several inches above the doorknob. There was a minute bulb, the size of a dewdrop, on top of the electronic device. It flashed red a moment after she slipped the card inside. An instant later, the card was spat back out and a soft *buzz* emanated from the little machine.

I stifled a laugh, but apparently not as well as I thought because Agent Ortiz turned to glare at me.

"Funny is it? I'd like to see some of your trade secrets now, mystery man," she said in a challenging tone.

"May I?" I asked, gently reaching out for the card.

She shoved it into my hand a bit aggressively. "In case

you didn't notice, I just tried that, smart guy."

I ignored her jibe, flipped the card over and around before sliding it into the electronic card reader. A second later, the tiny bulb flashed bright green, followed by a barely noticeable *clicking* sound. The card ejected, and I reached down to turn the doorknob. It turned and the door opened.

I turned to look back at a fuming Agent Ortiz, handing the card back to her. "You put it in upside down and backwards, but—"

"Don't you dare say it!" she growled.

"But nice try." I grinned.

Her look was all venom and spite at that moment. She pushed past me and into Herman's penthouse.

I followed her in, closing the door behind us.

"Wow…" she said, breathless.

I looked around and was blown away. As rich as Norman was, this guy must've been loads richer—it showed.

"This is much nicer than your place, Norman," she continued in awe.

"Yeah." I nodded in agreement.

The janitor's home was just…wow. The floor in the entry room was a cream marble with black flecks over every tile. Ahead of us, in the center of the room, was a ridiculously long, pristine, white leather couch. It must've been twenty feet long, designed to seat at least ten people, and then there was the other part. It ran off at ninety degrees, creating an L-shape. Atop the couches were extremely plump-looking cushions, arranged to alternate in their placement from white cushion to rich burgundy ones.

"Comfy," Ortiz mumbled idly after she had taken a look at the couch.

I walked over to the center of the living room and started to take in every detail I could, revolving in place as I did. The windows were small, square constructions with thick, white paneling between them, considerably smaller than most windows, but there were a great deal more of them in this home. About fifteen ran horizontally across the room. It seemed pointless to me; they could have just used one big, long window. Connected to them were another series of longer, narrower windows running upward at a canted angle. It gave the place a look that resembled a greenhouse, a ridiculously expensive greenhouse.

I leaned closer to the windows to examine them, running my fingers along every inch. I was looking for residue—namely soot. It would have been confirmation of my theory, but I turned up nothing.

I decided to examine the black circular coffee table directly in the center of the room, standing on its tiny nub-like legs. Nothing beneath or atop it, save for some brand new and unopened books. They weren't even out of the plastic wrap. Nearby was a small table meant for keeping decorative items on it, much like the vase and potted flowers it currently supported. It looked to be of similar make as the coffee table. In the corner was a classical piano and matching high, black, padded leather stool. Both of them were spotless as well.

I sighed loudly.

"Something wrong?" asked Agent Ortiz.

"Yeah," I muttered. "I haven't found what I'm looking for yet."

"Well," she began, "didn't the report say he died in the bedroom? You might find what you're looking for in there."

I looked at her astounded. I had completely forgotten about that. How had she remembered that little detail, but couldn't manage to put a keycard in the right way?

"So…are we going to the bedroom or what?" she asked impatiently.

"Thought you'd never ask, Toots," I quipped.

She rolled her eyes and snorted. "Not in your wildest dreams, pal," she laughed.

We navigated our way through Herman's lavishly decked out penthouse, passing by an unnecessarily large dining table with at least a dozen white leather sofa-looking seats strewn around it.

He had sofa seats for his dining table? The hell?

The table itself was a beautiful marbleized stone. I couldn't tell what it was, but it wasn't real marble, just looked like it. Strangely, it was still covered in bowls and dishes. Empty ones, but they were still out in placement.

We continued on, strolling through the kitchen next. Unlike the rest of the penthouse, the kitchen was surprisingly simple. It had expensive-looking, state-of-the-art equipment, of course, but the look itself was simple. Everything had an antiquated wooden look to it. It was homely in a way, clashing seriously with the rest of the home's bright white style.

The bedroom wasn't impressive, which was saying a lot considering the quality of the rest of his home. The floor was wood-stained to resemble the finish on a black, glossy showroom piano. It went well with the white, well, everything else. The king-sized bed was blanketed in white fabric. Its pillows were piled up and were, you guessed it, white.

This guy had no imagination.

It looked expensive but oddly simple compared to the rest of the house. It was sparse, just a bed and a small table at the foot of the bed. A small nightstand on both sides and that was it. Not to mention there was also a glass door leading out to the terrace overlooking Manhattan. Still, it wasn't much of a bedroom.

Then again, it had a bed and was a room. Isn't that all they are supposed to be? Maybe he didn't need or want much; he was shacking up with a model, according to Agent Ortiz.

"Kinda empty," stated Agent Ortiz. "I was expecting a bit more."

"I know," I agreed.

"What exactly are you looking for, Norman?"

"Stains," I answered, simply.

"Ah, what?" she asked, a bit taken back.

"Oh, soot stains. Not the, ah, other kind," I explained.

"Ah," she said, understanding.

"Yeah, sorry about that," I apologized.

"Why soot?" she asked.

"Confirmation of a theory, Agent Ortiz. Confirmation of a theory," I answered.

"And what theory is that?"

"I'll let you know if it turns out to be correct. If not, well there's no point in burdening you with more knowledge of what nasties are out there."

"Don't you think that I deserve to know, especially considering what I've witnessed?" she said, edgily.

"First of all, you haven't witnessed anything yet. Secondly, no," I replied.

"I'm sorry?" she said in a challenging tone.

"Look," I said, sighing. "If you want to talk about this, then let's do it later. Right, now we need to find something, anything. A clue, 'kay?"

"Fine. Later," she said with finality.

I nodded in agreement.

"I'm guessing his death wasn't listed as suspicious, right?" I asked her.

"No, just an older gentlemen's heart giving out during sex. It's kind of a cliché, but no," she answered.

"So it's a pretty good bet any evidence is still lying here," I said more to myself than her.

"Unless a cleaning staff member's been through here."

"Let's hope not. He died in bed, so I need the sheets to be dirty."

"Uh huh," she said, slowly.

"Not like that," I growled. "Now, come here and help me tear this bed apart. No, that's not a euphemism for us to shack up."

She laughed. "Yeah, don't worry. I didn't take it as one."

Was that an insult? Whatever.

We peeled back the sheets and I got my answer.

"Is that—" she began.

"Sure is." There was a small layer of soot. On a darker bedspread, it would've gone unnoticed, but on the perfect white sheets, it stood out a lot. It wasn't much, but it didn't need to be. I knew now, with a hundred percent guarantee, what we were dealing with.

"Damn," I muttered. "I was afraid of this."

"What? What is it?" she asked.

"A Djinn."

Chapter Eleven

This was bad. This case had just elevated from bad enough to dangerously worse. Djinn are heavy hitters in the supernatural world. Now I had to track one down and kill it before it could hurt any more people.

"A what?" asked Agent Ortiz, clearly baffled by what I had just said.

"A Djinn. You know, mythical creatures famed for granting wishes," I explained.

"A...genie? Like the blue genie from Aladdin?" she said, disbelievingly.

"Yeah, except it isn't blue, doesn't have a friendly temperament, and is not voiced by Robin Williams. Oh, just an FYI, Djinni is a female, Djinn is male," I responded.

She shook her head, "A genie? Really?"

"Djinn, I think, but it could be a Djinni," I answered.

"Grants wishes...genie..." she continued, unable to believe it.

"Yeah, they can bend reality on a small scale. They love making deals and granting wishes. Then they, well, the mean ones anyway, screw the person they made the deal with, normally having them die in some twisted way related to the wish," I explained to her.

"Uh, how and why?" she asked, still startled at the revelation that the Djinn actually existed.

"Well as to how, when a Djinn or Djinni makes a deal with someone, they sort of leave a bit of themselves on that person. They leave a residue. It's still a part of them however; it's like leaving a bit of their power on someone else. Anyways, this essence forms sort of a bubble around the person. It's a magical field that serves as a pipeline between the Djinn and the person who asked for the wish. The Djinn can reach out through it and continue to affect them, make their wish go bad," I explained.

"Like having an elderly janitor die while having sex with the professional model girlfriend he probably wished for?" she said, beginning to catch on.

"Yeah, exactly," I agreed. I thought about the will Norman had received from his father, the one indicating that Norman had always desired his father's car. It was obvious now he had wished for it, but got it at the expense of his father's life. I wagered Norman didn't know the cost going into the deal.

"So what happens when the person dies?"

"Well, the residue around them collapses, and here we are. Soot, and that's the most worrying thing of all," I told her.

"Why is that?"

"Because it means we're not dealing with some angry lowly type of Djinn—it's an Ifrit," I explained.

"A lowly type of Djinn? An Ifrit? What are you talking about?" she said shaking her head, a bit overwhelmed with all of the info.

"Djinns have castes, but they're not like societal castes where the only difference is their birth and stuff. Their caste system dictates their powers, their strength, and many times, their disposition. Ifrits," I said with a sigh, "are pretty high up and they're mean, like downright nasty mean."

"And how does the soot come into all of this?"

"Well, many supernatural creatures leave a residue—" I began to explain.

"Like the Wraith," she blurted out.

"Yes," I said through gritted teeth. "Like the Wraith." My anger at her interrupting me was obvious. If she cared, it didn't show. "Ghosts and many other spectral creatures leave ectoplasm behind," I continued. "Lore goes, Djinn are born from fire, Ifrits are born from the hottest and purest of flames, and a byproduct of fire is…"

"Soot," she answered, more to herself than me. I could see everything starting to click in her mind.

"Mythology around them states that Ifrits are one of the highest embodiments of fire. You know, created from the fires of creation, that kind of thing. They sort of have a superiority complex because they believe they came into the world first, before man and all. That, coupled with the fact that humans, like King Solomon, learned to bind them, and make them subservient. So yeah, they love killing us off if they get the chance and it really gets their rocks off getting us to do it for them."

She nodded in understanding. "Like granting wishes that cause ironic deaths," she said, glancing at the bed.

"Poor guy," I said softly. "He probably thought he was getting the deal of a lifetime."

"He was eager," Ortiz added, "What, with his age and occupation, I don't blame him."

"Yeah," I whispered sadly, "it made him a perfect target. He probably jumped at the chance."

"I still can't believe this," Ortiz said. "Wishes and genies and tigers and Wraiths…"

"Yeah, the Ifrit's behind 'em all," I said.

"It can really do all of that?" she said, stunned.

"Yeah, they're old. Really old, like near beginning of life on Earth old. They're heavy-duty players in the supernatural world too. They can pretty much make any lower, weak-willed creature their servant. Not to mention the whole part about warping reality on small to large scales, depending on their strength," I answered.

She blinked several times and then sat down on the edge of the bed, propping her arms on her knees and resting her head in her hands.

I went over and sat right beside her. Without another thought, I placed a comforting hand on her shoulder, much like she had done for me. "Feeling okay?" I asked.

She let out a dark laugh. "At this point, no. Not really."

"Welcome to a day in my world."

"No offense, Norman, your world sucks."

"Tell me about it," I agreed, dejectedly.

We sat there for several moments, before she spoke again, "So Djinn, they can only kill through their wishes?"

"Well, technically, I suppose they can kill in their human forms as well, but they'd be confined to—"

"Wait!" she blurted out, "These things can look like humans?"

"Yeah. Humans, animals, whatever. You name it, they can shift to look like it. But to answer your question, they can kill physically as a human would but they'd have to follow the same rules a person has to," I answered.

"I don't follow."

"Well, when they're in human form, they have to play by our rules. They would have to use the human body to kill. They can't rely on their powers till they shifted back."

"So they would leave signs? Like a struggle, someone being choked, bludgeoned, or maybe they'd use a weapon?" she reasoned.

"Yeah..." I answered, my thoughts were elsewhere though. *Norman didn't die in a physical manner. There were no physical signs, meaning he died from a wish, but which one? His father's car passed to him, and the money didn't kill him. Could it have been the youth?* That's when I realized just how poor Norman had died. He was an extremely unhealthy, older man who had wished for physical perfection. The toll the change must've taken on his body is what killed him. *Irony, perfect irony, wish to be perfectly healthy, and the shock of the change on your system kills you.*

"Norman, you okay?" Ortiz asked. "You look lost in thought."

"I am. I was," I responded.

"Oh okay, just wanted to point *that* out!" she said, jabbing a finger towards what she was talking about.

I followed her finger to where she pointed. There, on the glass-paned doors leading out to the terrace, was a small amphibious creature. It was massive for what is was, about one foot in length and covered in a hellish red, orange and yellow coloring. It looked as if someone had spray-painted a flame job on the amphibian. Its skin was secreting a viscous-looking substance that smelled horribly like petroleum. It clung to the glass door and stared at us for a moment, before convulsing in a little shiver. A stream of flames erupted along the ridge of its spine.

"Oh…well shit. It's a, um, a Salamander," I said.

"Really? Because where I'm from, they don't light on fire!" Ortiz exclaimed, taking a frightened leap back as she did.

"Yeah, they're beings that represent the element of fire. They travel in massive groups and well, just burn things. They're simplistic animals," I continued.

Her eyes widened as she turned to me. "How massive a group?"

"That massive!" I said, pointing in a panicky manner at the glass door. A dozen of the creatures had materialized from nowhere.

Agent Ortiz stood there in a stunned silence. So did I, as a matter of fact. I didn't expect this to happen.

The rest of the creatures followed the lead of the first and shivered terribly, until they, too, had a line of flames running down their backs. They slowly crawled down the glass door and onto the floor. Some fell rather unceremoniously, taking a shortcut as they plopped onto the wooden floor. Once there, the entire group shook once more in unison until their entire bodies burst into flames.

"Um, Norman," Ortiz began in an unusually calm tone. "What the hell do we do now?"

The entire floor began catching fire. Small flames were spreading out from the jelly-like substance the creatures oozed and left in their wake. The flames spread and licked their way up everything: walls, doors, furniture, and more.

"Now, we run!" I yelped, grabbing her hand and yanking her forcefully behind me. I led her past the small mob of flaming Salamanders, and we fled the room, avoiding the flames and small pack of fiery monsters. While not too fast, the creatures managed to put up a good chase, leaving their flammable gel-like secretion everywhere.

Everything started catching on fucking fire!

The majority of the upper levels of the penthouse were ablaze, and the rest would quickly follow. I had to get Agent Ortiz and myself the hell out of there.

"Come on!" I snarled.

She stumbled in the kitchen, and I helped her up as fast as I could. The pack of Salamanders was only yards behind us, rapidly setting the kitchen afire. Their ooze spread faster and faster across the penthouse. There was a *thwup* noise as a small glob of venomous looking green spittle landed in front of our feet. It proceeded to hiss and smoke…as it ate through the floor!

"You didn't tell me they could do that!" yelled Ortiz in an accusing manner.

"I didn't know they could do that," I yelped defensively. I yanked Ortiz's arm rather hard as I pulled her along with me, forcing her to break back into a run right behind me.

Soon all I heard was *thwup thuwp thuwp* as it began raining acidic goo. The floor became peppered with holes, leaving the surface beneath us brittle. We kept running, trying to avoid the flames and weak spots in the floor that were crumbling around us.

"How far does their spit keep going?!" Ortiz shouted over the roaring fire.

"I don't know," I shouted back. "It's supernatural, wouldn't be surprised if it kept going to the bottom!"

"I hate you for dragging me into this!" Agent Ortiz screamed over the sound of crackling and crumbling structures. Not to mention the typhoon of corrosive spittle raining down.

"Me? You involved yourself!" A fire alarm pierced the air, making it hard to be heard. I must not have noticed it before, what with the impending death by immolation and what not. The fire alarm must've given the Salamanders some offense because it fell victim to a cascade of acidy spit and shut up.

We raced through the living room. Jumping, diving and rolling over, through and past anything and everything in our frantic panic to escape. Nearly every inch of the penthouse was ablaze now, and, considering it was a rooftop house, one that belonged in a prominent hotel, it was a safe bet the fire department would be here soon.

Yup, they would be here just in time to pull our finely charred asses out of the burnt remains of this place.

I could see the door ahead, the flames hadn't reached it yet, but they were close. I pumped my legs furiously, hand outstretched, and reached for the door. I grabbed the handle and wrenched on it. "Dammit!" A white-hot searing pain lanced up my hand. I reeled back and looked at the imprint scalded into my palm. Gritting through the pain, knowing the wound would heal, I reached out again. I was about to turn the handle when I was impacted by Agent Ortiz and driven to the ground.

"Stay down!" she screamed as a series of *fwup* sounds flew overhead. A number of acid globs hit the door, dissolving the metal. A giant hole was quick to form in the middle and spread outward. "Come on," Ortiz said as she hauled me to my feet, leading me through the now-gaping hole in the door.

We were in for a helluva surprise though. As soon as we exited the penthouse, I saw the rest of the floor had already caught fire. Doors were flung wide open and I saw the fires blazing within the rooms. The fire alarm that had gone off in the janitor's home must've been linked throughout the hotel, setting off the others and warning the other occupants of the impending danger.

The sprinkler system came on—eventually—and tried to combat the fire but had little chance of success. This was a supernatural fire. Every time the fire was doused, it ignited once again. A blanket of steam filled the floor, making it somewhat difficult to see. The water in the system must've been depleted as the sprinklers stopped their downpour soon after starting, leaving the fire to continue its carnage.

The elevator was straight ahead of us, but wasn't the best route of escape—the door beside it leading to the stairs was. I sped forwards with Agent Ortiz just a few steps behind me, when the path before us erupted into a wall of fire.

"Jesus!" I shouted.

We ground to a halt. The flames stretched from wall to wall, licking their way from the floor to the ceiling, cutting us off from the stairs. They flickered for a moment, giving off the illusion they were fading away before snapping back into fiery clarity. Everything behind us was catching fire, not to mention the pack of Salamanders advancing towards us, while Agent Ortiz and I stood transfixed by the wall of flames. Something was moving within them; I could see something forming, taking shape deep within.

"Norman," gasped Agent Ortiz. "What the hell is that?"

It was hard to explain, but inside the massive wall of flames was another set of flames, almost like there was a shadow being cast inside the existing fire. I could barely make them out at first. The smaller ghost flames, if you will, moved separately from the surrounding fire. It formed a thin narrow tower of flames that filled out rapidly, forming the lithe figure of a woman. A petite foot and leg stepped out from the wall of flames, quickly followed by another. Soon there was entire woman of flames standing before us.

She was about the height of Agent Ortiz. Long locks of hair, made purely of fire, fell down her shoulders, behind her back and before her breasts. You could actually make out individual strands that were a multitude of oranges, yellows, reds and whites. Her eyes were pools of fire, set deep in her sockets, which looked like obsidian lines with glowing red cracks. Her mouth followed this pattern too. A wide demonic smile, lips made of volcanic rock and an open mouth with a fire burning within it. There were more obsidian-like protrusions running down her spine that culminated in a thin, wispy tail, stretching out like a whip behind her. It was lengthy and segmented with more bits of volcanic rock, looking more like beads strung between the length of her fiery tail. The floor beneath her feet was burning, but the flames weren't spreading towards us, no, they stayed centered around the creature.

"An Elemental," I whispered as more of a curse. As if the pack of Salamanders wasn't enough, I had to deal with an eldritch creature of fire; a physical manifestation of an inferno with the temperament to match.

The wall of flames behind the Elemental subsided and the pack of Salamanders stopped converging on us. The building, however, was still burning—we were surrounded on all sides by fire.

At least I knew one thing now: the Elemental was calling the shots with the Salamanders. It had enthralled them, and I had a pretty good idea what was pulling the Elemental's strings.

It cocked its head quizzically to the left, surveying the situation before she pointed forwards with an outstretched hand and wailed.

"Move!" I shouted, pushing Ortiz forwards as hard as I could. I sent her staggering past the Elemental moments before a gout of flames lashed out at the very spot she had been standing seconds earlier. The carpet burst into flames with a hiss and crackle. Steam shot up from the ground beside me. I could feel the heat from its strike, even amidst the already-burning building.

The Elemental spun in a slow, graceful manner to face Agent Ortiz, who was still righting herself. If I didn't do something—and quickly—it was safe to say that Ortiz was going to be incinerated.

"Ortiz! The stairs!" I shouted, indicating the emergency staircase several feet before her. Sadly, they were cut off to me, due to the Elemental standing right in front of me.

Agent Ortiz looked at the staircase. "What about you?" she asked as she inched towards the stairs.

"I dunno! I'll figure it out and meet you below. Now, go!" I hollered.

The Elemental turned back around to regard me, and then craned her neck back to look at Agent Ortiz. Ortiz was less than a foot away from the staircase now. I didn't know if the Elemental could understand human speech, but she seemed to have a pretty good idea of what was going on.

She pirouetted with supernatural grace and faced Ortiz again, letting out a high-pitched wail as she raised her fiery arms.

"No!" I snarled as I looked around for something, anything, to help me divert the Elemental's attention from Ortiz. There on the wall, this whole goddamn time, was one of those glass cases containing a fire extinguisher. I must've been too preoccupied to notice it before. What with the burning building, gaggle of incendiary Salamanders, and the Elemental setting this place ablaze. You kind of prioritize your own safety over finding the nearest fire extinguisher.

I dashed forwards, swinging my fist into the glass case. It shattered, driving shards of glass into my fingers and knuckles, slicing away at the tender skin I had received courtesy of the scorching doorknob. I worked through the pain and wrenched the fire extinguisher from its resting place.

The air suddenly filled with a very familiar sound. I leapt back as a torrent of acidy spit fell on the spot I had been just moments before. My sudden rush towards the extinguisher must've prompted the Salamanders from their idle state. Their projectile spit ate away at the wall and floor below us. I ignored the fact that the floor beneath me was literally crumbling away, and yanked the stupid health and safety tag and pin off of the extinguisher.

"Hey, ash-hole!" I called to the Elemental. It wasn't my best material, I admit, I must've been more concerned with trying to not be immolated than being witty.

It didn't matter how corny or stupid it was because it got the attention of the Elemental. It turned to face me, and I didn't hesitate. I depressed the handle and covered the Elemental in smothering foam. It staggered back and flailed wildly, screeching as it did. I didn't stop there though. I spun around and sprayed the pack of Salamanders behind me.

While doing so, I turned to look over my shoulder. Ortiz was still standing there, a mere foot from the staircase, staring slack-jawed. "What are you waiting for?" I snarled. "Go!" She nodded and bolted down the stairs.

I turned my attention back to the pack of Salamanders. They were entirely coated in fire suppressing-foam, but something as simple as a fire extinguisher wouldn't keep them down for long. The supernatural didn't play by our rules; the Salamanders and Elemental would be hurt for a moment, but that was about it. An angry hiss and wail confirmed my suspicions. I spun around to see the enraged Elemental rising back to her feet, burning a variety of blues and whites as smoke rose from her mass.

"This hotel has a no smoking policy," I growled as I depressed the handle again. The Elemental shrieked and collapsed to the floor beneath a layer of fire-resistant foam, writhing and flailing around. I turned to regard the pack of Salamanders, who had recovered and now were storming towards me. I pressed the handle to spray them down, but all that happened was a small amount of foam dribbling out of the nozzle. "Oh, well, shit," I murmured.

The entire pack leapt towards me, bodies afire and spitting a mass of material dissolving saliva at me. I did the only thing I could think of to escape. I looked down at the rapidly deteriorating floor and closed my eyes. *This is going to hurt.* I jumped up, tucking my knees to my chest, and moments before coming back to the ground, I kicked down with my legs, smashing them into the fragile floor. The result was instantaneous. The floor gave way, and I found myself hurtling down to the floor below.

I don't know how far the drop was. I'd wager somewhere from twelve to sixteen feet, and I don't know if four feet makes much of a difference in how much it hurts.

For the record, it hurt a damn lot!

I ended up landing on my side; my left shoulder and arm took the majority of the impact. I heard a sickening crunch in the area where my shoulder met my collarbone. The mixture of white-hot pain lancing up my arm and a deep throbbing throughout the rest of my body was overwhelming. Something either broke, or was dislocated. Knowing my luck, it was probably both.

I was tempted to lie there in agony, but I didn't have

that luxury. It was difficult to raise myself up. I couldn't lean
against the walls of the hallway since most of them were
engulfed in flames. I had seriously underestimated how
quickly the fires were spreading. If it continued at this rate, a
five-star New York hotel would burn to the ground. I dived
out of the way as a few more bits of crumbling ceiling fell
around me. A few bits managed to tag me, inflicting more
pain and caused me to lose my balance.

Screams filled the air, and they weren't coming from
me. I looked around frantically for the source. As I did, the
entire floor became more wreathed in fire…if that was even
possible. I hauled my broken and battered ass down the hall,
looking for the room where the screams emanated from.
Most of the doors on this floor were wide open, meaning
the occupants had fled. After making it down more than
two-thirds of the hallway, I found a room that was sealed
shut and fortunately, it wasn't a high-end metal door.

Most people don't really know how to properly kick
down a wooden door. They think they know, but they don't.
You aim for the spot right above the doorknob or handle;
that's where the wood is weakest and most likely to give.
Oh, you also don't ram into it with your shoulder. That's a
great way to injure yourself, especially if you've just fallen
twelve feet and are already injured. You take a good step
back, step forwards while pulling your arms back and
kicking with your heel at the spot I mentioned before. The
door won't come off its hinges like in some television
shows. What happens is that the wood around the doorknob
breaks and the door flings open dramatically. Of course, it
helps if you happen to have a bit of supernatural strength,
like I do.

The door flung open. Inside the room against the far
wall, where the window was, a mother and young boy
huddled together. The ceiling was on fire, as well as some of
the front portions of the room. I set my jaw, toughing
through the pain, and managed to sprint over to them. I
extended my arm. "Come on, this way!" I shouted.

She didn't grab my burned and glass shrapnel filled

hand, but instead grabbed onto my left forearm—the one connected to my broken and dislocated shoulder and collarbone. I didn't scream…aloud, anyway, but my teeth were grinding as she hauled herself up at the expense of my quickly diminishing pain threshold. She beckoned to her little boy, who shook his head. He sat there huddled up with his arms around his knees.

I didn't have time for this. I reached down and scooped him up with my burned right hand, throwing him over my good shoulder, and led them out of the room. I set the boy on his feet and gestured to the emergency stairs. His mother mouthed a silent thank you and took off with the boy. Common sense dictated that I follow them, make sure they got there safely, but I was too worried about something else. I hadn't seen Agent Ortiz yet. We were only one floor down. Granted, I had taken an excruciating shortcut to get there, but I should've run into her by now.

I began fearing the worst and started looking around for another fire extinguisher to arm myself with. Hotels of this grade were required to have them on each floor. Hell, some of them even had full-blown fire hoses. I was hoping I would be so lucky as to find one. It would put a hurtin' on any fire-based creature. I stumbled around for a few moments, struggling to see through the smoke, but eventually, I came across another extinguisher. I took the time to remove this one properly, rather than introducing a whole mess of glass into my fist, again.

After becoming properly armed, I began shouting, "Ortiz! Ortiz, you out there?" I shambled forwards in an awkward manner, the pain and damage to my body was taking a toll. Add to that the fact that the smoke and lack of oxygen were making it hard to breathe, I was beginning to get disoriented. If I was struggling this much, it made me considerably more worried about Agent Ortiz's well-being. Spurred on by that thought, I plowed through the dense smoke and supernatural-induced inferno.

I began coughing, which quickly escalated into a deep, painful wheezing, the kind that racks your throat until it's completely dry. "Ortiz!" I said hoarsely. "Ortiz, you there?"

No answer.

There was a clear patch of visibility through the smoke, and I saw another emergency staircase ahead. I banished the pain from my mind and lurched towards it. The fires around me intensified as I drew nearer, a sharp piercing wail overwhelmed me. It was louder than the damned fire alarm. The mass of flames flickered and waned out of existence for a brief moment before bursting back into clarity. A being jumped out of them, towards me!

I didn't have the strength to move out of the way, so I simply collapsed. Not heroic and badass, I know, but it was all I could do to avoid being immolated by the flaming devil woman. The Elemental soared over my prone form and landed several paces behind me. Before she had the chance to turn around and light my crippled ass on fire, I decided to capitalize on the moment. I scrambled to my feet and unleashed another wave of foamy wrath upon her.

"Ha ha!" I laughed, which caused me to cough heavily. "Where's your little lizard death squad now, bitch?" I said angrily, reveling in the fact that I had kicked an Elemental's ass.

I got my answer all too soon. About fifteen feet behind the Elemental's writhing form was an entire gaggle of the flaming amphibians.

"Oh...good, the whole gang's here," I muttered gloomily. I let out an exasperated sigh and solidified my grip on the extinguisher. I didn't know how many more rounds I could go with these things. It was starting to look like even if I did manage to find a way to kill them, I would die in the hotel fire.

Guns are loud. Seriously, really damn loud, and I forget that sometimes. I don't have the good fortune of being able to lug one around. So when one goes off by my ears, I notice. All I know is that, one second, I was staring at a mass of Salamanders coming at me, and the next, their numbers began to diminish.

Bang bang bang! In rapid succession. Shot after shot rang

out as Agent Ortiz's pistol was actually killing the Salamanders. The one at the head of the pack didn't so much drop dead from a perfectly placed bullet to the skull so much as it burst. When it did, the thing went off like a cherry bomb. Ka frickin' boom! She managed to drop eight or nine of them before the Elemental began to regain its composure. The remaining Salamanders had made it close enough to bombard us with their corrosive spit.

"Okay, good going there, but how 'bout we amscray before they decide to dissolve and or incinerate us, huh?" I said a little too loudly. I couldn't really hear myself; a gun going off point blank by your ears will do that to you.

I didn't make out what she said, but I understood her nod. She placed my arm around her and helped me limp towards the stairs.

I felt like passing out, but I knew I couldn't, not till we were clear of this mess anyway.

"Do you think I got them?" asked Ortiz. It came over muffled and distorted.

"I think so!" I shouted, trying to compete over the fire alarm and cope with being a bit deafened from the gunshots.

"I didn't know a bullet could kill something like that," she said.

"Me neither!" I shouted back as she helped me limp into the stairwell. We were on the eleventh floor, and I was battered pretty well. The descent looked pretty daunting. My legs were damaged and I didn't think I had a good chance of making it. Ortiz must've figured that out as well.

"Think you can make it?" she asked, biting her lip in a worried manner.

I snorted. "At this point, I think it'd be easier to roll me down the steps and meet you at the bottom."

"Now's not the time to be a smartass," she scolded; , there was a bit of a smirk edging its way across her face.

"Nonsense," I replied. "Impending death by immolation is the best time to be a smartass." *Not to mention it might be my last chance to be one.*

A series of *splats* hit the metal door behind us. Seconds

later, a sickening hissing noise filled the air. We turned our heads to see the door melting away. The Salamanders had caught up with us.

"How about you can the smartass remarks until I get you down these stairs without being turned into a puddle of goo?" Ortiz said.

I nodded in agreement as she helped me descend the first flight of stairs. We made good progress, clearing about three flights without interruptions from the Elemental or the Salamanders. Just as we were coming to the seventh floor, our luck ran out.

"Damn," cursed Ortiz as another wall of fire erupted in front of us, blocking off access to the rest of the stairs.

"Out onto the floor," I said, nodding at the doorway that would lead us into the corridor.

Ortiz helped me through, shutting the door behind us as a familiar wail rang out; the Elemental was right behind us. We hurried forward, away from the Elemental on our tails, and the air began to smell of ozone. The sound of superheated fire filled our ears as the metal door was blown off its hinges and into the wall opposite it. The door was streaked, not with fire but with what looked like molten lava, and was beginning to disintegrate.

Ortiz and I looked on in wide-eyed horror at the kind of power the Elemental had. If I wasn't so terrified, I would've been impressed by it.

"And how do we kill that thing?" Ortiz asked as she continued helping me limp forwards.

"We really can't," I answered.

"Can't?"

"Well," I began, pursing my lips whilst trying to figure out what exactly to say. "There's nothing here for us to kill it with. We'd have to fully smother the Elemental so it couldn't reignite or—"

I was slumping, struggling to hold myself upright as Agent Ortiz stopped supporting me. She spun around, gun drawn, and unloaded several rounds into the Elemental's body. Ortiz fired until her gun clicked and the slide retracted into the open position. Every shot managed to stagger the Elemental, forcing it to step back from the sheer force of the bullets, but I didn't think they actually did much harm. From where I was standing—well, slumping—the rounds passed harmlessly through its body. They were coming out the other end as flaming shrapnel, setting more of the building on fire.

The Elemental let out an angry howl and raised both her arms towards us. A mass of flames gathered around its wrists and hands.

"Down!" I shouted, the force of which caused further havoc on my sore and damaged throat. I collapsed to the ground, dragging Ortiz with me, just as two bolts of fire passed inches above our heads. The heat radiating from them was intense. It felt as if I had gotten instant sunburn on my neck.

Ortiz righted herself first, hauling me to my feet with force and speed, pushing me forwards and keeping me from stumbling awkwardly.

"You have another magazine?" I croaked.

"Yeah, but I don't think that thing is going to give me the time to reload," she replied through gritted teeth.

"Maybe if I ask nicely?" I joked.

"You try that, tough guy."

"Just be ready," I replied. Up ahead was another fire extinguisher—thank god buildings like this had to have one on every floor. They were becoming a real lifesaver. I rammed Agent Ortiz aside rather forcefully, but it got her out of the way of another potential strike as I scrambled towards the extinguisher.

"The hell!" blurted Ortiz angrily. She stumbled into a wall that had somehow avoided catching on fire.

"Reload, now!" I growled as I lurched forwards and swung open the glass case holding the extinguisher. I grabbed it by the top and yanked it out, aiming it at the advancing Elemental, and doused her in fire suppressant foam once again. The Elemental writhed, fighting off the smothering contents of the extinguisher as her flames sputtered.

"Reloaded!" called back Ortiz.

"How good are you at nailing moving targets?" I asked.

Ortiz caught onto what I was planning and scampered over to me.

"Wait till it gets back up," I explained. "Till then, let's keep moving but keep an eye out over your shoulder." Ortiz gave me an understanding nod. "No, no," I said, brushing off Agent Ortiz's attempt to help me walk again. Norman's body was beginning to heal, courtesy of my supernatural abilities. My hand was still covered in bits of glass and bleeding, but most of the pain was subsiding. My shoulder was feeling a bit better too. We covered the remaining half the length of the corridor before Ortiz motioned for me to look back.

The Elemental had gotten back to its feet and released a challenging shriek, but before it could launch another superheated blast, I hurled the extinguisher towards the creature. "Now!" I shouted. It tore my throat apart, causing me to cough violently again.

Agent Ortiz hit the extinguisher with a single shot the second it was inches away from the Elemental, and the effect was immediate. The highly pressurized container burst with enough force to knock the Elemental on its ass, but that wasn't the best part. The amount of concussive force, coupled with the fire-suppressing contents, wreaked havoc on the Elemental. It was blown back and doused in foam, landing a good five or six feet back, screaming in anguish as its flames waned. It was struggling to remain alight.

"That'll keep it down for a while," I said smugly, but apparently that wasn't enough for Ortiz. My ears were filled again with the thundering sound of her handgun discharging. She emptied the entire magazine into the already down and injured Elemental, every shot jarring the creature's body, making it jerk and flail more.

And then something unexpected happened, the flames that made up the creature's body subsided, they sank away into nothingness. The Elemental just faded.

I ran over to Ortiz and embraced her in a comforting hug. The building was collapsing around us, but clearly she was a bit shaken. I held her for a good, long moment before I heard her sniffle, and she gently pushed me away.

"You good?" I asked quietly.

She nodded, clearing her throat a bit forcefully. "Yeah," she said hoarsely.

I stared at her intently, trying to make sure she was truly fine.

She shook her head once. "Yes," she said in a firmer tone.

That was good enough for me.

"Come on," I said gently, gesturing ahead to another staircase.

I decided to take the lead this time, not wanting to put Ortiz in any more danger or expose her to any other shocking oddities the supernatural world had left to offer. She had been through enough already, more than any person should have to go through, and she was clearly rattled.

Who wouldn't be?

We made it to the staircase and began descending as fast as we could. The great thing about stone-walled rooms and stairs is that it's exceptionally hard for them to catch fire, making the stairs the safest place we could be during the debacle. Well, technically, I guess the safest place would've been outside the hotel and away from the fire.

After making it down to the fourth level, Ortiz placed a hand on my left shoulder. It still panged a tad, but I didn't let her see that. I turned to face her when she spoke. "Norman," she began, chewing on her lip thoughtfully before continuing. "That...thing. Is it dead?"

I didn't know what to tell her, Elementals could be killed, but it was damn hard to do. Most Elementals lived and rarely left an area that corresponded with their element. Most Elementals of fire stayed near volcanoes or, believe it or not, deserts. Some even appeared in the aftermaths of forest fires, but that was about it. The reason they stayed in such close proximity to such places was because, well, that's essentially what they were. That specific element that has been given physical form. As long as there was an abundance of that element around, they could, given time, reform. Not exactly a comforting notion to an already distraught Ortiz, or me for that matter. There was plenty of fire left in this building and chances were the Elemental would come back for us—and soon. Our only chance was to get out of the building.

Agent Ortiz fixed me with a nervous gaze. I couldn't decide what to tell her: the truth or a comforting lie? The truth would worry her more. I was fairly certain that the idea of the Elemental popping back would unsettle her. Though would telling her it was gone for certain, only for it to reappear when we least expected it be any better? I decided the truth would be best. It was better that she knew and was worried, albeit prepared, than feeling falsely secure and off her guard.

Never mind that the building was on fire and all. I was going to sit down and engage in a minor conversation.

Nice to know I have my priorities in check.

I took a deep breath before answering her question. "Yes and no. Yes, it's *gone*," I said, placing heavy emphasis on gone, "but only for now. It can reform from any of the fires around us. All Elementals work that way. If there's enough of their source element in the area, they can reform."

I watched her reaction. She suppressed a small shiver and nodded, more to herself than me. I think she was coming to grips with that notion in her head. I gave her some time to putter around in her mind. It's not like we were in danger of being consumed in a raging inferno or have a building collapse on us. No pressure.

"Right," she said hoarsely. She calmly raised her pistol and ejected the magazine she had spent on the Elemental and slapped a fresh magazine in.

I looked at her curiously, arching an eyebrow as I spoke. "Uh, how many of those things do you have?"

She gave me a wolfish smile but refused to give an outright answer. Fair enough. Not as if I had given her an abundance of straightforward answers myself.

We continued down the next flight of stairs to the third floor when something really unforeseen happened. There was a deep cracking and crumbling sound. I looked up to see the stone above us giving way. I knew there was still a small group of Salamanders left somewhere in the building, and that they were breaking much of it down with their acid spit. What I didn't know was that their spit had actually managed to begin breaking down the stone stairs throughout the building.

I flung open the door and grabbed Ortiz, pulling her through it just as some of the stone and metal structures above us gave way. We made it into the hall and heard a terrible crumbling noise, followed by a tremendous earth-shaking crash. It was like a small tremor.

"So," she said, "looks like we're not getting out that way."

"Guess not," I replied.

There were two staircases on most of the floors we had covered, so I was betting there was another way out. Ortiz must've had the same idea, because she took off down the hall without waiting for me.

I sighed and ran after her.

The hotel's condition was getting worse by the second. Now there wasn't as much danger from supernatural monsters as there was from immolation or falling structures pancaking us. Both large and small bits of ceiling, pipes, and even furniture were tumbling down from above, threatening to flatten us. We spent most of our time in that hall running, ducking, rolling, and diving. It took us longer than I would've liked, but we did make it to the staircase on the other side of the hallway. We bolted through it as fast as we could and raced down the stairs. The stonework was crumbling here as well. We decided that our best bet was to make it down to the second floor and back out into the corridor before more stone could collapse around us.

Both Ortiz and I made it to the second floor corridor, racing back across it hopefully to the stairway we were in earlier. I was silently praying that the earlier collapse had only blocked off the third floor and not the second floor entrance and passages.

None of that mattered, however, because as we navigated forwards, we quite literally ran into another problem. Ahead of us, and blocking off our route to the staircases, was a massive debris pile that was a fustercluck of materials. There was a flaming mattress piled atop broken piping, stone, kitchen appliances, and one of those Subzero fridges, which was completely lit up in fiery irony.

"Damn it," swore Ortiz, putting her hands on her hips as she turned to look at me. "What now?"

I didn't answer right away. My mind raced as my eyes frantically searched for a way out. I did a double take as I passed over a large glass cabinet that wasn't housing a fire extinguisher, but something considerably better. The cabinet held a thick and lengthy hose. The kind some buildings carried to put out heavy fires, similar to a firefighter's hose. It couldn't clear the blockage for us, but I was thinking it just might help get Ortiz and I out of here. There was a room opposite it, and I had my fingers crossed that it was in ideal condition to get us the hell out of the hotel.

Fortunately, the room was left open. I motioned for Ortiz to go inside and see if she could get to the other side safely to crack a window open. She complied and raced into the room while I ran over to the glass case containing the hose. It was heavy-duty enough to support at least one of us. That was good enough, not to mention it was long enough for what I had planned.

Ortiz shouted back from the room, "Window's open. Now what?"

"What's the distance down?" I called as I unraveled the hose and began making a wide and loose lasso of sorts with it.

"About fifteen, maybe twenty feet," she answered.

I slipped into the room right behind her, dragging the

heavy hose with me.

"What's your plan?" she asked without bothering to look back. She leaned out the window, looking down at the scene unfolding before the hotel. A mass of emergency service vehicles and personnel gathered outside, attending to people and trying to suppress the fire from outside. It was a lost cause though. The building, I mean. From the amount of damage it had sustained, it was obvious that it wouldn't be safe to enter until the fire was out.

While Ortiz fixated on the scene outside, I threw the now-lassoed hose around her waist, pulling it tight until it constricted around her midsection.

She turned her head to look at me, her face thoroughly perplexed. "What in the hell?"

That's when I pushed her out the window...

It sounds bad when you say it aloud, but trust me, it was a good idea at the time!

"Hold on to the hose," I shouted as she tumbled from the window.

She screamed a string of obscenities. I think some were directed at me but I wasn't sure. I think it was safe to assume that though. After all, I did just push her out a window.

I held on tight to the hose, working to lower her carefully at a steady rate. A federal agent pancaking into the pavement below would really get me in trouble. Once she was safely on the ground, which I got confirmation of via her continued swearing at me, I pondered my next move.

"Great," I grunted as I gave a few forceful tugs on the heavy hose. While the hose could take my weight, I wasn't so sure the fastenings that held the hose to the wall fixture could. I didn't really have a choice however. The room around me would deteriorate soon enough and I would go with it. I didn't bother tying the hose around myself, I wasn't sure if this was going to work, so I didn't want to be stuck in it if I didn't have to be. Taking a firm grip, I sat on the windowsill, climbing out backwards so I could rappel down the building.

That was the great thing about my body-hopping experiences. I was once inside an Army Ranger, so I knew all manner of helpful techniques.

I began traversing the building wall, actively trying to navigate away from windows and anything that might lead me into contact with the fire. After making it halfway down the second story, but still a bit off from the first, something really unfair happened. One moment, there was a great deal of tension on the hose due to my weight and the next, well, the tension was gone and the hose was no longer taut. There was also the unmistakable sensation of falling. Everything rushed upward while I tumbled down. I was still holding onto the hose though. Well, the now severed hose. I didn't really know how it happened, only that I was holding onto half a hose as I fell.

I should've been screaming. I know I yelped, but I should've kept yelping, but I didn't. More than anything, I just swore—loudly, I might add—for all the good it would've done me.

So I tumbled and swore my way to the ground, landing with a *splat/crunch*, which is really the only way to describe it. The kind of sound you make when you fall from a building while swearing, and crash to the ground with a rubbery fire hose is distinct. It's a sonata of pain. All I know is that I sort of landed on my already injured side and a bit of my back. There were obscured blurry images of people and lights over me. It went black immediately after that.

Chapter Twelve

I felt a pair of soft hands cupping my right hand, the one that had been punctured with glass and burned. It was a delicate, yet firm, and rather comforting grip. I groaned as I opened my eyes. Bright lights flooded everything and I instantly shut them. When I opened them again, I gave them time to adjust to the lighting, and was soon able to get a good look at my surroundings. The walls were a light salmon color with golden-brown wooden paneling decorating the walls. It gave the place a warm look. I was lying on a rather comfortable and plush bed, several thick pillows beneath me, and a thick white blanket atop. A series of tubes and wires were connected and inserted into my body.

"Nice to see you up," said a soft feminine voice.

I looked over to my right, to the woman who squeezing my hand. She sat in a simple wooden chair with a thin-padded covering in navy blue upholstery. Her dark brown eyes looked worried, and there was a tired look on her face. Made sense, we had both gone without sleep for…however long it had been up to this point; I wasn't sure at the moment. Her chestnut brown hair looked disheveled. I was more surprised it wasn't singed.

"Hospital?" I asked, my throat hoarse and dry, but my body didn't seem to be in as bad a shape as I feared it would be. I must've healed quite a bit while resting. They do say sleep is oh-so-important.

She nodded.

I flexed my left hand and rolled my shoulders. There was a pang of pain, along with the sensation of pins and needles. Yes, I *had* been healing while I slept, and I still was. Good, I needed to be fit to move.

Agent Ortiz brought a glass of water to my mouth, and I sipped slowly. I knew better than to guzzle away and thus choke. I didn't jump out of a fiery building and survive an encounter with a group of hellish creatures only to die from a glass of water now.

She gave me a moment to hydrate myself before asking, "How are you feeling?"

"Like I fell out a burning building onto pavement, you?" I grumbled.

"Like I was pushed out of a burning building by a maniac," she retorted, a small smile playing across her face.

"Yeah," I said a bit gutturally. I took a moment to allow the water to work its mojo. "Sorry about that," I apologized.

She didn't say anything, but instead looked down at the multicolored floor. It was a mixture of red, green, black, and blue tiling. It gave the place a bright look.

I didn't need any sort of powers to know something was wrong, so I asked.

"The fire department's still checking the place out. You'll be happy to know that the entire place wasn't burnt down," she said.

"But?" I asked, fearing her response.

"But," she said, chewing her lip, "there were a few deaths." She looked like she was struggling to find words. "Some people didn't make it out." A melancholy look overcame her beautiful features.

I felt the heat rising in my face, feeling angry and a fair bit guilty too. Those people died because of the Elemental—no, the Ifrit. That monster was out to get me, and any other innocent people it could out of sheer spite, but it attacked the hotel because of me. They died because *I* was there. My stomach felt queasy, and it wasn't from the injuries or the painkillers they were administering.

Ortiz was somehow able to read my thoughts. She gave my hand another reassuring squeeze and said, "Norman, it wasn't your fault."

I turned my head away from her. I wasn't used to this. I always worked alone and avoided people for this reason. In all of my cases, I had never once gotten anyone else involved. It was a cold, hard approach, but it spared me from news like this. I didn't know how to handle this. It was certainly a first for me. Sure, I had worked with other creatures before, sometimes with a person too, but never this closely. And never did I get someone like Agent Ortiz involved in something like this, but now I had, and everything that happened was on me.

I decided to change the subject. "The feds," I croaked. "They involved yet?"

She shook her head. "Fire department's still combing the building, trying to determine the cause and its source and...looking for remains."

I rose from the bed, using my elbows and forearms to support myself, but a hand placed on my chest pushed me gently back down.

"Nuh-uh, you're staying here, Norman," said Agent Ortiz in a tone that left no room for argument. Then again, this is me. Like hell I wasn't going to argue.

I brushed her hand aside and propped myself back up, yanking off the wires connected to me.

"You just fell out of a building!"

I ignored her, shaking my head to clear out some of the medicinal cobwebs that had been placed there. Things like painkillers and drugs don't affect me much. Mostly, I don't need them.

Of course, I do happen to feel a great deal of the pain inflicted upon this and any other body I inhabit, which is totally unfair. I have my theories on why that might be though, like whoever's pulling my strings finds it highly amusing. My many lives are run by some cosmically empowered asshole.

Point being, I was in much better shape than Agent Ortiz thought I was, and I was going to make that abundantly clear. I righted myself until I was sitting at a ninety-degree angle, stripping those little suction cup things off my chest and tossing them off the side of the bed.

"You're insane, Norman. You're lucky to still be alive!"

"Come on. Let's go," I added as I gingerly stepped out of the bed, ignoring her comment.

She shook her head in disbelief. "You don't get it, do you? You're going to kill yourself like this. I think you should do a stint in a mental institution after this."

I shrugged nonchalantly. "It's been suggested many times before."

She sat there in shock, watching me flex my hands, roll my shoulders, and go through a few stretches to see just how much of Norman's body had recovered. "You're...okay?" she said in a confused tone.

I nodded. Technically, I wasn't entirely better. There was some general stiffness and pain, but I could still function.

"How?" she asked, stupefied.

"I'll tell you about it over dinner...breakfast?" I said uncertainly. "What time is it?"

"A little after one in the morning," she replied.

Damn, I thought. I had been out for a while. I still had a bit of time left, but I was starting to push it. I needed to hurry as I wasn't keen on starting a confrontation with an ancient magical creature during daylight hours. Better to keep this fight in the dark, lest more people like Agent Ortiz get involved. I would have to step things up—and fast.

I walked towards the door when Ortiz cleared her throat rather pointedly. I turned around and found her staring rather intently at my backside. She looked up at me with a raised eyebrow. *Right...* I was in a hospital, dressed in one of their tie-on gowns. Seems like someone had forgotten to tie the backside up. So, there I was, struttin' away with Norman's rear end thoroughly exposed.

"You might want to put some pants on, Norman," she said with a bit of a snicker. "You don't want to give some poor old ladies in here a heart attack."

I snorted. "Only old ladies, huh? No federal agents finding it an amusing sight?"

She shrugged. "I took an appreciative glance. It's not like you men don't do the same."

She had me there.

"In a bag in the bathroom," she said, reading my mind before I had even spoken.

I nodded my thanks, cinched up the back of the gown, and hobbled into the bathroom. Ortiz's laughter filled up the room behind me. My clothes had been stuffed rather unceremoniously into a plastic bag hanging from a small towel rack. I undid the knot on the bag and pulled my clothes out of it. Stepping out of the gown, I started to dress.

"Ugh," I grunted after a quick damage assessment of my shirt. It was covered in soot, sweat stains, singe marks, and dust. Beggars can't be choosers though, so I slipped it on, suppressing a hygienically concerned shiver as I did. The pants weren't any better, but I slipped them on as well. I couldn't be running through the mean streets of New York with my borrowed ass hanging out and on the line after all. I didn't bother changing the socks though.

Sure, they were the standard ridiculous hospital socks—purple and embossed with anti-slip grips in the shape of dog paws—but none of that mattered. Why? Because they were clean. So I tossed Norman's old socks in the trash, slipped into his shoes and stepped out of the bathroom to face a concerned Agent Ortiz.

"Are you sure you want to leave, Norman? You really shouldn't be moving. You *can't* be moving," she said.

"I promised."

"What? You…promised?" she said, clearly confused as to what I was referring to.

"Yeah," I said, cracking my neck with a groan. "I promised back in the hotel that we'd talk after we got out of there." I gestured to our brightly colored and comforting surroundings. "We're out of there now, so I guess it's time to make good on my promise." I stepped towards the door and looked over my shoulder. "You coming?"

She gave a small snort. "Sure, what the hell? After

everything I've seen and been through today, a little food"—she paused to yawn—"and some more coffee would be a nice change of pace."

I gestured at the door and gave an exaggerated bow. "Well then, this way Agent Ortiz," I said, finishing with a flourish of my hands.

She rolled her eyes. As she walked past me, she stopped. "You know, it's customary that when a man takes a woman out for food," she said, letting the sentence hang in the air for a minute, "to not look completely like shit." Her eyes twinkled and I could see her resisting the urge to smile as she walked out of the room.

I snorted and left the brightly colored hospital room behind. Moving quickly, I fell in step behind her, trying to look straight ahead as we walked down the corridor, and not at the people staring at me. I got a series of odd looks and garnered a few gasps as well, not surprising. Here I was, walking through the hospital in tattered, torn, singed, and dirty clothes, as if I had just escaped a burning building. Well, I had, but they didn't know that. I was more surprised some nurse didn't run up to me, forbidding me to leave. At least until they were certain I was a-okay. They were probably busy with the other people who had escaped the building fire though.

"So where are we going?" asked Ortiz, breaking my chain of thoughts.

"Huh?"

"Where. Are. We. Going?" she said much slower, enunciating each word as if I were a small child.

"No idea." I gave an indifferent shrug. "Whatever's open at this time, I suppose."

She scoffed and muttered under her breath, but made sure I could hear it, "Men...they've got no idea on where to take a lady after a hard night."

I laughed, which set her off, and then we were both laughing rather loudly. A bit too improperly given our surroundings, but we didn't care. It felt good to just laugh, given what we had both gone through. There's something rejuvenating about laughter. Laughter heals a great deal of pain. It really does. I've traveled the world, mingled and tangled with all manner of supernatural things. With all of that, I've learned that laughter can help with a lot of things.

Take my word for it.

We continued walking, laughing, and drawing stares until we left the hospital grounds and hopped into Agent Ortiz's car. The laughter faded into silence. Neither of us knew what to say. We had both just been through so much. So we sat in silence as she drove, watching the many lights and buildings of New York pass by like a scrolling marquee.

"So," said Agent Ortiz, breaking the silence I had been somewhat enjoying.

"So," I replied.

"When we get to this diner, what exactly is off limits for me to ask?"

I shrugged. "What makes you think anything is off limits?"

"Don't give me that Norman. We both know you haven't been entirely honest or upfront with me from the start."

I tried to protest, but she took her right hand off the wheel and held it up, motioning for me to be quiet. I was. Damn, I really needed to learn how women did that.

"I'm not saying I have a problem with it, per se. I get it," she said.

"You...get it?" I replied, thoroughly confused. I had no idea what she thought she got...say that five times fast.

"Yeah, Norman, I get it." she repeated, shaking her head. "After sampling a bit of your world today, I get where you're coming from."

"No..." I said. "No, you really don't, Agent Ortiz."

"Fair enough," she replied. "But I understand you not wanting to share everything or wanting to be completely open and honest with me."

"And...you're okay with that?"

"Oh, god no!" she exclaimed.

Great. She's never gonna let this go.

As if she could read my mind, she verified my assertion. "I'm never going to let this go, Norman."

I let out a sigh. The kind of sigh you do when you give up on some things, like the hope that the federal agent on your tail will give up her relentless pursuit of you and all things supernatural. Yeah, that kind of sigh.

"But," she added, "I'm going to give you time. I know it can't be easy to trust people in your line of work."

"No, it isn't," I said. "Hell, there are some monsters I trust more than people." I instantly regretted saying that.

"Gee, thanks, Norman. You really know how to make a woman feel special," she joked. I could tell she really wasn't upset.

"I didn't mean you—"

"I know," she smiled. "But would it kill you to extend a little trust to the woman who saved your life?"

"Saved *my* life?" I yelped, a bit taken aback. "Hold on there, missy! Didn't you faint in the presence of that Wraith?"

She stared icy daggers at me. I didn't care, so I continued on.

"Didn't you flip out back there in the hotel too?" I added.

The car jerked to a frightening halt as she slammed on the brakes. Car horns went off behind us.

"What the hell?" I yelped. Why did women do things like that?

"I'm sorry there, tough guy, but I clearly remember saving your ass when you were crippled and pinned down by a...what did you call it? An Elemental?"

Ortiz was right. She did shoot the Elemental, thus saving my ass, but now my pride was on the line. "Yeah, you're a real Annie Oakley," I quipped. "In case you forgot, it was my idea to throw the fire extinguisher at it and—"

"Which I shot!" She sounded a bit defensive, but she wasn't really. I could see a light smile on her face.

"Thank god you didn't miss, what with your hands trembling and all."

My left arm began to throb, just for a moment or two. She had punched me lightly, but when I looked at her in mock fury, her gaze was focused on the road since she had started driving again. She stared ahead, a bit too intently. Her jaw was clenched in what looked like anger, and it took me a moment to realize she was doing it to suppress a massive smile.

"You're a jerk," she said, stifling a small laugh.

"Yeah? Well, you're," I began, not quite sure what to say. I was too busy trying to suppress a laugh of my own.

"Careful now," she said. "Don't hurt yourself over there."

That's pretty much how the ride went. We traded barbs and teased each other the whole way. It was…nice. It was new. I wasn't used to this, but wow, was it a departure from what I was used to. We drove on like that, laughing, arm punching. Well, she was punching me. I had enough sense *not* to punch the driver. After about ten minutes or so of nonstop humor-filled travel, she finally decided on the place to eat, since I was particularly clueless.

The diner was located in the most miniscule parking lot I had ever seen, and that's saying something in New York. There were spots for maybe ten cars tops. It would have been insignificant, really, if it wasn't for the fact that the diner itself was an altered, antiquated subway train car. It was, well, interesting. How many diners have you seen that are actually old public transport vehicles?

It was painted a myriad of bright colors, which created a gaudy and still somehow homey look. The oval billboard on top was pearl white. Its scarlet lettering had a mustard yellow outline that read: Dino's Diner. The roof was bright white, but faded into, I swear to god, a relish green. I think they painted the place using actual condiments, but somehow, it worked. The square glass windows had lavender paneling around them. It sat above the burgundy stripe running along the bottom half of the car, which was painted baby blue.

It was the most jarring sight I had ever seen, and I've

seen quite a lot. Yet, I was transfixed by the place. I don't know why. It just felt comfortable, which was a new sensation for me. I had never allowed myself the luxury of comfort. In my line of work it's a death sentence. Enjoying the occasional sensual massage shower doesn't count.

I was flabbergasted that she chose this place, and it must've shown on my face, because the very next instant she spoke.

"What?" she said defensively.

"This place?" I asked incredulously, jerking a thumb towards the diner. "Seriously?"

"Seriously," she replied, flatly.

"Why?"

"First of all, they're open every day, all day, throughout the year—even holidays," she answered.

Had to admit, that was a really good opening point. Not that I should've been arguing, considering I was starving.

"Secondly, they serve breakfast, lunch, and dinner items at all times of the day," she said with a bit of a ravenous growl.

"Does…does that matter?" I asked, honestly confused if that was relevant. "All I need is some more coffee and anything edible so I can keep going without crashing and burning."

She looked at me as if I were hopeless. "Come on," she said, stepping out of the car.

I popped out of my side and followed her through the doors. They actually opened horizontally, like they did on subways.

The place was empty and thankfully so. I didn't want to see it full. There was hardly any room, but then there never is on a subway car. The faded, cream-colored counter bore a dizzying array of bottles and containers, undoubtedly holding all manner of kitchen condiments and supplies, and took up most of the room. In front of the counter was a straight line of the typical burgundy, vinyl-topped stools to sit on. Behind the counter, stretching from one end to the other, were a series of surprisingly clean and gleaming cooking appliances, stoves, grills, and griddles, and the like.

"Nice to know they keep the place clean," I muttered below my breath. It was enough of a comment to earn me a sharp elbow in the ribs, courtesy of Agent Ortiz.

"Just sit down and shut up," she said in a lighthearted tone.

We plopped down on stools beside each other. She leaned forward and rested her arms on the counter while I continued to look around. The floor was a shocking checkered pattern of cotton candy blue and pink. Along the wall with sliding doors were a few circular tables with heavy padded purple and white-striped diner seats on either side.

When the hell did I step out of the supernatural world and into a cartoon? I wondered.

"I thought the same thing too," Agent Ortiz said.

"Huh?"

"Something out of a cartoon, right?"

"Uh yeah...how'd you know?" I said, surprised.

She snorted. "Everyone thinks the same thing when they come in here."

"What'll it be, Camilla?" The boisterous voice nearly caused me to leap back from the counter—nearly. I am a seasoned professional paranormal detective, after all. Nothing scares me whatsoever.

I got surprised is all. The guy came out of nowhere, which is saying something considering he was a helluva lot of guy. His face had, well, let's say a generous amount of mass. Laugh lines around his nose and eyes. His heavy, full cheeks gave him a jolly look. He had bright amber-colored eyes that radiated a kind, nurturing look. A salt-and-pepper raggedy head of thinning hair sat atop his thick, solid head. Scant wisp-like eyebrows hung above his gleaming eyes.

He stood there with a big frog-like smile that played across his massive face, his thick meaty hands clasped atop his enormous belly. This guy made Santa Claus look small. Short, beefy, muscular arms and a squat-like figure made his physique look intimidating, but like I said before, the man's face shone with kindness. A fatherly manner hung around him.

"I'll have a Scrooge," she said in a tone used to speak with old friends. I didn't need to be a detective to guess they knew each other pretty well.

He didn't bother asking me what I wanted, but instead turned around and fired up a bunch of burners before hobbling off to a back room.

"Uh…what's a Scrooge?"

She ignored my question and asked one of her own. "So, what are you getting?"

I looked around and laughed. "Whatever doesn't send me to the coroner's."

"Wrong place," she smirked, sliding me a small folded menu.

I nodded a thanks, swept it up and began flipping through it. I finally decided to try a piece of pumpkin pie and the chocolate, coffee-infused milkshake, killing two birds with one stone.

The mountain of a man returned a few seconds later, carrying a mass of food items that he placed on and in different skillets, and pans.

"Uh…" I began.

"Rich," whispered Agent Ortiz.

"Rich," I said. He grunted, indicating that he heard me, I guess. "Can I get the chocolate coffee thing and a piece of pumpkin pie?" I asked. He was a big guy. I didn't want to make it sound like an order, even though it was a diner, but like I said—really big guy.

He gave another affirmative grunt.

Just moments ago, he was smiling and cheerily greeting *Camilla*, being on first name basis with her and all. But me, I got grunts. I leaned over to whisper to Ortiz, "He not like me or something?"

"Oh, don't mind him," she whispered back. "He's like that till you get to know him."

"And," chimed Rich, who had apparently overheard the whole thing, "I'm really protective of her." He jabbed a meaty index finger towards Agent Ortiz.

"Hey, man!" I exclaimed, throwing my hands up. "I just met her!"

"Relax, Rich," she said. "We're just working together; nothing more." Her words were more successful in calming Rich down than my own.

"So...? That mean I'm getting my shake and pie or...?" I asked with hesitation. My answer was what I took to be an affirmative grunt.

Ortiz leaned over again, "Sorry about him," she whispered. "I've been coming here ever since I was a small girl, so I've known Rich forever. He's like a father to me."

I mouthed a silent "Ah."

"So," she said nonchalantly, "we going to talk now?"

I cast a nervous glance over to Rich. He was busying himself with making whatever culinary concoctions Ortiz had ordered. He may have seemed busy, but clearly his hearing was sharp and his attention was somewhat focused on me.

Ortiz caught my glance. "Don't worry. He's done listening in. You were just a new curiosity. Once he's cooking, he's only cooking. That's all."

I rolled my shoulders and shrugged. "Fire away," I said. I didn't want to start the conversation. I felt it better if she asked and I answered.

"Well..." she said, rolling the word around on her tongue. "We established that you don't remember your real name."

I nodded a silent agreement.

"And you told me you don't remember how long you've been doing this," she said, with just a hint of disbelief in her voice.

Again, I nodded.

She chewed on her bottom lip, her gaze wandering around our surroundings. "Okay," she said, more to herself than me. "How about we start with how you're fine after falling out of a burning building."

"I... I'm not exactly normal in the physiology department."

"Yeah, I figured that part out, strangely enough." She offered a grim laugh. "What I want to know is why, or how?"

"Honestly?"

"Honestly," she replied.

"I really don't know. Chalk it up to a beneficial side effect of doing what I do." It wasn't a complete lie. I mean I knew why I healed, but not the details. I healed because my superiors, whoever they might be, wanted me to be able to put my body through its paces during my work.

Her eyes narrowed, as if searching to see whether I was telling the truth or not. As I said before, there was something a bit off about her. She had, so far, demonstrated an uncanny ability to separate fact from fiction. Agent Ortiz broke the few moments of silence. "Okay, good enough for me. For now, at least."

I let out an inner sigh of relief.

"Do you know how far you can push yourself?" she asked.

I shook my head. "I honestly don't know how far, just that it is considerably farther than a normal person."

"So, what? Working around this supernatural crap has rubbed off on you or something?" she said in a confused tone.

"Something like that," I said vaguely.

"That's not an answer," she growled.

"It's all I can give you, sorry."

That seemed to placate her a bit. "Fine, moving on," she said.

I rolled my hand with a flourish, indicating for her to continue.

"Do you always work alone?"

I thought carefully before answering that one. I didn't want to reveal the existence of Church to her, but it was obvious she could tell when I was lying. I pondered for the best way to phrase it. "For the most part, yes, I do," I said. "I never really have much to go on." That much was true though, seeing as Church wasn't exactly a talkative or informative fellow.

Her eyes narrowed again. I had an inkling she knew I wasn't being completely honest with her. I felt guilty, and it was strange. I had lied to officers, law enforcement, and federal agents before, but she was different. I had shared a foxhole with Ortiz. She had risked her life for me, even with me having lied to her. What's worse is that she knew I had been lying to her, and she still risked her neck to save mine. I really did wish I could come clean, but I just couldn't. Not yet.

If she was angry with me for giving her some clever word-play, she didn't show it and moved on. "So..." she began slowly, her voice softening as she spoke, "have you had to deal with people dying before?"

I looked away from her, from the counter, from everything really. I shut my eyes tight and thought, or tried to. I didn't know what to think, what to say. I had always been detached in my work, never allowing myself to get involved. When I worked, I worked, that's it. It was a mission, clear and cut. My job was to use a body, track down whatever creature was doing harm, kill it, and move on. Rinse and repeat. I have never been involved enough to know if innocents were being harmed on the sidelines. The only victims I knew of were the ones the creature responsible had already killed, such as the victim whose body I was inhabiting.

Ortiz seemed to regret asking the question because she was quick to apologize. She reached out and grabbed my shoulder, giving it a comforting, reassuring squeeze.

We sat there for what seemed like forever, in complete silence. The only sounds came from Rich's hustle and bustle as he cooked up a storm.

"Anything else?" I asked a bit too gruffly. I felt enough quiet time had passed; I wanted to get this show back on the road.

"Yeah," she said as she rose from her seat and walked towards the exit, leaving me a little baffled. She walked right out the door and towards her car, returning moments later with my journals and the binder Gnosis had given me. "You never told me where you got this from," she said, waving Gnosis' collection of information in my face.

"It's, uh, well, it's complicated," I somewhat answered.

"Try me," she said in a firm tone.

Just then, with the best timing I had ever witnessed through my many lives, Rich came over and plunked down a plate containing Ortiz's, um, meal? I say it like that because I'm not entirely sure what it was. All I know is that Rich's decision to come over that very moment spared me having to tell another lie.

So, thank you, you disgruntled massive man.

"Enjoy it, Camilla," he said in his booming voice and placed a large clear glass of sparkling, fizzy, golden drink on the table.

She pulled the plate closer to her. "Oh, I plan on it, Rich," she said with a hungry smile.

Rich gave me one look, sniffed, and returned to the room at the back. Guess my food wasn't quite ready yet; probably wasn't a priority to him.

I looked back at Agent Ortiz's whatever-it-was and curiosity, coupled with the desire to derail the conversation, got the best of me. "Uh…what the hell are you eating?"

She lifted the large sesame seed bun and revealed the burger's—and I use that word lightly—inner workings. Underneath the bun was, I swear to god, a miniature pancake coated in thick, gelatinous, golden-brown syrup.

"Is that…a pancake?" I asked incredulously.

"No, it's a Rich's pancake," she said in a tone that implied it made all the difference in the world. Must've been one helluva pancake, but still it was *just* wrong; an opinion I gave voice to.

"A pancake inside a burger? Sacrilege!" I hissed in mock outrage.

She ignored me and continued to peel away the bun. Several thick strips of syrup-coated bacon nestled beneath the pancake. Under that was the meat of the burger, a thin fried chicken breast, and around it, a cluster of scrambled eggs with what looked like boiled potato chunks. The entire whatever the hell this thing was ended the same way it started—another pancake followed by a burger bun.

I looked at it and at her slender frame, absolutely stupefied. Like hell she was going to eat all that.

Seconds later, she proved my assertions wrong. A fork and knife materialized out of nowhere, and she dug into it in an animalistic manner.

"Uh…should I leave you and your monstrosity of a burger alone?" I joked.

She replied with a low growl.

I shut up.

After a few moments of her devouring her breakfast, lunch and dinner combination burger, she reached over to take a sip of her fizzy drink. She released a relaxing sigh after taking a few sips of it.

"Any good?" I asked.

"Mmmm, pineapple," she said. A blissful look crossed over her face.

Never knew they made pineapple soda.

Agent Ortiz took a few more sips and then cleared her throat rather loudly. I guess the reprieve from the interrogation was over. Lucky me. "So, Norman," she said, picking the binder of information up again. "Where did you say you got this again?"

Ah, she was pulling that old trick. I knew that one. Using the break in conversation to distract me, and then ask me a question in a manner that made it seem like I had already answered her. All I had to do now was recall the answer and repeat it back to her, except for the fact I never told her. It was a nice try though.

"I didn't," I replied rather simply.

"But you're going to?" she asked, raising a questioning eyebrow as she reached to take another sip from her soda. It was a long, exaggerated sip, and she never broke eye contact while taking it.

I got the message. "Fine." I sighed. "I'll spill."

She stopped taking a sip, dug back into her burger, and

chewed a bit, all while completely ignoring me until she was done. She then turned back to address me. "I had a feeling you would."

I grunted. "Yeah, well, you're not getting the whole story."

"Yes, she will. She'll find a way. She's good at that sort of stuff," said a booming Rich. He stood before us, though how he managed to get so close while remaining so quiet was a supernatural mystery in and of itself. He held a ginormous, thick, frothy chocolate milkshake in one hand and a small plate in the other. He placed them both down, gave Agent Ortiz a smile, and me a grunt, turned, and walked back into his room.

"So, Norman?"

"Pie," I said simply.

"What?"

"Pie first," I repeated, picking up a fork and digging into the slice of pumpkin pie Rich had provided. The fork sank in without any resistance. My god, it was soft. It cut through the crust effortlessly. I brought the dark orange piece close to my mouth, salivating at the sight of it as I gently blew the wisps of steam away. I bit into the piece and almost fainted from the pure joy of it. It was amazing! It tasted like Christmas; there was no other way to describe it.

I ignored the sound of Agent Ortiz tapping her impatient foot against the steel legs of the stool. I lazily stirred the straw through the immensely thick milkshake, eyeing Agent Ortiz from the corner of my eye. She was getting really agitated. Too bad. It was my turn for some playful payback. I took a long and exaggerated sip just as she had done. I shouldn't have done that though. While the drink was mind-blowingly good and energizing, it was icy cold and my brain paid the price.

"Ackh." I winced. My palm flew to my forehead, compressing and rubbing it.

"Serves you right," muttered Ortiz in a playful tone.

"Yeah, yeah," I grumbled as I continued massaging my head.

She waited for my wincing to subside before continuing. "So, you going to tell me or what?"

"I have a source. He's got access to information networks all over the world—the normal and not so normal," I explained.

"Your source have a name?" she asked, the intrigue in her voice abundantly clear.

"Yup."

She arched an eyebrow, waiting for an answer I wasn't going to give unless prompted. She sighed. "And his name is?"

I cut off another piece of the pie and shoveled it into my mouth. "Ohh, it's so good!" I murmured through pieces of pie. She exhaled in frustration but kept her composure fairly well. I reached over and began sipping the shake, slower this time however; I'd learned my lesson. "Ahhh." I sighed in satisfaction. "So, where were we?"

"Your source's name?" she asked politely but through gritted teeth. She was trying to be nice, but I was making it difficult. Oh, well.

"Sorry," I said.

"Sorry?"

"Yeah. Can't tell ya," I replied.

"Why not?"

"Would you consider my work important?" I asked her.

"What does that have to do with—" she started before I cut her off.

"Just answer the question. Yes or no?"

She inhaled deeply before answering. "Given all that I've seen and experienced with you today, yes, I feel your work is important."

"Thank you," I said, pausing for effect. "I'm in the investigation business, same as you, and I need sources of information. The thing with information brokers is they like to keep their identities a secret. The one bit of information they *don't* want to share is who they are. If I am to remain on their good side, I can't share that info, especially since I really need their info from time to time," I finished, nodding at the binder in her hands.

"Fine," she conceded. "Fair enough."

"Sorry, he's not too big on sharing, or anything else for that matter," I said, trying to suppress a laugh.

Ortiz gave me an odd look, but then she would. She didn't get the joke. She didn't know Gnosis, but she let it go.

"So," I said, "anything else you wanna ask?"

"Yeah, you have an idea who this monster of yours might be posing as?"

"Tough one," I replied. "I'm not sure, but we have established it's got some way of getting in contact with museum employees. My bet is that it's one of them. I just can't figure out who."

"Well, you mentioned that one victim, who you've failed to identify to me by the way. He died what, several days ago?" she asked.

I nodded in agreement but remained silent. The poor, unidentified stiff she was referring to was sitting right next to her.

"And then there's the janitor," she muttered to herself. "He died within the month."

"Yeah," I agreed.

She didn't hear me, I think. Instead, she brushed our plates aside and slammed the binder onto counter between them.

"Hey!" I exclaimed indignantly as my pie was pushed away from me.

Still ignoring me, heavily engrossed in the binder, she flipped through page after page. "This!" she said, sliding the binder over towards me and pointing at the page.

"Marsha Morressy," I read in a befuddled tone, not seeing her point yet.

"She's one of the museum's employees. She works under you right?"

I waggled my hand in a so-so gesture, implying we had worked together in some capacity, or at least technically. Perhaps Norman had worked with her. I, on the other hand, had only just met the gal.

"Well, look here," she said, pointing a bit further down the page.

I followed her finger and read the contents. It said exactly when Marsha had begun working for the museum.

"Near about a month," I murmured.

"About a month," repeated Agent Ortiz. "A time frame that coincides perfectly with the deaths of the janitor and your mystery man."

"Hmm," I said as I pondered the possibilities. I had to admit Ortiz had a good point, but something didn't sit well with me about that theory. I didn't know what; it was just a feeling. Over the years I've worked this gig, I've learned to trust those feelings. On the other hand, I've also learned to follow up on any and every lead possible. You might not get the answers you want, but you might learn something helpful. Something inside me, or from Norman's memories, didn't quite buy the idea that Marsha was responsible, but it wouldn't hurt to pay her a visit.

Nope, it would *only* be extremely awkward having your boss show up in the wee hours of the morning, with a federal agent, and accuse you of being an Ifrit. What could possibly go wrong?

My face must've shown signs of the mental Olympics I was performing because Ortiz chimed in. "You have to admit, Norman, it's pretty convenient for her to start working there just before the murders start happening."

"Yeah, you're right," I sighed, jerking a thumb towards the door. "Let's pay and go."

Agent Ortiz let out a merry chuckle. "You mean, let's *just* go. I eat free here." She let out the faintest of smiles at that.

My eyes widened in gleeful surprise. "Well then, it seems I'm going to have to make a habit of eating with you more often."

She gave me a wolfish smile. "Sounds good to me. Gives me more time to question you."

Damn, I completely fell for that one. "Uh…on second thought, maybe we should be more focused on going to question a possible monster, rather than me?"

"Yeah, all right there," snorted Ortiz. "I'll save you for later. You're not getting off the hook that easy."

This time my sigh wasn't suppressed, bringing another smile to Agent Ortiz's face.

"Come on, Norman," she said, rising from her stool and walking towards the door.

I stood up and started to follow when someone cleared their throat rather forcibly. I turned around to see Rich's massive frame. He looked down at our plates and then up at me expectantly. "I uh..." I looked out of the window to see where Ortiz was. "She said that she, uh, eats for free."

He gave me a grunt and picked up the plates, stacking one atop another, scooped up our glasses, and shuffled towards his mysterious back room.

"So...this mean I don't have to pay?" I called out behind him.

No answer, just a series of *clinks*. Guess I was free to go then. I took one last confused look at the back room, wondering if he'd come back out having changed his mind. When that didn't happen, I exited the diner rather quickly and hopped into Agent Ortiz's car.

Ortiz had already started the car while I was inside. She shot me a quizzical look when I entered. "What took you?"

"Ah, Rich gave me a look that was rather ambiguous. I didn't know if he wanted me to pay or not," I answered.

"Oh," she said. "Yeah, sorry about that."

"Maybe you should've said something to him before we left?" I hinted.

"Maybe," she said. Her expression was neutral, but, I swear, even though it was dark outside, her eyes shone with humor.

"Is that payback or something for me not being completely honest with you?" I asked.

"Or something," she smiled.

I gave a dismissive grunt. "Let's just get to Marsha's place."

She nodded in agreement and put the car into reverse.

I cast a worried glance at my left forearm. My little blackout had cost me a fair amount of time. Three hours left...

Chapter Thirteen

"Are we there yet?" I groaned in annoyance, attempting to break the silence we had been driving in for nearly fifteen minutes.

"Cute," said Ortiz rather dryly. "Real cute."

"Yeah, well," I began, "I'm on a tight timeline, so if you'd be kind enough to—"

"To what? Drive you to the apartment belonging to one of your employees, who may or may not be some sort of evil genie with a penchant for burning things down? Is that it?" she snapped, her eyes never wavering off the road for once, to my great relief.

"Sorry," I said, throwing up my hands as a gesture I had had enough, hoping that would placate her somewhat.

She let out a heavy exhale but otherwise remained silent.

"Where's her place anyway?" I asked.

"Didn't you look at her information?"

"You can't answer a question with a question!" I said.

"She's got a place down in Midtown," answered Agent Ortiz. "That's where we're headed now."

"So, uh...how—"

"Don't you dare ask me how long!"

I shut up that instant, not even finishing my sentence.

She jerked a thumb over her shoulder, pointing to the seats behind us. "The binder's back there. I need you to find her exact address for me."

I nodded and reached back for it, picking up the binder Gnosis had provided me with. I flipped through it until I found the page with Marsha's life story on it. Seriously, this thing had every piece of conceivable information about her.

I hadn't gotten the chance to delve into the file yet, but, man, this was impressive. The information listed every possible detail, from Marsha's first recorded fillings at the age of five, to her first boyfriend at age thirteen, and it kept on going right up until the very day I had asked Gnosis for this bundle of info. Credit card transactions, phone calls, everything—I mean everything—was in here. I knew Gnosis was good, damn good, but this was on the verge of stalker-like and definitely illegal.

Nice to know I have acquaintances who are willing to break all manner of rules and can provide me with a helluva lot of solid info.

"Well?" asked Ortiz, shaking me out of my Gnosis-appreciation daze.

"Oh yeah," I replied quickly, scanning down the page and repeating the info Ortiz had asked for. "East 39th Street is where we're headed."

"East 39th," repeated Ortiz. It was a light whisper, more to herself and for herself than anything else. "Does it say what apartment number?"

"Yeah, 204. Nice little studio number," I answered.

"At least it's not on the twelfth floor," she commented flatly.

"Afraid we might have to jump out of another building?" I quipped. "Hey!" I exclaimed. My shoulder began throbbing, courtesy of Agent Ortiz's totally uncalled for punch.

"I didn't *jump* out of the last building, did I? Somebody pushed me out of a window!"

"Hey, I did that to sa—" I started defensively.

She pursed her lips in mock curiosity. "Now, who was that?"

"Alright, alright," I conceded. "I pushed you out a building. I'm sorry…again,"

"Damn right," she muttered under her breath, but there was a smile playing across her face.

"Happy you managed to force me to apologize for something I've already apologized for?" I asked,

"Very," she said, still smiling.

"Let's just hurry up and get there, please," I growled, tapping my forearm to accentuate my waning timeline.

Ortiz didn't offer a reply; she set her jaw and sped up.

The ride wasn't too lengthy, but it was longer than I had hoped. We had burned through a little more than half an hour.

"Which one?" asked Ortiz as we drove down East 39th Street.

I looked out the windshield, trying to spot Marsha's apartment complex. It only took a few seconds for me to find it. "That one," I said, pointing to the nearest building.

Ortiz didn't respond, just a simple nod to let me know she had heard me and acknowledged the building I was pointing at.

The building wasn't too difficult to describe, even though it was dark outside. There were plenty of lights to illuminate its features. It was your average cookie-cutter building, made of large ruddy brown-red concrete with massive panels of glass windows. That was pretty much it; the building was rather simple. I say this because not all apartment complexes in New York are art deco nightmares.

Ortiz pulled into the building's underground parking complex, pulling into a reserved spot right near an elevator.

I shot her an oblique look. "Uh, pretty sure we can't park here. See, there's letters and all saying we can't." I gestured to a sign.

She looked at me, rolling her eyes. "We'll be fine. Stop worrying."

"Whatever you say, it's not my car," I said with an indifferent shrug.

"No one's up at this hour. The spot was clearly empty so it's not being used and we won't be too long."

"Unless we get another visit from our fiery friend."

"Don't even joke about that," she said.

"With my luck, it's bound to happen. It really is," I told her.

"Well, your luck sucks."

"Tell me about it," I mumbled in agreement. I stepped out of the car and onto the pavement.

Ortiz got out and headed straight to the elevator without so much as a backward glance. Speaking over her shoulder, she said with a chuckle, "Remember where we parked."

I snorted, but mentally jotted down where we were. *Wrongly parked in a spot clearly reserved for someone else and next to a rusted Ford Bronco.* I jaunted after Ortiz, falling in step behind her as she entered the elevator.

"So, how you do plan on stopping her?"

"If it is her," I said.

"You're not sure it is?"

I shook my head. "No. No, I'm not."

"Why don't you think so?"

"Just a feeling. A hunch." I said.

"You trust it?"

I shrugged. "I have in the past—always served me well."

She chewed on her lip. I could tell she was mulling through her thoughts, so I left her to it.

We arrived on the second floor within a minute or so, stepping out onto the fairly thin, hard, gray carpet lining the hallway.

Agent Ortiz pointed at one of the doors.

I followed her finger. The door was numbered 245; Marsha's apartment was 204. I scanned the doors and figured out which way the numbers were descending, giving a head nod to Ortiz to follow.

We walked for about a minute before coming to Marsha's door. It was a pleasant surprise because her door was wooden. Now I know that that's such an insignificant thing to most people, but for me, well, now I had a door I could break down…if it came to that, of course. Breaking down doors for kicks and giggles is also known as "destruction of property," and some people seem to have a problem with that.

Ortiz walked up to the door and glanced back at me. "How do you want to play this, Norman?"

I rapped my knuckles on the door several times. "How about like this?" I grinned.

She rolled her eyes and muttered a simple "smart ass" under her breath, but I heard it.

We waited a few moments. It was late or early I guess, depending on how you viewed things. Marsha would probably take some time answering the door. After waiting for long enough, I knocked again, this time noticeably harder and louder. A few moments passed again. No sound or response from within. Ortiz and I exchanged a nervous glance.

"You don't think she's on to us do you?" she asked.

"Or worse," I whispered. "Maybe the Ifrit's got her."

"You're just a ray of sunshine, aren't you?"

"I can be," I said. "So what now?"

Ortiz didn't answer, but fished through her coat pockets and removed a small black zipped up pouch. I knew exactly what it was—a government-issued lock pick set. My hunch was correct. Seconds later, she unzipped it and produced a torsion wrench and a rake pick.

"This is breaking and entering, you know?" I whispered to Ortiz.

She produced a low snort and replied. "It's only entering. I'm not breaking in."

"Still, this is fairly illegal, even for a fed."

She shot me a vicious glare as she slipped the torsion wrench into the lock and applied a light amount of pressure. She then slid the rake pick beside it and began moving it rapidly. Even though this would work, it was still taking too long for my tastes. Marsha could've been in danger…or *the* danger.

I cocked my leg back, visualizing where my heel would strike, right above the doorknob where the wood was weakest. I sent my heel crashing forward, the wood around the lock splintered. The door gave way and opened…much to the dismay of Agent Ortiz.

"*Now* it's breaking and entering," I said.

One second I was standing there all smug-like with a

broad smile on my face, and the next I was being jerked by my collar by a pissed off Agent Ortiz. "What the hell is wrong with you?" she hissed.

I shrugged. "Lots. Lots and lots of things."

She shook her head and gave me a reproachful look. "Someone could have heard that. You could have tipped her off," Ortiz said, voice dripping with disdain.

I gave a mock bow and flourish of the hands in the direction of Marsha's apartment. "Then we best get inside—ASAP."

She gave me another disapproving look and muttered, "You belong in an insane asylum, you know that?"

"Maybe my next case."

She ignored my comment and entered Marsha's apartment. I followed right behind her, looking back into the hall cautiously before closing the door as quietly as I could.

Chapter Fourteen

Marsha's apartment was nice; small, but nice. A quaint and cozy aura hung around the place. We walked over her cinnamon and nutmeg-checkered wooden floor in the dining/living room. Since the place didn't have all that much space, Marsha seemed to have gone to great lengths to maximize what space she did have. In the middle of the room was a circular mahogany table with miniature shelves running between its legs, serving to hold a small collection of various books. Against the wall was an old, faded gray couch with amber pillows resting at either end. Above it was another small, but lengthy, shelf made of simple stainless steel. Even though there were clearly signs of someone living there, the place felt strangely empty.

Ortiz nudged me in the ribs with an elbow, giving me a puzzled look and a shrug.

I shook my head. I didn't know how to respond. It seemed that we had come to the same conclusion: clearly, there was no one home.

"You think she left?" Ortiz whispered.

"I'm not sure," I whispered back. "Maybe she heard us and thought it was a break in, might be hiding."

"And whose fault is that?" hissed Ortiz.

I rolled my eyes and pressed forwards, passing a small, metal table surrounded by high mahogany chairs. I motioned for Ortiz to check out the kitchen, which was nothing more than a narrow inlet along one side of the apartment walls. While she was busy with that, I moved on to the bathroom. A small, red bathroom mat sat on the white and black-checkered floor before the sink and toilet. I swept the place over, looking for any residue of soot, but turned up nothing. I brushed the bathtub's red and white striped curtains aside to check the tub as well, but found nothing.

I let out a silent curse, not that I was hoping to find something here because that would implicate Marsha and—

My chain of thought was interrupted by a sharp and sudden gasp, I almost didn't hear it, but the walls of this place must've been thin. I bolted out of the bathroom and to the only place in the apartment we hadn't searched—the bedroom.

"Marsha!" I shouted as soon as I entered. There, not more than five feet away from me, was Marsha Morressy atop her bed. She was being strangled…by nothing but thin air. Her pale green and blue blanket was on the floor. Marsha writhed violently on her bed, dressed in a simple pastel purple nightgown. Her legs were kicking up and down, her hands clasped to her throat.

"Ortiz!" I shouted desperately. I ran over to Marsha, trying to restrain her and figure out what the hell was going on. Her eyes were bulging. She was horrified and so was I. I couldn't do anything. Tears streamed down her cheeks as I still struggled to hold her. Her eyes shone with recognition, and with a silent plea for help.

Ortiz came running in within seconds. "My god," she whispered in horror.

"Help me, Ortiz" I said hoarsely. "Help!" I shouted.

She ran to the other side of the bed, pinning Marsha's arms down as I tried to find out what was causing her to choke. It was hard to see if there was anything lodged in her throat with the room being so dark, and I didn't have time to go flipping on light switches. I hopped onto the bed and straddled her waist, intertwining my hands. I began administering a series of abdominal thrusts. When her gasps began to slow, I almost breathed a sigh of relief—almost. The gasping didn't stop so much as change to a gurgling sound, and Marsha's frantic writhing began to slow and weaken.

"No. No, no, no, no—fight it!" I cried as her struggling ceased. Seconds later, Marsha Morressy stopped moving altogether. Her eyes, still wide and filled with horror, stared back at me. I shut my eyes and turned my head away. A mixture of sorrow and some of the greatest anger I had ever felt surged through me.

"Norman," said Ortiz in a soothing whisper. "You couldn't have done anything."

I don't know what came over me, but the next instant I turned to face Ortiz and said, "You know that, huh? You know that!" My voice echoed through the bedroom.

She looked taken aback. Even in the dark, I could see her eyes widening in shock.

It wasn't fair. Ortiz had come to help me try and save Marsha and I was taking my anger out on her. Here was someone who resolved to help me in my line of work, when by all rights she should have already arrested me for breaking all manner of laws. She had put her life on the line for me, the so-called badass who could solve this case. I was not used to this. I worked alone, always have. I'm not good with people and even less adept at handling failure.

I was ashamed; I couldn't look her in the eyes when I muttered my apology.

"It's not your fault, Norman," she said gently. "Look."

I turned to look at what she was pointing at. I hadn't noticed it at first because I was so preoccupied with trying to save Marsha, but it was hard to miss now. Surrounding Marsha's delicate and deceased frame was a thin layer of soot. Hell, it was everywhere. The bedspread was peppered with the stuff. Her fallen blanket was caked in it, even her clothing.

Anger erupted inside me once again. Marsha had been another victim of the Ifrit. This thing was really starting to piss me off!

Ortiz sat beside me on the bed, speaking in soft tones, "What do we do now?"

"Phone," I said gruffly.

"What?"

"Give. Me. Your. Phone," I growled slowly.

She reached into her coat and pulled out her cell phone, handing it over to me. Without muttering a single word of thanks, I began dialing.

"Who are you calling?"

I ignored her and listened to the phone ringing, praying they would answer. After what felt like an eternity of annoying rings, someone finally answered. "Graves," I said rather brusquely.

"Who's Graves?" asked Ortiz.

I ignored her as a familiar voice came on the phone.

"I thought our business was done, Graves," said the voice.

"Fuck that!" I snarled. "You're helping me till I'm done. *That* was the deal, Pint Size!"

I could almost see Gnosis' eye's narrowing on the other end. When he spoke, it was in a deadly quiet whisper. *"People"*—particular emphasis on people—"don't really speak to me that way. The ones that do, well…"

I couldn't give a damn about his threats. Gnosis could and would make good on them if he felt he was seriously wronged, but I die all the time so screw him.

"Don't threaten me!" I growled back.

"Threaten?" whispered Ortiz, leaning and trying to listen in.

"I saved you. *You* owe me!"

"You can't keep dangling that over my head, Graves," was his all too calm reply. It sounded as if he really didn't give a damn about my problems.

"Not like I have to dangle it that high," I retorted.

"I'm hanging up," he replied.

"Wait!"

Silence; silence, as in no click, meaning he hadn't hung up.

"I'm dealing with an Ifrit," I said. I didn't hear a reply per se, but a sharp inhale of breath more like a hiss. That revelation had caught him off guard.

"Well, that…changes things," he said slowly.

"It does, huh?" His quick change came as a surprise to me. I couldn't quite believe he was ready to help me now.

"Yes, I supplied you with information to help you deal with it. If you are unsuccessful, it may come after me—after it's finished with you, of course."

So the little bastard was more concerned with his own safety. Fine, so long as he helped me take it down. "How do I kill it?"

No answer.

"Do the same rules apply to an Ifrit as it does with a normal Djinn?" I asked.

"An Ifrit is an ancestor in many ways to the Elemental you encountered," he explained. "That's why it can control such creatures with ease."

"How do you know about that?" I asked, thoroughly surprised.

"Really, Graves?" he scoffed. "You should know by now how good I am at my job. It's why I am where I am."

"Fine, whatever," I growled dismissively. I didn't have time for his bragging. "How do I gank it?"

"Graves," he said in an exasperated tone, "an Ifrit's old enough to be considered primordial. You don't *gank* it."

"Well, I'm open to suggestions, I'm assuming silver dipped in blood of a victim still does something, right?" I said.

"It won't kill it like a normal Djinn, but it will hurt," he replied.

I sighed with relief. "That's a start."

"Not much of one," said Gnosis. "Hurt and kill are not synonyms. You are aware of that aren't you, Graves?"

"Then?" I said, letting the question hang in the air.

"A mortal king found a way to bind Djinns in the past," he answered.

"Solomon? He's sort of dead, you know. Real dead."

When Gnosis spoke, he adopted the tone of someone speaking to a rather dimwitted child. "I am aware of that Graves. It is my job to be aware of such things...or did you forget?"

My teeth ground against each other. "Give me something, Short Round, or I'm coming after you next!"

"Eeek," replied Gnosis in mock terror.

"Give. Me. Something. Useful. Now," I said, emphasizing each word slowly, dangerously, making sure he knew I was getting really angry now.

The next instant, the phone vibrated against my ear.

"What the hell?" I pulled the phone away from my ear to see a little symbol appear. It was indicating I had gotten some message, or file, or some other crap. I'm not a phone guy obviously.

"The seal," Gnosis said.

"What?"

"The. Seal." He repeated, albeit much slower. He must've really thought I was stupid or something. The little ass hat.

I fumbled with the phone, tapping the screen with my fingers as I struggled to make whatever he had sent me appear.

Agent Ortiz grabbed the phone from my hands. "Give me that." She did…something, and then handed the phone back.

There was an image on the screen. It looked like an ancient scrawling; a circle in which there was a series of intersecting lines resembling a compass, or a very thin star. "Great," I muttered sardonically. "What do I do with it?"

"Use it to trap the Ifrit," he said, pausing before adding, "forever."

I let out a low whistle. "Forever, huh? Well, I'm assuming I can't throw the phone at the damn thing, so how do I use it?"

"Put the genie back in the bottle, so to speak," he replied.

"And uh, how exactly do I do that?"

"Whoever releases an Ifrit can force it back into its vessel by making an unselfish wish," he answered.

That actually made sense. Ifrits preyed on the greediness of humankind, granting selfish wishes to enrich whoever asked. In the end, they all went horribly wrong. A case of tragic irony, and these things got off on it. A selfless wish was the exact opposite, like water to fire. I mentioned earlier that the supernatural are really big on rules and traditions. Hell, a fair few of them bind me as I am. So, trapping a creature whose whole M.O. was getting people to make selfish wishes, really could be as simple as getting someone to make a selfless wish. It's like changing the rules in the middle of a game. It's a disruption and in the case of the Ifrit, it would hopefully be disruptive enough to its energies that it would be forced back into its vessel.

"Thanks."

He didn't reply. There was just an audible *click*, and the phone went quiet.

"Well, talk about bad phone etiquette," I murmured.

"Look who's talking," replied Ortiz, reaching out to take her phone back.

"There a way to make sure you don't lose that picture?" I asked.

I can be an antiquated soul at times.

Ortiz replied with a nod. "What is it exactly?"

"A seal," I answered. "If we can get the Ifrit back into its vessel, whatever that is, we carve or draw this seal on it and trap the thing forever."

"And how exactly do we get it back into the vessel?" she asked.

I sighed. "That's the hard part. We have to find whoever let it out and convince them to make a selfless wish."

"You mean force them to give up the possibility of getting any more wishes?"

"Yeah," I replied.

Ortiz closed her eyes and let out a heavy breath. "That's not going to be easy."

"Tell me about it."

"Anyone who's become accustomed to having their wishes granted isn't going to give that kind of power up just because we ask them to, Norman."

"I know," I sighed.

"We still don't know where or who this thing is."

"I know that too," I said through gritted teeth.

"So what now?"

I looked back at Marsha, crestfallen that she lay there dead because of me, in a way. It took me a moment to realize my fingers were digging deeply into the meat of my palms. When I spoke, it was a harsh and rough tone, "Now we find who let the Ifrit out. Find one, find the other."

Ortiz chewed her lip again. She did it every time she was nervous or engrossed in deep thought. I was hoping it was the latter. "Well," she murmured more to herself than me, "it has to be an employee of the museum."

"All of the victims have been museum employees," I added, continuing her train of thought.

"And Marsha," Ortiz said a bit weakly, pausing for a moment. She shut her eyes tightly before deciding to speak again. "And Marsha, she had work experience with Middle Eastern culture right?"

"Dammit!" I roared, bolting up from the bed in absolute outrage. *How could I have been so damn blind?* I thought, cursing my stupidity.

"I know who's behind all of this. I know who the monster's posing as!"

Ortiz didn't utter a word; she got up from the bed and was standing beside me all in an instant. "Come on then," she said, tugging on my arm.

I all but ran out of Marsha's apartment. It was a brisk pace at the very least, stomping towards the elevator. Once inside, Ortiz gave me a gentle poke in the shoulder to get my attention.

"Who were you on the phone with?"

I debated telling her the truth. I couldn't tell her about Gnosis. She had his number on her phone now, but I was sure he had ways to prevent people he didn't know from contacting him. "The..." I paused, trying to choose my words carefully. I didn't want to reveal any more about Gnosis than I had to. "The information broker I told you about."

"The one responsible for that binder?" Her eyes widened, eyebrows rising in surprise.

"The very same," I replied.

"Hmm," she said through pursed lips.

I already knew what she had in mind and was a bit curious to see the results myself. "Try it," I said with a shrug.

She pulled her phone out and redialed Gnosis' number as the elevator reached the parking complex. I could hear her phone going through the series of usual rings. We stepped out of the elevator together and began walking, all while waiting to hear the result of her call.

"That's weird," she said.

"What is?"

"A recorded message—informing me the number's no longer in service," she said, casting me a suspicious look. "But it was the number *you* dialed..."

I merely looked at her and gave a confused shrug.

"Fine," she resigned with a sigh.

Gnosis was clearly living up to his reputation.

Ortiz unlocked her car with the remote key fob as we walked towards it. I took a deep breath before opening the passenger door. Marsha's death flashed through my head. I couldn't tell if it was just me, or a bit of Norman's memories. I could tell he cared for her, I could feel it. The combination of feelings was overwhelming. It was why I went to great lengths to stay away from people the victim knew. At times, it wasn't possible, but still, I tried. I didn't want to have to sort through a myriad of emotions that stemmed from both myself and the victim. It was too much. You have to be detached in my line of work.

I must've stood there thinking for a good while because Ortiz piped up. "You getting in or what Norman?"

I shook my head and muttered to myself, pulling on the door handle. I was just about to sit down when I heard a *dong*. I looked over the roof of the car to see the elevator door opening.

"Fanfuckingtastic," I swore when I saw what was exiting the elevator. It—and I use the word it because no other word really applied—was the shape of a woman, but that's about where the differences ended. Her shapely feminine form was nude and wreathed in flames. This was the creature responsible for burning down an entire hotel and I suspected, for cutting the hose I had tried to rappel down the building with.

She was the reason I had learned the fallacy of one of Newton's laws first hand. Graves falls from building. Graves hits pavement; pavement does not hit back with equal force, but a million times the force, causing Graves serious brain damage, evident by the fact I'm referring to myself in third person.

Ortiz and I barely escaped the first time. Hell, I thought we had successfully ganked the Elemental.

Ortiz's breathing picked up its pace. "N-Norman, please tell me that's not what I think it is? I thought we killed it. We killed it, right?"

I was a blur of motion. I heard Ortiz's question, but it barely registered. I dived into the back of her car and retrieved my items. "Move!" was the only reply I gave her, and I shouted it as loud and as harshly as I could. I hoped it would snap her out of her fear-induced reverie.

It worked. One second, Ortiz was utterly overwhelmed and distraught, and the next she was back in the game. I retrieved my journals, the binder of info Gnosis had given me, as well as the silver fire poker Ortiz had left on the backseat. In the front of the car, Ortiz stretched her body across the driver seat and over onto the passenger seat, reaching for the glove box.

"What are you doing, Ortiz?" I shouted.

She ignored me and yanked the glove box open. I had no idea what she was getting as I had already pulled myself out of her car and was keeping an eye on the Elemental. The flame-based woman had stepped out of the elevator and did a lazy, yet graceful, spin to face us. Her head swiveled in an eerily slow manner. She stared at me for a few moments, regarding me as if it were the first time we had met.

Creepy. You think she'd remember the person she tried to burn alive and cause to face-plant into the pavement. Most women would remember...I think.

The Elemental let out an ear-splitting wail. Guess she remembered the part about us dousing her ass in foam, shooting her, and then blowing a fire extinguisher up in her face.

"Ortiz, you might wanna move—now!" I screamed as the Elemental swung her arm in the direction of the car.

All I heard was a "Got it!" from Ortiz. She scrambled through the passenger seat of the car, diving out as a row of flames burst onto the hood of the car. They quickly danced their way across the body of the car until most of it was engulfed in fire.

"My car!" shouted Ortiz.

"I told you something bad would happen if you parked in that spot!"

"Not now!" she snapped back as she began digging through the small purse she had retrieved from her glove box.

"A purse?" I shouted incredulously. "We're in danger of being immolated and you saved your purse?"

Ortiz ignored me, her attention drawn to her flaming car and the Elemental that had caused it. She stood, eyes transfixed on the scene. I knew what was going on. She was on the edge, torn between fear and self-preservation. I had seen her lose her composure before, back in the hotel; I wasn't going to let that happen again.

I ran over to her and knelt beside her. We were between her car and the rusted Bronco. I took her shoulders in my hands and shook her lightly. "Ortiz. Hey, come on. I need you get a grip."

Her eyes blinked several times and then she moved with a sudden surge of speed, brushing me aside and forcing me to collide with the Bronco's door.

"Ow!" I yelped.

Her hands flew out of her purse and produced a

diminutive, gleaming, silvery gun. A palm-sized, snub-nosed revolver, and she had it pointed near the rear end of her car.

A sharp wail drew my attention to what Ortiz was aiming at. The Elemental's slender and fiery figure had crossed the back end of the car and now had us pinned. We were stuck in the narrow space between the car on fire and the rust bucket. You know the saying about a rock and a hard place? Well, in our case, it was a flaming rock and a hard place with a living flamethrower staring us down.

Just as the Elemental raised its arms towards us, my eardrums cried out in pain as Ortiz let loose with her little hand cannon. My hands flew up to my ears as the gun erupted, filling the air with the sounds of twin reports.

Ortiz had wreaked havoc on my eardrums by firing off her gun next to me in the hotel. Now, she fired off a mini cannon, and underground parking lots are really good at amplifying sounds. Needless to say, I think my eardrums would be pressing charges against Agent Ortiz. I mean hell, car alarms were going off everywhere!

At least my eyes were still working; the twin rounds had entered the Elemental's face only a fraction of an inch apart. Damn, that was some good shooting. The two rounds distorted the Elemental's features as her face erupted into twin plumes of miniature flames streaming out of her head. My head was still in a tizzy as I saw the Elemental collapse to the concrete. Her body spurted little geysers of fire everywhere. Maybe she was dead, or dying. I could hope at this point.

Ortiz turned back to face me and helped me up. My hands were still clamped over my ears. I think my eardrums were doing somersaults inside my skull. Those gunshots really knocked my noggin around. I wasn't focusing on her though, I was too occupied by the flames edging their way around the body of the car. They would inevitably cause a very loud, and problematic, *boom!*

My journals dropped to the floor. I brushed her aside and turned quickly, bringing my fist back in what seemed to have become my signature move of late. I plunged it through the Bronco's driver side window.

"That's vandalism!" shouted Ortiz, although it came over as muffle thanks to my mangled eardrums.

I shot a quick glance towards the Elemental. She was now pulling herself back together, so I decided to speed up with breaking some more laws. "If you don't like that," I called to Ortiz as I unlocked the door and slid into the vehicle, "you're really not going to like this next bit."

Ortiz noticed what I had, that the Elemental was getting back up. She unloaded another two rounds into the creature—this time in her back. The Elemental jolted violently before collapsing once again.

I capitalized on the situation and ripped apart the bottom of the steering column to reveal a mass of wires. Hotwiring a car is easy. It really is. All cars have voltage coursing through them even when they are off; it's how radios save settings. What you have to do is find the appropriate wires, strip 'em, and touch 'em together. It bypasses the need to use a key, telling the starter motor to engage and light up the spark plugs, thus starting the combustion process. On a nineties Bronco, that process is ridiculously easy.

"Yes!" I shouted triumphantly as the engine thrummed to life. "Ortiz!"

"What?" she shouted back.

"Get in the Bronco!" I roared as I put the thing into reverse. Ortiz ran around the other side and swung the door open. "Come on," I implored as she began tossing an assortment of things into the vehicle. My journals sailed rather unceremoniously through the air and landed somewhere in the Bronco, prompting a scandalized "Hey!" from me. Then came the silver fire poker...something which seriously should not be thrown. It nearly caught my ankle, falling short by just a few inches. Next came the info binder Gnosis had given me, which I noticed received better treatment than my own items as it was carefully lobbed onto the dash.

"Alright," panted Ortiz. She hopped in and jammed her

seatbelt on, slamming the door shut as she did.

I slid the Bronco out of the spot as fast as I could. The vehicle lurched to the side a bit as I sped out and away from the ticking time bomb that was Ortiz's car. I continued backing up the Bronco until we were literally up against the rear wall of the parking complex.

"What are you doing, Norman?" Ortiz asked, staring at me like I was insane. "We have to get out of here!"

"Just wait and watch the fireworks," I replied with a smirk,

She glanced at the Elemental and then at her car, realizing what I had meant. "Fireworks?" she growled, arching a dark eyebrow. "That's my car!"

"Was," I said. "Past tense."

"It's still there!" she snarled, pointing a finger towards it to accentuate her point.

I guess I was simply running ahead of things.

The Elemental was striding towards us when Ortiz's car blew, and, man, was that something!

You ever hear of that expression of holding on to your teeth? Well, now I know what it meant. The force of the explosion shook everything. My jaw rattled, and I tasted copper where I must've bit my tongue or the inside of my cheek. Windows burst on nearby cars from the sheer force, and my ears begged for mercy. My eyes got their fair share of suffering too; they were temporarily blinded by the sudden flare of light in the dark complex.

Ortiz had a death grip on my right arm, her nails digging into my flesh. She mouthed some words, I think. Maybe I really had gone deaf.

"Norman..."

Nope, not deaf, I thought.

Her voice came through as a distorted whisper. I shook my head violently, which really doesn't help, physiologically speaking. It's more psychological than anything. A message to the head that says, *Get your shit together!*

"There," said Ortiz. I was struggling to hear her, but made out her meaning as she pointed to the Elemental. The explosion had sent the thing crashing into a massive work van opposite Ortiz's now flaming scrap of a car. It had been driven into the double doors at the van's back end. The upper half of her body was somewhere inside the van's spacious trunk. But the Elemental wasn't out of commission yet. Her lower half twitched and seemed pretty functional.

"Norman," Ortiz said, a hint of desperation touching her voice. She was starting to get overwhelmed again, and who could blame her? The Elemental wouldn't go down permanently, no matter what we threw at it. "Please, let's just go," she pleaded.

I wanted to make sure I got this thing, lest it surprise us again, so I waited. It was a hard thing to do. I could feel Ortiz's nervousness and didn't want to put her through anything else if I could avoid it. I shut my mouth, teeth upon teeth, setting my jaw in another psychological ploy to make sure I didn't back out of doing this.

The Elemental's arms slid out from inside the van's trunk. It pushed itself out from where it was firmly wedged, descending with eerie slowness. Its head snapped in our direction, and this time, there was no angry wail or warning. The monster charged towards us with a burst of speed I have never witnessed, crossing several car lengths in an instant.

I slammed the car into first gear and floored it. The Bronco lurched forwards like the heavy, powerful monster it was, accelerating as the Elemental charged towards us, the flames on its body dancing violently.

We collided hard. The Elemental's upper body *thunked* into the front end, its arms crashing down onto the hood, but not bouncing off as I hoped. They dug into it, tearing at the metal. I mashed the pedal down as far as I could and the Bronco picked up more speed. "Hold on!" I shouted to Ortiz as I slammed on the brakes. We both shot forwards only to be stopped by our belts. The Elemental wasn't so lucky. She flew forwards and smacked into the pavement, rolling viciously until she came to a stop, struggling to right herself.

I felt a tight squeeze on my arm. Ortiz held it in a strong grip. I turned to face her. Ortiz's jaw was firm, and she was steel-eyed. "Get that bitch!" she exclaimed, venom and anger dripping in her voice.

That was all I needed. I stomped the accelerator and shifted. The Elemental wasn't on its feet for more than half a second before the full force of the Bronco *thudded* into it. There was a loud *thwump* and the car rocked as the Elemental's form vanished beneath it.

Ortiz spun back in her seat, craning her neck to look out the rear window.

"Well?" I asked, stepping on the brake to slow the monster-killing Bronco down.

"It's down, but something weird's going on."

"Weird?" I asked, cocking my head in confusion.

"Yeah, the fires on its body are fizzing, like when you spray water on a firework, or something like that," she answered.

I turned to look for myself. The Elemental was immobile. The only movement was the flickering, waning of fire struggling to remain alight. Moments later, they fizzled out and the Elemental faded from sight. All traces of her gone in an instant.

Ortiz let out a sigh of relief and her arms wrapped around me. "Thank god!"

"Thank the Bronco," I patted the dash. "Built Ford Tough. Too bad O.J. had to ruin their rep."

Ortiz let out a small laugh. Felt good to make her laugh, especially after what we had just been through.

"Let's get out of here before the cops show up," I suggested.

"Good idea," she smiled. "You're already responsible for disturbing the peace, endangering the general public, arson, destruction of property, and breaking and entering."

"Don't forget grand theft auto," I added, putting my foot back on the gas as I drove the Bronco out of the parking lot.

She looked at me, shook her head in mock

disappointment, and tried to stifle a laugh. She failed. Moments later, her laughter infected me and we were laughing for what seemed like forever—just laughing and driving. It was amazing. We had just escaped another near-death scenario and here I was laughing.

I had never been able to do that before—to laugh with someone. It really helped terrible things like that fade, even if only for a few moments.

"Ahh," I sighed, rubbing a hand under my nose for no reason.

Ortiz let out a relaxed laugh and induced sigh of her own. "So"—she paused for a moment—"what now?"

That question sobered me up. We were quite a bit away from Marsha's apartment complex now, so I pulled the Elemental-crushing Bronco over. As the vehicle lumbered over to the side of the road, I gave Ortiz the name of another employee to look up. She flicked through the binder, and once she found the employee in question, I asked her to read a small piece from the relationship section.

"Marital status: single," read Ortiz. She continued listing things that only served to confirm my suspicions, but the piece I really needed was what she said last: "No next of kin."

My fingers curled around the steering wheel, knuckles whitening. I could feel my heart racing. Damn, I was angry. "Bastard!"

"What?" Ortiz asked in confusion.

"We're going shopping," I replied.

"For...what?" she asked hesitantly.

"Cigarettes."

"You've lost me," said Ortiz.

"I've got a theory that needs testing," I said. I put the car back in gear and took off, searching for the nearest store.

Chapter Fifteen

"Thank you," I grumbled in a sardonic tone, snatching the pack of cigarettes out of the cashier's hand. I swiped Norman's credit card from the card reader and stormed out of the shop, leaving a bewildered attendant and Ortiz behind.

"You know," Ortiz said, panting after having to chase after me, "you really have a way with people, Norman."

I turned to face Ortiz, "Thirteen dollars! You oughta charge him with extortion!"

Ortiz shrugged. "Hey, free enterprise. What can you do?"

"Punch him in his squirrelly little face and take the one cigarette I need?" I muttered below my breath. "I mean, seriously? When did a pack of cigarettes become more expensive than gas?"

"Yeah, a real people person," she added sarcastically.

"People suck," I said in a flat tone.

Ortiz decided not to comment. She followed me to the Bronco and clambered into the passenger side whilst I started the gargantuan beast up.

I headed towards the museum, mulling things over in my head, like how I was gonna confront the Ifrit, and what to do if things got dicey.

Of course Ortiz decided this was the best time to break my concentration with an unnecessary question. "So, these cigarettes are important why?"

Smartassery always served me well in the past, so I replied as such. I took my right hand off the wheel and waggled it in a spooky manner. "Trade secret," I replied in a mock serious whisper. I went so far as to hold a finger to my lips with a "Shhh!" afterwards.

This elicited a sigh of resignation from Ortiz. "Fine. Keep your mystery mojo crap to yourself."

"Thank you. I will," I said cheerily.

Ortiz didn't respond immediately. She plopped her purse down on her lap, unzipping it and reaching inside. She pulled out several loose rounds and inserted them into her diminutive revolver. "Oh, Norman?" she said in an eerily calm tone.

"Uh…yeah?" I answered a bit uncertainly. My eyes wandered from the road to her revolver and back again. This was a creepy way to have a conversation with a guy.

"Just wanted to let you know," she said, all sugary sweet, "that if you keep something from me that results in another fiasco like the Elemental thing—"

Ooooh boy, I knew where this was heading.

"You're the next person I am going to shoot," she said, in an all too-sweet and nice tone. I swear I got cavities from the tone of her voice alone.

I'll admit it caused me to convulse a bit. Yes, a little shiver actually ran down the back of Vincent Graves. Women can do that to a guy, especially when holding a gun and threatening to shoot you.

That's when it occurred to me that the only experience I could recall spending time with a woman of late, was the one going on right now…sitting in a car with a woman threatening me with her hand cannon.

I needed a new life.

Anyways, when threatened by a woman with a gun, always resort to smartassery or changing the subject, like so.

I gave Ortiz a bewildered look. "You keep loose ammo and a revolver hangin' around in your purse?"

She shrugged nonchalantly. "A girl's got to keep three things in her purse; mascara, concealer and lipstick," she rattled off in quick succession.

I rolled my eyes. "None of those are a deadly weapon,"

She ignored my quip and continued, "A tampon—"

"Whoakay!" I said, nearly throwing my hands up at that revelation. "Too much info there."

"Men," she scoffed with a shake of her head. "Compact mirror, wallet, I.D, keys, emergency twenty dollar bill…" she rattled off, showing no sign of stopping.

It was at this point I began holding up some fingers, trying to figure out what equated to three in her head. She didn't care; she kept on going while I silently kept count.

"Cell phone, mints, a small pack of tissues, and a backup gun," she finished.

"Ortiz, maybe you and I have a different understanding of the number three, but, ah, them's a helluva lot more than three things in your purse," I reasoned.

She looked at me like I was the insane one. "The lipstick, concealer, mascara and mirror count as one thing," she said like it was obvious.

"Oh yeah, of course," I said, taking on a tone of mock understanding.

"Emergency makeup kit."

I rolled my eyes. "And the other hundred and fifty?"

She shrugged. "Split them into two more emergency sets."

I shook my head. Of course, it's so simple. A bazillion items in a woman's purse equals three.

Suddenly I had remembered one of the items she was carrying. "Wait," I said, in pleasant surprise. "Did you say lipstick?"

I must've looked really happy, and strangely so, because a slightly confused look crossed her face. "Uh…yes," she said, giving me an oblique look.

It was all we had at the moment, but it could just work.

"Is there a particular reason you're so interested in my lipstick, Norman?" she asked hesitantly.

"Huh?" I replied, coming out of my thoughts, "Oh, yes and no."

"First the cigarettes, and now you're gunning for my lipstick?" she muttered quietly. "You going to tell me why? Or is this another weird magic thing?"

"Weird magic thing," I smiled, waggling my fingers once again in a spooky manner.

I could see her bristle in her seat. The non-answer got under her skin. She was definitely not accustomed to not knowing things. It made sense though; her job was to investigate, to ferret out answers. Not knowing something could really rankle a person.

Welcome to a day in my world, Ortiz. Hell, I never got the answers upfront when I asked, and I suspected Church always had them.

I heard her exhale again. "So, Norman," she said, getting my attention.

"Yeah?"

"What have we got in store for us when we get there?" she asked a bit apprehensively. I could see her tightening her grip on the undersized, yet definitely not underpowered, revolver. Her eyes were wide, not with fear, but uncertainty.

Sure, I couldn't tell her everything. God knows I wanted to. I couldn't tell her anything I wasn't certain of. It could put her in more danger, like letting her know my plans for the lipstick. Yes, I know lipstick isn't inherently dangerous, but if she knew what I had planned for it, she might take it upon herself to do it, and that would put her in danger.

But I could tell her about the dangers posed by the Ifrit. Well, the ones she wasn't already aware of. Like its ability to enthrall a bunch of exceedingly dangerous monsters. Oh, and the ability to grant wishes and then have you killed from wherever in the world. It doesn't even have to be remotely near you. Once you strike a deal, you're essentially dead.

"Alrighty then," I said, pursing my lips as I thought about what to say. "Well, you already know about the Ifrit being able set a bunch of supernatural hitmen after us?"

She nodded.

"It can also bend reality to a certain degree, and—"

"Just how far exactly can it bend reality?" interjected Ortiz.

I inhaled sharply, thinking the question over as I really wasn't sure myself. "Well, I honestly don't know."

"Gee, what a wonderful source of information you are," she said with a lighthearted laugh.

"Hey!" I exclaimed indignantly. "I can't have all the answers; I've never dealt with an Ifrit before!"

"Well, what do you think? Based on what you have seen and dealt with, Norman?"

"Hmm," I pondered aloud. "Well, at the very least I know that it has the ability to sic a frickin' tiger on me."

"About that," said Ortiz. "How exactly did all of that happen? You still haven't explained it; you just blamed the Ifrit."

"You know that Golden Tiger restaurant?"

"Yes," Ortiz answered hesitantly. "I've been there before. Nice place."

"Ever notice those little tiger statues outside?"

She nodded.

"One of those was our rampaging tiger."

"That's…a joke, right?" she said, her voice ringing with disbelief.

"After everything you've seen, seriously?"

"Right, of course," she muttered to herself. She began chewing on her lip again. I knew she was thinking, so I kept on driving, remaining silent until she decided to share her thoughts. "So, we know it can mess with reality on a fairly significant scale," she said. "Enough to bring an inanimate object to life."

"Then there are the wishes," I chimed.

"What about them?"

"Well, think about it. They are massive alterations of reality. In granting a wish, an Ifrit's rewriting a person's life. That's a major perversion of reality."

"Yeah," she said, pausing for a moment before continuing. "Like being a janitor one instant and a multimillionaire the next."

"Exactly."

"So we might not even be able to put up a fight? Is that what you're saying Norman?"

It was a possibility, one that we had to be prepared for.

"It could go down that way, Ortiz. I mean, whoever let the Ifrit out could just wish us dead," I said.

"Then why haven't they?"

"I think they have."

"The Wraith and Elemental, you mean?" she said, catching on to what I meant.

"Yeah, my guess is that it can't just poof us away or something. At least when we're this far away." What I didn't say, however, was how it had almost ripped my soul out of Norman's body. That was excruciating, so much so that I had blacked out. It gave me a sense of just how powerful the Ifrit was. It didn't need to physically interact with me; it could just pull me from existence. At least it tried to, anyway.

Somehow, Church had prevented that. He never bothered to explain how either. I was beginning to get a sense of how Ortiz must've been feeling when I didn't explain things to her.

"So how exactly do we stop it if it can do all of that?"

I slowed the Bronco down and pulled to a complete stop. I turned and reached into the rear seats, retrieving the silver poker.

"We're going to use a fire poker…on a creature that can bend reality?" Ortiz asked, her face a monument of incredulity.

"I told you," I said firmly, trying to give my words some more weight so they sank in. "Silver hurts a lot of things in the paranormal world."

"And…this," she said. "Can it hurt or kill the Ifrit?"

"Not like this, no." I answered her.

"Then what good is—" she started saying, before my actions caught her attention.

I held the fire poker firmly in my right hand, whilst placing the sharp barb at the far left side, on my left palm. It hurt like hell when I slid it towards my other hand. The barb grazed the skin at first, but it dug deeper as I applied pressure. Soon, there was a long narrow gash across my palm, blood welled and seeped down the end.

"What are you doing?" asked a bewildered Ortiz.

I winced before speaking. Compared to everything else I had undergone recently, the pain wasn't excruciating, but it was still an annoyance of sorts. Think about it, getting punched hurts far more than a paper cut, but a paper cut still hurts doesn't it? Those suckers are really annoying. That's what this was—a big, honkin' paper cut.

"Like I said before, silver hurts many things. To hurt the Ifrit, well, it needed something extra," I told her.

"Blood! You need to use blood?" she asked in disbelief.

"Blood holds a lot of power in the supernatural world," I explained, not telling her the whole truth however. Gnosis said the blood of a victim would work. The janitor was obviously out, on the account of not having access to his body. Plus, he'd be all dried out and starting to get all corpsey...not sure if that's the medical term for it. Marsha was out because...well, there was no way I was going to mutilate her body just to get some blood. There was a bit of poetic justice in bleeding her to put a hurting on the Ifrit. I couldn't do it however. I just couldn't. What I could though, was bleed myself. Norman was a victim, and one who I had a damn good amount of access to. Since I had the ability to regenerate any body I inhabited, it made sense to use his blood. I was a walking armory of sorts...except for the fact that every drop came at the cost of causing myself pain.

Does that make me a masochist?

I had to leave Ortiz ignorant of the victim part. That would have been a little too much for her to handle, not to mention the fact we were about to walk into the proverbial lion's den. I didn't need to get her confused and worked up before that, so I left out a few details. It was for her own good.

I slid my bleeding palm across the upper portion of the fire poker, coating every inch of it in Norman's blood.

Ortiz visibly shuddered at the action. She had been through a lot of truly terrifying experiences recently, but I guess self-mutilation always gives a person the heebie-jeebies.

Every time I slid my lacerated palm across the metalwork, it stung—it stung a helluva lot, but I bore it. Oh, I grunted a bit, that was expected though. It was uncomfortable having the metal slide and rub against the sliced flesh, preventing it from trying to seal up.

"Are…you okay, Norman?" she asked in a soft breath. Her hand reached out to grab my right wrist, the one holding the poker.

In silence, I grasped the pronged side. Pain lanced through my already injured hand as part of the prong nicked the torn flesh. I grimaced through it and handed Ortiz the poker, giving it to her by the handle, the only side not coated in blood.

"Are you alright?" Ortiz repeated.

I winced once again. My hand had a slight burning sensation, and I had an overwhelming desire to itch it. "That'll keep you safe. You can hurt the Ifrit with it."

"Thank you Norman," she responded in a gentle voice. "Now, answer me," she said in a firmer tone. "Are you alright?"

"Peachy," I replied rather casually. The shallow cut hurt, but it was nothing to get angry over. Better to play it down than have Ortiz concerned over an insignificant cut.

"Okay then," she said with a simple nod, hefting the silver fire poker. "Will this really work?"

I shrugged to let her know I wasn't completely sure. "That's what I was told by my source, and before you ask, yes, I trust him."

Her hands tightened around the base of the shaft. I knew she was going to keep a death grip on the thing. After all she had been through, she wasn't going to let go of something that could wallop the Ifrit.

I exhaled to clear my head and psych myself up for what we were about to go get ourselves involved with. Wrapping my hands around the steering wheel, I slipped the vehicle out of neutral. Ortiz reached over to grab my semi-bloody hand. The blood that had welled up in my palm had dried and caked up. All that was left was a dark red line with a layer of thin, crusty blood.

"Is...is that going to heal like...? Well, is that going to do whatever you did to get better after your fall out the hotel window?" Ortiz asked. She was clearly a bit perplexed as to what I could do and recover from.

"Yeah, quicker too," I said. I removed my hand from hers in a gentle gesture, placing it back on the wheel. "Let's get going again, huh?" I whispered.

She gave a silent nod of agreement.

I pulled the hulking vehicle away from the curb and we continued on to the museum, and to the confrontation I was beginning to dread for Ortiz's sake.

Chapter Sixteen

A familiar sight greeted me as I pulled the Bronco into the west parking lot of the museum. I parked beside a pastel yellow Lamborghini Miura. Norman's ill-gotten Miura, I mean. An estimated seven-figure car that came at the cost of his father's life.

There was a bit of rustling in our vehicle. Ortiz was fidgeting a bit, looking uncomfortable. Her face was a mask of apprehension. Now we were finally here, about to face and attempt to kill the Ifrit, it must've been unnerving. I placed a reassuring hand on her shoulder and gave it a firm squeeze. "You'll be fine, Ortiz. I promise," I said in a near whisper and as matter-of-factly as I could. I wanted there to be no doubt in her mind that she would come out of this okay.

She closed her eyes and murmured something unintelligible to herself before turning to address me. "Promise me something else too."

"What?"

"That you really, truly are going to come clean about everything—"

"Ortiz...I can't." My voice sounded more like a plea—a plea to tell her to drop it.

"Everything you can," she said, speaking over me. "I know there are some things you just can't talk about. Not yet anyways."

I nodded a silent agreement.

"Please," she pleaded. "If I'm getting involved in this crazy world, I really need to know more."

"You plan on making a habit of this?" I asked,

surprised.

She looked away, staring out the Bronco's window at nothing, a long lost sort of stare. I knew what she was really doing was getting lost in a series of important thoughts. I remained respectfully silent, which is fairly hard for me to do.

"I'm not sure what I'm going to do after this," she said, breaking the silence, "But after seeing all of this, what actually happens, I don't know if I can just sit back and not get involved." Her voice became stronger as she spoke; by the end of her sentence, her words were like steel.

Wow, here was a woman thrust blindly into the supernatural world, she had been through a boatload, and still wanted to keep going. Honestly, I felt a bit ashamed. I didn't show it or say anything. I had been doing this for so long, bouncing from one body to the next, one case after another, that I had began to lose touch. Somewhere along the line, I think I stopped caring as much about the people—people who should've been the priority, lives to be saved.

No, somewhere down the road I became too fixated on the monsters. The supernatural predators who preyed on people, the ones I was supposed to hunt down, the ones I was obsessed with killing. Ortiz had reminded me of what I was really supposed to be doing. I couldn't look her in the eyes at that moment, so I turned to look at my knees.

"Norman," she whispered.

"Yeah," I croaked.

"Promise me," was all she said.

My lips parted, but no words came out. I nodded, which might not seem like much, but it was a promise to tell her what I could when this was done.

Her arm reached out, her fingers softly pressed beneath my chin, turning my face towards hers. Still, I couldn't bring myself to meet her eyes. "I promise," I whispered, forcing the words past the lump in my throat. "I promise to tell you whatever I can when all of this is done; I swear it, for whatever that's worth to you."

A long moment of silence passed between us. She lowered her hand from my face and sat back in her seat. "A lot, Norman. That's worth a lot. Thank you."

After all the dishonest things I had said in front of her, she still had faith in my word. She still had some level of trust in me. A nauseating sensation churned inside my stomach and I hated it. I pushed my thoughts and feelings aside. This wasn't the time to get lost in my head or feel guilty. I picked up my journals, holding them tight and turned to Ortiz. "You ready?"

She gripped the poker in one hand, while in the other hand, her fingers clasped around the handle of her ear-assaulting revolver. She looked at me, steely-eyed. "Ready." Her tone was all courage and iron.

I breathed deeply, preparing myself mentally for whatever possible things we would face. "Alrighty then," I said as I swung the Bronco's door open and hopped out.

Ortiz let out a low whistle of appreciation as she walked by the Lamborghini.

I smiled. "Like it?"

"Yours?" she asked, wide-eyed with surprise.

"You didn't think I walked here every day, did you?" I couldn't tell her it was mine flat out. Ortiz was a human lie detector. She would catch that lie outright. The car was Norman's. Well, originally his father's. I couldn't tell her I got the car from Norman, who I currently inhabited, who happened to get the car when his father died because Norman decided he wanted the car. Awkward.

A ghost of a smile appeared on her face. "You really like your non-answers, Norman."

I waggled my hands in a so-so gesture.

She let out a small snort and laughed as I opened the door of the Lamborghini and fell into it. The seats were low and Norman was pretty tall; there really was no graceful way of entering. I leaned over and opened its glove box, inserting my journals into it for safekeeping. After climbing back out, I saw Ortiz was giving me a quizzical look. One eyebrow arched, posing a silent question.

"Safekeeping for my journals," I said. "Figured it'd be better to keep 'em in there until we're done. Chances are we'll probably be leaving in that, what with your car getting blown up—"

"Thanks to you," she said in annoyance.

"Blame the Elemental. Like I was saying, we can't exactly continue driving a stolen Bronco."

She didn't say much, just scoffed with lightheartedly and proceeded to the nearest entrance.

Jogging after her, I silently prayed the museum doors I had unlocked on my previous visit were still open. I had visited the place after normal operating hours yesterday. It was the next day now, but it was still early morning or late night—whatever.

Ortiz brought out her lock picking kit once we reached the doors; I cut her off, drawing a suspicious glance from her.

"What are you doing, Norman?"

I reached out for the handle and pulled gently. "Come on," I whispered. The door opened.

"Yes!" I bellowed in triumph, eliciting a shut the hell up punch from Ortiz in my shoulder. "Right sorry...yes," I whispered.

Ortiz shot me a reproachful look, shaking her head in disapproval as she brushed past me and entered the museum. I slipped in right behind her.

We walked in silence for a few moments, traversing the corridor as quietly as we could. Everything was disconcertingly quiet. I got the distinct impression I was being watched. It's spooky being in a museum after hours— the eerie silence, and remains of massive creatures everywhere. They gave off vibes like they were watching you. Ortiz's eyes were darting everywhere. She seemed to be in a hyperaware state, trying to take in everything around her.

I reached out to grab her shoulder, intending it to be a reassuring gesture. Apparently, that was the wrong thing to do. The new throbbing sensation in my arm told me that.

"Dammit, Norman," she hissed. "You scared the hell out of me!"

"Hey!" I hissed back in defense. "I was trying to calm you down. You looked spooked."

"I was spooked... I *am* spooked," she replied in a harsh voice.

I threw up both hands in a placating gesture, hoping she would stop trying to verbally slay me and focus on helping me find and gank the Ifrit. It worked. Soon, we were back to walking the corridors in eerie silence; the only sounds was that of our footsteps *clacking* across the polished stone floor.

We were drawing near the guard's desk when I picked up on an overwhelming, and all too familiar smell. It was acrid, with a hint of heat. It overpowered my nostrils and made my eyes water. There was a coppery smell to it, like the burnt residue from fireworks. It was foul. A fustercluck of all sorts of disgusting. As we drew nearer, there was a tinge of sulfurous odor as well.

"Oh my god," whispered a mortified Ortiz, her hands flying up to her mouth. Whether it was in shock or to prevent herself from vomiting, I wasn't not sure. Probably both. The stench was unbearable this close.

"Damn," I muttered as I approached the guard's desk. I had known the source of the smell before seeing the body. You never get the smell of burnt flesh out of your mind, and sadly, it's something I've smelled before. It's heavy and thick; almost a taste—leathery, overpowering, and just plain noxious.

I couldn't get a proper look at it from the front of the desk. The still smoldering body was curled up—well, more shriveled—on the ground behind the desk. I walked around, holding my breath as I approached. The stench grew unbelievably stronger the closer I got. I knelt beside the body. My eyes were really watering at this point. This person had been recently immolated; there was a fair bit of heat radiating from the body. The ground around the poor guy had scorch marks too.

A sharp pang pierced my skull. A flash of images and

sounds ran through my mind. I knew this person, or rather, Norman knew the person. "Rick," I said in a somber tone. Rick had been an idiot, sure, maybe even a bit of a prick, but he didn't deserve this. His body lay there like someone huddled up with their blanket, his hands close to his chest as if he were trying to curl up and away from the flames.

"Ack!" I gagged. It was getting hard to breathe, even through my mouth. There's a reason burning flesh is one of the worst smells in the world. You'd think it would smell of cooking meat, but you'd be wrong. Meat is processed, bled. Most of it is skinless, and it certainly isn't full of iron-rich blood, living and working organs, hair and nails. All those things burning in tandem give off a series of horrible smells that mix to form an olfactory assault. When hair and nails burn they release a smell like sulfur, which is bad enough on its own. Add bacteria-filled organs, such as intestines, and you get methane, the gas responsible for horrendous flatulence, and according to some scientists, global warming.

So you can imagine what it was like to be this close to a charred body that was still somewhat hot, odors fuming out of it.

"Norman," Ortiz croaked. "That looks like it was done by—"

"No." I knew what Ortiz was hinting at. She was afraid the Elemental had come back. It hadn't. This was the work of the Ifrit. It was here. Hell, it had never left the museum. "*It* did this, Ortiz. The Elemental's gone." I tried to say it as definitively as possible. I didn't want to leave any doubt in Ortiz's mind that the Elemental was done for.

She closed her eyes. I could see them watering. I guessed it was the smell and sight of Rick's body. "How?" she asked. Her voice was a bit rough; the smell was really getting to her.

Instead of responding to Ortiz's question right away, I rose, beckoned for her to follow me to lead her away from Rick's charred body. I gave her a moment to collect herself. I didn't need that long to recover. I've had the misfortune of coming across this before. A few deep breaths were enough for me to forget about it. Just forget, not stop smelling it however. The smell of burnt flesh and hair clings to your nose. Literally, small particulate matter stays there.

There was a guttural sound of someone trying to clear their throat. That or gagging, followed by a loud clatter and *clang*. I nearly jumped out of Norman's skin. Ortiz was doubled up, clutching her stomach, revolver still in her hand. The silver fire poker had slipped from her grasp, causing the clatter I heard.

I placed my now healed left hand on her back, slowly and calmly rubbing it. "You okay there?" I asked as sympathetically as I could.

There were a few heavy coughs, but then gingerly, she righted herself. "Yeah," she said, still sounding a bit rough. She knelt down in order to pick up the fire poker, but I held up a hand, motioning for her to stop.

She had almost just thrown up. I wasn't going to make the lady bend back over to pick up a silver pointy stick. I was going to be a gentleman and do it for her.

I dropped to one knee and retrieved the poker, handing it to Ortiz by the side I hadn't bloodied earlier. Fortunately, the blood had dried, but still, you can't hand a lady a bloody…well, anything really.

"Thanks," she said a bit shakily. "So what happened…to that man?"

"The Ifrit, that's what," I growled.

"Why? Do you think he knew something?"

"No." I could feel my lips peeling away from my teeth in rage. "He didn't know anything—"

"Then why?" interjected Ortiz.

"He's a message…to me," I said bitterly. "A message that I'm getting close and that I need to lay off."

Ortiz lifted the fire stoker to her chest; her knuckles were white from gripping it so tight. "Like hell we're going to lay off!" she snarled.

"Damn straight," I agreed, leading the way as we walked towards the warehouse section of the museum. This was where I had first encountered Marsha. The poor girl had just transferred here; she didn't deserve any of this. Now she was dead, in part because of my ineptitude. I wasn't going to let that one go.

"Norman, you okay?" Ortiz had a sixth sense on reading people. She could tell I was distraught about something.

"Yes and no," I replied.

"Wow, another non-answer. You love making a habit out of this."

"I was thinking about Marsha."

"Oh," she said, pausing for a moment. "You feel responsible, don't you?"

"How can I not?" I barked. That was unfair; Ortiz didn't deserve the brunt of my anger. I needed to direct that at the Ifrit.

"Did you do everything you possibly could to save her?" she asked in a strangely neutral voice. It was devoid of almost any tone.

"You know I did. Hell, you were there, Ortiz."

"I know," she breathed in a soft tone.

"So, what's your point?" I asked, irritated.

"My point," she said firmly, "is that you're not responsible for her death. My point, Norman, is that you did everything you could to save her."

"But—" I began before Ortiz waved me off with an aggressive swipe of her hand.

"Honestly," she muttered under her breath. "What is it with men? It's not hard to understand. You. Are. Not. Responsible!" Her eyes and tone burned with fiery resolution. Hell, she made me believe it. She *actually* made me believe it.

I'd never really noticed the kind of person Ortiz was until that moment. She was the extraordinary kind—the kind you don't meet every day. The kind you stick up for, and with, when things get rough. The kind of person who would stick by you when things got supernaturally rough.

"Thanks, Ortiz," I said with a cough, trying to mask any sentimentality. I'm a monster killer, not a sentimental mush bag.

Ortiz let out a rather loud snort. "Don't get all emotional on me, Norman. Men have about a difficult time with that, just like they do with…well, everything." She said that last bit with the hint of a chuckle.

"Emotional? Me?" I exclaimed in mock outrage. "I do seem to remember you turning into a little girl every time—"

"Ass," she muttered as she punched my arm—again!

I rubbed my recently pummeled arm, opening my mouth to protest.

"Oh, stop your whining…wimp."

"You throw a good punch, Ortiz, but seriously," I stopped for a moment, trying to get the words out and really mean it. "Thanks. For Marsha, I mean."

"No problem."

"Just wanted to say it is all. What, with the possibility we might get incinerated pretty soon," I remarked.

"Look at you, Mr. Positive," she said sardonically.

"Hey! I am positive… Positive we're going to be immolated," I said.

She shook her head and let out a small laugh. "You're hopeless."

I shrugged. Didn't know how to reply to that one, so I kept walking, heading towards the hall at the end of the warehouse section we were in.

"You still haven't explained how the Ifrit was able to do that," Ortiz said. "That looked more like the—" She looked like she was suppressing a shudder.

"The Elemental," I finished for her. "I know."

"So?" she said, urging me to continue.

"It wasn't. That thing's dead—"

"But?" she interrupted.

"But…" I began slowly. "My contact reaffirmed what I already knew, like I told you back in the janitor's place."

"Yeah, I remember. Ifrits are old spirits of fire and smoke or something, right?" she said.

"Try ancient—damn near beginning of time ancient.

Kind of like the great-great-grand-ancestor to the Elemental," I explained. "The Elemental's like a sparkler compared to the Ifrit."

"You have a heck of a way of getting a girl's confidence up, you know that?" Ortiz muttered.

"Sorry," I replied half-heartedly.

"Don't be sorry, Norman. Just tell me we can do this."

"Uh, what?" I replied, caught off guard by the request.

Her eyes fixed on mine. "Tell me we can do this."

"We can do this, Ortiz." I nodded. "We'll come out just fine." I said as firmly as I could. It was hard though, I didn't know if it was true. It certainly wasn't a lie. It was possible, but didn't seem likely. Still, I didn't see the point in not saying a few kind and motivating words. Hell, it might've been that hearing those words pushed her to make sure she did make it out fine.

Ortiz exhaled deeply, a weighty sigh of relief. "Thanks," she said, standing a little straighter.

"Uh, no problem, Ortiz," I responded. It seemed to have done the trick; she stood a bit more confidently than before.

"I just hope this thing works," she said, sending the poker through a few practice swings as we continued walking.

"So do I," I muttered under my breath, too low for her to hear. I had just told her things would be alright, no need to start causing her to doubt me or the weapon I had given her.

We cleared the warehouse and most of the hall, walking towards the room I visited earlier. I signaled to Ortiz with a nod of my head, pointing to the door.

She replied with a nod of acknowledgment.

"You ready?" I asked in a hushed whisper.

Nod.

I twisted the handle as quietly as I could, releasing the catch from the lock and then put all my weight into it. The door flew open.

Chapter Seventeen

I didn't exactly get the badass reaction I was hoping for as I burst into the room. Neither of the two people inside seemed the least bit perturbed about my entrance, but then, why would they?

James was lying slumped against the legs of one of the massive tables, upon which were dozens of items for the upcoming exhibit. His features had a sunken look. He had aged since our last meeting, looking forty years older—at least. He had looked a bit haggard before, the result of pulling one too many all-nighters. Now? James looked utterly emaciated, like his life force had been sucked out of him, which in a way is exactly what was happening to him.

"Not looking too good there, are you, James?"

He craned his neck to look at me, an exceedingly difficult move for him to make. His movements showed signs of fragility. "Norman?" he rasped. It was more a question than an exclamation of surprise. I didn't think he was capable of being surprised in the state he was in. It didn't matter anyway. I was pretty sure he couldn't even see me, or anything else for that matter.

"God!" Ortiz gasped when she saw him.

James' entire face was gaunt and hollow looking. Massive rings of blue and black shadowing circled his eyes, as if he had been socked too many times in the face, minus the swelling. His skin clung to him with unnatural tautness. It looked stretched. It was a seriously disturbing sight.

A wisp of smoke caught my eye and I turned to face the other person in the room. She was dressed in the same manner as our first meeting: black leather jacket hung over her strategically slashed shirt, baring the skin of her chest and taut stomach beneath, equally distressed jeans that led to a pair of oversized studded black combat boots. She sat on one of the tables, having brushed many of the artifacts unceremoniously aside. Her legs dangled over the edge as she regarded Ortiz and I.

Her molten brown eyes narrowed as I stepped towards her. Her posture changed, becoming more rigid as I approached. A few tendrils of smoke wafted out of her mouth, and her left pocket, where her hand was stuffed as if concealing something. It was a nice act, but I wasn't buying it anymore.

I reached into my pocket and removed the pack of cigarettes I had bought earlier, smacking the container until I was able to pull one out. She arched an eyebrow in surprise when I held the cigarette in front of her, inches from her mouth. I arched an eyebrow of my own, surprised it wasn't obvious to her. "Well?" I said expectantly.

"Well, what?" she snapped haughtily.

"Can I get a light?" I asked quietly.

Her haughty demeanor faded, and an unfocused look came over her. She looked startled by the question. "Uh...what?" she said, looking completely baffled. You'd have thought I was speaking in a foreign language from the state of her reaction.

I breathed out slowly. "Can I get a light?" I repeated, only much slower and with more emphasis.

She stared at me with her mouth agape, just as startled as she was before. It's funny, because she hadn't had a problem giving me attitude before. Hell, five seconds ago, she was giving me one, and now she had conveniently forgotten how to speak?

I clapped my hands together. "Come on. Chop, chop! I need a light," I feigned in an impatient manner.

She looked terrified, operative word being looked. She wasn't going to pull anything else over on me again. "I...uh...I..." she stammered.

"I...you...uh...ahhh...what?" I snapped.

A soft hand fell on my shoulder, gripping it lightly. "Hey, Norman, take it easy on the kid," Ortiz whispered.

I ignored her and continued eyeing the girl, waiting for an answer.

"I don't have my lighter anymore," she replied. "I tossed it when I heard footsteps outside."

"Why?"

"Because you already caught me once. I didn't want to get in trouble again," she said, lowering her eyes from mine in a sheepish manner as she hopped off the table. "I'll leave, and I promise I won't come back," she said as she tried to walk past me.

My hand shot out, grabbing her around her upper arm rather strongly. I shoved her back against the table with a good amount of force. "Oh, no. You're so not leaving, doll! Sit!" I commanded.

"Norman!" Ortiz was scandalized by the way I was treating the poor little girl. "What the hell are you doing?"

I continued ignoring her. I figured the best way to get her to understand would be to simply show her. I turned my attention back to James' daughter, who was now sitting on the table once again. "Turn out your pockets," I ordered with an edge in my voice.

She did, after a little hesitance—first the right one, which revealed nothing, then the left. I found what I was looking for—the cigarette she had stashed. She held it up rather weakly, her hand trembling in fear. She was a fantastic actress, but then again, so were most of the monsters I'd hunted. "Sorry," she mumbled apologetically.

I snatched the cigarette out of her hand. It was old, hell it was ancient. Comparing it to the brand new one in my other hand, I noticed a helluva of difference. The pristine, white upper portion was severely distressed and yellowing; this thing had been stowed for a long time, and not properly. But the real kicker was that it had never been lit. At least, not properly. That was all I needed.

"That's funny," I said with a grim laugh.

"What?" Ortiz and James' daughter asked

simultaneously.

I held the cigarette up for Ortiz to see while turning my gaze on the girl. "When did kids start smoking these things backwards?"

"Huh?" was the brilliant reply I got from the young girl.

"Ortiz?" I said, tilting my heads towards her. My tone made it more of an open question.

"The butt's been lit, but the rest is...fine?" Ortiz said in confusion.

"Yup," I confirmed. "You know what I think?" I turned back to the girl. She opened her mouth to speak and I held up my hand, silencing her. "I think this is the same cigarette I saw you smoking yesterday. Hell, I think this is the only cigarette you've been smoking. And I'm pretty damn sure that you haven't been smoking it at all!" I said, my voice getting louder as my anger took over.

"But—" she pleaded, leaning forwards and casting a nervous glance towards Ortiz, as if she were going to save her.

"I also think it's not a new trend for kids to light up cigarette butts and put them out on their tongues," I said, raising my voice higher than hers. I turned my head slightly towards Ortiz and asked in a much lighter voice, "It's not, is it?"

She shook her head.

Right, then. Just had to make sure. Kids are doing all manner of stupid things these days.

"What I think," I growled, "is that you don't have a lighter because you haven't been smoking. Not by the standards of mortals anyways."

"What are you talking about? You're crazy!" she shouted in a terrified, shrill voice. She turned to face Ortiz, pleading, "Help me! He's insane!"

I shot a glance at Ortiz. She was biting her lip, a sign that she was carefully observing and weighing the situation. She took a step back and remained silent, deciding to stay out of it and allowing me to continue.

Looking back at the now teary-eyed girl, I picked up

from where I left off. "I think the reason this cigarette looks like it's ten years old is that you've been keeping it for appearances. You don't carry a lighter because you don't smoke cigarettes. *You* just smoke!"

"I...don't. I... I..." she stammered and cried.

"Gun!" I barked.

Ortiz gasped. "What?"

"Give me...your gun, Ortiz."

She hesitated for an instant, but gave it over.

"Oh god!" cried James' daughter. "You're gonna kill me!" She turned to Ortiz, her eyes showing desperation. "Please..." she whimpered.

I arched an eyebrow at Ortiz, asking the silent question if she was going to intervene or not. I could see her struggling with this, but she didn't get involved. She squeezed her eyes shut and let out a profound sigh. I took it as a sign that she was going to let me do my thing, but that she wasn't entirely comfortable with it.

"All right," I snarled, pointing Ortiz's revolver dead center in the girl's face. My action elicited a large shriek from her as well as another plea.

"I didn't do anything!" she cried. "I didn't—"

"Didn't do anything?" I roared, spittle flying from my mouth, my lips quivering. "You're the reason James is lying there with the life sucked out of him!" I gave a quick nod to the emaciated figure lying against table. "You're the reason I was nearly eaten by Tony the fucking Tiger! You're the reason I was ambushed by a Wraith in all my naked glory!" I continued shouting, the gun shaking in my grip. "You're the reason the museum janitor is dead, the reason Rick is dead. You're the reason..." I broke off, struggling to say her name aloud.

I tightened my grip on the revolver and pushed it into her face, the barrel rested on the tip of her nose. "You're the reason Marsha is dead!" I snarled in pure fury and reached out with my free hand, grabbing her mouth and giving it a violent shake. The gun never wavered from her nose.

"Norman," Ortiz said in hushed whisper. I could hear

the concern in her voice. "I think you're going a little—"

I cut her off with a gesture; I knew where she was going with this. One simple show of my hand was enough to get her to understand what was really going on. The hand I had just grabbed the girl with—the hand Ortiz was currently looking at—was covered in a fine, powdery black substance. An all too familiar substance. It had coated the scene where I had killed the tiger. It was on Marsha's bed, the janitor's bed. Hell, it was on the will back in Norman's place.

The whole damn thing had been staring me in the face the entire time. I just hadn't realized it. I was too obsessed with finding a monster in a monster's form. I wasn't looking for a wolf in sheep's clothing. Not all creatures can take human-like form. I didn't know what to expect on this case, so I guess I expected the obvious. I expected the easy, the simple, and I expected wrong. And my expectations had cost two people their lives, and if James didn't make it, three people would've gone down.

I thumbed the hammer back on the revolver. "You're the Ifrit I've been looking for," I said, my voice dropping to a sharp whisper. My finger was now placing a bit of pressure on the trigger. "I think I'm going to put a bullet in your head," I said quietly.

Ortiz didn't move. She would've been motionless save for her tightening her grip on the fire poker and bringing it in front of her, holding it at chest level.

That's when something weird happened. Okay, weirder than being chased by a golden tiger across the streets of New York, being caught naked in Norman's townhouse by a Wraith and pretty much everything else that had happened. The girl, the Ifrit had a small smile on her lips.

I had a gun on her, and she was smiling.

It's always disconcerting when a person, or monster in this case, has a smile on their face when you have a revolver pointed at them.

Her voice was exceptionally clear when she spoke. No more whimpering and tears, but rather a deep, smoky voice. "Well," she said, sighing, "it was inevitable."

I nearly leapt back when I saw her—its—eyes. They were smoldering! Not like oozing with sexuality and come-hither eyes; they were on frickin' fire! Her pupils dilated, taking up most of her eyes, darkening into pools of onyx. I could actually see lines of ashy gray and fiery orange flecks throughout her eyes. It gave them the appearance of two pieces of charcoal that were on fire. Even after seeing that, I didn't move the gun from her face. I was seriously freaked out, but I had a gun in her face. I had the gun.

Not like it did all that much to terrify her.

"Yes, I seem to remember killing you—*twice,* in fact," she said in her smoky, husky tone. She placed heavy emphasis on twice. Guess she was counting the time she tried to tear my soul out of Norman's body... Well, she failed.

I sucked in a breath and held it.

"Norman?"

I threw Ortiz a quick glance, but couldn't meet her eyes.

I was afraid of this, of her finding out how not normal I am, at least before I'd had the chance to explain it to her.

Ortiz bristled. "What is she talking about? She's...killed you?"

"Ooooh," said the Ifrit with a delightful peal of laughter. Her volcanic eyes beamed brightly, and she kicked her legs like a little child. "He didn't tell you, did he? Yes, I killed him once—twice in fact. He should be dead now, but obviously something happened there," she said, pushing her face against the barrel of the revolver. "Tell me what happened, Norman?" she said with a predatory smile.

"Norman, what's going on?" Ortiz's tone was nervous, and taking a bit of an edge to it. "What the hell is going on?"

"Oh, yes," laughed the Ifrit. "Tell her, Norman. Tell the human what's going on. I must admit. I'm curious as well. Maybe if you tell, if you're a good boy, I'll end you quickly. You can see that mortal cow... What was her name ag—"

The reverberating sound of the gunshot filled the small room. The Ifrit's beautiful face rocked back violently, causing her body to fall back across the table. Ortiz swore, having jumped when the shot went off.

"Marsha," I said in a deadly whisper. "Her name was Marsha."

Chapter Eighteen

"Is…is it over?" Ortiz asked in a quiet voice.

I shut my eyes and released a deep, shaky sigh. "Yeah," I said, my voice coming out a bit rougher than expected. "It's over."

Ortiz pursed her lips. "I thought the plan was to seal that thing up. I didn't think it would be so easy to kill."

I shrugged.

"Didn't your contact say something about trapping it?" she pressed.

"Guess he was wrong," I said dryly.

"And…" she began, in obvious confusion. "What was all that stuff about you dying?"

"Yeah, we'll talk. I promised, so yeah, we'll talk." I sighed, heading past her and towards the door.

Ortiz grabbed me by the arm. "What about him," she said with a nod towards James.

"Leave him."

"You can't be serious?" Ortiz sounded a bit scandalized.

"He brought this on himself," I replied, still sounding rather harsh.

"But—"

I waved her off. "But nothing. He's the reason three people are dead, and that's counting only the employees!" I said, my voice picking up a great deal of heat. "He's the reason I was nearly assassinated by a Wraith, devoured by a tiger, and trapped in a burning building with you. People died in that fire, Ortiz. People died!"

She looked at me with a stubborn expression, but I could see a hint of sadness in her eyes. When she spoke, it was a gentle whisper. "At least call an ambulance."

"Fine," I said begrudgingly. I shrugged my way out of her grip and headed for the door.

"Uh, Norman?" she said, getting my attention once again.

I looked back over my shoulder at her. "Yeah?"

She pointed at the Ifrit's corpse. There was a small wisp of smoke from the center of her face; right where I had shot her. "That doesn't seem right..." she said trailing off into silence.

"No," I murmured, "it doesn't." I approached the body sprawled lifelessly over the table. As I looked down at the Ifrit's limp figure, I noticed something else. The bullet had gone straight through her, but there wasn't a hole in the wall behind her. I had shot her with a .357 at point blank, yet the round hadn't impacted the wall behind her?

Where the hell did it go?

I raised Ortiz's snub-nosed revolver and aimed it at the Ifrit's still chest and was about to squeeze the trigger.

The body surged forwards, both of her hands clamping around my forearm and wrist with pressure akin to hydraulic machinery. In one smooth movement she pushed down and forwards, forcing me to kneel with my arm bent backwards, the pistol pressing against my chin. It hurt too much to scream. My teeth ground against each other as I struggled.

She was still smiling; the hole in the middle of her face wasn't really a hole anymore. It looked like a tunnel that was flooding...with molten hot lava. The dark hole in her face filled with the fiery hot liquid, spouting bits of smoke and steam. The lava coalesced inside the empty spot like a filler. Within an instant, the hole in her face was perfectly healed, restoring the missing nose and everything else that was blasted away by Ortiz's hand cannon.

When she spoke, her voice changed from smoky to downright disturbingly baritone—and distorted. It was the voice I had heard in Norman's office. "Well, that was unpleasant," she said, applying even more pressure on my arm. The barrel of the gun dug deeper into the soft tissue beneath my chin. "What's that human expression?" she mused. "Ah, yes, a taste of your own medicine." She released one of her hands from my forearm and slid it over the hand that was still on the trigger. Her other hand applied an excruciating amount of pressure on my arm, keeping it in place.

A seductive smile slid across her mouth as a slender finger slipped into the trigger guard next to mine. I squeezed my eyes shut.

"Bang," she whispered.

The gunshot was loud. This was like the bajillionth time a gun had gone off near my head. My arm wrenched as the shot went off. I was hurled several feet back, opening my eyes as I crashed and slid along the floor. The Ifrit was howling, holding her left arm with her right hand. Blood and steam billowed out of a long gash in it.

"I don't think so, bitch!" growled an irate Ortiz. She held the silver, blood-encrusted poker I had given her earlier. Standing a few feet in front of me, she clutched the thing in both hands like a club.

I struggled to my feet a bit groggily. "What happened?"

"I charged her just as she was about to pull the trigger. She saw me, threw you, I hit her and the gun went off," she rattled off in rapid succession.

"Ah," I said as I stood up straighter. "Guess that answers whether or not that thing works."

"Guess so," Ortiz replied.

The Ifrit's eyes were really blazing now; the intense, fiery lines that had filled her pupils were spreading into her eyelids. The skin around her eyes looked like it was beginning to crack. Lines ran through them like miniature flaming fissures. She was absolutely seething. "You dare strike me?" she roared in a voice that reverberated around the room. Hell, the artifacts and doodads on the tables were shaking!

Ortiz's face began to lose its color; she was going to lose it again, like she had with the Elemental. I reached out and gave her free hand a reassuring squeeze. "Hey," I said softly, "keep it together. We'll get this bitch together." Ortiz gave me a nervous glance, but her jaw hardened and she gave me a firm, resolute nod.

Good.

The Ifrit flung her arms at her sides like an impetuous child. "You touch silver and blood to me! To me?" she roared again. Her voice was giving my ears a serious beating; it was like a boom box inside my ear canal. "Mortal sow!" she hissed at Ortiz.

"Sow?" Ortiz said casting me a curious glance.

"It means female swine," I replied as neutrally as I could.

Ortiz's eyebrows shot up in surprise. "Pig?" Her features hardened even more. "The bitch just called me a pig?"

"Seems that way," I answered, still in a carefully neutral tone.

Ortiz didn't respond, vocally at least. Her eyes narrowed and nostrils flared.

The tension was palpable—seriously. Ortiz had cut the Ifrit, and the Ifrit had called Ortiz a pig... I'm surprised the entire room didn't spontaneously explode.

I decided to stick my neck out and break the tension; I'm smart like that. Okay, suicidal. "So...uh, why aren't you dead?" I asked the Ifrit.

She cocked a quizzical eyebrow.

"You're in the form of a mortal," I continued. "Last time I checked, if a Djinn impersonates a human, they play by human rules. Headshot equals dead."

The Ifrit threw her head back and howled with laughter. "Djinn?" she mocked, "I am Ifrit!"

Ifrits are big on pride, real egotists; they believe they are the greatest, oldest, best, entitled, and all that childish jazz. I figured I'd get to its head; mess with its pride a bit. "Uh, what's the difference? You're all just glorified magical gofers," I said with a mild shrug. "Go for this, go for that. I snap, you get it, right?"

Apparently that was pushing things a bit too far.

You know those cartoons where a character gets so mad that they start shooting smoke out of their nostrils? Well, that's pretty much what started happening here.

Her entire face turned a horrendous red. The fiery lines around her eyes expanded, spreading into her cheeks, forehead, and temples. The damn thing's face looked like a bright red piece of pottery with a helluva lot of cracks. Chalk it up to bad craftsmanship.

"Cockroach," she hissed.

I turned to Ortiz with an expression of mock indignation on my face. "Cockroach?" I exclaimed. "The bitch just call me a cockroach?"

Although her tone was as neutral as my own had been earlier, Ortiz smirked. "It seems that way."

"I am not some slave, or something to be bound and used—I am Ifrit!" she spat, as if saying that explained everything.

"Yada yada yada. You still haven't explained why you're not dead. I mean, a normal Djinni in mortal form wouldn't be having this conversation. You'd be, you know—*poof*— smoked. Get it?" I said with a bit of a chortle.

"I. Am. Ifrit!" it repeated…again, much louder than before. Its basso, booming voice shook the room up some more; it hurt to hear it. Ortiz swayed a fraction, but it was still noticeable to me. Her arms fidgeted a bit, resisting the urge to drop the fire poker and cover her ears. Good thing, too. I wouldn't have been comfortable with her dropping the only thing that could hurt the Ifrit, maybe even gank it.

"Broken record much? Repeat, repeat, repeat," I quipped with an exaggerated sigh. "How's about you answer my question, huh? Why aren't you dead?"

"I am Ifrit," she began.

Oh my god. I groaned. On the inside, of course. I didn't want to be roasted alive.

"The rules of Djinn do not apply to us, to me. I am above them," she said practically dripping venom and hate at this point. It was obvious she didn't think much of other Djinns. Her face was all scowly like. Her lips peeled back in a really unattractive manner.

"Look at you, bad girl! Above the rules and everything," I said in a mocking tone. I arched an eyebrow, giving her a sideways look.

She was fuming now. Her entire posture was tense. I could see her chest heaving in her anger as she stood there sneering at me.

"So, bullets. They can't kill you, but they hurt, right?" I asked.

The question caught her off guard. She shot me a confused and unfocused look.

I unloaded the rest of the revolver into her chest—center mass for the win. Each round tore into her with ease, the impact of the rounds staggering her, jolting her body until she was up against the wall. She fell slowly, her upper body slumped against the wall, leaving a trail of…well, it was certainly not blood. It was some viscous-looking, orangey fluid that was giving off steam, but it wasn't setting fire to anything. That was good.

"Grab him," I said to Ortiz, nodding to James. He was now prone on his back and looking like he was going to pass out. Ortiz rushed forwards, helping me get James and half carry, half drag him towards the door.

We actually made it to the door, and were just stepping out when the inevitable happened.

"Mortal!" she said like a whip crack.

I sighed. "Of fucking course," I muttered sullenly. I stopped supporting James, leaving the brunt of his weight on Ortiz, not that there was much weight on him at the moment. He was a living scarecrow, and the living part didn't seem like it was going to be very long.

"Norman, what are you doing?"

"Take him and keep going," I answered.

"Take him where? We won't get far like this," she replied.

"I'm going to stay here and stall her. Get him to the guard's desk. Hide him there."

"It's going to be a long walk there, especially like this—

"

"Then I'll have to do a good job stalling her," I said, turning back to face the Ifrit who was rising shakily to her feet. Guess the bullets did hurt a bit, even if they didn't do as much harm as the poker.

"Norman..." Ortiz hesitated. "You want the—"

"Keep it," I said, knowing damn well that she was talking about the fire poker. "You might need it. You know, in case..."

She understood what I meant and hobbled off with James slumped against her. I gently shut the door behind her.

"So..." I said slowly. "Just you and me, huh, Hot Stuff?"

"I'm going to enjoy roasting your flesh until it crackles. I'll do my best to keep you alive so you can feel me peeling it off, bit by bit," she finished in an uncharacteristic whisper.

Most people would've been frickin' terrified after hearing that. I'm not really a person though, so I wasn't terrified in the slightest. I was fucking flippin' out! That was all kinds of nasty.

I suppressed a shudder. "Wow, that's an awful lot of work. I thought your kind were big on the whole killing us with ironic deaths sort of thing."

"I'm willing to make an exception for you," she purred. It was strange, and awful, hearing that come out of a young girl's mouth with a supernatural boom box echoing voice.

The bullet holes in her chest were healing. I could see it happening through the torn fabric of her shirt, not that there was much there to begin with. Her shirt was more slash with bits of fabric than fabric with bits of slashes in it anyways.

"It was foolish of you to let the woman leave with the silver weapon. You couldn't stop me with it anyways, but now..." she said, letting the words hang in the air as she started doing something really unexpected. She leisurely slipped out of the leather jacket and brought her hands up to her chest, clawing at the scanty fabric.

"Uh…yeah," I gulped. "That's me. Foolish."

She tore the shreds of fabric from her body, standing naked from the waist up. Her taut midsection completely was bare, as well as her breasts. A seductive smile played across her lips. It would've been an attractive sight if her face hadn't looked like a piece of pottery held together by superglue. Then there was the fact that her eyes were now twin pools of flames.

Creepy.

"So…uh, I guess the only way to stop you now is to get you back in the bottle, huh?" I said weakly.

Her smile widened as she leaned forwards, giving me a fantastic view of her chest as she began slipping off her boots. Her smile grew further "You won't find squeezing me back into my vessel an easy task."

"Well, you know, if it were easy, ah…" I trailed off. Wow, I was really, ah, well, you know, taking in the sights.

She slipped off her pants, making quite a show of it. Soon she was completely naked before me. Like really naked, like, wow…naked.

It's not often I have an attractive woman giving me a strip tease, even if she's a primordial monster that just threatened to cook and filet me. Okay, maybe I shouldn't have been entranced by it as much as I was.

I blame my anatomy.

Then again, so does every guy.

"Hmm," she mused, putting a finger up to her lips. "How to burn you without killing you?"

"Uh, well, you know what they say about having your cake and eating it, so uh, maybe we settle with one out of two?"

She tilted her head sideways, and her smile widened to an impossible length, which was really creepy. "Mmm," was all that left her mouth.

"Let's go with the not killing me part, and maybe being a good girl and hopping back into your vessel?" I suggested.

The slightest flicker passed over her face. No sudden movement of her head or anything else, just a swift glance with her eyes to the table on the far left of the room. It was too fast to notice. Well, for most people, I mean.

I followed her glance subtle-like. It was one of the tables I had looked over when I had first met James. What was oblivious to me at first was now a big glaring neon sign. Hidden in plain sight, on the table, was the Ifrit's vessel; the oil lamp on its side like it had been discarded. I know it was such a cliché, but then again, most of these clichés and stereotypes started with a little bit of truth. Djinn are known for being trapped inside brass lamps because that's really what they were trapped in long ago.

Unfortunately for me, the knowledge on how to trap a Djinn was lost a long time ago, at least as far as I was concerned. All I had was the knowledge that I had to find a way to get James to make an unselfish wish. A wish that's sheer contradictory nature clashed with the purpose, the energy, that fueled the Ifrit.

Water and fire, if you will. The act of doing that would banish the Ifrit into its vessel, provided I got my hands on it, convinced James to make the wish, and, oh yeah, managed to find a way to scrawl a seal on it, permanently trapping the bitch. Even if I managed to do most of that, I had no way of actually sealing it. It's not as if I could shove a cork in the hole and I certainly didn't have a Sharpie on me to scribble the seal.

Well, one problem at a time.

"Someone's found my vessel. Oh dear," she said coyly, which sounded so odd in her freakishly deep and resonating voice.

"Uh yeah, so," I said snapping my fingers several times. "You wanna hop back in and call it a day?"

It seems that snapping your fingers like you're giving orders isn't the smartest thing to do to a creature that's been bound into servitude and harbors immense resentment towards the human species.

Her features twisted into a really ugly—okay, uglier—scowl. "No. Now—what is the expression? We dance!"

Uh oh.

She sauntered forward at a relaxed pace, making a big show of it. Her hips swayed and her face, well...it was falling to pieces, literally. She was, I think for lack of a better term, shedding. The lines running through her face burst into long lengths of flames, causing the skin to fall off in bits and pieces. Thin, long shreds began slowly and gracefully falling to the floor, swaying and dancing as they did. The pieces that fell looked like glued-on bits of skin, paper-thin, cindering around the edges and smoldering as they shriveled up and burned away to nothing.

I could see her face, her real face I assumed, as the rest of the skin fell away. Her hair lengthened and condensed into thicker locks. It shifted into varying hues of reds, oranges, and yellows as it fell to the small of her back. The skin beneath her was a burnished red. It shone in certain places, even under the dim lighting of the room.

Her ears elongated, tapering off near the ends. The twin pools of fire that were her eyes became two opaque orbs of solid jet black.

Her thin, black lips spread into a massive shark-like smile, filled with jagged, pointed teeth. They looked like shards of razor sharp obsidian, matching the color as well.

This was seriously disturbing. She was looking at me like a piece of meat. Not the way a woman looks at you as in the whole seductive, sexual nature sort of way. She looked like she actually wanted to eat me.

A devilishly long and forked tongue snaked its way out of her mouth, sliding its way down her still human-looking neck and ending up near her chest. It hung there for a second, before trailing its way back up, taking the, um, scenic route, around her breasts and up to her mouth, where she made the obviously noticeable action of licking her lips.

Normally, that would've have been a sensual and arousing thing for many a guy to see. Well, minus the whole forked tongue and demonic face part. In my case however, it triggered thoughts along the lines of, *I'm so gonna get eaten.* Not exactly what I'd like to happen when trapped in a room with a naked woman. Well, two-thirds of a naked woman, once you gloss over the monstrous head with razor-sharp teeth.

"My, what big teeth you have," I said with a nervous laugh.

Her eyes gleamed. "Oh, I know this one. All the better to eat you with!" she said in her booming deep voice.

Yup, so gonna get eaten! Who knew the Ifrit had time to brush up on nursery tales?

No sooner than I had finished that thought, the rest of her body became riddled with those fiery lines I had seen on her face prior to it falling apart. Her skin began splitting violently, shreds of flesh began tearing apart and falling to the ground in the same manner it had with her face.

I've heard of trying to shed some pounds before, but that's taking things to a whole new level.

All of her human skin fell and burned away, revealing a body that wasn't all that different from the mortal form she had taken. Her breasts and torso looked the same, only they matched the burnished red of her face now. Well, that and her breasts were partially covered in glistening, black scales. Her torso looked no different, except for the new paint job. The arms became slender, with forearms sporting long, bony protrusions, as were her elbows. They looked like spikes made from volcanic rock. Her fingers had lengthened and become skeletal, the tips tapered into sharp points. There was definitely flesh there, but it looked like bone, which was odd.

She studied her hands as if she hadn't seen them in a long time. Well, it was probable she hadn't, not in that form anyway. She flexed them several times, holding one in front of her face for inspection, like some women do after a trip to the nail salon.

Her legs had significantly lengthened; she was now as tall as I was. Her kneecaps were now some irregularly shaped rock, bone-like lumps that matched the color of her jet black eyes. The feet looked like something out of Jurassic Park—very raptor-esque, elongated toes with very sharp talons at the end. One of them looked like it was hinged, a curved switchblade.

Great…

Then there was the tail. Yeah, she had a thin, yet powerful-looking, whip of a tail. More of those obsidian-looking protrusions ran along it. They started from the base of her skull and ran down the entirety of her spine, right to the tip of that mean-looking extra appendage of hers. She gave me a demonstration of it too—how considerate—as she cast it out at a nearby table. The sound of it was identical to a whip crack; it cut clean through the dense wood.

"I really should've kept that poker," I muttered miserably below my breath.

Chapter Nineteen

The air around her shimmered. I could see waves like the kind when you're stuck in traffic during a heat wave. The temperature in the room went up. Man, it went up a helluva lot! It hadn't even been a minute and I could already feel myself sweating. My clothes were clinging to me.

She opened her razor-lined, shark-like maw, and I saw inside her throat. It looked like the pit of a volcano. She leaned forwards and exhaled.

"Holy shit!" I yelped as I dove out of the way. A superheated blast of air glanced the area between my neck and shoulder. My clothes weren't burned, but my skin certainly was. It felt as if someone had touched a red-hot skillet to my neck.

The Ifrit tilted its head from side to side, surveying what she had done before letting out a boisterous laugh. "Is it hot in here, or is it just me?"

"You"—I panted—"it's really just you." Her footsteps made a noticeable sound as she crept up behind me with an air of confidence. I didn't bother looking at her, but eyed her vessel, and something else I had overlooked. I lunged forward as her clawed hands reached out for me, and I grabbed the Shamshir I had seen earlier. In one swift motion, I turned, slashing blindly at her outstretched hand.

I missed the hand, but the blade hit her square in the forearm, cutting into it before passing through and leaving me with half a sword.

The other half of the blade, the top pointy part, the important part clattered to the ground uselessly. Did I mention the section where the blade had severed was melting? The portion I still held was melting too; a thick molten-orange metal sludge ran down the length of the ruined Shamshir.

"Well," I sighed, "that sucks."

The Ifrit held up her arm, looking rather curiously at the gash in her forearm—the gash that was now healing. She looked at it like it was nothing more than an insignificant mosquito bite, something to be noticed, itched and then forgotten about. I guess in a way it was just that.

That wide, shark-like smile returned to her face. "Expecting something different to happen?" she asked, showing rows of obsidian, dagger-like teeth.

I suppressed another shiver. "Yeah, a few things," I said sullenly. "You know, hoping I got lucky and you'd have half an arm? Maybe some divine intervention and you were just smoted, smited, smitten? Is that the word, smitten? Anyways I was hoping that you know, poof and—"

Her claw-like hand darted out, grabbed me by the throat, and lifted me off the ground. Her sharpened digits dug into the soft tissue of my neck.

"Glurck!" I gasped as I struggled against her vice-like grip. It wasn't doing any good though, and worse than that, my neck was starting to burn! Never mind the fact that her grip was so hard her claws were actually drawing blood. Her hand was emitting heat. Being touched by it felt like sticking my neck inside a furnace. I could feel my skin blistering, and it hurt—bad. It was worse than sunburn, and I was getting really, really thirsty.

"Oops," she said with a small laugh, releasing her grip on me. I fell to the ground, landing in a crumpled heap. "I forgot. I promised to burn you without killing you, didn't I? Seems I'm a little too enthusiastic."

"Yeah," I rasped, trying to rub my throat, but a single touch caused it to erupt in pain, never mind the fact it felt like all the saliva in mouth had dried up. She was toying with me. She could kill me oh so easily, and she knew it, but she was going to take her sweet time doing it.

Lucky me…

I coughed several times as I struggled to get up; my throat was so dry that the coughing made things worse. Each one felt like it was tearing my throat apart. The pain from that, coupled with the burns on my neck, would have been enough to cause most people to scream at the very least.

I'm no stranger to pain. I've been beaten up, shot, burned, hit by vehicles...the list goes into infinity. I can tolerate a lot. That's not bragging—it's fact. This, however, was unbearably painful. If I could've screamed, I would've, but I was struggling to talk, so screaming was out of the question. Hell, my coughs were killing me. What would screaming have done?

"No clever retort?" she asked with amusement.

The bitch was enjoying this.

"What's that expression? Cat got your tongue?" Her ear-splitting laugh echoed inside the room.

I told her to go fuck herself, except it came out more like the sound a pining dog makes. It was more like a really high-pitched wheeze or a really bad whistle.

Talking seemed not to be an option, at least for the moment. If the fight went on for a bit, then I would probably heal enough to talk, not that I wanted the fight to be drawn out. I'm not a fan of losing, and I'm definitely not keen on having my ass kicked into and in overtime.

So I decided to talk with my fists. I balled up my left fist and swung as hard as I could. It connected with the Ifrit's jaw. Her head rocked fast and hard to the side. The impact caused her to stumble a bit. I know how to throw a punch. I was inside an Olympic-level boxer once, not to mention all the years of throwing them in the first place.

Of course, I also have memory issues, some more severe than others because I had forgotten all too quickly what had happened to my throat. The second I finished following through on my punch, I was yanking it back in pain. My knuckles and fingers were scalded. A brief second of contact, and my fist was burned.

The Ifrit righted itself in a leisurely manner. My punch

apparently served only to stagger her, not causing any real harm. She made a clucking sound. "You don't learn very well, do you, human?"

No, no I really don't, I thought.

Without warning, all of my breath was knocked out of me as she spun with supernatural speed and grace. Her whip-like tail snapped into me, sending me soaring towards the wall.

Oww! Was the only thought capable of going through my head as I impacted the wall and fell to the table below, scattering the artifacts everywhere. One item managed to stay on the table though. The dull, brass oil lamp, and it was only an arm's reach away.

I stretched for it, snatching up the Ifrit's vessel. That elicited a helluva reaction from the Ifrit.

"My vessel!" she roared, body flaring in anger. I could see her skin erupt into white and blue flames before they subsided. After her skin returned to normal, clouds of smoke hung around her, but I got an idea of just how pissed she was when she swung her tail overhead, bringing it crashing down on the table I was currently lying on.

I rolled out of the way as wood shattered and splintered, but the sheer impact jarred my body. Man, this chick was violent! The second the table split in two, gravity did its thing and caused me to roll towards the now collapsed middle of the table. I fell once again to the floor.

She let out an incoherent scream as she reached out for me with both arms.

Fuck that!

I scampered to my feet and away from her grasp. I lurched towards the door. I swung it open and then slammed it shut behind me.

Now, I'm no coward. I wasn't running so much as luring the Ifrit to a larger section of the museum where I would have more room to maneuver. It's called tactics. I ran down the length of the hallway and into the massive storage section, looking around frantically for a place to duck behind.

On the far side of the room were a series of massively long, but not so high, containers. I sprinted towards them, diving over the top and landing behind them. I scrambled up and against the backsides of the containers, keeping my profile low, so when the Ifrit passed by she wouldn't be able to see me.

That's not hiding by the way. It's obtaining a secure position from where to launch an ambush. Whether or not I actually launch one is irrelevant.

The sound of water hitting a hot skillet filled my ears repeatedly; it was in sync with how her footsteps sounded. The Ifrit was drawing closer.

"Where are you?" boomed its voice. "I'm not in the mood for a hunt."

I held back the grave temptation to yell back "Marco!" Wisdom triumphed over my witty sense of humor; besides, it wasn't like I could really yell at the moment anyway.

The hissing sound of pressurized steam got louder. The Ifrit was really close now. I shouldn't have hid there, I should've kept going through the room, but I needed to buy Ortiz as much time as I could.

"Are those crates fireproof?" asked the Ifrit.

Shit! How? I wondered as I jumped to my feet and started running.

The crates exploded with the force of a grenade. I knew what that felt like, having once been near one.

I landed several feet away. My entire body throbbed and part of my midsection stung horribly. There was a large piece of wood, from the crate no doubt, protruding from my side. I didn't try to remove the wooden shard that was currently making me into a Graves shish kabob. Hell, I couldn't even move, so I lay there in agony, blinking my eyes and trying not to twitch. Everything was just hurting.

"Aww, poor little human!" she cooed in false sympathy as she sauntered towards me, clearly savoring my pointy predicament. She stood over me now, her hellish features blurring in and out of focus, which tends to happen when you've got a jagged piece of former two by four going through you.

I reached for the piece of wood impaling me, hoping to pull it out and try stabbing her with it. I was itching to see how she'd liked it.

Being the kind of monster she was, she thought it best to lend a hand. "Here, let me assist you with that," she said sweetly, grasping the large piece of wood. It smoldered the second she touched it. As disconcerting as that was, what she did next is what really pushed me over the edge. In one swift movement, she wrenched the wooden shrapnel out of me, tearing it out so forcefully that I made another discovery.

Minutes ago my throat had been burned, preventing me from making any sort of coherent noise. Turns out that I had healed from some of the damage already, enough to let out a vocal expression of my pain. "Gaaaaaaaaah!" I screamed. That hurt, and I am an expert on getting hurt. When I say something hurts, it really hurts.

"Ooooooh!" she said merrily, sounding like a child who had just opened a Christmas present. "That looked excruciating."

It was...

She was really getting off on hurting me, but then that's what did it for Ifrits. Getting us to kill ourselves or doing it to us the old fashioned way. Either worked for them.

"Let's fix that for you," she said, her booming voice making my head spin even more. She was so close, not to mention I had just endured a minor explosion. She reached out towards my gaping wound. I tried to squirm away from her, but the most I was able to do was flop in place like a weak fish. Her index and middle fingers dug their way into my injury. Heat radiated from them, burning my insides quickly and painfully.

She was cauterizing my wound!

This was far more painful than having the wooden shrapnel yanked out of my torso. Cauterizing a wound this severe is like jumping into an Antarctic pool of water...naked. The second it happens, your body goes into shock and everything contracts horribly. Then there's the pain. The kind of pain that's so excruciating, it's literally mind-numbing. You don't know what to do. You can't think, and it's so painful you can't even scream; you endure it in silence. By endure it, I mean not pass out because it's really tempting and most likely to happen.

All of that happened in an instant; unbearable pain and heat as she as pulled out of my wound. "There," she said, oh so smugly. "I promised I would keep you alive until I've had my way with you."

I told her to fuck off; it came out as, "Gah!"

She bent over at the waist, bringing her obsidian eyes mere inches from mine. I gazed into the empty pools of black. "I'm sorry, what did you say? It was...incoherent." Although her tone was neutral, those demonically black eyes glistened with delight.

I could feel the heat emanating from her face. I felt it wise not to piss her off this close to my borrowed visage. Instead, I asked her how she knew where I was. "How?" I managed to wheeze.

"How did I know you were hiding behind those?" she said, interpreting my single syllable question perfectly as she nodded to the demolished crates.

I gave a weak nod.

"My vessel," she said simply. "I can sense it."

Great. I was walking around with an ancient magical GPS device.

The Ifrit stepped back and allowed me to get back to my feet. It took a while, but I was able to wobble to a standing position. That's when she swiped at me with her tail. I didn't try to dive out of the way. I was too weak. Nope, I simply went limp and fell to the ground. Her tail snapped harmlessly over me.

Holding on tight to the Ifrit's vessel, I crawled away as fast as I could. She must've found the sight amusing, because she didn't pursue me with as much gusto as I thought she might. I kept crawling, breaking into a sweat from the effort, while the Ifrit ambled behind, taking her sweet time.

As I continued reenacting the military's infamous belly crawl towards the hall leading back to the museum, I noticed a series of appliances nearby. One of those heavy-duty, deep-set metal sinks, with all manner of faucets to clean yourself up. Nearby was a small pan with a hose attached to it, one of those safety eye wash things for when you get something in your eye you're not supposed to. Next to it was one of those safety showers, in case you spill something hazardous on you, and next to that, mounted on the wall, a fire extinguisher.

Thank you OSHA.

OSHA is the Occupational Safety and Health Administration. They're the ones responsible for making sure every workplace, ranging from a tiny auto repair shop, to a massive museum, are kept safe. They're also the ones who make sure those workplaces have things like fire extinguishers everywhere—to put out fires or, smother demonic, fiery, primordial monsters.

Either or.

I pushed myself up, teetering as I tried to right myself. Once I was able to do that, I lurched towards the extinguisher. Pulling the extinguisher from its resting place, I whirled around. Okay, it was more of an awkward spin. I ripped out the stupid health and safety pin, and aimed the extinguisher at the Ifrit.

She kept advancing, a calm expression on her face despite the fact I had the bane of all things fire in my hands—the almighty foamy fire extinguisher.

"Uh, you might want to stop now," I panted, waving the hose-like attachment at her. I continued motioning, accentuating the fact that I had something that could really put a hurtin' on her in my hands.

The Ifrit stopped. Wow, and all I had to do was ask? Who knew? She regarded me with a neutral expression, then out of nowhere, her black lips slowly spread into a gigantic smile. "Go ahead. Make my day, mortal."

Oh wow, seriously? A Dirty Harry reference? Did she

get cable service all those years trapped in her vessel? "Okay, I'll call. Do you feel lucky? Well, do ya, punk?" I snarled in my best Clint Eastwood voice.

"I most assuredly do," she purred.

"Enough of this coy crap," I growled, depressing the lever on the extinguisher. I aimed the rubber hose and wide, bell-like attachment towards her. She was doused completely in fire suppressant foam from head to toe, waiting for the inevitable shrieking and writhing in agony.

Yeah…that part never really came.

She stood there in a mountain of foam, looking like a giant mound of snow, but that's all. The Ifrit didn't so much as twitch beneath it all. The foam around her eyes vanished when she blinked a couple of times. The pools of jet black contrasted greatly with the rest of her foam-covered body.

"Well…" I said as my face contorted in confusion. "Um, that wasn't supposed to happen."

Her shark-like smile returned, black lips and obsidian teeth appearing from underneath the foam. "Wasn't it?" she asked in delight.

I sighed. "Not really, no."

"What were you expecting to happen?" she asked, still smiling. She was clearly overjoyed by my continual failure to stop her. Hell, I was having trouble just trying to hurt her.

"Oh, I dunno," I said, shrugging nonchalantly. "I was kind of hoping that you'd be on the floor writhing, screaming and twitching in pure agony."

"Ah," she said understandingly, "like the Elemental?" She chuckled at that last bit.

"Kind of," I replied flatly.

She laughed again, even louder, "I am Ifrit."

Not again. Seriously, the supernatural seem to have a broken record disorder or something.

"The Elemental is nothing," she said disdainfully. "A tool, a mere shadow of what I am. Nothing more than a means to an end."

"I thought it was your offspring in a way?" I asked.

"Offspring?" she scoffed, "A tool. One that failed and

nothing more."

"Wow, you're a shoe-in for 'Mother of the Year,' aintchya?"

She ignored the jibe, and the temperature in the room took a sudden spike, way hotter than it had been in the small room before. I was starting to get dizzy—well, dizzier—just standing near her. What really shocked me though, was what was happening to the foam covering her body. It began to liquefy, sliding off her body and pooling on the floor around her feet.

The heat was becoming unbearable. I was already in bad shape, and now I was sweating out the precious fluids I needed. My throat was beginning to feel dry again.

"What do you plan on doing now?" she asked with a Cheshire-like grin on her face.

I managed a weak smile and shrugged. "Dunno. Something like this—" I grabbed the extinguisher by the hose and swung it as hard as I could at her head. Though the extinguisher wouldn't do any real harm, that wasn't the point. The sheer impact caused the Ifrit's head to snap sideways. It hit her with enough force to cause her to collapse to the ground. The extinguisher was crushed on impact however. The metal was now slag, but with enough material and heft to it for me to lift the melting extinguisher and slam it back across her head again, just to make sure she'd stay down for a bit.

The second strike caused the can to become a complete pile of molten material, but it did the job. The Ifrit was flat on the floor—for the moment. I capitalized on the moment and hobbled my sorry, beaten, borrowed ass down the hall, towards the main part of the museum, praying the Ifrit would stay down long enough for me to reach Ortiz.

I had limped halfway down the hall when there was a headache inducing roar. Hell, the walls shook!

"Great," I muttered. "She's up."

I continued limping towards the door leading to the guard's desk. I barreled through the door. Alright, I fell into it, really hard, causing it to fling open. "Ortiz!" I shouted.

"Ortiz!"

I grabbed my sides as I struggled towards the guard's desk. The damage to my throat was definitely healing, but my sides were still aching. The worst of the pain had subsided however. "Ortiz!"

Chestnut brown hair popped into sight from behind the guard's desk. Ortiz's face came into view followed by the rest of her. Her eyes were worried. She stood there, clutching the silver, blood-encrusted poker, still gripping it in both hands like a baseball bat. "Norman?" she breathed, sounding shocked to see me. Her eyes drifted to my midsection, and they widened considerably. "What happened to you?"

"Long story. Hand it over, Slugger," I panted, nodding to the weapon in her hands.

She didn't leave the desk, but extended a single arm, holding the poker towards me.

I hobbled over to her, taking the weapon from Ortiz. I was going to need it. My hand trembled as I wrapped my grip around the spiked rod. Man, was I in rough shape. Well, technically I guess Norman's body was, but then again, I was in it and I was the one hurting.

Semantics suck.

Ortiz definitely took note of my bad condition because she looked me over with concern. "What happened to you?"

To which I repeated, "Long story. The Ifrit will be here any minute. No time for storytelling."

"Then make it a short one," she replied firmly.

I sighed. "Explosion, impalement, no longer impaled, she stuck a finger in me—"

"What!" exclaimed Ortiz in a mix of confusion and shock.

"Cauterized wound, painful, and now here we are playing twenty questions," I continued as if Ortiz hadn't interjected.

"Well you look like crap," Ortiz said seriously.

"Flatterer."

"I'm serious, Norman. You don't look like you're up for

this," she said firmly.

"I'm really not," I said wearily. "How's James doing?"

She pursed her lips, a worried look coming over her face. "You might want to take a look for yourself," she said softly.

I leaned on the top of the desk for support and walked gingerly around it to the other side. James was lying on the floor, huddled up in some sort of fetal position. He looked like hell—still emaciated, still elderly, and just frail. His breaths were long and shallow. If the Ifrit didn't kill him, well, he'd die soon enough from the looks of it.

I looked at Ortiz. "He say anything yet?"

"Lots, actually. Bits and pieces, some incoherent, some not," she replied.

"Any of it useful?"

Ortiz didn't respond. Her gaze transfixed on a sight behind me. Her eyes widened as she spoke. "What the hell is that?" she yelped, pointing a finger down the hall.

I turned around as fast as I could, my torso twinged a helluva lot. Coming down the hall towards us was the Ifrit. Her whip-like tail swayed from side to side, a predatory fixed smile on her face.

"That," I said sighing, "is round two."

Chapter Twenty

"Is…that who I think it is?" asked Ortiz, still in shock at the sight before her.

"Yeah," I said sullenly. "Yeah, it is."

"So…round two?"

"Yeah."

"Who won round one?" Ortiz asked.

"You know," I said, "the judges are still debating that one. I had my moments."

"That bad, huh?" she replied.

"Worse," I answered as the Ifrit drew closer, still taking her sweet time to cross the hall. It was like watching a lioness stalk wounded prey; no rush, just savoring the moment.

"What now, Norman?"

Without taking my eyes off the approaching Ifrit, I reached back and handed Ortiz the oil lamp. "Take it," I said hurriedly. "Keep it hidden. Keep it safe." There was no word of acknowledgement from Ortiz, just the sensation of the vessel being removed from my grasp. "And stay down." I walked back to the front of the desk and headed towards the Ifrit. I was seriously hoping to keep her as far away from Ortiz and James as I could.

"Norman!" called Ortiz.

I turned my head to look at her, but kept walking forwards. "What?"

"What do you want me to do?"

"Keep the vessel and James safe. Hell, see if you can get him to make a selfless wish. That'd be great," I told her.

"Norman," she said again, although now her tone had

changed to seriously worried.

"Yeah?"

Her lips pursed again, turning her face into an anxious mask. "Just...just don't die," she said.

I snorted, trying to show a bit of bravado. I didn't want to worry her any more than I had to. It's not like this was the moment to tell her that I die all the time. "Don't worry," I called back. "I won't," before muttering under my breath, "I hope."

Ortiz bit her lip nervously before giving me an assuring nod. I think the nod was more for herself than me, but I responded with a reassuring smile before she ducked behind the desk. I turned my attention back to the Ifrit, who had now stopped and was regarding me carefully. Her eyes were drawn to the silver in my hand.

I twirled the silver rod in my hand with a bit of a flourish, stretching out my other hand and taunting her with a beckoning gesture. It got her attention. She approached, albeit warily this time. Good. She knew I could hurt her, and, boy, did I intend to.

"You know it cannot kill me, mortal?" she said, more as a question.

"I'm not planning on killing you with it. I am, however, planning on beating the living crap out of you," I responded, a smile playing across my face.

I guess she didn't like that idea as much as I did, because she surged forwards with monstrous speed, swiping at me with her claws.

When at risk of fire or being mutilated by an ancient spirit of fire, what do you do?

Stop, drop, and roll.

Which is exactly what I did. Dropping to my knees, I rolled forward and under her strike. My torso panged as I performed the maneuver. It wasn't as bad as before though. Thank you, healing powers.

I bounded back up to my feet and swung the poker in a wide arc, connecting lightly with her abdomen, but still connecting. My strike grazed her. An extensive, shallow cut appeared across her midsection. She reeled back and howled in fury, smoke wafting from her injury.

"Insect!" she roared in pure fury. Her eyes glowed with an inner fire. The deep black eyes contained an orange glow now. She pressed one of her clawed hands to the cut running across her stomach, her body heaving as she breathed in deeply, and oh so angrily.

"Careful," I taunted, waving an admonishing finger at her. "You know the thing about insects, right?" I asked, giving her another flourish of the poker. "They can really sting." I grinned.

A deep, guttural sound burbled in her throat. One snarl later and she was lunging at me, her clawed hands swiping at me in a furious blur.

"Whoa!" I yelped, leaping back and narrowly dodging each swipe. "Was it something I said?"

Another snarl and another flurry of swipes followed.

I must've really riled her up. I have that effect on some people—monsters too.

She swiped at my face with one of her hands; I felt the heat emanating from her razor-sharp fingertips as they harmlessly sailed by, but I wasn't paying attention to her other hand. That's the one that got me. She swiped upwards, obsidian talons raking their way up my torso, chest, and nearly my throat. If I hadn't already been jumping back, her claws would've lodged deep in my intestines, rather than just leaving a series of lengthy gashes across my body.

I reeled back in pain, nearly dropping the silver weapon as I clutched my chest. My hands came away with nothing however. It was a stinging and searing pain, but there were no fresh trails of blood, just long scars. The heat from her body instantly seared the wounds shut. Not the most efficient way of killing someone. Cauterization stops the bleeding, so I guess she couldn't bleed me to death.

A silver lining of sorts. It's not much, but when you're in a business like mine, you have to look for some positives here and there. Otherwise, it's all gloom and doom.

"Good hit. Good hit." I panted. "Go again?" I goaded

her with another gesture of my hand. I was hoping the next exchange would go better than the last one. If I kept trading blow for blow with the Ifrit, I'd be dead soon.

Her tail whipped out lightning fast and towards my face, darting in and out like a rapier. I had trouble avoiding it. I danced around the tail every time it lashed out. It came in so fast that I didn't have time to follow up with any strikes of my own; it was like trying to swat a hornet.

Okay, I thought, *enough of this dodging crap!* I took a chance and dove at the Ifrit's legs. She sidestepped away, but not before I was able to jam the spike of the poker into her knee. The hard, crystalline protrusion atop her knee shattered as the spike pierced it. Her leg buckled, and she came toppling down, howling in fury. I wrenched the weapon out of her leg and did so aggressively, much like she had done to me with the piece of wood earlier. My doing so elicited another shriek from her.

"Serves you right, bitch," I muttered as I rose to my feet, taking a moment to recover my breath. The Ifrit was in a heap next to me, her hands clutching at her royally damaged knee. The wound wasn't closing up like when I had shot her with Ortiz's revolver earlier. Smoke and a black ichor substance oozed out of it.

That'll keep her down for a bit. I raced back over to the desk Ortiz and James were hiding behind. One of my hands grabbed my sides in an unconscious gesture. I wasn't hurting down there as much as I was before. I was healing quite nicely. Good. The sooner I got back to one hundred percent the better.

"Ortiz," I gasped, hunkering down besides her. "Get your phone out. Oh, and I need your lipstick—now!"

A bewildered look crossed her face. "You…what? Norman, now is not the time to act out some cross-dressing fantasy," she said. Still, she pulled out her phone and began digging through her veritable treasure trove of a purse with its bazillion items inside.

"Now's not the time to argue with the guy with the know-how and the plan on how to gank this thing," I snapped back in irritation.

"Oh," she began with mock surprise, before dryly adding, "so there is a plan? And here I thought you were making it up as you went along."

Technically, she was right. I was making it up as I went along. It's not as if I had a ready-made plan for if an ancient Ifrit was released and started murdering people. But as a paranormal investigator, it's always good to have a plan ready. If that's not possible, then give the impression you have a plan.

"Yes, I have a plan," I replied defensively.

"What might that be?" Ortiz asked as she continued rummaging through her clusterfuck of a purse.

"You give me the lipstick and find a way to make that photo my contact sent you pop back up on your phone," I said hurriedly, cautiously inching my head above the desk to take a quick peek at the Ifrit.

"The seal?" she asked as I was trying to catch a glimpse of the Ifrit over the desk.

"Yes, the seal," I replied a bit tersely, which caused her to stop her purse excavation and shoot me an angry glare. "Sorry," I murmured. "I'm a bit tense. Running out of time, 'bout to be immolated, you know?" I prattled as I watched the Ifrit moaning on the floor in agony, grasping her ruined knee. I let out a sigh of relief and turned back to Ortiz, who gave a sideways shake of her head, as well as letting out an exasperated huff of air before resuming her dig.

Ortiz's movement ceased, and she pulled her hand back out of her purse and with an air of triumph. "Here!" She shoved a small golden cylindrical container into my hands. Her fingers began a crazed dance across the icons on her phone. Finishing her maddened finger tap dance, she held it out in front of me. On the screen was an image of the seal Gnosis had sent me earlier, a seal rumored to have been crafted by King Solomon himself—the man who, in legend, discovered the way to trap Djinns in the first place.

The seal wasn't too complex in design. In the very center of it were a series of intersecting lines. Two lines ran perpendicular to one another, like a giant plus sign. Two more lines ran diagonally through the first two, a giant X of sorts. At both ends of every line was a unique symbol, and around the entirety of that, there was a circle, around which were ancient writings. Four distinct words that meant...something, I guess. Knowing the words wasn't important, at least not for this seal.

"Hold that for me, please," I said to Ortiz as I removed the top from the lipstick. There was a silver band around the middle of the container with some design. I gave it a quick twist and a deep strawberry red tube protruded from the container.

"Need me to tell you how to apply it?" Ortiz quipped with a rather neutral expression, but there was enough of a twitch in her lips to let me know she was stifling a smirk.

"Cute," I replied dryly. "Really cute."

"I can be," she said in exactly the same tone I had used when she was questioning me about the tiger fiasco.

I ignored her and held up the Ifrit's vessel before me. Taking the tip of the lipstick, I pressed it against the vessel and watched as the tip began to deform, leaving a reddish smear atop the brass.

"The hell are you doing?" asked a scandalized Ortiz.

I continued to scrawl a copy of the image from her phone onto the vessel, using her lipstick in lieu of a Sharpie. It's not like we had one. Make the best with what ya got.

"You couldn't have used a pen?" she muttered bitterly.

I did my best to copy the image as perfectly as I could. "Do you have permanent marker in your purse?" I asked.

"No, but—" she began.

"Lipstick it is, then," I said, holding up her now ruined lipstick to accentuate my point, before returning to finish drawing the seal.

"YSL," she muttered angrily under her breath.

"Uh, W.T.F?" I said slowly, emphasizing each letter as I drew the individual, diminutive symbols onto the seal.

"It's the brand. It's thirty dollars," Ortiz said edgily.

Now it was my turn to be scandalized. "Thirty bucks!" I

exclaimed, holding the lipstick up before my eyes in a useless attempt to see why it was so expensive. For the life of me, or in my case, for my many lives, I still can't figure out why makeup is *that* expensive. "It's like three ounces, Ortiz!"

She shrugged as if that was normal. It's not. Shaving cream is several dollars. I know, I've checked. I once had to use a can to kill something.

"Thirty dollars for a couple ounces. Drug dealers need to start selling Avon," I prattled to myself as I completed the seal. Well, nearly. It still needed to be empowered.

Ortiz let out a nervous bark of laughter. "Done?"

I waggled my in hand in a so-so gesture. "Sort of."

Ortiz fixed me with a blank stare, waiting for me to elaborate.

"It needs to be empowered. You know charged, like a battery in a phone," I explained. "Otherwise, it won't work and is essentially nothing more than lipstick."

"It *is* lipstick," Ortiz responded in a matter-of-fact tone.

"I know," I said impatiently. "But empowering a seal also serves to protect it. It's like laminating something. Otherwise, somebody could ruin the seal and render it useless."

"Isn't it useless now?" she asked.

"Yes," I replied through gritted teeth.

She raised a singular eyebrow expectantly.

"All seals need something to, well, activate them."

Ortiz snorted. "What, like magic words?"

I shrugged. "Some, yes. This, no. Seals are different, but they need to draw power from somewhere—this one needs blood."

"So...you're going to...?" Ortiz began, letting the question hang in the air.

I nodded, putting the vessel down on the floor and tossing Ortiz her ruined bit of lipstick.

"Thanks," she replied sarcastically, catching it and brusquely flinging it into her purse.

I held out my left palm and picked up the poker with

my right, taking in a deep breath as I was about to slice the soft skin open.

That's when the air around us grew hot, continuing to increase in temperature until it was literally searing. Then, well, the entire desk exploded! A burst of superheated air erupted around us, sending Ortiz, James, and myself flying through the air. I didn't really see it all happening so much as I felt it. One second I was about to finish the seal on the vessel, and the next second, I was impacting the ground, hard.

"Ugh..." I groaned as I pushed myself off the floor. "Ortiz?" I called out gruffly, sputtering as bits of desk confetti rained everywhere, including into my mouth.

A voice groaned back in response, "A little shaken, but fine. You?"

I spat out more bits of desk, shook my head and blinked several times, looking ahead to where the desk was moments before. There was absolutely nothing left. Not a scrap. A whole desk was just...gone. I'm pretty sure there's some scientific law about not being able to completely destroy stuff and what not. The Ifrit did not seem to care much for the laws of science. The supernatural rarely do.

The Ifrit stood in the space where the desk had been; standing, but barely. Her knee still oozed the black ichor-like substance. Her leg was twisted in a horribly wrong angle, while her foot...well, pointed sideways. I could tell by the way she was standing that it still must've hurt like hell. It was clear she was putting most of her weight on the other leg. That...and she was absolutely seething.

"Not fine, Ortiz." I sighed. "Not fine at all."

"Mortal," boomed the Ifrit in that awful, reverberating voice. "I've changed my mind."

I cast a nervous glance at Ortiz, who despite just being in a mild explosion, looked fine. James, on the other hand, well, he definitely did *not* look fine. James was in pretty rough shape before the desk was blown apart. Now? He was lying on the floor like a rag doll—limp and lifeless in a small puddle of blood pooling around his head.

Ortiz followed my gaze to James' limp and bleeding form; she gave me a curt, silent nod before crawling towards him.

"So," I said as I turned back to the Ifrit, trying to keep its attention fixed on me and not Ortiz. "What did you change your mind about?"

"Killing you," she hissed as she made her way towards me. It took her a bit of effort considering one of her legs pointed in the wrong direction. What really surprised me was that she wasn't dragging her leg, but walking on it. Badly. yes, but still...ouch!

"Well, that's good," I said with a sigh of relief. "I wasn't all too fond—"

"Slowly," she added. Her charcoal lips widened into a voracious predatory smile. "I'm going to forgo pleasure and kill you quickly."

Well, that sucked.

"Oh...uh...well," I stammered as I got to my feet and backpedaled. "You know what they say about making rash decisions."

An obsidian eyebrow quirked in amusement, and that shark-like smile of hers widened, revealing more of her jagged, gruesome teeth. "What can I say?" She upturned her wrist, opening her palm. Seconds later, a pale light burst into existence. A small ball of intense white flame floated an inch above her palm, no bigger than a softball. It just sat there, in the air; streaks of white streams danced atop the sphere. "I'm a bit of a hothead," she added, giving a flip of her fiery-hued hair to really make her point.

I would have appreciated the fact that she had made a joke, if not for the fact that there was a white-hot fireball sitting in her hand with my name on it.

A scraping sound drew the Ifrit's attention along with my own. Ortiz had reached out and whisked the Ifrit's vessel off of the floor. She held it firmly in her grasp. Surprisingly enough, the seal was still perfect. Not a smudge, mark, or blemish to ruin its design. All it needed now was a bit of blood, and it would become permanent.

Nice going, Ortiz. All I had to do was put the Ifrit down again and finish the seal. Yeah, all.

The Ifrit had noticed the little lipstick markings on its vessel, as well as their significance. "Mortal," she said, but not in her usual booming and demanding voice. There was a hint of a plea in her tone.

"That's me," I chirped pleasantly. "Little old mortal who's going to stuff you back in the bottle."

The Ifrit's features changed. Her glossy eyes widened almost in horror, as she cast what looked to be a worried glance towards Ortiz, before turning back to me. "Do not," the Ifrit said firmly, but not so firm that it was a command; it sounded more like a strong request.

I barked with laughter. "Why the hell not?"

"Do not," she repeated, pausing for a long moment before adding, "please."

That last one nearly had me hitting the floor in laughter. She was begging for mercy? After all she had done? "Ah ha," I sighed. "That's rich. You're asking me for mercy? Ahhh!" I finished with another laugh.

She just stared. No reply, just that terrified look on her face. It was priceless.

"You want mercy?" I asked incredulously. "You want to, what, be spared?" I continued to speak, my voice hardening. "How many people did you give mercy to, huh?" I shouted, fists clenched, fingernails digging into the soft flesh of my palms. I thought of Marsha, of Ortiz having to endure all of this, of the innocent people who had died in the hotel fire.

Again, silence was her response.

When I spoke, my voice came out as a low, venomous growl. "It's no less than you deserve, to be trapped for an eternity, no hope or way to escape."

"Deserve!" barked the Ifrit in disbelief, breaking her silence. "Deserve! You think *I* deserve this?" she continued in outrage. Her body shook, and the intensity of the flames in her hand increased. The little white ball of flame began to pulsate ferociously.

"I think you deserve to die," I said acidly. "You've murdered innocent people. You're a monster—literally."

"Did my kind deserve to be bound, to be enslaved by yours?" she snarled. "Murder?" she scoffed at that bit. "What do you think your kind used me for?" The Ifrit let out a bitter laugh. "Don't pretend to be so noble. Your kind are the murderers. Your kind used mine to kill your own. Your kind used mine to enrich your own lives, to impoverish others. Do not presume to lecture me about what *I* deserve!" she roared.

"What, someone ages ago made you their bitch, and you take it out on innocent people?" I roared back. "Cry me a river."

"It's no less than *you* deserve," she replied in mockingly sweet voice.

"What?" I barked, the muscles in my throat quaking. "You want me to feel sorry for you? Is that it? You *were* bound—get over it! You're free now. You had a choice. You still have a choice. You didn't need to do any of this!" I shouted.

"Choice?" she exclaimed haughtily. "What choice?" she sneered. "Do you know what it is like to be a slave? To be bound into servitude? To cater to the whims and desires of another being? Do you know what it's like to have no control over your own life, to be put to work by another? Your kind has stolen my life, and this debt must be paid!"

Wow, looks like I wasn't the only one getting the shaft. Then again, I didn't go around killing people out of vengeance and spite.

Her eyes met mine. "I have no choice," she said with utter finality.

I sighed deeply. "Then neither do I," I finished softly.

The pulsating ball of fire sank from the Ifrit's hand as she lowered her arm. Like an autumn leaf, it fell gracefully, weightlessly, weaving its way to the floor. Upon hitting the ground, it began to compress and flatten out. It widened across the tiles until it was a pool of blindingly white flames dancing across the museum floor. I was impressed by the fact it hadn't set the place ablaze. The pool of flames sat there for a moment, harmless, almost as if they weren't real.

The flames receded, and I breathed a sigh of relief. When they were a little more than an inch high, bulbous shapes resembling the original ball of flame formed inside the pool. They took form fast. Some grew to the size of footballs; others were as large as poodles.

"Uh, Norman...those look familiar," commented Ortiz, breaking the silence she had kept during my verbal exchange with the Ifrit. The balls had formed stubby legs and were beginning to resemble amphibious creatures: Salamanders with a ridge of flames across their backs. Only this time the, creatures and flames were completely white.

"Yeah," I croaked. "Yeah they do."

The Ifrit thrust her head back defiantly. "Kill them," she bellowed in fury. "Kill them both!"

The creatures shimmied together, and the ridge of flames along their backs burst into larger ones. They released a single chorus of high-pitched wails and charged.

"Why do the monsters never take the option to go down without a fight?" I muttered.

Chapter Twenty-one

"Ortiz!" I barked. "Amscray!"

She hesitated, looking down at the vessel, to the Ifrit and approaching horde of Salamanders, and then to James. He was still lying on the floor, but the bleeding had stopped.

"Ortiz!" I barked again.

She started backpedaling, but didn't take her eyes off James.

"Leave him!" I shouted.

"But he's—" She argued.

"I know!" James was our best bet at stopping the Ifrit. A selfless wish would bind the Ifrit, and, with our help, it would be permanent. None of that could happen if James died…but then, none of that would happen if *we* died.

In the end, I didn't give Ortiz much of a choice. I ran over to her, grabbed her arm, and pulled her along behind me.

"What now?" she asked.

"How 'bout running? You know, staying alive?" I nodded towards a section of the museum up ahead.

"Take this," she panted, handing me the vessel as we ran into the small mammals section.

Taking the vessel was a bit hard while running for my life, but I managed. I even managed to cast a quick glance over my shoulder without running into some priceless museum thingamabobs.

The Salamanders were fast, much faster than the ones we had encountered in the hotel. Strangely, and fortunately, they weren't secreting that napalm-like acid and setting the entire museum on fire. Guess the Ifrit didn't want to set the alarms off and bring in the authorities. She wanted to keep things contained, fine by me. I didn't want to be partially responsible for burning down a museum.

A sudden succession of reports rang out, nearly causing me to fumble. The gunshots were even louder than the ones Ortiz had made before. I looked over at her as we ran and saw her brandishing a 1911 series handgun. No doubt discharging those famed wallop-packing .45 caliber rounds.

The hell did she get that from? I wondered in amazement. It seemed Ortiz's purse, like many a woman's, really did have no end to it.

Two more gunshots rang out, dropping a pair of Salamanders pursuing us.

"God, I hate these things," cursed Ortiz.

"Yeah," I panted, "they suck. By the way, Ortiz?"

"Yeah?"

"Where'd you get the gun? Most magicians pull bunnies out of their hats, not ear-blistering handguns out of purses."

"Security desk," she said briskly, turning to discharge another round before speaking. "Dug through it," she clipped and then fired off another round. "Figured it'd be handy." She finished her statement with another gunshot.

"No arguments here," I bellowed, trying to talk over the sound of yet another gunshot.

"We can't keep doing this, Norman."

"I know," I replied through gritted teeth.

"Then what do we do?" she asked desperately.

"I'm thinking. Just keep shooting!" I shouted back.

Another succession of shots rang out. "Think fast!" Ortiz shouted, "I'm running out." That's when I heard the noise.

It was hard to discern what that noise was at first. What, with Ortiz and I running for our lives, shouting and the gunshots—who notices a ring tone?

"Ortiz!" I shouted, trying to compete with another gunshot.

"What?"

"Your phone," I said, pointing towards the source of

the noise.

"What?"

"Your phone!" I screamed, jabbing my finger at it again.

She looked a bit surprised that someone would be calling her at this hour, but she pulled out the phone anyways, an angry look came over her face as she glanced at the screen. "Seriously? Telemarketers at this hour?"

"What?"

"It's a blocked number. Who else?" she replied, moving her thumb over the little red button to hang up.

A sudden notion occurred to me.

"Wait!" I blurted out, shocking her into nearly dropping the phone. I didn't wait for her to respond before I snatched the phone from her hands and answered. I ignored her angry muttering, wincing as another gunshot went off.

"Yeah, uh, hello?" I shouted. My hands cupped around the speaker to make sure they, whoever they were, could hear me.

"Graves," said a very familiar deep voice.

"God, have you got great timing. Look, I'm being chased by yet another pack of—"

"I know, Graves," interjected Gnosis.

"You know? The hell can you possibly know that?" I asked in surprise.

He inhaled deeply before answering, clearly irritated by something. Well it obviously couldn't have been me, because me, irritating? That's absurd.

Anyways, before he could respond, I cut him off. "Wait, scratch that," I said. "You got anything that can help me out?"

Another gunshot rang out.

"Dammit, Ortiz!" I shouted, covering the speaker to prevent Gnosis from hearing me. "Can you cut that out?"

Ortiz didn't reply. Well, not with words. She did shoot me a deadly glare that pretty much conveyed more than words ever could.

I pointed at the phone, opening and closing my hand several times to resemble a talking gesture, then silently mouthed the word "important," pointing in the direction of where the Ifrit was.

She nodded and stopped shooting.

"Sorry about that," I panted. I was having to run harder now that Ortiz had stopped capping those fiery sons of bitches.

"Tell your federal agent friend to conserve her ammunition," Gnosis said.

"Uh, why?"

"You're going to need some, Graves." He paused for a moment. "To kill the Ifrit."

"What?"

Ortiz shot me a curious glance.

I held up a finger, telling her to give me a moment. "Ah, could you repeat that, sounded like you said *kill* the Ifrit?"

"What?" blurted Ortiz.

"I know. That's what I said."

She looked at me and gave a slow, disapproving shake of her head.

Right, then, no time to be funny; back to business then.

"You heard what I said, Graves," he said testily.

"Yeah, well, then hurry up with it," I panted impatiently. "Kinda busy trying not to get immolated here!"

"You're aware of the properties of human blood?" he asked.

"Yes," I growled. I was getting angry now; he knew that I knew that.

"Rounds covered in the blood of a human of pure soul," he informed me.

"Great," I muttered to myself. "Where the hell am I going to find a pure soul?"

"That'll take some time, Graves—"

"Uh, sorry, wasn't asking you. No offense."

He didn't answer.

"So...blood and bullets. Anything else? Does it matter where we put 'em?" I asked. "We talking headshots? Pump 'em full of lead? What?"

"The latter," he answered.

"Uh, there a magic number or something?"

"A full magazine should be sufficient, Graves."

I nearly choked. I had to empty a full mag into the Ifrit? Hell, the way Ortiz had been shooting, we'd be lucky to have half a magazine.

"Uh, one sec there, pal," I told Gnosis as I turned to Ortiz. "Hey, Bonnie, how many rounds you got left?"

"Bonnie?" Ortiz mouthed silently with a quirk of an eyebrow. She ejected the magazine, frowned, and then held up three fingers.

I sighed. "Uh, small problem there, Chief," I said to Gnosis. "We've only got three shots left. What do we do?"

"Make them count," he said as if it were obvious.

"Gee thanks, and after that?"

"You still have the original option," he replied.

"Yeah, convince James to make a selfless wish and give up the power of a really powerful Djinni," I snorted. "Like that's going to happen."

"Graves," he said firmly, ignoring what I had just said. "You know the power of human blood." It wasn't a question this time.

"Yeah."

"For a pure, truly pure, human soul, magnify it, exponentially," he said quietly. It was almost a whisper, and I swear there was a hint of fear in his voice. Gnosis wasn't one to get scared, or to show it at least.

I didn't know what to say, but then again, when has that ever stopped me? "So, uh...it can do some pretty nasty stuff, huh?"

He let out a frustrated sigh.

That answered my question.

"Graves, the potential it carries, especially when used as a weapon is..." he trailed off, inhaling deeply before continuing. "This can be used to harm a great deal of creatures."

"What, like a one-size-fits-all-monsters kind of deal?" I said in surprise.

"Yes," he whispered, "with a few exceptions."

I let out a low whistle. This was some powerful stuff. That is, if you could get your hands on some blood belonging to a pure human soul. Not that many of those out there.

I felt my anger rising when I realized what this meant, what it could have meant if I had learned this long ago. "Why didn't you tell me about this before? Hell, why not yesterday?" I said, trying to keep my voice neutral, but failing.

No answer.

"You were afraid I'd use the knowledge to kill anything and everything I wanted. Not much could stop me, right?" I said, understanding the reason why Gnosis had kept this from me.

"Knowledge is power, Graves. You know that."

Damn, this was powerful stuff. A way to kill almost any monster, or at the very least cause them serious harm. I could see why he was apprehensive about me knowing this.

It was hard saying the next words to him, really hard, but I managed to get them out. "Gnosis, I won't misuse what you've just told me. You have my word."

That may not have seemed like much, but it was. I may not be the nicest guy, but there's a reason I have a great deal of contacts in the supernatural world. That reason is my word. It's good. It always has been, and there are lots of monsters out there who can attest to that.

"See that you don't," he warned. "And, Graves?"

"Yeah, yeah, I figured. This squares us, huh?"

"No. Now, you owe me one," he said with utter firmness.

"Hey, wait a—"

There was an audible click as he hung up the phone.

Who knew that such a small…being, could be such a large ass?

We rounded the corner and ducked out of sight behind a rather large and probably extinct ancient mammal. It kind of looked like a bear mixed with a wolf and a really gnarly temperament. I dubbed it the werebear.

Ortiz elbowed me to get my attention. She was chewing on her lip and looking at me expectantly. "So?"

"Well, I think I might've found a way to kill this thing," I said slowly.

"Great, what is it?" she said hurriedly.

"Maybe," I added after she finished her last sentence.

"Maybe?" she exclaimed before letting out a frustrated sigh. "Alright, it's not like we have much choice. What is it?"

"Bullets," I said. She shot me a glare and, a look that implied that I was an idiot. "Covered in the blood of a human of pure soul."

That last part caught her off guard. The angry look slipped off her face and was replaced with confusion.

"What is it with the whole blood thing?" she asked, irritated.

Wow, that was a big question with a big answer. How the hell do you explain something like that to someone with little to no knowledge of the magical, the supernatural, and the just not normal?

"There's power, Ortiz. Power in a person's blood, in every person's blood," I said. "Some people can tap into it. It's what's behind warlocks, witches, and the like."

"Witches?" She let out a derisive snort and then caught my eye. Ortiz sighed. "You're not kidding, are you?"

I shook my head. "There's energy, life force, chi, mana—call it whatever you will, Ortiz—and it lies within every person."

"I don't see how this helps. How's it work?" She rubbed her temples in frustration. This was probably giving her a headache.

I exhaled before explaining further. "Ortiz, blood is a more powerful source of…well, power…than anything else today in modern science. If you can tap into that, or find a way to use it, you can do a lot."

"Like…make mystical mumbo jumbo bullets that can kill a monster?" she said hesitantly.

I nodded. "Yeah—or worse."

Her eyebrows shot up in surprise. "Worse?"

"I'd rather not get into it, Ortiz. Blood can be used for all sorts of things—rituals and more. It can be used to hurt monsters...or people."

She bit her lip pensively, but otherwise didn't say a word.

"The blood of someone pure of soul, well, it kind of multiplies that potential to a whole 'nother level. The potential for good or bad..." I said, letting the last words hang heavily in the air.

"Okay," she said, nodding more to herself than me. "So we're playing with magical fire, or something similar right?"

I nodded.

"And we could get burned—bad?" she continued.

I nodded again.

"So we're just going to stick with blood and bullets, I'm assuming. Right, Norman?"

Another nod.

"So," she muttered to herself. "Where do we find someone who's pure of soul and get our hands on their blood?" she asked, raising her head to look up at me, only to find I was staring back at her.

"Me?"

"Well, it sure as hell isn't me," I snorted. "You're all I've got." I shrugged.

"Gee," she said in a dry tone. "You really know how to compliment a girl, don't ya?"

"Ortiz," I sighed. "You were thrust into a supernatural shit storm, stuck by me through an inferno, been chased by fiery monsters, trusted me, and more. What do you want me to say? If that ain't pure of soul, I don't know what is." I didn't realize I was saying all that until I had actually said it. Silence hung in the air after I did.

A wry smile came over her face. "That'll do, pig. That'll do." Her voice turned to a whisper. "Thanks."

I nodded quietly.

The air filled with the disconcerting sounds of hissing. Pools of corrosive acid landed near us, eating away at the tiling around us.

"Ooookaay," I said. "Do or die time, Ortiz. For the record, I prefer do, to die."

Ortiz ejected the magazine of her pistol and thumbed out the last few rounds, lumping them into her left palm. She looked at her right hand, a bit worried; she closed her eyes and took in a deep breath, calming herself down before she moved her hand closer to her mouth. Ortiz took the soft thin tissue that ran between her thumb and forefinger and placed it in her mouth. She bit down hard and winced. "Son of a bitch!" she cursed as she pulled her hand out of her mouth. Blood welled up between her thumb and index finger. "How much blood do I have to coat these things in? I don't want them soaked, not sure if the gun will fire."

I rolled my shoulders in a shrug. "Just roll 'em around a bit I guess, then let them dry. Shouldn't take long."

More hissing sounds filled the air, and another series of corrosive blobs landed near us, closer to the corner we were hiding around than before.

Damn those things were getting close!

"Good," Ortiz muttered as she clenched her bleeding hand into a tight fist. She closed her eyes as more blood seeped out. "We don't have a lot of time." She tossed the three remaining rounds from her left hand into her blood-covered right, rolling the bullets around quickly before slipping them into her pocket to dry. She slammed the empty magazine back into the gun. It made it easier to move than having to carry the magazine and the pistol separately. She held up the ammo-deprived handgun in front her face, giving it a slight twist in the air and frowned. "This won't do us much good now."

"Yeah, it's essentially a paperweight till we get those rounds back in it," I replied.

"Even so," she started, "we've only got three."

"Make 'em count," I said with an indifferent shrug, echoing what Gnosis had said.

Ortiz sighed in frustration.

I offered a weak smile. "You could always pistol whip—"

"I think I'm going to, Norman—right across your head!"

I snorted. "If we get out of here in one piece, Ortiz, you can pistol whip me all you want."

"Don't tempt me." She smiled, holding up the gun in a mock attempt to hit me with it. It was good to see her smile. Even in the midst of all this, she managed to cling onto her sense of humor. That was good. She'd need that; we'd both need that...and the bullets too.

Her smile slipped, turning into a painful grimace. I frowned and noticed her flexing her right hand over and over. I looked down at my tattered clothing and tore a wide strip from my ruined shirt. Folding it half, I made it thicker.

"What are you doing?" hissed Ortiz. "Come on. We need to move." Another series of acidy globules struck the floor beside us.

I peeked around the corner and saw the Salamanders were no more than ten feet from us now. Upon seeing my noggin poking around the corner they launched another volley of noxious corrosive spit. "Eek!" I yelped as I pulled my head back just in time. A series of *splat* noises hit the wall next to me. Bits of it crumbled right before us.

"Norman," she said a lot more firmly. Before she could say anything else, I grasped her right hand and pulled it towards me, prying it open. I wrapped the strip of fabric I had torn from my shirt around her palm.

I tied it off and beckoned for her to follow me. "Come on, Bonnie, there's a Djinni that needs a-killin'!" I said as I jaunted down the hall that would allow us to circle back to the Ifrit.

She shook her head and tried to suppress a smile as she jogged beside me. "You know Bonnie and Clyde got shot, right?"

"Well, they went down fighting," I replied, "and that's the point."

"Actually," she said as we continued moving towards the end of the hall, "they were ambushed. Didn't put up much of a fight."

"Okay, fine," I whispered back, "but we're doing the ambushing here, and we are definitely going to put up one helluva fight."

Ortiz's eyes and face turned to solid steel. "Damn right," she growled as she fished the bullets out of her pocket.

The blood on the rounds had dried. It doesn't take long once blood is exposed to air, especially when it's small amounts. It generally takes a few minutes, not to mention the fact that some of the blood must've been absorbed by the fabric of Ortiz's pockets. The bullets weren't really caked in blood. The brass rounds still shone under the museum lighting, but there were a few splotchy smears of red on each one.

Ortiz ejected the magazine and thumbed the rounds back in, slamming the magazine into the handgun with an audible *click*. She closed her eyes and took several deep breaths before she pulled the slide back on the pistol and chambered the first round. Ortiz stared at me, eyes unwavering and her jaw set. She was ready to do this, but I still had to ask. I had to hear her say it.

I stared right back at her. "Ready?" I asked in a quiet and reassuring whisper that contrasted the steely look I gave her.

She took a deep, calming breath and nodded silently.

I gave a jerk of my head towards the end of the hall, motioning for her to come on. I ducked into a crouch and crept forwards.

As I turned to check on Ortiz, a flurry of movement at the end of the hall caught my eye. "Shit." Ortiz turned around as well, noticing what I had. The Salamanders had rounded the corner and were looking straight at us. The few remaining Salamanders jiggled in unison before letting out a collective shrill shriek and surged towards us. They sent a wave of their corrosive spit hurtling through the air. "Move!" I bounded to my feet, grabbing Ortiz by the collar and forcibly hauling her with me. I shoved her around the corner, following right behind. The mass of acid spit landed behind us, but the violent sound of the hiss sent shivers up my spine. *Man, that was close!*

Both Ortiz and I looked straight down the current hall and to the open area that lay at the end of it. We had gone around two hallways, circling back to where we had last seen the Ifrit. The only problem was that this hall was narrow. Walls on both sides meant we couldn't see the entirety of the opening ahead, nor could we see the Ifrit.

"Careful," I whispered to Ortiz as I took point and began jogging forwards, cradling the Ifrit's vessel in my hands. Ideally, I would have liked to move at a slower pace, but with the Salamanders advancing behind us, that wasn't an option. I didn't want to be pinned between them and the Ifrit. Ortiz ran behind me, both hands on her gun. She held it waist level, barrel aimed down at the floor.

Once we made it to the end of the hall, I looked back to Ortiz and gave her a knowing look, to which she nodded in response. I turned the corner with a burst of speed, charging into the open area and then skidded to a halt.

The Ifrit was standing about thirty feet in front of me, but that's not what made me freeze. She wasn't paying me any attention, but I was certainly fixated on what was going on. Her entire left arm had reverted back to her earlier disguise. It was human, completely bare, and without a shred of clothing. It bore the hideous scar that she had received courtesy of Ortiz.

The transformation went a little past her arm to a bit of her chest; the rest of her body remained unchanged however. It was still a burnished red that shone in certain places. She still had volcanic rock-like protrusions and that shark-like mouth with the obsidian teeth. Her leg was still ruined. The gaping hole I had made was still leaking that disgusting black motor oil-like fluid. And it was still the wrong way around.

It wasn't hard to figure out why the Ifrit had decided to shift its arm back to its human form. She couldn't touch anything without burning it, and right now she was holding James. The Ifrit had her hand in a vice-like grip around his throat, holding him off the ground effortlessly. His limp form dangled from her supernaturally strong hold. She brought his mouth close to hers, her dagger-lined mouth spreading into a wide predatory smile as she brought him nearer. That's when things got weirder than they were already.

The Ifrit squeezed harder on his throat, forcing him to open his mouth as he began to gag. She exhaled deeply, and smoke billowed out of her mouth. It didn't behave like normal smoke. It didn't waft through the air, but condensed into thick, almost liquid-looking streams. They resembled a bunch of smoke-like tendrils really. They darted towards James, forcing their way into every orifice they could find, slithering forcibly into his mouth, ears, and nose. His body jerked and spasmed violently. It was like he was having a seizure. Horrible gagging noises came from him as the smoke forced its way inside.

What I saw next really boggled me. James was having his body reconfigured in some strange way. The first time I had met him he had looked a fair bit older than his actual age, but that was due to his haggard and disheveled appearance. I chalked it up to stress and overtime. Moments ago, he had looked like a frail elderly person who should've been on their deathbed. And now, he was starting to regress, slowly. His elderly features became noticeably younger.

Smoke continued pouring into his body. His seizure-like movements intensified, and I quickly understood why his body was spasming out of control. The smoke inside him was moving around his body in a grotesque fashion. It looked like there was an army of snakes writhing beneath his skin. There were long cord-like bulges visible beneath the features of his face, pulsating and moving under his skin.

Within seconds, James had gone from a decrepit-looking ninety-year-old to a much younger, albeit still feeble looking, sixty-year-old. And he was getting younger by the second. I'm sure the Ifrit would have kept going if Ortiz hadn't come around the corner behind me, gun drawn at chest level, and pointed square at the Ifrit.

"Wha... Nor... What...what are you doing?" stammered a completely horrified Ortiz. She was transfixed by the sight of James spasming and gurgling helplessly. His face contorted in agony as he continued to get younger. Ortiz's aim wavered. The barrel of the gun sunk for second, before she regained her composure and brought it back up to level. "Put. Him. Down!" she said in a tone that was all iron and ice.

"I'm doing him a favor," replied the Ifrit in a cheery manner. "Don't you want me to restore his youth?"

"Put. Him. Down," Ortiz repeated, just as firmly.

"I don't think so," the Ifrit said as she tightened her grip on his neck. She stopped the flow of smoke coursing through, and into, James, halting his youthful regression. "I'll kill him if either of you do not do exactly as I say," she said in a venomous tone, accentuating her point by digging her fingers deep into his throat. The action elicited a sharp, painful gasp from James.

There was a part of me—an angry part—that wanted James dead for starting all of this, for letting everything get so out of hand. Part of me that wanted to say, "Yeah, go ahead!" I suppressed that part. Plus, I knew Ortiz wouldn't stand by and let that happen. Ortiz was a fed, but more than that, she was a good person. She wouldn't let James die if she could help it. But part of me still wondered what would happen if James did die? Why didn't the Ifrit kill James long ago and be done with it?

Ortiz sighed in frustration, breaking my chain of thoughts as she conceded. She raised both her gun and free hand into the air.

"You," the Ifrit snapped at me. "Bring me my vessel."

I scowled at the Ifrit as I took a step forwards, and then I noticed what was lying on the floor between us. It must've landed there after the Ifrit had blown up the guard's desk— the silver, blood-stained poker was all but ten feet away from me.

She must've noticed it too, because the next second, her voice rang out loudly with authority. "Stop!"

I didn't. I continued walking towards the silver weapon.

The Ifrit's fingers dug deeper into James' throat, drawing blood this time. She even gave a series of small but harsh shakes, jerking him like a rag doll to make her point.

"Norman," called Ortiz in a pleading tone. "Stop."

I ground my teeth in pure aggravation, but I stopped.

"Good," replied the Ifrit. Her mouth spread into that hideously large and disconcerting smile once again. "Now, place the vessel on the ground and kick it over to me," she instructed.

I knelt slowly, placing the vessel on the ground. I set it down on its base, trying to figure out a way to kick it over to her without having the seal scrape across the museum floor. I couldn't risk screwing up the seal. It wasn't even empowered, not to mention the fact that I didn't know if I would get another chance to inscribe it should this one be ruined. I pulled my foot back to kick the vessel across the floor, but as my foot was about to connect, I stopped.

I hesitated. Something wasn't right. I couldn't tell what, but I could just feel it.

"Mortal," hissed the Ifrit impatiently, giving James another violent shake. "What are you doing?"

"Norman," whispered Ortiz. "Do it. We can't let him die. We need him."

"Yes, Norman," the Ifrit purred triumphantly. "Do it. *You* need him." She heavily emphasized you, as she repeated Ortiz's words with such glee.

A deep, guttural burble formed in my throat. It never left my mouth, but it was audible nonetheless.

The Ifrit's smile grew wider after hearing the anger rising in my throat. She enjoyed seeing me mad. Good, because I was planning on getting a helluva lot madder.

I looked down at the vessel and drew my leg back. A thought struck me, and I stopped once again. "No," I growled.

"What are you doing?" both Ortiz and Ifrit shouted simultaneously.

After the sudden outburst in stereo, only the Ifrit

continued to speak. "Stop playing games!" she commanded, her body quivering with rage. "Give. Me. My. Vessel!"

"No," I repeated with iron-hard firmness.

"I. Will. Kill. Him," she said, speaking slowly, threateningly and emphasizing each word, making her threat clear.

"Yeah?" I snarled defiantly. "Go ahead!" I dared.

"Norman, what the hell are you doing?" shouted a panicky Ortiz.

I turned back to face her, shooting her wolfish smile and a wink, one I was hoping had gone unnoticed by the Ifrit. Ortiz didn't say anything in response but chewed nervously on her lip once again. I understood backing this play of mine went against her conscience. She couldn't, and wouldn't, let James die if she could help it. She was trusting me now, not just with finding a way to take down the Ifrit, but with her own morals and beliefs. If my plan didn't work, and James did die, there'd be hell to pay, and I wasn't just talking about the Ifrit. On the other hand, if my suspicions were correct, Ortiz and I were just about to gain something very important.

Leverage.

"You heard me! Go ahead and kill him!" I said in a challenging tone.

The Ifrit moved her fingers into a new position on James' throat before squeezing it to the point of drawing a bit of blood. She was making quite the show of hurting James, but that last maneuver had an awful lot of care in it, considering the fact that she kept threatening to kill him. Too much pressure from her fingernails in one spot, and she would have already pierced something vital. So far, all she managed to do was break the surface layer of his skin, causing splotches of blood and red scratch marks. Now she had repeated the process in a different spot. Oh sure, she drew blood, and it looked bad, but we all know looks can be deceiving. She could make all the effort she wanted at bleeding James, because bleeding ain't killing, and I'm proof of that.

I was done buying her act.

She tightened her grip further, really tightened it. Not just digging her nails into his flesh, but actually crushing his throat. James began to spasm more violently. His legs kicked all over the place and his face lost some of its color. He wouldn't be able to take much more of this in his weakened condition. Part of me wanted to stop it right there, but I held my ground and decided to roll the dice.

It wasn't like I was gambling with much, only a man's life. Then there was Ortiz, and me as well, so our lives too. Oh, and the prospect of losing the only guaranteed way of sealing an ancient Djinni with severe anger issues.

See, nothing much…

Boy, I hoped I was right.

I'll admit, I was about to start sweating bullets when James' eyes stopped bulging and fluttered. He wasn't gasping desperately for breath either. It was quieter, shallower. But before things got any worse, the Ifrit loosened her hold on James, right when he was on the brink. James didn't start gasping for air, which would have been a good sign, but he didn't die either. He had passed out from the lack of oxygen.

"Be careful, mortal," the Ifrit warned. She flexed her fingers around James' throat. "A little more," she gave a quick, firm squeeze to his throat, "and he *will* die."

I gave an indifferent shrug. Behind me, Ortiz mumbled a string of curses under her breath.

"Last chance to do as I say, mortal," she cautioned. "Remember…you need him." Her tone was full of pleasure as she turned to look at Ortiz. "Your companion won't let me kill him, will she?" asked the Ifrit, savoring Ortiz's predicament.

Yahtzee! I had just gotten what I needed.

"And what about what *you* need him for?" I asked.

The Ifrit's wide, pleased smile slipped away, replaced by a look of complete bewilderment. The question had caught her off guard.

It was my turn to smile, and I made it a big one.

"What's the matter?" I taunted. "Cat got your tongue? I asked you a question. What do *you* need him for?"

"What...do you mean?" the Ifrit asked hesitantly. I could hear the confusion her voice.

"My god, are you dense!" I said with an air of exaggerated drama. "I mean, what do you need him for? Why is he still alive at all? Why not kill him the moment you were let out? You've killed a small group of people already, so why is he still alive?"

No answer. She stared back at me in silent confusion.

"See, I don't think you will kill him," I said, the Ifrit's eyes narrowing in anger. She gave another dangerous-looking squeeze to James' throat. "Oh, I know you want to kill him," I continued, "but you won't..." I trailed off as a new thought occurred to me. "Or...you can't, can you?" I said in sudden realization.

If the Ifrit was confused and in shock before, I sure as hell had no idea what she was now. Her features were totally blank; I mean completely and utterly dumbstruck.

"I was wondering why you only killed a few museum employees instead of a whole mess of people," I said.

"Explain," demanded the Ifrit. Only her voice didn't have the authoritative strength that it had before. Her voice was little more than a whisper. It trembled. She was afraid.

"You've been loose for what...about a month now, give or take? And in all that time, you've never once targeted a regular museum visitor. Only the people James knew. Hell, you were never far from James. You never once tried to leave the museum. You could've killed me at any time, but you didn't. You always got something else to do it. First the tiger. Then you enthralled the Wraith."

"*You* were one of the people I killed. As you said, the list is very small, so why then are you still alive?" she asked, leaning forwards curiously.

"Don't change the subject!" I snapped at the Ifrit. I could feel Ortiz's eyes boring a hole into the back of my head. "Why didn't you leave the museum? Get away from James? There's a whole world out there for you to kill and get your rocks off with your whole revenge against humans thing."

"Norman," hissed Ortiz. "I don't think you should be encouraging this thing to go on a killing spree."

"I'm just making a point Ortiz," I said calmly.

"And what is your point?" asked the Ifrit, her voice taking on a booming tone again.

I fixed the Ifrit with a steely gaze. "My point is all of it, everything I asked, why didn't you do any of it?"

Her creepy, knife-filled mouth worked silently in confusion. "I…did not wish to be revealed. I…preferred exacting my revenge in concealment," she answered hesitantly.

"Yeah huh," I said disbelievingly. "And you needed concealment why exactly? What could've stopped you? Hell, we've barely been able to stop you. You're one tenacious bitch, I'll give you that." The irony of asking all the questions was that I was answering them as I followed through my chain of thoughts. I was realizing more and more as I continued. "You never left the museum…because James never did—did he?"

The Ifrit resumed her silence.

I understood it now. "All that talk about hating humans, about them binding you, it wasn't just about the vessel, was it?" I asked more to myself than the Ifrit. I was thinking aloud now, and was on a roll. "James didn't just let you out, did he? Whatever was done to bind you in the vessel, bound you to it—and to whomever lets you out, isn't that right?"

Her features twisted into a mask of pure fury.

"It was never about concealment, at least not for you. James never left the museum because he wanted to hide *you*! He didn't want his little secret getting out, but it got out anyways, didn't it?"

"Norman, make sense!" shouted a thoroughly perplexed and irate Ortiz.

"The Ifrit never left because James never left. It's been stuck here because James didn't want to risk anyone else finding out. That's why it hasn't killed a bunch of museum goers. It's only attacked people James knew. It's tethered to him," I explained. I turned my attention back to the Ifrit. "James kept you on a bit of a short leash, didn't he?"

"He thought he was in control at first," sneered the Ifrit.

"But he does have a bit though, doesn't he? That's why you've never tried once to deal with anybody other than a full-time museum employee. He kept you close. The only people you could get your claws on were the ones who spent a lot of time here."

"Yes," she growled bitterly.

"Obviously, things got out of control. Let me guess. After James got his wishes and a taste of your power, he couldn't give you up," I reasoned.

"Obviously," replied the Ifrit in a snide tone.

"But he realized the danger you posed, and was too afraid to do anything about it. So he huddles up in his little room and busies himself with his work, turning a blind eye to you." I said, all of it making sense now. "You go around prowling the museum, seducing some people with your offers, killing only a few, barely satisfying your appetite. You feed on that stuff—their suffering, their pain—but James kept you close."

My lips twisted into a taunting smile. "You must be starving!"

Her scowl deepened.

"But wait!" I blurted out. "What the hell was I chasing back at the park?"

"A shadow," the Ifrit answered in a voice completely devoid of any tone.

A shadow is essentially a physically tangible illusion. They're real to an extent. They can be touched and interacted with, but in the end, they're still fake. Not many creatures can conjure them up, but an Ifrit wasn't an ordinary creature. At least now my theory was confirmed. The Ifrit never did, nor could, leave the museum.

"That explains all of it, doesn't it? James is your anchor. Your one connection to our plane of existence and whatever place your vessel locks you up into. Because, no offense, girlfriend, but there is no way you're physically squeezing all that ass back into that bottle," I quipped.

She was absolutely livid now. I mean I could feel her temper—literally; the room grew insanely hot. I was sweating within seconds.

"So, you're bound to James," I continued. "Wherever he goes—you can go. If he doesn't leave, you don't leave," I paused. "So, no James..." I said slowly, letting the importance of it hang in the air. "No you."

The Ifrit's opaque eyes widened.

"So, you can beat him, torture him, grant any and all of his wishes, feed off him, do whatever it is you were doing to him with all that smoke. But. You. Can't. Kill. Him." I said in a smug tone. "Meaning you've just lost your only leverage," I finished with a wolfish smile.

Apparently Ortiz had really taken my earlier comment about making her shots count to heart. The report of the first shot surprised us all, especially me considering the fact I felt the disturbance of air as it whizzed dangerously close to my ear. It rocketed towards the Ifrit with deadly accuracy, impacting the creature right in its left eye. The round shattered the jewel-like eye with explosive force. Crystalline shards spurted out as the round pierced the Ifrit's skull. That's when Ortiz and I witnessed the truly devastating effect of using blood-covered rounds. The Ifrit's head jerked back brutally as plumes of silver-white fire, erupted from her eye socket. Tinged with red, the sinister micro-explosion disfigured the area around the Ifrit's left eye socket, as well as the upper portions of her lip on that side of her face.

The Ifrit didn't make a single sound the moment Ortiz's first shot struck her eye. The only movement was James dropping to the floor as she released hold of him. That and having her head snapping back.

I let out a low whistle of appreciation. *Damn good job, Gnosis!*

Ortiz didn't waste a moment. While I was mulling around in my head, paying compliments to an asinine gnome, she was busy firing off her second round. It struck dead center, several inches beneath the breastbone. A perfect shot to the solar plexus. The Ifrit's entire body jerked in an odd fashion. Her body snapped into a rigid state with her chest thrust forwards, her head and arms fell back. It was similar to the pose a gymnast strikes after a dismount. Another plume of silvery white and red fire burst from the Ifrit's body, leaving a gaping hole in her chest.

The third shot rang out, hitting the Ifrit in the liver. She doubled over just as a third and final plume of fire erupted from her torso. Ortiz and I stood there—motionless, watching as the Ifrit just hung silently in her doubled over state. There was no movement. Seconds later, as if in slow motion, the Ifrit's form sank to the ground, folding into a lifeless heap.

I crept forwards cautiously. Smoke billowed out of her jagged, deformed mouth. As it poured out, her features began to shift. Her lengthy, fiery-hued hair receded and darkened. Within seconds, her hair was the exact same shade and style as when she was posing as a human. The rest of her body soon followed. Her glimmering red skin returned to a fair complexion. The obsidian protrusions disappeared, as did her tail. Lying in a crumpled mess before me wasn't the body of something out of a fiction story, but a young, naked woman.

"Is…is it over?" asked Ortiz cautiously.

"Yeah," I said hoarsely. "I think it's over."

Ortiz decided to go perfectly limp and plop straight to the floor. She fell into a comfortable cross-legged position, hunching over as she propped herself up on her balled-up fists. Her elbows rested on her thighs. "Thank god," exhaled Ortiz in complete exhaustion. "It's finally over."

"Not exactly," I said firmly. "What about him?" I gave a sharp nod towards the unconscious form of James.

Chapter Twenty-two

"Right," Ortiz muttered as she calmly rose to her feet. "What about him?"

"You can't take him in, can you?" I asked, already knowing the answer.

"No," she replied bitterly. "I can't charge him with any of the deaths. There are no solid links."

"Or believable ones," I snorted.

"True," she replied.

I looked around the museum and then back to Ortiz, shooting her a wide grin. "Destruction of public property?" I suggested.

She smirked. "I think I could make that stick."

I cleared my throat and stood up straight. "Assaulting a respectable citizen?" making a mock gesture of straightening a tie as I said it. It's not like I had a tie to straighten. Hell, I didn't even have a complete shirt left!

Ortiz quirked an eyebrow. "You know, if you want to press charges for that, you're going to have be questioned again. You sure want to be dragged into that?"

"If you take him in," I said, nodding towards James, "aren't you going to be dragged into worse?"

"You already dragged me into worse," she chided, casting a wide glance around the museum and nodding to the Ifrit's corpse.

"Ah, good point," I conceded, "but seriously, how are you going to explain any of this. How are you going to explain why he looks like he's in his sixties?"

Ortiz's face became a pensive frown. "I can't."

"Then...maybe, oh I don't know, don't file a report?"

She looked at me like I had just committed some form of heresy. "I *have* to report this, Norman. Rules," she said, as if that explained everything.

"Ah, screw the rules," I said in animated voice, making a disregarding motion with my hand.

"You're speaking another language now," Ortiz said in an exasperated tone, but there was a small smile on her face.

"Alright then," I said with a sigh as I knelt to scoop up the Ifrit's now useless vessel. "How's about we all go to the hospital first, then decide?"

Ortiz pursed her lips as she thought for a moment. "Works for me," she agreed. "And then…a nap."

I let out a bark of laughter. I could've used one as well, but now that my case was done, I would be pulled from Norman's body and shoved into another meat suit, just as soon as I visited Church and wrapped things up.

I walked over to James, bending over to grab him by the elbow. "Come on grandpa," I groaned as I lifted him to his feet. "We're going to the hospital!" I said cheerily. "Imagine it," I groaned as I continued hauling him up. "Drop dead gorgeous nurses ready to give us sponge baths and all-you-can-eat Jell-O!"

James stared at me. "I…I…" he wheezed feebly.

"You…?" I asked, confused.

"I…feel her," he rasped weakly.

"You…feel her?" I said perplexed. "The hell does—"

The air was forced out of my body as the Ifrit's sprang forwards with all her mass and speed, colliding hard with my mid-section. "*Oomph*," was the only sound to come out of me. James slipped from my grip and sank to the floor wearily. There was a cracking sound around my torso, and a couple more as I slammed into the hard museum floor nearly a dozen feet away.

I tried to shout, "Why won't you die?" Only it came out as, "Hrngh!" courtesy of cracked ribs…as in a lot of them.

Ortiz was a blur of motion, racing forwards with the pistol held high, like a club. She drove it towards the Ifrit's skull in a furious pistol whip. The Ifrit was having none of that however; with a lazy upward flick of her wrist, she slapped the pistol out of Ortiz's hand with ease.

The Ifrit lashed out with her palm at Ortiz's chest, but she bobbed to the side. The blow glanced Ortiz's shoulder, sending her into an out-of-control sprawl towards the ground.

There was a noticeable *thunk* as Ortiz's pistol landed a few feet in front of me. I gritted my teeth, using my feet and elbows to inch forwards. Hell, just breathing was an effort. Happens when you've got three or four cracked ribs. It doesn't take much imagination to understand how much pain I was in as I crawled on my stomach, grinding my already broken ribs across the unforgiving tiled museum floor.

It hurt like hell!

I had barely moved across the floor. The pistol was at the edge of my arms reach, but I had nothing left in the tank. I made some incoherent groaning noises as I reached for the weapon. My fingers brushed against the cool metal of the handgun. I grimaced as I twisted my body, the pain was too overwhelming to describe as I angled my right side closer to the pistol. I tried once to grab the gun, my fingers running across the grip, but not far enough to actually grab it. I raked the diamond-beveled grip with my fingernails. It began to slide forwards. Using what little strength I had left, I grabbed it, pointing it towards the Ifrit.

Freeze! I shouted with authority, except it came out as, "Fwee!" It was more of a pained wheeze. Whatever. I had cracked ribs and was only a few letters off. I had a damn gun pointed at the Ifrit. She got the message.

She tilted her head to the side as she regarded me. She stood there, naked. What was once an absolutely gorgeous body, was now hideously deformed. There was a softball-sized crater enveloping one side of her. It had taken away her eye socket and a part of her upper lip. It was a grisly sight. Bits of tissue hung down, and I could see parts of her gums and teeth. The missing chunk of lip gave her a perennial snarl. Then there was the fact that the wound was leaking the same tar-like ichor her earlier wounds had oozed.

In fact, her entire body was coated in the stuff. The wound on her arm, the gaping hole in her chest and liver, not to mention the knee I had pierced earlier. Don't get me started on the foot, it just looked...wrong. It had been bad enough when it was twisted in her other form. Now in her human form, it was just...well, grotesque.

She must've noticed the expression on my face as I looked at her. "What's the matter," she purred, her voice back to a husky, seductive feminine one. "Don't you find me attractive?" She gyrated sensually, or it would have been if she didn't have fist-sized holes in her face and torso that were weeping motor oil.

I took a deep breath and worked really hard on making sure my next words came out coherently. "Damaged...goods," I wheezed, before having to take a number of shallow breaths.

She gave an indifferent shrug and spread her lips into a ravenous smile. The damaged part of her lip peeled away from her mouth as it stretched. Her smile would have been intoxicating before, but now it was downright bone-chilling. "That weapon really hurt me," she pouted. "Too bad it's empty." Her one eye twinkled as her smile transformed into something more malevolent.

She walked towards me when I shook my head side to side, disagreeing with her last statement. "Ngh," I wheezed. I had meant to say no.

The Ifrit stopped walking and let out a hearty laugh. "Please don't lie. If you had anymore left, you would have used them before," she said as she began approaching again, somehow managing to make her hips sway, even whilst dragging her twisted leg behind.

Damn, that takes skill.

I held up a single finger, indicating I had one shot left.

The Ifrit actually threw back her head and laughed dismissively. "You're bluffing."

I shook my head.

"It's a shame really that you don't have any more

ammunition," she said, frowning. "That was, by far, the most painful thing I have ever felt."

"Grhngh!" I groaned in pain, which translated into: Good, you psycho skanky demonic murdering bitch! I wish I did have a few more rounds so I could cap your ass more thoroughly this time!

It wasn't too far off from what I said.

"We saved one," chimed Ortiz, who had risen back to her feet, clutching her shoulder tightly and grimacing.

The Ifrit cast a lazy glance towards Ortiz before disregarding her with a roll of her head and eye.

"Just in case," added Ortiz in a tone that made our claim sound like solid fact.

Ortiz to the rescue!

The Ifrit let out a callous laugh. "And what good will that do you?"

She was buying the bluff. Good.

"You attacked me three times, and I still live," she snarled.

For now I muttered. It came out as, "Frngh."

"Although my powers have been diminished," she sighed. "I cannot regain my other form until I heal."

Boo fucking hoo.

"So again, what good is your one last chance?" she chortled.

I looked past her and pointed a finger in the direction I was looking.

The Ifrit followed my finger to James, and she let out an angry hiss. "You wouldn't!"

I pointed my finger at Ortiz and shook my head side to side, conveying the message that Ortiz wouldn't shoot James. Jerking my thumb to my face, I smiled, nodding my head up and down, letting her know that I sure as hell would. I'd shoot him and damn both their asses to oblivion.

Her posture tensed, her mouth hung agape, and her single eye was wide in terror. She looked alarmed. It was a good look for her. A better look would have been dead—like permanently, but we were getting there.

"Mortal," she said, her lips trembling. "A chance..."

That left me confused. I cocked my head to the side in bewilderment, to let her know that I had no clue what she was talking about.

"A chance for all of us to walk away," she said in a pleading voice.

Oh, this was going to be good.

"A wish. Anything. Any wish," she implored. "Ask for anything, and I will grant it in exchange for my freedom and my life. Ask!"

If I could have laughed without blowing my ribcage apart, I would have. One simple threat to shoot James, and she had gone from the bimbo of death to begging for her life. It was great.

"Anything, simply ask," she beseeched.

I was going to ask if I could have her fuck off, but that probably wasn't going to happen. What the hell could I wish for anyways? I wasn't that stupid. I knew it would come back to kill me. It was a pointless exercise, and I think some part of her knew that too. But, if she could buy herself time, why not go for it?

I was going to answer her with a string of obscenities, but couldn't manage it. Instead, I settled for grunting, "Hrngh!" I shook my head back and forth. Oh, I gave her the finger too.

Her body tensed up again, though I don't know how that was possible. She must've been coiled tighter than a spring.

I cocked the hammer on the pistol and made a show of steadying my aim on James.

The Ifrit turned her worried gaze towards Ortiz, upturning and extending her open palm in a friendly gesture. "Law keeper," she pleaded.

Law keeper? How come Ortiz was law keeper and I was mortal?

"Law keeper," she begged again. "A wish, any wish," she added as a small light burst into existence in the middle of her palm. It hovered like the orb she had conjured before, only it wasn't nearly as big. It was about the size of a quarter, and didn't look so menacing. There were no pulsating dangerous flames. It looked like a ball of glimmering white light.

She thrust her hand forwards in a gesture that beckoned Ortiz to take her deal. The Ifrit's face was frozen in a state of worry.

To her credit, Ortiz didn't look like she was tempted, not even for a second. "One wish, huh?" she scoffed.

The Ifrit nodded fervently in silence.

"Yeah okay..." Ortiz said.

I knew she was kidding, taunting the Ifrit, but I couldn't have predicated what came next.

"I wish I didn't have to deal with you, with any of this," she snorted, rolling her eyes to make her point. She focused her eyes on the Ifrit again, shooting her a venomous, hate-filled glare. "You're pathetic," she spat, "I wish I didn't have to put up with your sorry ass."

You tell 'em girl.

The Ifrit's attention turned back to me as my smile grew wider. I waved the gun at her before steadying it back at James. I was hoping Ortiz would come up with something, because my bluff was about to be called.

The Ifrit's head darted back and forth between us in a nervous frenzy. She looked absolutely petrified until, finally, it began to change. She cast another glance, looking at Ortiz then me. Her features shifted into ones of understanding. She looked at Ortiz again and then back to me, as if suddenly realizing something. Her smile returned and grew wider.

She turned back to Ortiz, holding her open palm towards her and whispered gleefully. "Be careful what you wish for."

No...

The little ball of light hissed angrily through the air and...

...struck Ortiz above her breast, sinking into her heart. Ortiz was frozen in perfect stillness for a moment. Her mouth started moving silently, strangely, as if she had forgotten how to talk. Her face completely perplexed. "Na... Norman?" she whispered, confused. Then she sunk to the ground. It was slow, like watching a snowflake drift to the ground, only to melt.

"Oh god," I gasped, both in shock and pain.

The Ifrit let out the loudest, cheeriest laugh I had heard yet, overwhelmed with delight. "Wish...fulfilled," she said with the twisted smile of hers that resembled a snarl. The Ifrit let out another bout of uncontrollable laughter.

"Oh god, Ortiz," I breathed. "Oh, god."

The Ifrit's body shivered with sheer pleasure and ecstasy as she spoke. "It seems I have regained my leverage," she laughed. "I can bring her back of course..."

I glared at her in cold, hard rage.

Her remaining eye twinkled with maniacal glee. "Provided," she said as she walked towards James, "you allow him, and I, to live, of course."

Of course...

I wanted to rip her throat out, but I couldn't even push myself up off the ground. All I did was lay there, holding the pistol in futility, wishing I had more rounds.

"But first things first," the Ifrit said between a fit of youthful giggles. She leaned over James, bringing her mouth closer to his. She cast a naughty look over her shoulder towards me. I only saw half her face, the undamaged half, as she spread her lips into a devious smile. "Oh, it's quite alright," she said in a wicked tone. "You can peep." She slipped one hand around the back of James' head and forced his mouth to meet hers.

She pressed her lips against his, hard. James' body jerked in reaction the second their lips touched. Familiar tendrils formed and writhed under his skin. He moaned in agony, his body spasming out of control, but she held him there with little effort. Her arm snaked tightly around him, holding his mouth against hers. There was no chance for him to break free. His features continued contorting until, very soon, he returned to how he looked when I first met him.

He didn't look to be in perfect health. James was still worn-down and gaunt, but he was at least back to his actual age. The Ifrit pulled her face away from his. I could see a mass of the black ichor substance on James' face. Long, thin streams clung to both their mouths, hanging in the air between them.

Ew…

She ran a slow, affectionate hand over the top of his head before making a tight fist, yanking him hard by his hair. James yelped in pain, and the Ifrit let out a laugh of delight. "Good," she purred, turning back to address me. "I wanted him youthful and lucid, so he could see all of this," she murmured seductively, waving her arm at the scene around us. "I wanted to him to see that," she gestured at Ortiz's fallen body. "I wanted him to know everything that's happened is on his head. I want him to feel anguish, to feel responsible, to suffer." Her tone had quickly changed from pleasure to anger. "Then I'm going to feed on him again. Slower. It'll be so much sweeter this time around."

She was one twisted bitch.

"Oh, James," she called in a singsong voice.

He groaned painfully, but seemed aware of everything around him. "Norman?" he said, in utter shock when he noticed me.

I feebly waved the gun at him in a weak welcome.

The Ifrit looked down at James. "Pay attention now," she said, addressing him like a schoolteacher did a child. She walked over to me, dragging her damaged leg and leaking viscous, tar-like ooze all over the place. When she was directly above me, she slipped her good foot under my body, right under my damaged ribs and flipped me over in one swift motion.

I landed on my back. A jolt went coursing through my spine, into the back of my ribs and up through the front. I didn't scream, because what would have been the point? I couldn't have anyway. My mouth hung open in pained silence as a rush of air left my lungs.

"Ooooooh! Did I hurt you?" she asked in an apologetic tone that was completely insincere.

I tried to reply, but all I ended up doing was blinking several times.

What's Morse code for fuck you?

I felt an intense pressure on my throat as she slid her foot over it and pressed down. I couldn't even gasp for air. All of it had been knocked out of me when she'd flipped me over, and now she was pressing down on my windpipe. My right arm began a frenzied dance, flailing around to point the gun at James in an attempt to scare her off.

"Oh no," she chided as she bent over, subsequently putting a bit more pressure on my throat. She slapped the gun out of my hand.

It was odd, really. Kind of symmetrical in a way. I had started this case trapped in a coffin, running the risk of dying by suffocation. And now here I was at the end of the case, having the life snuffed out me of via suffocation.

Symmetry sucks.

I started feeling woozy. It was calming really. Everything just sort of began to fade, like falling asleep when you're dead tired. It was just so...easy.

I heard something in the background, but it seemed so far away. A voice shouting. "Stop it! You're killing him!"

The pressure on my neck subsided. At first, my vision began to focus, and then I was gasping for air on pure instinct, unable to control the frantic breathing causing my chest to expand and contract deeply. Oh yeah, that was great for my busted ribs. Every necessary breath caused me a bout of agonizing pain.

"What are you doing?" exclaimed James, distraught at what was going on.

"Killing him," she replied rather nonchalantly. "Like you said, remember?" She placed her foot back on my throat and pressed again. The pressure was firm, but much softer than before; she was going to take her time.

I really hated her.

"Stop!" James shrieked.

And she did.

The Ifrit jerked her foot off my neck like she had been scalded. "What?" she snarled, her mangled lips quivering and flapping in anger. "Why?"

"I...I changed my mind," muttered James feebly.

"You changed your mind?" the Ifrit said, bursting into uncontrollable laughter. "It's too late for that. Look around you!" She made a point of gesturing towards Ortiz's body.

"Who...who's that?" he stammered.

"One of your mortal law keepers," she replied lazily. "I killed her."

"You...why? What happened?" he continued stammering in confusion.

"Lots," she shrugged. "Why are you so surprised? After all, you did all of this. *You* let me out. *You're* responsible for all of this, James."

"No...I..." he muttered weakly. "Marsha? Where's Marsha?" he asked loudly, looking around frantically, as if he expected to see her here.

"Aww," the Ifrit purred. "I'm sorry to tell you this, but Marsha is...dead." Her face lit up in pure amusement upon seeing James' reaction.

"Dead? No...I..." He sobbed uncontrollably.

The Ifrit abandoned me and walked over to him, grasping him gently by the chin and forcing him to look at her as he cried. "Oh yes," she whispered, pleased. "I killed her, but...you knew that would happen eventually, didn't you?" she asked smiling. "I told you there was a price for my power, but, I can bring her back."

The weight of that last statement snapped James back to reality. His eyes widened as he stared at her.

"But first, why don't you tell him?" she said merrily, nodding to me, "what it was *you* wished for?"

James mumbled something I couldn't make out.

"Louder!" snapped the Ifrit.

"Marsha," James whispered.

I didn't know what to think.

"She died because of you," she told James, causing his

features to distort into an anguished mask. "Don't worry too much though. It was never real. It was a strong infatuation, yes, but never love," she laughed. Turning back to face me she said, "That's what he wished for—love." She laughed again, much louder this time, as if it was one of the funniest things she had ever heard.

"I just…just wanted to be loved," he sobbed.

Who doesn't, pal. Who doesn't? I thought.

"I can bring her back, remember?" she reminded him. "All it would take is another life, a life for a life," she informed him. She looked at me, a hungry smile on her face. "Maybe…his?" she suggested.

James looked at me with his tear-stained, puffy, red face then desperately at the Ifrit, weighing the situation.

"Him for her," she said. "What do you say, James? All it takes is a wish."

I made every effort I could into speaking, "James," I rasped, drawing his attention. "It…it won't be real. You know that."

"I…know…but—"

I cut him off. "Look…around you," I panted. "At her." I nodded to Ortiz. "She didn't deserve this. She's dead because of *you!*" I made sure to put heat into those words. To make him understand. To make him feel guilty. This guy's conscience needed a wake up call, and I was going to give it to him.

"I…I…" he stammered.

"Is this what Marsha would want?" I asked, working hard to say that complete sentence.

He froze, his head bowing over in shame. "No," he mumbled quietly.

"Then stop this," I pleaded.

"Stop this? Look at him," the Ifrit barked incredulously. "He won't stop this. He can't. He's pathetic!"

Way to win him over to your side.

"James…please…" I begged. "Stop this."

James shut his eyes tight and breathed deeply, rising slowly to his feet. He opened his eyes and addressed the

Ifrit. "A wish," he said, his voice firmer than it had ever been.

The Ifrit's face lit up with glee. She hadn't noticed what I had, the defiant look in James' eyes.

"Anything," she purred.

"A life…" he said, pausing for a moment as he collected himself, "for a life."

"Of course," replied the Ifrit.

"I wish for Ma…" he started, but then cast his gaze over to Ortiz's fallen body and inhaled deeply before beginning again. "I wish for her life," he said pointing to Ortiz's body, "to be restored. My life as payment, and"—his jaw tightened before he continued coldly—"and I want you gone."

Nothing happened for a moment. There was no flash of spectacular blinding light, no smoke, nothing. Everything was perfectly still, like a painting, for a while at least. Then James turned to face me, a look of remorse on his face.

"Norman," he whispered. "I'm sorry. Sorry for everything. Sorry for"—he broke off for a moment—"sorry for her," he said nodding to Ortiz. He took in a deep, heavy breath before adding, "I'm sorry for Marsha. I'm so sorry…"

His whole body shuddered as if the room temperature had dropped below freezing. His eyelids fluttered and a lengthy, quiet breath left his body. I watched as James' body fell in complete silence for the final time as he died, died trying to fix all the damage he had done. He couldn't bring Marsha back, the janitor, Norman, nor the people who had died in the hotel fire. But he gave his life to bring back Ortiz. I hoped it was a good enough deed to put the Ifrit away for good.

The Ifrit, however, well, she didn't decide to go so quietly or peacefully. Hell, she didn't even mutter so much as an apology. She glared at me in cold, hard fury. Her entire body was riddled with hairline cracks that burned orange and seeped smoke. She looked like was falling apart right before me. That perennial snarl of hers widened as she screamed furiously at me. "Do you know what you've done?

Do you?" she shrieked.

Yeah, I thought smugly. *I put genie back in the fucking bottle.*

More hairline cracks appeared across her body. Smoke was billowing from every inch of her. "You called me a murderer," she screamed, body shuddering. "You've just damned me to an eternity of slavery! That is no life! No life at all!" She sounded like a teenager throwing a fit. "Who's the murderer!?" she screamed, pointing an accusing finger towards me. "I didn't ask for this!"

Neither did I.

That's when I noticed the stream of moisture cascading down her cheek, trickling from her single eye. "I didn't ask for this," she sobbed. "Your kind took everything from me. Your kind did this to me! Who's the murderer? Who's the mur—"

She froze, taking quick shallow breaths as if she were suffocating. Her body jerked wildly for a moment before the cracks riddling her body flared brightly and violently. She threw her head back, screaming at the ceiling as her body burst into a mass of smoke tinged with flecks of bright orange flames. It wisped gracefully towards her vessel. Seconds later, the mass of smoke and fire coalesced into a narrow stream as it filtered into the brass oil lamp, making a sound much like a light breeze did.

And then she was gone. That was it. No trace of her from what I could see.

I struggled to push myself up to my knees, and I crawled on all fours to Ortiz's still prone form. My head hovered directly above hers, looking down at her calm, frozen, and beautiful features. "Ortiz?" I whispered,

There was a deep gasp. Her body arched backwards before lurching forwards with surprising speed. Her head shot forward like a missile, colliding with my frickin' nose!

The sick, wet sound of cartilage breaking filled my ears. Warm blood trickled out. Between that and my ribs, I thought I was going to faint, or at least vomit.

"Oh my god! Norman—your nose!" she exclaimed in shock.

"Grhngh!" I moaned unintelligibly. Translation: Goddammit, Ortiz!

She completely ignored what I said and looked down at her chest in amazement, running her hands over the hole in her clothing, completely baffled. She looked at me uncertainly. "I...died?"

I nodded aggressively, while pinching my nose hard, trying to stop the blood.

"I'm...alive?" she said in disbelief.

I grunted an affirmative.

"How?"

I grunted.

"The Ifrit?" she asked in shock.

I gave another nod and another grunt.

"Is she...?" Ortiz asked, not bothering to finish the question.

I nodded.

"For good? You're sure this time?"

I shot her an angry glare and nodded more aggressively.

"And... James?" she whispered.

I shook my head.

"You know you can talk, right?" she said impatiently. "I heard you whisper my name."

Yeah, before you head-butted me in the nose! I thought. Aloud, I said, "It hurts."

"Such a wuss," she teased.

I get no respect.

Ortiz rose to her feet and walked away from me. She approached the lipstick-covered oil lamp, kneeling down to pick it up. Ortiz encircled it in both hands and then jerked back, dropping the vessel.

I gave her a "what gives?" kind of look.

"It's...really hot," she murmured as she brought her hands to her mouth and blew on them.

"Wuss," I teased lightly.

Ortiz snorted and knelt down again. She removed her coat, wrapping it around the oil lamp before picking it up. She brought it over to me and set it down before sinking to her knees beside me.

The seal was perfectly intact.

"So, since you seem to be conveniently bleeding, care to do the honors?" Ortiz asked, keeping her tone carefully neutral. I couldn't help but notice the smirk on her face.

I glowered at her and made a childish face.

She laughed.

That set me off, and we just laughed for what seemed like forever. God, it felt good to laugh and be done with all this. Well, almost done.

I took one of my blood-covered hands and pressed it against the seal. An intense heat enveloped my hand, yet there was no pain. I pulled my hand away to find the once smudgy lipstick seal now looked as if it had been part of the brass vessel from the very beginning. It blended perfectly with the metal, save for the slight tinge of strawberry red.

A gentle tingling sensation ran across my forearm. I shot a quick glance at it. The big, black number one was quickly losing its clarity. Moments later it faded. I started laughing, louder this time. I couldn't help it. That close to the finish line and I pulled it off. Ortiz stared at me like I was a lunatic, which only made me laugh harder. I held my healing ribcage and laughed until I couldn't laugh anymore.

"Now," I sighed, "it's really over."

"What are you going to do with that?" Ortiz asked, pointing at the now sealed vessel.

"Kill two birds with one stone," I replied.

"Huh?"

"I'm going to turn this in and keep a promise I made you," I said.

"Oh?" she said surprised, arching a dark chestnut eyebrow in curiosity.

"Yeah. Feel like going to church?" I smiled.

Her eyebrow rose even higher.

Chapter Twenty-three

Since it wasn't too far from the museum, I decided to visit the building I had first visited when I had contacted Church. I pushed past one of the large wooden doors with Ortiz right behind me, and entered.

Ortiz brushed against my shoulder as she moved up beside me, vying for a better look.

It was a small church, but beautiful. The vast majority of it was a dark, cherry wood. From the intersecting ceiling beams, to the walls and the pews, the place had a sensation of warmth to it. Two chandeliers hung across from one another, bathing the wooden church in a soft glow; an archway in the front of the church contained several intricate and angelic paintings. Stained glass windows ran along the sides of the building. All in all, it wasn't such a bad place to be after everything we had just gone through.

Sitting in a pew at the very front of the church was a lone figure. Chin-length, wavy, blonde hair hung behind him, and I could see he hadn't changed his shirt. It was still the full-length, white-collared shirt from before. There was an almost unnoticeable movement of the shoulder, gently bobbing as he moved his arm side to side. He must've been writing. He was always writing something.

"Who's that?" asked Ortiz in a hushed whisper.

I held up a finger, motioning for silence. I didn't want to disturb Church. I gave a quiet nod, beckoning her to follow as I quietly approached the front of the church. About halfway there, I felt something slump against me. I turned to find an unconscious Ortiz resting her full body against me.

I gave her a gentle shake. "Ortiz?"

"Sorry," said a soft, kind voice.

I turned to look at Church. His frosty eyes, tinged with hints of blue, calmly looking back at me; a few blonde locks of hair had fallen over one side of his glasses. He was standing with perfectly straight posture, his hands clasped in front him.

I turned my attention back to Ortiz, ignoring Church for the moment. I bent at the knees and slipped a hand underneath her, in an effort to pick her up. The second I tried to exert even the tiniest bit of force, my entire ribcage lit up with scorching pain. I grimaced through it, but, man, was it hard.

"Please," Church said quietly, stepping forwards to take Ortiz from my arms, lifting her effortlessly, as if she weighed next to nothing.

For the record, all women always weigh next to nothing. One of the most important survival tips I've ever learned.

He held her tenderly, like she was something fragile, as he carried over to the nearest pew. He laid her down to rest. All of this happened without the slightest hint of effort. So Church had apparently found time to hit the gym between his regular job of bossing me around.

"I'm sorry, Vincent," he said quietly, "but she's not ready to meet me yet."

"You did that?" I asked in a tone that was both surprised and impressed.

He gave a simple and quiet nod of the head.

Huh, cool.

"You know..." I began slowly. "I promised her answers."

"I know," responded Church in his ever-so-quiet voice.

"She helped on this case."

"I know," he replied again, just as quiet and softly as before.

"She risked her life for me, Church. Hell, she saved it too."

"I know, Vincent."

"She deserves answers, Church," I said firmly.

"She does. Just not yet. When she's ready," he replied with a quiet firmness, signaling the end of that part of our discussion.

"Fine," I said holding up both my hands in resignation. "This is the part where I turn in the vessel, you say 'good job, Graves,' and give me a pat on the back?"

A flicker of a smile crossed Church's mouth. "All but the last part, Vincent."

I gingerly made my way over to Ortiz's resting body and removed the vessel from her arms. I turned around and handed it to Church.

"Good job, Graves," he smiled as he took it from me.

I couldn't tell if he was patronizing me or not.

Church walked back to the pew he had been sitting on when Ortiz and I had first entered, putting the vessel on it before returning to me. He stood there completely motionless and just stared at me.

"So, uh, I've got some questions, Church," I said slowly.

"I know."

I exhaled heavily, frustrated by Church's response, which wasn't all too smart since it caused a painful twinge in my ribs.

"Acting in anger is like picking up a hot coal with the intent of throwing it at someone else, Vincent. You must first burn yourself in order to burn the other person," he said, spouting his Yoda-isms in his soft, slow voice.

"Tao of Church?" I snickered.

"Words of Buddha," he replied calmly.

Oh...

"So, where to begin?" I asked with a light shrug.

"With your first question, preferably," he responded...to a rhetorical question.

I sighed on the inside.

"You pick which cases I'm supposed to work, Church." It wasn't a question when I said it.

He nodded affirmatively in silence.

"So why this one?" I asked. "I mean, I don't get it."

"What don't you get, Vincent?" he asked, sounding like a parent trying to help a child with a complicated problem. It was a kind and understanding tone.

"All of it, I guess," I replied with a shrug. "The Ifrit. The short—really short—timeline, but mostly the Ifrit."

He stood quietly and motioned for me to continue explaining.

"I'm not used to, well, I've never dealt with anything this bad before. That Ifrit was in a whole 'nother league," I said.

"Yes, I'm sorry," Church said.

"This case was just, I don't know, a lot for me," I continued.

"Yes," he whispered.

"There was so much going on, so many people involved. I'm not used to people, having to watch out for them. I work…used to work—"

"Alone," he said, finishing my sentence for me. "I know, that's one of the reasons why."

One of the reasons why…? I thought to myself in confusion.

"Uh, Church," I began hesitantly. "What the hell are you talking about?"

"Vincent, the Ifrit and short timeline were a test. A test that you needed. Something to push you, to see if you can handle it," he explained calmly.

"A test?" I growled. I jerked my head over to Ortiz and snarled. "She *died* in this *test!* It was a damn miracle that James decided to bring Ortiz back to life at all. He could have just as easily wished Marsha back, and Ortiz would have died for nothing!"

Another painful lance shot through my torso, and I gritted my teeth.

Church gave me a knowing look.

"Yeah, yeah," I growled. "Anger, coal, burned. I got it."

"Vincent, it wasn't a miracle what James did at the end. It was *you*," he said, "Both of you," he said, nodding to Ortiz. "James did the right thing because of what you and she did, together. Your words and actions changed him."

"Yeah," I muttered dismissively. "A helluva lot of good it did me. People still died, Church." I sighed, thinking about the innocent lives lost in the hotel fire.

"I know," he replied sympathetically. "I'm sorry, but I'm surprised to see you so upset about it, Vincent."

Who the hell isn't upset when people die?

"Of course I'm upset, Church!" I snarled, "My job is to protect people from this kind of stuff..." I trailed off, realizing what I had just said, what Church had been hinting at.

For the longest time, hell, just yesterday, I had constantly been telling myself that my job wasn't about saving people. I wasn't supposed to get involved in their lives. My job was solely, strictly, to nail whatever supernatural thing was responsible for murdering the stiff I inhabited.

All of that changed within a day of working with Ortiz.

"Vincent," Church began, "this wasn't just a test. It was a reminder."

"A reminder?"

"A reminder that your job has *always* been to protect and help people. You forgot that sometime back. You had to remember to care about other people and not just the case," he explained.

It was suddenly so very obvious to me. "You arranged for me to meet Ortiz, didn't you?" I asked, already knowing the answer.

"You needed to learn how to trust people again, how to work with them, but no," he answered. "I didn't arrange for you to bump into her, but I hoped."

"You hoped?" I asked incredulously.

"Vincent, one of these days you will learn that hope is all you really need," he said. "You're my hope, Vincent."

Okay...just a little uncomfortable.

"Uh, Church, you're not hitting on me right now, are you?"

He rolled his eyes and actually snorted. "No, Vincent.

Don't flatter yourself."

Gee, way to let a guy down easy there, Church.

I tried to bring the conversation back to the important stuff. "So, what did you mean about me being your...uh, hope?"

"I need your help, Vincent," he replied simply.

"With what?"

"Forces unseen. Something dangerous, more so than anything either you, or I, have ever faced. Something I *cannot* intervene in, alone, at least," he explained, without really explaining.

I rubbed my temples in both frustration and fatigue. "Church," I said as patiently as I could. "Ambiguity is really overrated at whatever the hell o'clock it is in the morning."

He didn't respond.

"And what does any of that have to do with this case? And why it was such a pain in the ass?" I asked. "Why couldn't you have, oh, I don't know, asked me for help?"

"You can't help. Not in your current state, Vincent."

"My...current state?"

"This case was to help you remember the person you were, the person before you died," he explained.

"Who I was? I... I don't get it, Church?"

"Kind, caring, would risk his life for others, and always put them first," he continued.

My head started hurting. He knew who I was? He knew about my old life?

"This case was to help you regain your humanity, the things that make a soul something more," he said. "Like caring for others."

"My humanity? Church, give me a straight answer! I deserve one!"

"If you can regain it," he said. "You can regain your old life, your memories, your body..." He said some more things, too, but I stopped listening after that point.

I had a shot at getting my old life back? My...body.

"Only then can you help me, Vincent," he continued.

"Well, job done," I said. "I passed your test and

everything, Church."

"No," he replied. "You can't just reclaim your past life just like that, Vincent. It has to be earned. There's much more for you to prove, Graves. This is just the beginning." He sighed heavily.

I closed my eyes, rubbing them hard with my hands as I tried to make sense of everything Church had just told me. I had a chance to be…me again, to get back everything I had lost.

"Church," I said, opening my eyes. Except when I did, he was gone. The entire place was empty, save for Ortiz and I.

"Way to drop a bombshell on a guy and then leave," I muttered as I approached the pew he had been sitting in. I removed both of my journals from the coat I had been wearing, placing them down on the pew. I knew they would be taken care of.

I returned to where Ortiz was resting and sat beside her, weighing everything Church had told me. My head reeled at his revelations as well as what they meant.

I could have my old life back, but then I would have to help Church. But still… I could have it back.

A soft, tingling and gentle tugging sensation enveloped my body; it was time to leave Norman's body. I could feel my soul being pulled from Norman's form. But all I could think about was what Church had said.

"There's much more for you to prove, Graves. This is just the beginning."

Fan-friggin'-tastic…

Thank you for taking the time to read this novel.
You can find out more about the author at the
website below.

www.rrvirdi.com

What reviewers are saying about Grave Beginnings:

"I believe R.R. Virdi belongs with other Urban Fantasy greats like Jim Butcher. The Grave Report is sure to go far and only pick up more fans with each successful novel. I can't wait to see where R.R. Virdi will take us next." — A Drop Of Ink Reviews

"Fast paced, humorous, with action and drama on every page and paragraph, this paranormal thriller is reminiscent of one of my all-time favorite authors. This is like Jim Butcher's The Dresden Files but with a flavor all its own. RR Virdi is fame-bound with this series. If you like Jim Butcher, you'll enjoy this one. Highly Recommend." — CD Coffelt — Author of The Wilder Mage

"A fast paced story with great characters, I loved the story and fell even more in love with the future possibilities... Virdi maintains both the suspense of the case at hand, and the character's past and current transformation, making us feel both for the victim and the investigator. He excels at action scenes - I have rarely read books with such well-described yet fluid action scenes." – Shadow and Clay Reviews

If you enjoyed this book, please consider leaving a review!

CPSIA information can be obtained
at www.ICGtesting.com
Printed in the USA
LVHW101408210722
724000LV00003B/139